had all been masters of ships he hadn't been able to pass for his second mate's ticket although, at her insistence, he'd sat times beyond number. What she could never see was what Sam and the examiners saw too well: that although he was a first-rate practical seaman he simply had no head for books and figures. Besides, he was completely lacking in the ambition and the fierce desire for brass so typical of Bramblewick character. So long as he could get a berth on a ship with officers that didn't try to "ride it over him" too much, with a spell ashore once a year to see his old mother (a mixed joy on his part), so long as he could get a reasonable amount of ale and all the baccy he wanted he was content to let others have the bossing and the brass. He spoke at last, slowly, ponderously, like a very old man.

"It'll be Tom's last call tonight, anyway. Tide's just right for him fishing. He'll be away down the landing scaurs."

The coastguard said,

"He was there last night. I saw him from the watch-house and got the telescope on him. He had a little lantern to bait his hook by. Must have been half frozen standin' there. 'Tisn't as though he'd got sea-boots on. Looks like to me as though he's gone a bit cracked."

"Well, maybe it will sober him before he gets home," said Jonty. "I'm sorry for his missus, you know, and his little lass. I doubt Ella Moorsholm made the mistake of her life when she wed a Bransby. She was a fine lass. Is yet! She holds her head up in spite of what's happened."

The smith grinned and said sarcastically,

"He's fetched her down from Up-Bank though. There's not much to hold her head up for, spot where they're living now. . . You know," he added, more seriously and without sarcasm, "it's my belief that Tom Bransby's about at the end of his rope. He's got a queer look in his eyes. There'll be one night he'll be going down the scaurs fishing when he's full of drink and there'll be folks looking for his body washing up on the next tide."

The landlord came in with the drinks. All had ale except Captain Christopher, who had a glass of rum and water steaming hot with a lump of sugar in it which he crushed and stirred with a spoon. He took a sip at it and then he remarked to the company,

"Tom's in a bad way and no mistake. I'm sorry for the lad as well as for his missus and bairn. From all accounts he was as good a ship's master as ever came from this spot."

"You're right there," put in Sam, now lighting his pipe, "you're right there. I sailed with him."

"Aye," the captain went on. "And folks can say what they like about the Bransbys. They were all hard drinkers, we know, but there was never one of 'em that couldn't take it. And I reckon it wouldn't have let young Tom down but for the war and what he'd gone through before it happened. He'd seen his own father, John Henry, and his young brother Harry blown up and burnt to death. His two other brothers were drowned. He'd been torpedoed twice himself apart from that mine that blew up his father's ship. By rights he ought to have had at least one voyage ashore after that last do. Chap that spoke for him at the inquiry said that and the president agreed, and none of 'em had owt to say against his previous record. It was hard luck even if the case was proved and Tom admitted being drunk on the bridge and doing something the cabin boy could have told him was wrong."

The coastguard was an Essex man and a comparative newcomer to Bramblewick. He asked the captain,

"Were any lives lost?"

"Nay. Neither was his ship or t'other one, but salvage came into thousands of pounds. Lloyds would see to it that Tom wouldn't get a ship again, and anyway the court suspended him for two years. It served him right of course. I'm not saying otherwise. Ships aren't to be chucked about by men who can't carry their liquor. For myself the time I was at sea I'd never touch a drop, watch above or below."

"Save it for ashore, eh?" the coastguard laughed, raising his glass. "Here's health to you, Captain!"

The captain acknowledged the toast by taking another sip at his own glass. The other three also drank, and the smith remarked as he wiped the froth from his moustache with the back of his hand,

"You're right, Captain. If a chap can't take his liquor he'd best leave it alone. Now I reckon I can put away as much as most chaps, but no one's ever known me late at the smithy next morn, nor botching a job either."

There was an arrogance in his voice that was not lost on the others. He was not a popular man in the village. For one thing he had too high an opinion of himself, and the fact that his opinion was in many ways justified made no matter. He was acknowledged to be the best blacksmith in the district. He was also an exceptionally skilled all-round mechanic: capable of fixing anything from a sewing-machine to a gramophone or traction engine. He was a bit of a naturalist and taxidermist.

He was a great book reader. The books he read were chiefly scientific and philosophical, borrowed from the Burnharbour public library, although he had a good collection of his own. He was a socialist and, what was only a degree worse in the estimation of the village, he did not believe in God or a hereafter and was ready to argue his disbelief with anyone, parsons included.

Long Jonty laughed. He was a simple, honest, generous man. He had a long nose and big prominent teeth which were still sound and white. He liked his ale, but it never made him quarrelsome. He had married, late in life, the widow of a jobbing mason called Peacock who also had been a man of great stature. She herself was very short, almost a midget, but she had a tongue like a whip and was complete boss of her second husband as she had been of her first. She didn't mind him coming home slightly tipsy every week night. She liked a bottle of stout herself at suppertime. But she was a church-goer and a strict Sabbatarian, and on Sundays Jonty always had to be in his "best" with a stiff collar and tie, and he was obliged to accompany her to evening service and then go straight home although most of the pubs were open from half-past eight till ten. Polly had some reputation as a midwife. Both of them were very fond of children and it was a pity that neither as Polly Peacock nor Polly Scaife had she produced a family herself. . . Jonty gave the smith a quick, almost challenging, look when he said, still laughing,

"I'll not say I've never been mastered by ale. There was that time they were having a pig-killing at Matty Brewster's and I got so much into me I fell in the beck just below his stackyard, with the postbag too, and damned

6

if I could read the names of half the letters when I got 'em out."

There was general laughter, and then Sam Bunny said, "I couldn't count the times I've been carried on board ship, especially out foreign, where mostly you get wine and not ale. And I won't say it won't happen again... But to get back to Tom Bransby. You know I sailed with him more than two years on the *Northgate*. Tom drank a bit then when he was ashore. But I never once saw him the worse for it on board ship and I can tell you I never want to sail with a finer chap. Now take that time we picked up that Spanish steamer in the Bay of Biscay. It was a hell of a gale with seas like mountains and snow, too, coming in blinding squalls. We were homeward bound. Ground--nuts from West Africa. You'll know what ground-nuts are for a cargo, Captain. You might as well just be in ballast and no cargo at all. We were making no more than five knots when we got her distress signals. Her engines had gone and she was just wallowing, with the seas coming over her sides as if she'd been fast ashore. You couldn't have done owt with a boat. There's a lot of chaps wouldn't have risked what Tom did, bearing down from the weather side on to a ship out of control and getting close enough to heave a line aboard. God—we came within feet of her at one time, and if we'd touched both ships would have been riven in two. But they got our line all right, and we got their hawser, and we got her head slewed round to the weather. Three times over the hawser broke, and as many times we got her in tow again and we fetched her into Brest in the end. But it took us four days, and I'll bet Tom wasn't off the bridge for more than twelve hours the whole time."

"You'd make a nice packet of money out of it, didn't you?" asked the coastguard.

"Aye. We all did well of course."

"It would be out of that Tom bought his house Up-Bank," put in the smith. "I hear he's got a bill of sale even on his furniture—that is, what was left of it when they flitted Down-Bank. Aye—he's made a mess of things all right!"

There was nothing in the smith's manner or in what he said to make the others feel that he had any particular spite against Tom Bransby: it was his natural churlishness. But Captain Christopher was on the defensive. He had not finished his drink, but he sat with his two hands clasped on the silver head of the Malacca cane he always carried when walking and now held perpendicularly between his knees. His hands were white and the veins stood out on them like the roots of a shrub bared by heavy rain. He was very old but he spoke with greater precision and speed than the comparatively youthful Sam had done, and he looked squarely at the blacksmith.

"Aye. Maybe you're right and Tom's made a mess of things. But he's the first of his family to lose a ship through his own fault. For that matter he's the first master, aye or mate or second mate or engineer either, from this spot to get into that sort of trouble. Back as far as anyone can go there's been Bransbys here. Fisherman Bransbys, sailor Bransbys, it doesn't matter which—they've all been chaps you could rely on and never mind their faults. They've all been boozers. But that's never stopped them doing their job. And they were good-hearted too. Take John Henry, Tom's father, and Matt and Zach and John's three brothers Charley and Joe and Steve, and their father, aye and old Jake Bransby the hardest boozer of them all. You say you can put your ale away, Knaggs, but what's ale to rum, and not the stuff that's in that glass but real Jamaica. I've heard my father say that Jake could drink a bottle of it at one go and still be on his feet."

"I've heard tell of old Jake Bransby," said Sam. "Wasn't him who took the lifeboat out one day when he was getting on to be eighty years of age?"

"A fisherman, was he?" asked the coastguard.

"Nay," the captain answered. "Jake was no fisherman. He was a ship's master and owner too. Him and his two brothers they owned two brigs and a topsail schooner between them. I served my time on that schooner. *Jane Bransby* they called her after Jake's missus. Smart craft she was too. But Jake had retired then. He'd made his brass. Mind it wasn't until his missus died that the booze really got him. They say that it was her who'd always kept him up to the mark. He'd always been gentle as a lamb with her and when she died he sort of lost hold of himself. Remember there were twice as many pubs in this spot then and there were no restrictions either except closing at half-past ten at night and during church and chapel time on Sundays. Ale was tuppence a pint. They say you could buy a bottle of Jamaica for half a crown."

The others laughed ironically and the coastguard said,

"Tuppence a pint! God's truth—wonder anyone ever *was* sober!"

"Why, from all accounts, very few of 'em ever was, when they were ashore," the captain went on. "Except on

Sundays. Apart from one or two downright wasters, and I doubt if they were sailors or fishermen, they were all God-fearing men, either church or chapel."

"You mean they made up on the seventh day for what they did on the other six," the smith put in sarcastically. "Sitting in church or chapel dressed in their best and looking as though butter wouldn't melt in their mouths. There's plenty like that these days, never mind going back to when ale was tuppence a pint."

"I mean nowt at t' sort," the captain retorted with asperity. "I mean that although they drank they did their jobs. They were *men*, all of 'em, and they behaved themselves mostly. They could curse and fight same as most men. There was nowt namby-pamby about them. But give 'em a job and they'd do it and no boasting about it when it was done. I remember that lifeboat do. I was only a lad but I remember it as though it was only yesterday although it's nigh on seventy years ago."

The captain took another sip at his glass. Whatever the smith felt at the spirited counter-thrust to his sarcasm he said nothing and the captain had no need to glance at the others for encouragement to go on.

"Jake," he said, "was a great big fellow and he'd got a voice on him like a bull. He stood over six foot high and even when he'd turned eighty they say there wasn't a chap in Bramblewick dared have picked a quarrel with him. His beard wasn't even white then. Not that he was one of the quarrelling sort. None of the Bransbys ever were, but they'd not let anyone sit on them, or play 'em a mucky trick. Jake always kept his small change in his trousers pocket. He'd never pass a bairn in the street without giving him a penny to buy goodies, and of course no one ever went short of a pint when he was in t' pub. It was come one come all with him. . .

"Aye, I remember that day. I reckon I'd be about ten years old, still going to Gaffer Bulmer's school, and it was a Saturday, for with another lad I'd been along the shore seeing if any wood had washed up. There'd been a north-easterly gale blowing for several days but it had backed to west and the sea had calmed enough for the cobles to get off to their crab pots. They hadn't been to 'em, of course, while the gale had been blowing, but they'd got them in deep water well away from the scaur ends. Well, you know what lads are. We'd been dawdling about, picking up bits of wood and scratting among the tangles washed up at the cliff foot for owt we could find and not particularly noticing what was going on at sea or that the wind had changed again and was blowing south and then south-east. As you all know a south-easterly wind's about the worst thing you can get here, especially if it comes on top of a northerly ground swell and there's a spring tide as there was that day. It was that tide that made us hurry to get round Hutton's Nab on our way back, and it wasn't until then that we noticed a crowd of folks standing on the slipway, looking out to sea. Then we saw the cobles—two of them close in to the landing.

"There'd be about twenty cobles fishing from this spot then. All of 'em were off including Tommy Coulson and his brothers. Tommy was coxswain of the lifeboat then, Will was second coxswain, and Fred, of course, one of the crew. There wasn't one of the regular crew ashore. The crowd on the slipway was mostly old men with some women among 'em with shawls over their heads, and all of them were quiet and looking very anxious. Most of the cobles were a long way off and you couldn't make out the men who were in them. But those other two were just outside the landing scaur posts, and the seas were already breaking between the posts, and even I could tell they couldn't get through. They weren't trying anyway. Their sails were set. They must have decided to leave their pots and make for home soon as the wind had changed. They must have seen they were too late, though. They'd gone about and were trying to beat out to sea again and make for Burnharbour."

"I've seen that happen myself," put in Sam. "A south-easter shuts the landing quicker than a north-easter, even if it's not blowing half as strong."

The captain stirred his rum, and took another sip at it.

"And there was a north-easterly ground swell to start with this time, remember," he went on. "But I didn't know what a fix they were in. I was too young to know that it wasn't the seas breaking across the landing mouth that was troubling them. Their danger was t' rough ground along Low Batts cliff. A lee shore, and seas were already breaking along it as far out as Low Batts Head. Tommy Coulson's was one of the two cobles. He must have seen what was coming and he'd reckoned it was his job to be ashore quick to get the lifeboat out in case anyone else got into trouble. There was Reub Winspear and his two lads in t' other coble. One of 'em had only been married a few weeks before to a lass who'd come as a servant to the Manor House. She came from London, and by rights she oughtn't to have married a fisherman for she was dead frightened of the sea. She was standing among t' other women, only she hadn't a shawl on, and I can remember now how white her face was.

"Well, as I said, it was that lee shore they were bothered about. That was on their port tack. They were going as near the breakers as they dared, with their sails close hauled, then going about for a longer reach to starboard and of course drawing farther to sea each time. But t' wind was freshening every minute and t' sea was getting rougher. There were times when one of them would sink in between two waves and you'd see nowt but t' top of its mast and sail, and when it did show again it was listing so that anyone would think it was bound to capsize. Both cobles were on the port tack, and every one on the slipway was sort of holding their breaths when Jake Bransby came down the slipway. He'd got two of those regular wasters with him. They used to follow him from pub to pub, sponging on him for booze. He was singing and shouting, and—I told you he had a voice like a bull—he was so drunk he was holding on to one of the chaps to keep himself steady. He came right down to where t' other folks were standing, and then he stopped close to an old fisherman and gave him a slap on his back and laughed and shouted at him to come and have a drink. He hadn't noticed yet what was happening out at sea. But he must have done soon after.

"T' cobles had just reached the end of their port tack, about three lengths from where the seas were breaking. Two men in each of them were pulling their starboard oars to swing them on to the starboard tack, and bearing straight down on them was a great squall of wind churning up the sea like an engine blowing off steam. I saw that squall strike t' first coble, and it was just as though a great lump of cliff had fallen on it. Its sail didn't flap or quiver. It was just struck flat and the coble itself seemed to jump out of the sea as it went over. Next minute you could see it and t' other coble too, floating keel up and chaps who had been in them bobbing up and down in t' water trying to hang on to whatever they could. I don't know if it was seeing what had happened that suddenly brought Jake to his senses, or whether it was hearing that chap's wife. She was standing just alongside Jake. She gave out a great yell, and then she fainted dead. One or two women went to help her, but as they did Jake roared out,

" 'Come on, you bastards! Get t' lifeboat down. Don't stand there deeing nowt.'

"And with that he swung round knocking one of those wasters who had followed him on to his backside, and he paced up the slipway, shouting again,

" 'Come on, all of you give a hand, breeches and skirts!'

"Jake had stiffened himself up just like a soldier. You wouldn't have thought that a minute or two before he'd been near dead drunk! He'd never had much to do with the lifeboat. That was always a fisherman's job in those days. But he took charge as though he'd been at it all his life. And he didn't stand for any argument either. There was a scuffle among the old fishermen for belts, but two coastguards came rushing down, and Jake told two of the oldest chaps to hand over their belts to them. He knew it was going to be a tough pull to get to those cobles before they drifted into the breakers. . . Well, the tide was halfway up the slipway, and as you know that's about the worst time for getting Bramblewick lifeboat out. Tide sweeps straight across and if t' boat loses way after it's left the carriage it's likely enough to be swept into the old coastguard's wall and be smashed up."

The captain paused for another sip at his glass. There had been no regular fishermen employed at Bramblewick since the end of the war, and since a powerful motor lifeboat had been stationed at the nearby port of Burnharbour the local station had been closed. The coastguard said,

"It must have bin a wicked job, Captain, and with a scratch crew."

"I reckon there never was a worse spot than Bramblewick for getting a lifeboat out with the tide up," Sam put in. "No wonder they closed the station when motor lifeboats came in."

"Pulling boats never were much use," said the smith. "An engine's worth a dozen men with oars any day."

He had been listening to the captain's narrative with impatient deference. He was not a good listener. He would have rather been talking himself, arguing, laying down the law. But none of the others challenged his assertion. The captain went on,

"Aye, of course. But there were no motor lifeboats then. And even if there had been, if she'd had to come all the way from Burnharbour she'd have been no use. Once those cobles had drifted into the breakers chaps still hanging on to 'em were as good as as gone. Everyone lent a hand—even us lads. But it was Jake who did the job! Old Jake Bransby, and him only a year short of eighty years of age. Fishermen aren't like sailors. They're not used to taking orders. Although in my time Bramblewick lifeboat never failed to carry out a job I've never seen a launch when there wasn't a lot of haggling, never mind who was coxswain. But there was only one voice this time and it was Jake's and he didn't pick his words either.

Jake knew about every swear there was. He was the only one who didn't wear a lifebelt. He had no oilskins either, and only a hard felt hat on his head. When the carriage was far enough down the slipway he shouted to the crew to get in, and he climbed up himself and took t' rudder yokes, and stood watching t' breakers coming in, watching his chance for a calmish spell. But he didn't get one. A great sea came rushing up and broke clean over the boat and carriage. It knocked some of the launchers flat and it half-drowned t' chap who was standing under the stern waiting for Jake's order to knock out the steel pin that holds the boat keel to the carriage. And that sea did worse than that. It slewed the carriage round so that the boat was aiming broadside on instead of head on to the next sea. If Jake had waited for that sea, boat and carriage too would have been smashed against t' coastguard wall. But he yelled down at the chap to let go. Pin was knocked out. T' boat slid down and backwash of that first sea helped it, and gave old Jake and an old fisherman who was acting second coxswain to him just time to sweep her stern round with t' steering oar so that her bow met t' next sea almost head on. They couldn't have done it with the rudder, of course. She stood up almost on end but she weathered it all right. She almost went from sight down the back of that sea. When she rose again crew were at their oars and Jake was roaring at them to pull like hell. All that had happened to him apart from a drenching was that he'd lost his hat. It washed up t' slipway and one of us lads got it to keep for him, maybe thinking of what he'd give for it when he got back.

"In all the years I spent at sea I never saw a finer bit of

seamanship than that. Mind he was a Bransby. It was in their blood. They were always a bit better than others when it came to a test. He made those chaps pull as they'd never pulled in their lives before! And he steered through the seas that were breaking almost all the way in from t' landing mouth as well as any fisherman could have done, although all his service had been in ships. And all the time those cobles were drifting in to the breakers. Everybody on shore was quiet again. Everybody was watching. I could only see the cobles. But there was an old chap who had a pair of glasses, and he said he could make out three men, two hanging to one coble, and another to what he said looked like a rudder. He couldn't make out which of 'em it was, and it was a good job that London lass had been taken home. T' other women weren't sort to scream or faint, in spite of 'em being so anxious.

"Well, they got to the cobles. They came at the first one from t' landward side, of course, so that for a long time lifeboat hid her. Then the chap with the glasses said he could see some of the crew leaning over the side, and then he yelled that someone was being hauled aboard. He couldn't tell who it was, but that didn't matter for he soon said they'd got three men in from that coble, and it wasn't long before he shouted that they'd picked up lot of them—one from the rudder, the other two from second coble. So that London lass's chap was safe too..."

The captain paused to drain his glass. Then he went on,

"But that's not end of what happened. T' lifeboat couldn't land while t' tide was high, and so with those half-drowned and frozen chaps aboard Jake decided to follow t' rest of the cobles—they'd all been too far out to see what had happened—and make for Burnharbour. They had a sail of course and a gale behind them. They'd make port in under an hour and, as t' train didn't leave for Bramblewick until five o'clock, naturally they went to the pubs. Well, I doubt if Bramblewick had ever seen such a do as when that train came in. Everyone was up to the station including t' vicar and t' Wesleyan minister. I believe the idea was that there'd be a sort of thanksgiving service on the platform so it was a surprise for them all that practically every man jack of the fishermen was tight, and of course Jake too. Jake didn't mind a thanksgiving, but his idea was to have a procession not to church or chapel but round to all the pubs. Some of the women seized their own husbands and got them away from him, but a lot of them followed Jake and seeing that it was Saturday night with all the farmers down for marketing it was worse than any fair night and even when t' pubs turned out they went on singing and merry-making. Well, that was the sort of chap old Jake Bransby was. He was a drunkard all right. Before he died he lost all his brass too. He made a lot of daft investments it seemed, not in shipping shares, which were things he knew all about, but in things that had been advertised in the papers. But there was more than summat good about him! As there was about all the Bransbys."

"He must have been a tough 'un, Captain, and no mistake," said Jonty. "I've heard plenty of tales about old Jake, but that one's the best."

Sam Bunny nodded his head. "T' captain's right," he

said. "There is summat more than good about the Bransbys, or what's left of 'em. Tom's all right too, if he could only pull himself together."

The smith was grinning sardonically.

"Aye," he said. "But what happened next day, Captain—it was a Sunday, wasn't it? Did they have that thanksgiving service you mentioned? What had the parsons to say about it from the pulpit? Did Jake go to chapel?"

The captain's eyes flashed and he rapped his cane on the flags angrily.

"You're a cantankerous devil, Knaggs," he said. "You think you know a lot. Maybe you do but you don't know everything. You say there isn't a God. But there's plenty has lived longer than you in the world and say there is, and has plenty of proof too. What you ought to have done was to have gone to sea. You'd have learnt things there that they don't teach you in books. They all of them did go to church or chapel and there's no shame in telling it. I was at chapel with my mother and Jake himself was there, least at evening service, looking prim as a judge. I don't remember what the preacher said, but I do remember they sang 'Eternal Father', and that Jake joined in, there was no mistaking his voice. And I remember that that Winspear lad was there too with his wife, with her face still white as a sheet. And I remember that Jake was on the booze again next day, but what of it?"

The smith laughed this time rather sheepishly.

"No harm meant, Captain. I've got nothing against the Bransbys. And we don't want to start an argument about religion this time of night. What about another round? There should be time."

The landlord had just opened the door.

"There isn't," he said. "It's closing time so let's have your glasses, lads. Clock's just struck."

The company rose. The smith, a little crestfallen, bade the rest good night and was the first to go out. In the gas-lit street, which was roughly cobbled and just wide enough for the brewer's dray to bring its monthly load to the Mariner's cellar, the others parted. The captain lived on the North Cliff, Jonty's cottage was in the same direction and they turned right and upwards, Jonty slowing his postman stride to the captain's steady pace. Sam Bunny lived in an alley leading from Bennison's Steps at the south side of the village; the coastguard had a long climb from the dock to the new station built still higher up, and the two of them walked together to the dock from which the slipway slanted to the shore.

It was a dock only in the sense that it was a shelter for small craft. The cove from which its name derived had been the mouth of a small stream escaping to the sea through a ravine in the shale cliff. But in the days of Bramblewick's prosperity as a fishing port no space had been left on the sides of the ravine for further building, so the stream had been arched over and more cottages built above it leaving space only for the one road which led from the bank, followed the course of the invisible stream and widened out just before it reached the slipway top to give room for the lifeboat house and (once) for a fair number of hauled-up cobles.

There were no cobles now: only a few light pulling boats used for hire in the summer holidays. The lifeboat house was empty. The place was deserted but for one elderly man coming from the street that led from the gasworks and now walking up the main road. It was Ned Turnbull: stoker at the gas-house and lamplighter. He carried a ladder and he was starting on his round of putting the street lamps out. Some of the lamps were on posts; some were fixed by iron brackets on the cottage walls. They had incandescent burners but these had been fitted into the old lanterns which had been made for naked jets and the original taps had been left as they were. Bramblewick wouldn't have liked the idea of a pilot jet burning all day just to save the lamplighter carrying a ladder with him on his double round.

The two men stopped at the slipway breakwater, opposite to the old coastguard station. From here they had an uninterrupted view across the bay. It was October and there was a chill in the air, but there was no wind and the sky was starry. The tide was down and the curving scaurs, dark against the starlit creeks that divided them from each other, were visible to low water, marked with the white teeth of a gentle ground swell which made a low continuous booming. The two scaurs which formed the old fisherman's landing led almost directly seawards from the slipway bottom. The oak posts which used to mark them at all states of the tide in the old days had long since washed away. But near the end of the northern one a flickering light was visible and the coastguard said,

"That'll be Captain Bransby, eh?"

"Aye," Sam answered. "That'll be Tom. He's always down there when t' tide's right. Only thing that will keep him out of the pubs. For myself I never had much interest in fishing. Tom was always mad about it. When I was with him on the *Northgate* and we got to an anchorage it would never be long before he had a line over the side."

"Do you think he's all right? Think there was anything in what the smith said? It's a slippery spot that. There must be two fathoms of water close to where he's standing now."

Sam laughed dryly.

"Take no notice of Will Knaggs. He's a bloody know-all is that chap. Tom can carry his liquor as good as any other of the Bransbys could. He knows those scaurs as well as any fisherman. He could walk down them blindfolded." And then he added, thoughtfully, "If Tom fell in it wouldn't be by accident."

"What do you mean—ending himself?"

For a moment Sam stared at the light in silence. Then he shrugged his shoulders and turned, and the two of them walked on past the lifeboat house to where an alley led upwards to the left, and Sam said slowly,

"I don't believe he would. I don't believe he would. He's got overmuch sense has Tom."

"Well I hope you're right. Pity to see a man like that letting himself go. But blimey he does get on your nerves in a pub, doesn't he? I'll put the glasses on him when I gets up to the watch-house. Good night to you, Sam."

"Good night!"

They parted on their respective ways. Their footsteps died and there was no sound in the dock save the low booming of the far-off surf. Then after a while there were footsteps as Ned Turnbull came back down the road. He set the ladder against a corner of the old coastguard station and his footsteps were duller as he climbed the wooden rungs. A moment's silence, then six more dull-sounding steps as he came down. He shouldered the ladder and again his steps were loud as he walked through the dock and turned up the gasworks road. They faded and again there was only the sound of the sea. The dock was dark now. The gables and chimneys of the surrounding cottages stood out against the starshine. Seawards there were only the navigation lights of a ship on the horizon, and the faint flicker of Tom Bransby's lantern on the landing scaur end.

2

IT WAS an old-fashioned candle lantern, with one of its panes cracked and mended with a strip of brown paper. He had placed it on a pile of flat ballast stones so that the light from its clearest pane would shine on his rod which he had leant against another pile of stones, its tip (conspicuous with the white porcelain fair lead on it) three feet above the surface of the water. But there was enough light from this and the other panes to illuminate the bareish patch of level scaur on which he stood: a shallow circular toffee tin half-full of sand worms; a knife; an old and tattered fishmonger's bass containing tackle, spare leads, hooks and snoods. He was wearing ordinary walking boots of good quality. The heels and soles of them were worn down and they were sopping wet so that when he shifted his balance from one foot to the other they squelched and the air bubbled from the lace holes. His trousers too were wet as high up as the knees. He wore a dark gaberdine raincoat of naval pattern with a belt. It was shabby and the button had gone from the collar which was turned up but loose so that his throat was exposed. His cap was pulled down over his forehead. The light was below him and the shadows it cast accentuated the deathly pallor of his skin, his hollow cheeks and deep-sunk eye sockets. His hands were thrust in the pockets of his raincoat, but now and again he took one out and blew on the naked clenched fist and thrust it back again, at the same time slightly raising one foot and pressing on the other. His knees were trembling. But not for one second were his eyes averted from the gleaming porcelain ring on the tip of the rod, which never moved, although the line which slanted down from it swayed gently from side to side to the motion of the spent waves that broke continuously on the ends of the scaurs at the landing mouth.

He was not drunk. Alcohol had long since ceased to produce in him the ordinary effects of intoxication. He drank only to deaden and (with a vain effort) to kill a gnawing agony of mind from which he had suffered since that awful moment, more than two years ago, when he had felt the first impact of his ship on the plates of the other one. It did not produce complete forgetfulness. It stupefied him so that the pain itself became remote and endurable and the memory of what had happened, then and afterwards, unreal and dreamlike and possibly untrue. It gave him too the illusion, at least, of physical warmth and energy: warmth enough to withstand the shock of the cold night air after the stuffy heat of the bar-room; energy to walk with only a slight unsteadiness down the slippery scaurs with their many crevices and weed-hidden pools to his favourite fishing place. It gave him control over his numbed hands so that he could bait the hook dexterously and make his cast so that the sinker would drop just clear of a sunken patch of tangles inside where the surf was gently breaking. It gave him, above all things, the hope and anticipation of pleasure, the assurance that before long he would see that bright little ring jerk and the rod bend to the struggle of a hooked fish. He knew that the cod always came in when the tide turned, and already the gentle swaying of the line was more pronounced towards the land. Beneath the ledge on which he stood the level of the water was slowly rising.

But the illusory warmth of the drink he had consumed was draining from him like oil from the reservoir of a high flaring lamp. He was not aware as yet of the physical cold except as a minor discomfort in his feet and hands which he countered with an almost reflexive movement. He was starting to think again: the dream was becoming real, and involuntarily he allowed his gaze to shift from the rod to the seaward horizon, to the lights of the northward-passing ship, its red side light brighter than any star. He looked back at the rod, but it was steady, and the red light drew him again irresistibly, and he was back on the bridge of the ship, with the red light of the other ship, like a demon eye, glaring in the darkness close on the starboard bow.

The helmsman, old Pete Petersen, and the third officer who had been on the bridge at the time, had each given evidence against him. Pete was a naturalised Norwegian whose home was in Hull. He was a fine seaman with more than forty years' experience, ten of them in Arctic whalers. He was a man of fine character, sober, reliable, scrupulously honest and loyal too. He had sailed with many Bransbys in his time and he had a great respect and personal liking for Tom. It must have been an ordeal for this grand old sailor, who had so many English seafarer friends and was married to an English-woman, to stand in the witness-box and say what his strict honesty compelled him to say, and he had done his best in the course of his evidence to suggest mitigation.

"D' ship she come verra quick. I tink d' vind blow d' smoke from her funnel, and dat and d' driving rain 'ide her lights. D' vind vas behind her and blowin' verra strong. She come sodden like dat and d' captain make mistake, he tink *I* make mistake in turnin' to starboard. Ve can all make mistakes sometime. . ."

But that, prosecuting counsel had pointed out, although possibly true was opinion and not evidence. Pete's admissible evidence was in every detail a corroboration of what the third officer Mr Lawson had said. He too had shown a pathetic reluctance to testify against a man he liked. He was young, had only got his second mate's ticket and it was his first voyage as an officer, but he had been an apprentice under Tom, and would much rather have testified to his master's kindness and ability as an instructor in the arts of seamanship and navigation.

But what had it mattered how any of them had felt? Tom himself had given his own evidence without any appeal or suggestion that there were mitigating circumstances. There were not, either from a seaman's or from a legal point of view. It was not a mitigation that he was under the influence of alcohol while on the bridge of his ship. He was not drunk if drunk meant incapable of walking and standing. But he had been drinking most of that evening. He'd had a strong nip of whisky before he'd come on to the bridge. He'd just got there when he saw the lights. No—not the lights, but the single red one, and he'd heard the lookout man hail, "Light fine on the starboard bow".

It was probable that both vessels were proceeding in such a direction, and at such a speed, that a collision would have happened in any case. The vessel on the starboard bow had the right of way; it was incumbent on the other to avoid it and the obvious procedure was to reduce speed, to turn to starboard and pass under its stern. The third officer had sprung to the telegraph to signal "full astern", and instinctively old Pete had put the helm over. He would have done it without the third officer's command. Tom could not remember whether he had countermanded that order. If Pete and the third officer said that he did he would not deny it, but he did remember and he did admit pushing Pete out of the way and seizing the wheel and deliberately turning the ship back to its original course. The going astern of the engines had made no appreciable difference to the forward speed. He admitted complete responsibility for the collision. . .

He was still not consciously aware of the cold, but he had huddled his shoulders as though instinctively trying to conserve what was left of that illusory warmth inside him. The tide was flowing fast. The water had risen to the level of the ledge. It was creeping insidiously over it. It was over the welts of his boots. The bait tin gave a series of little jerks then moved smoothly towards the stones holding the lamp and grounded temporarily near the bass which was partly awash. But he did not move except that the shaking of his knees seemed to extend upwards to his shoulders. He had turned to look at the red light again, and now it was not the memory of the collision that possessed him but that of a ship on fire, burning from end to end and with a cloud of crimson smoke billowing upwards from her holds, lighting the sea around so that it was like a sea of blood. He had seen it from the piece of wreckage to which he had clung after the first explosion of the mine had split the part of the deck on which he had been standing and blown him overboard.

Although he held a master's certificate he'd been sailing mate then under his father's command. It was the second winter of the first war and the ship was not in convoy. She was homeward bound, chiefly with case oil from Mexico, and she had struck the mine about fifty miles off Ushant. It had exploded apparently amidships on the port side. The engine-room and stokehold must have flooded instantly and she heeled over to the port side to a considerable extent, but the oil was already on fire in Nos. 2 and 3 holds, the hatches of which had blown off. It had happened just before midnight during the third officer's watch. He had been having a last look round before turning in. His father, John Henry, had been on the bridge with the third officer and Tom had wished him good night from the bottom of the companion ladder. John Henry rarely left the bridge at night for more than half an hour when they were in wartime coastal waters, and he never undressed. Harry would have been in his bunk and asleep, dreaming no doubt of home. He'd been on the bridge with Tom during his own watch which had ended at eight, and he'd been talking excitedly about the presents he'd bought at Galveston for his mother. He was only seventeen, the baby of the family, a bit spoilt but a grand lad and already promising to be as good at his job as any other of the Bransbys. He'd be on his way home, with the other apprentice, as soon as the ship got into port. His father would see to that.

No one would ever know how they died, but it was unlikely that they were killed in the first explosion. The apprentices' quarters were on the starboard side near the galley. They may, on awakening, have rushed forward, but the flames from No. 3 hold would have driven them back. There could have been no escape aft. Tom had seen figures moving on the bridge which was not so badly damaged but the foremast had crashed down on it with its derricks and the only way to the safety of the sea was blocked with a tangle of torn plates and twisted rigging. He was badly hurt himself. He could not swim but he had made a wild effort to grab a piece of floating wreckage that was nearer to the ship. He wanted to get back to it to help. But he went under and the object he clutched at with the frenzy of a drowning man was the piece that he had left. When he was able to look again he saw nothing but the red flames and the smoke, and he had only the strength to haul himself flat on to the wreckage so that it supported him without the clutch of his hands. It was the flames that he remembered when he regained consciousness in the skipper's cuddy of the British tug which had rescued him and the three other survivors. The red flames and the smoke and his hate— hate for the devils who had done it! . . .

The bait tin was afloat again. It had spun round the stones and was now heading like a toy boat over the hidden scaur edge to the deep water of the landing. The water was over his ankles and lapping the bottoms of his trouser legs. He still did not move. His eyes were on the rod. The slack of the line was curving towards the shore. It was vibrating, but only with the drag of the tide. The rod was steady. He was thinking of Harry now. They'd always been pals. Before he'd married Ella it was always Harry he thought about when he was away at sea. It was always Harry he'd brought things back for. There was that Swedish knife he brought from the Baltic, those leather deck boots from Rotterdam, a real Indian bow from Vancouver. Always when he'd come home he and Harry had gone off on expeditions together: bird nesting or trout fishing if it was spring, poaching rabbits or cod angling if it was winter, or maybe making a day of it at Burnharbour and going to the pictures. It was the death of Harry more than of his father that he'd wanted to avenge. It was a hate and a fierce lust for vengeance that made him chafe at the days he had spent in hospital while a deep ragged wound on his back mended. It was hate that had sent him to the Naval Recruiting Office his first day out of the hospital to enlist in the fighting Navy. They would not have him. He was told that he should have joined the R.N.V.R. in peace-time if he'd wanted a naval job in war. If he wanted to kill Germans, to beat the devils, his best job was the one he was doing. There were plenty of berths going, masters' too, with his qualifications, and anyway they were giving all British merchantmen guns soon. There'd be plenty of chances of a scrap when the Huns got their new U-boat fleet going. . .

The opportunity for vengeance had never come. He

had been torpedoed twice, but on each occasion the U-boat had given no indication of its presence either before or after the attack. Other local skippers with less of a score than he had to settle had had running fights with surfaced U-boats. One skipper he knew had rammed a U-boat that had just sunk two ships out of a convoy and had had the satisfaction of seeing some of the devils in the sea, shouting to be saved. Save them? That was something he would not have done. Would any of them have saved Harry and his father from the flaming oil? Hate? You'd got to see someone you loved tortured and murdered to know what hate and wanting vengeance meant. You could get hardened to losing someone when they died naturally, but you couldn't forget, and you couldn't forgive, a murder. But what good would it have done if he'd told the court that it was his hate that had made him drive his ship into the other one? What would they have said if he'd told them that it was not because he was drunk, but because he wasn't drunk enough that he had done what he had done? They'd have said he was mad. They'd have been right too, but in a different way to what they meant. Could he have told them that since the end of the war he'd never been on the bridge of a ship at night and seen the lights of another ship approaching without that madness coming over him: that mad desire to ram it?

He had seen a doctor. The doctor hadn't laughed. He'd made him sit with his legs crossed and he'd tapped him just below the knee-cap with a little rubber mallet, and he'd gone all over his body testing his reflexes and his eyes and his blood pressure and had asked him enough questions to fill a book. He had told him that he was suffering from some sort of neurosis, which meant that his nerves were strained and used up and that the only cure was complete change and rest. He'd best go easy on the bottle, too, and smoking. The fool didn't realise that whisky was the thing that enabled him to control his mad impulses and discharge his duties as the master of a ship with competence. As for a change and a rest he'd tried one voyage ashore and it had made him worse. It had been in the spring. He'd gone for a walk one day to Matty Brewster's Wood (it was too far and too rough a road for Ella and Jane). It was daffodil time and when he got to the wood and saw the first patch of them down by the beck under the bare, but golden, budded oak trees he'd remembered the last time he'd been there with Harry (they'd come fishing too), and he'd hurried on, not daring to pick a flower, to the Falcon up on the moors and he'd got so tight they'd put him to sleep in the barn till morning!

As the illusory warmth oozed out of him the craving for the physical fuel of it began to possess him again. He thought of the flask he had hidden under a loose slab in the wash-house floor. He had done it cunningly, waiting until Ella had gone to fetch Jane from school. Still staring at the rod he noticed out of the tail of his eye that the water had now almost covered the bass and was only a few inches from the lantern. The bait tin had long since floated out of sight, but he did not notice its absence. Nor did he notice that the water was up to the hem of his raincoat. It was as though some nerve link between his senses and his mind had been severed and that the impulses had to travel by a longer and slower route. His eyes travelled from the lamp to the rod again and perceived a more significant thing: that the rod butt and the reel were under water and becoming buoyant, thereby changing the rod's balance against the pile of stones. At last he moved, and by doing so discovered how deep the water was round his legs. He knew he must go. He bent forward to seize the rod, but before he had touched it the long-anticipated thing happened. The tip jerked forward and sharply back again, and then forward and down to the water. It was as though an electric impulse had shot through him. He grasped the rod with both hands just as it bent over. He straightened himself, slid one hand down to the reel and pressed a finger against it to check the spin. He raised the rod point up and struck at the fish, got the feel of it and then let the line run out a bit. When he checked it again he felt its size and knew it was big.

He was alert and energetic now, in complete command of himself. He knew that the fish was too big to be lifted direct from the water, that it must be played and then dragged, not lifted on to the bare rock. There was no such rock within the area of the lantern's light. The scaur was submerged for a long way shorewards, and by sight it would have been impossible to tell the deep from the shallow water. Every inch of it was familiar to him, and holding the rod in both hands he started to move shorewards, playing the fish skilfully. He left the lantern and his gear. He could wade back for them once the fish was landed. It made a rush that bent the rod like an archer's bow and made the line sing. He checked it very gradually, moving step by step along the invisible scaur edge. This did not run continuously straight. There were numerous clefts in it, some of them deep. But none was wider than a man's stride and he knew exactly where they came and all the time he was reaching shallower water. The fish fought savagely, yet it was forced to obey the moderate drag he kept upon it and move shorewards. A few feet away from where he knew it would be safe to land it he started to reel in, ready to ease off if it made a sudden last effort to break away. He checked again while he took a few more careful strides that brought him to the dry scaur. He stopped. The fish, finding itself in shallow water, made its expected rush seawards. He let the line spin out and then checked slowly. But the rod did not bend as he applied the full check. The line had gone slack. He raised the rod, reeling in furiously. The fish had gone. . .

He did not curse or make any gesture of anger. He continued to reel in until he came to the broken end of the line, without fish or hook or sinker, and for a moment he stood where he was. But he was shaking again from head to foot. It was as though the excitement of hooking and playing the fish, which for the time had completely obliterated the pain of his thoughts, had consumed all that had been left of his nervous strength. He started to sob like a sick and tired and unhappy child. Then he remembered the whisky and a shred of courage and hope came back to him. He clenched his chattering teeth and started to walk up the scaur towards the slipway, one numbed hand holding the rod at the trail, the other thrust in his raincoat pocket. He had forgotten his bag and the lantern, which still gleamed on its island of stones just short of where the incoming surf was now breaking. He walked unsteadily, wearily, and his boots squelched at every footfall.

In the village itself, whose nearest cottages straggled along the cliff edge northwards of the slipway, there were no lights, but high above a solitary light shone from the coastguard watch-house on the hilltop. It disappeared as he drew into the shadow of the cliff and reached the slipway foot. He swayed as he walked up it, and he lurched sideways into the breakwater wall and nearly fell, but he carried on, up to the dock and past the lifeboat house to where Sam and the coastguard had parted, and he took the steep alley that Sam had taken, known as Bennison's Steps. As its steps twisted and turned upwards between the tight-packed cottages the sound of the surf which had followed him grew less, but the squelching sound of his own footfalls grew louder, and echoed between the walls. As though the sound scared him he stopped suddenly, and then went on, treading more lightly, and when he reached the corner of an alley on his left he stopped again, leaning against a wall. There was a light in the downstairs room of a cottage half-way up this alley, showing through chinks in the blind. That was Sam Bunny's. Three cottages up, on the same side and last of the row, was his own. He could see no light in it. He hoped that Ella had gone to bed and was asleep.

He was panting with the exertion of his climb up the steep main alley, and he leaned wearily against the wall. But he knew he'd be all right once he'd got the drink inside him. It would be all right if Ella was asleep. He started off again, treading furtively, almost tiptoeing as he passed the Bunnys' window. He was on good terms with his late bos'un, and if Sam heard him passing he'd be out wanting to know if he had caught any fish.

He could hear Mrs Bunny's high-pitched unpleasant voice nagging her son as she did every night when he got home from the pub. He became even more furtive as he moved on, treading so lightly that there was only the squelching of his boots and his own heavy breathing. Then he saw there was a light in his own downstairs room, and he stopped a few yards away from the doorway at the opposite side of the alley. Ella was waiting up for him. The wash-house was at the back and there was no way to it except through the cottage itself. He was afraid of her. He wasn't when he'd got enough whisky inside him. Then he could endure the scorn which he believed was behind everything she said and every look she gave him. That was what he hated. She'd never go for him. She'd never tell him straight out that he was a waster. But when he'd had nothing to drink he just knew that behind all her politeness and seeming kindness she was just hating him and despising him. When she saw him now the first thing she'd notice was that his feet were wet. She'd want him to change. She'd want him to have something to eat and some hot tea. But she'd know what he really wanted, and she'd hate him because of that. She wouldn't know that he could get it though. Once he'd got that flask he'd be all right.

The thought of the drink again gave him the courage and strength to move. He leant his rod against the wall and he opened the street door and closed it behind him. As he fumbled for the latch of the inner door it opened. He was so dazzled by the light that he did not immediately see his wife still holding the door and her voice startled him.

"Oh, I am glad you've come. Jane won't go to sleep till

you've said good night to her, Tom. Listen to her."

There was no anger, no disapproval in her voice. Nothing to suggest what he knew she must really be thinking: that he'd been on the booze all day, as he had been every day of the last week and hadn't earned a penny to pay for food or coal or rent or clothes for her and Jane; that her husband, Captain Thomas Bransby, once about the dandiest-dressed sailor belonging to Bramblewick, in uniform or "private", looked like a tramp begging at the door for a crust; Captain Thomas Bransby, late owner of The Hollies, New Avenue, Bramblewick, now tenant at a rent of two shillings a week of a hovel scarcely fit to house pigs. . . He did not look at her. He moved instinctively towards the fire that she'd evidently made up expecting that he'd come back wet and cold (using, he noticed, a tarry log he'd fetched up from the beach a few days ago). Then he heard Jane's voice from upstairs, reciting the twenty-third psalm:

". . . *He restoreth my soul. He leadeth me in the path of righteousness for His name's sake. Yea though I walk through the valley. . .*"

"You'd better go up to her, Tom. You know she'll never go to sleep till you've said good night to her. She's got that psalm on her brain. It's what she's been learning at Sunday School."

His eyes were on the door that led to the wash-house. But the reciting went on and the real warmth of the fire gave him a new, if transient, strength and self-confidence.

"Take the candle, Tom. She's really half asleep so don't start talking to her. See that the blanket's well tucked in behind her shoulder. . . You look wet through. I'll get some dry socks for you. Your slippers are by the fire. There's tea in the pot."

He did not look at her or speak. He took a candle which was lying lit on the table. The staircase door was open. There was no door to the second flight of stairs which led from the bedroom to the attic where Jane slept. The child heard his squelching footsteps and stopped her reciting to welcome him.

"Daddy—Daddy. Come and kiss me good night."

He swayed drunkenly as he climbed the attic stairs, and he had to pause for breath. Then he mastered himself, reached the top and advanced across the floor towards the tiny bed. The bed and the bedding, a coloured rug on the floor and a small painted dressing-table to match the bed were new-looking and expensive. Ella had bought them at a good shop in Liverpool when she had gone with Jane to see him off on his last disastrous voyage. They had been kept back from "The Hollies" sale. . . He put the candle down on the dressing-table. Jane was sitting up, holding out her arms to him. For a moment he hesitated to move to her. He had a sense of shame and remorse, something that Ella had never roused in him since he'd started going downhill. Ella's affection, her sympathy were put on: a mask hiding what she really felt. There was nothing put on about Jane's love. She just loved him, that was all. And he loved her and he was ashamed for her sake that he had let himself go. She was beautiful. The candle-light made a sort of radiance round her that reminded him of some picture he had seen long ago of the infant Christ.

She was so clean and fresh-looking. Everything about her seemed to glow: her wavy golden hair, her cheeks, her big wide-set grey eyes, her red lips and even teeth.

She was smiling at him, lovingly, with eager delight.

"Come on, Daddy. Kiss me!"

He had left his hat on the kitchen table. He wiped his hands on his coat and he bent down and hugged her round the shoulders, careful not to let her feel the chilliness of his hands and, deliberately keeping his own face in the shadow, he kissed her on the brow and pressed her head very gently on to the pillow. She turned her head away from him and shut her eyes contentedly and yawned and murmured,

"Good night, Daddy!"

The words "Good night, Jane" nearly stuck in his throat. He tucked the blanket round her shoulders, then he stood back, looking at her, loving her. Then he thought of Ella, waiting for him, and the whisky. He started to shake with cold and his fear of her and he lurched and bumped into the dressing-table as he reached for the candle. She was kneeling by the fire when he got down, holding out a pair of socks to warm. She half turned her head towards him and in that moment he noticed more than ever he had done before how like her face was to Jane's. Her hair was only a shade darker than Jane's and it had the same wave in it. She had colour in her cheeks too, and her lips were red and her teeth strong and white, and if it hadn't been for her eyes and the knowledge which he knew was in them he could have felt as he had felt towards Jane: shame, remorse, and perhaps a penitent love. But he could not meet her eyes, and she, knowing that, looked at the fire again when she said,

"You seem to have got her off all right. Sit down and get your boots and your socks off, Tom. You look frozen.

Did you get any fish?"

He had to pass behind her to reach the wash-house door. He knew that what she really meant was, "You've been in the Mariners all night until it was fishing time. You've spent enough on drink today to buy Jane at least a pair of shoes. You know we've next to no money left and you can't even bring a fish back with you". He said,

"No, I had no luck. I'll take my things off in the wash-house."

He had the candle in his hand. As though to show his wife that there was nothing the matter with him, he braced his shoulders and walked with an exaggerated steadiness towards the door. But he misjudged the distance and collided with it and had to grope for the latch. She glanced at him but said nothing and continued to hold out the socks to the fire. He got the door open, stepped into the wash-house and closed the door behind him with an unintentional bang that made her jump slightly. She kept her eyes on the fire, however. She could hear him moving about inside the wash-house. She heard him kick against an empty bucket, and then there was a short silence followed by a low thud, repeated twice. She heard him moving again. He was fumbling with the latch. The door was opened. She did not look until he had lurched half into the room. Then she got up and swung round half facing him. He still had one hand on the latch handle to support himself. He did not shout. His voice was so hoarse it was scarcely audible.

"Where is it?" he said.

She looked at him quite steadily and her voice was calm, conciliatory.

"Where's what?"

"You know what I mean. Where's that bloody flask?"

He let go of the latch, but he swayed and had to grasp it again. She did not answer immediately. She glanced at the fire as though from its light and heat she too was drawing courage. Then she turned again and spoke quite calmly,

"If you mean that flask that was under the stone, Tom, I've taken it. You're getting enough of that stuff without fetching it home. It's time you stopped it, Tom. You've got to stop it, if not for your own sake, then for Jane's. . . Come on, Tom. What's the use of getting vexed? You're killing yourself with drink. You haven't had a decent meal all day. You look frozen. Come and sit down by the fire and change your things and have a cup of good hot tea. It'll do you far more good than that stuff."

He was shaking violently. He had managed to shut the door. He was half-leaning against it with his shoulders crouched, his hand still clutching the latch. He looked desperately ill. His lips were grey, his face corpse-like in its pallor. But his eyes blazed with rage.

"I don't want your bloody tea. I want that flask. Do you hear? I want that flask. I've got to have it. It's the only thing. Where is it? I'll—I'll kill you if you don't give it to me."

He let go of the latch, but again he had to seize it to stop himself stumbling forward. Without apparent fear she moved towards him, and she put her hand on his arm. Her voice was still calm and soothing.

"Stop it, Tom. It's no good getting vexed. You know you're ill, and you'll be worse if you don't get your things changed. Whisky would only make you worse. I can't give it you anyway. I've thrown it down the sink. Now come and sit down and don't make any more fuss about it. Come on, Tom."

She put her other hand on his arm and started to pull him gently. She looked at his hand still clutching the door. He let go, but as she felt his full weight, he shot that hand out straight at her unprotected face. She fell without a cry, backwards. He saw her head strike the fender, then saw her roll half over with one arm swinging across her breast to lie with the other. He staggered back against the door, felt for the latch, missed it, and slowly collapsed into a sitting position. Then he leaned forward and moved nearer to her on his hands and knees, his head nodding grotesquely as though he was playing a game of bears for Jane. The sounds he made too were grotesque, deep in his throat, inarticulate. He moved until he was close to her shoulders. He put out one hand and touched her, and withdrew the hand sharply as though what he had touched had burnt. Then he looked at her head. Her hair was loose, and part of it lay over the rail of the fender, glinting in the firelight. He touched it and he felt a wetness. He lifted his hand up and saw a dark stain on it. The noises in his throat suddenly became articulate.

"Ella—Ella. I'm sorry. I didn't mean to harm you. I didn't mean it! I didn't mean it!"

He wiped his hand on the sleeve of his other arm. He put both his hands on her shoulder and tried to move her round so that he could see her face. There was no blood on it. But there was a dark bruise just above her chin, her cheeks were white and her eyes were shut. He went on gasping, "Ella—Ella" and he touched the back of her head again, but he could not tell where the blood was coming from for her hair was now matted. He was seized with panic. "I must fetch the doctor," he gasped. "Oh, Christ, I've killed her. I must get the doctor." He glanced towards the street door, the inner door to which Ella had left ajar. There was a sofa against the wall. He got up into a crouching position, then moved to the sofa, and steadied himself against it with his hands as he moved towards the door. All the strength seemed to have gone from his legs, however. When he reached the end of the sofa he sagged down again and he had to move on his hands and knees to the outer door. He reached up his hand for the latch. He thought of Sam Bunny. If only he could get the door open he could shout down the alley and Sam could fetch the doctor. He made a supreme effort to heave himself upright. He was successful, but he could not lift the latch without leaving go his hold, and he started to sink again. And then he heard voices outside, and a rapping on the door itself. He gasped, "Come in—come in," and the latch lifted and the door swung back gently. On the step was Hutchings the coastguard and, close behind him, Sam Bunny. The coastguard was carrying a hurricane lantern, but he was dazzled by the light from the room and he could only see Tom in silhouette as he crouched holding to the door. He was the first to speak.

"Why—it's you, Captain. Glad to see you and no mistake. Thought you'd blinkin' well got drowned. I've bin watching your lantern from the watch-house. Saw the tide comin' round it, and then it go out. Went down the landin' but saw no sign of you. So I thought I'd best come up and see if you'd got back. Sam, here, hadn't heard you passing, had you Sam? So you're all right, eh?"

He grinned. Then they both saw Tom swaying and as

he half-turned and the living-room light caught his face they saw the terror in it. They both moved to support him. He gasped at them,

"Ella—I think I've killed her. I didn't mean it. Fetch the doctor—quick—lying there—I didn't mean to hurt her—inside—fetch—"

He sagged down, babbling, "I didn't mean it." The coastguard took charge.

"Christ," he said. "Something bad's happened. You hold him, Sam. Got him? Fetch him inside. Christ—she's there on the floor."

He strode into the room. He knelt down by the woman's body, looked at her face, saw the blood on her hair. He was cool, and skilled in first aid. He parted the matted hair, found the source of the still welling blood in a cut just above the temple. He stood up. Sam had got Tom through the doorway. His collapse was complete but he was still babbling.

The coastguard had served as a naval P.O. through-out the war and had been in battles.

"Shove him on the sofa, Sam," he said quickly. "*He'll* do no more harm."

He seized a clean towel from an airing rail above the fireplace. He knelt down again and expertly mopped the blood round the cut, and then pressed the towel against it. He looked at her face, saw the bruise and noticed a faint tremor of her lips. She was breathing. Sam had dragged Tom to the sofa. He heaved him on to it and, very scared, looked at Ella.

"Is she dead?"

"Blimey no. But it's a case for the doctor. Constable too, I reckon. He must have knocked her down. She caught her head on the fender there. Only a skin cut on her head, but it'll need some stitches. You fetch him, or the constable could ring him."

"Aye. I'll go. But I'll not believe Tom tried to do her in on purpose. He was never that sort. I reckon we can do without police. Phone box in dock's nearer than station. I'll be off."

"Tell him they're both bad. I won't say he's not worse than her. They've got a kid, haven't they? Can't have made much noise about it or she'd be awake crying. Ask your mother to come along, case she's needed."

Sam was already at the door.

"She'd be no good. I'll go for Jonty's wife. She's the one for a job like this. God, I'm glad she's not dead. But I'll swear Tom didn't mean it anyway. I'll not fetch the policeman."

He went. The coastguard relaxed the pressure of the towel on the wound. The blood was showing signs of congealing. Clearly it was only a superficial wound. He left the towel on and took a cushion from the nearest chair, and very gently raised her head and slipped it underneath. He took his thick reefer coat off and put it over her. He knew that it was important to keep an unconscious person warm. He looked at her face again. Her lips still quivered. He could hear her breathing, see the rise and fall of her bosom. No, Tom hadn't killed her. She might be suffering from concussion, but she wasn't dead and she wasn't dying. He was glad that Sam wasn't going to fetch the policeman.

The long row of ribbons on the coastguard's breast showed that his service had begun long before the Great War. He'd served on the South African station during the

45

Boer War, and previous to that on the East Indies and China stations. He'd had plenty of experience of life—and death. He'd been in battles. He'd also seen famines and earthquake and volcanic disasters, and plague and cholera and yellow fever epidemics. He'd known what personal suffering and unhappiness was. In the Great War he'd lost all of his three sons, two in the Navy, one in the Royal Artillery. Mercifully for her his own wife had died before the war came, so she had missed that, but their younger daughter had lost her husband, and the elder one who kept house for him now had hardened her heart against marriage and was as a consequence short-tempered and cantankerous and difficult to live with.

The ribbons of the Distinguished Service Medal and (on his right breast) that of the Royal Humane Society were a testimony to his personal courage. He had gained the first in the Dogger Bank action. He had been awarded the Humane Society's medal during his pre-war coast-guard service for descending an overhanging sea cliff down a rope ladder in pitch darkness on a stormy night to rescue a shipwrecked sailor. He'd never had the education or ambition to rise above the rank of Chief Petty Officer in the Royal Navy. But he had a wide experience and a deep knowledge of life and one of the biggest things he had learnt was tolerance. The sight of the woman lying unconscious on the floor did not anger him. He felt a compassion towards her, but he did not think of her as the single sufferer. As he pressed the towel gently against the wound he glanced round the little room with its damp walls and meagre furniture, remembering what he had been told about the Bransbys' come down, of how the captain and Sam had stuck up for him in the pub. He noticed on the airing line a newly washed and ironed child's dress and he thought of the child asleep upstairs still ignorant of what had happened. It was a pity that this sort of thing could happen to a young couple. A pity that Tom couldn't get hold of himself. When drink led to violence it was high time to lay off. Yet many a chap's nerves had gone in the war. He'd seen that for himself. There'd been a big chap, one of his own gun crew, who'd cried like a kid when he'd seen his mate's arm blown off during that Dogger Bank do, and another that went raving mad and had to be put in irons coming back. It was something more than booze that had got Tom Bransby where he was.

He saw that the bleeding was now definitely checked. He got up and looked at Tom. He was lying as Sam had put him on his back, with one arm reaching down and the hand touching the floor. His eyes were shut. He was trembling all over and his lips twitched spasmodically as he babbled. . . He was in a bad way. Worse, perhaps, than his wife. Booze, and eating nothing probably, and then standing down there on the scaurs in the cold. Enough to kill anybody. It was either pneumonia or D.T.s—perhaps both: he was certainly delirious. He noticed Tom's boots, and quickly he took them off, and his socks. His feet were like those of a drowned man. The coastguard rubbed them vigorously, then he fetched the socks he'd noticed in the fireplace and, with difficulty for the wool stuck to the clammy skin, he put them on and he fetched some old coats that were hanging behind the street door and wrapped them over his body, lifting up that hanging, dead-seeming arm and making it snug. Then he stood over him, pitying him, pitying his wife and kid too, wondering how long it would be before the doctor came, still glad that Sam wasn't fetching the policeman.

Yet what was going to happen if the doctor got them both right again? Would a do like this give him a fright, put him off the booze for ever? He'd sounded sorry enough for what he'd done with his "I didn't mean it". Of course he didn't. They never did when they were tight and half crazy. What was he babbling about now? With his eyes half on Ella the coastguard listened to the jumble of sounds he was making in his throat, most of them indistinguishable as words. But there was one sound repeated over and over again and it was like "Harry", and there was another that might have been "whisky", and he articulated one complete sentence with an extraordinary vehemence, *"ram the bastard"*. Funny, the coastguard thought, that this was the chap who'd sat all night in the Mariners and never spoken a word. . . Well there was nothing he could do but wait for the doctor and Jonty's wife. Don't move—more than you can help—a physically injured unconscious person! Treat for shock. Keep warm. Give no stimulant. The doctor would need hot water. The kettle was on the hob. When Jonty's wife came they could fix up about the bed. She made a sound and he moved towards her. She was coming round. Trying to speak. And he could hear Sam running back up the alley.

3

THE REVEREND DAVID IVOR JONES, minister of the Wesleyan Methodist Chapel, was a post-war newcomer to Bramblewick. He was the son of a Glamorganshire miner, born in the Valley of the Taff, but his father had been killed in the pits when he was only six and he had been brought up by a schoolteacher uncle in Birmingham who, himself a local preacher, had effectively directed the boy's course through school and college to the ministry. He had never gone back to Wales. He remembered the squalor of his home, a four-roomed cottage housing a family of nine: one of a row of several hundred such, built like steps on the side of a bleak hill. He remembered the grime and the overcrowding and the noise, and a strike and starvation, and he remembered the day his father was brought home from the pit, and his mother weeping, but she was expecting her eighth baby then, and her uncle had taken him away after the funeral. Three weeks later the uncle had gone back to a second and, this time, a double funeral. David, however, had stayed where he was and by the time he realised that his mother was dead his Aunt Mary had more than taken her place in his affection.

Aunt Mary had been English. Uncle Glyn had been long enough in England to have lost his Welsh way of speaking. This second, and more permanent and highly respectable home of David's, his school and college, the years he had spent with a Wesleyan Mission in the East

End of London and as a minister on various circuits in the cities and industrial areas of the Midlands and Yorkshire, had Anglicised his speech and to a certain extent his outlook on life. He was not a snob and he certainly was not ashamed of his humble origin. He was too conscientious a Christian for that. But South Wales had become to him as it was to most Englishmen: another country where distressful things were going on now that the war-boom was over, but nevertheless foreign and remote.

Yet in many ways the Reverend David Ivor Jones was still, at the age of fifty-two, as Welsh as his name. His principle inheritance from his collier home was shortness of stature and a chronic weakness of health. Without his remembering it he had come through three strikes and three periods of semi-starvation during his childhood. It was not that he suffered from any specific malady. It was just that he had little resistance to the germs that were going the round except those to which a previous attack had made him immune. Thus from childhood on he had suffered from measles, scarlet fever, rheumatic fever, German measles, chicken-pox, mumps, quinsy, jaundice, and every one of the various types of cold and influenza. He had missed diphtheria and typhoid, but to make up for this he'd had pleurisy three times and it was the last attack which had decided him on his doctor's advice to give up a city ministry and come to the north east coast with its dry and bracing climate.

Although so short and narrow-chested, he had an imposing appearance, particularly in the pulpit. He had long, wavy, silvery hair which he wore brushed back like a poet. He had a very deep forehead, a thin handsome nose, a fine and expressive mouth and chin (he was clean shaven) and clear grey eyes which gleamed with a true Celtic ardour when he was reading from the Bible. But it was a poet's ardour rather than a religious one. He had a deep smooth sonorous voice with which he could make the Bible's lovely phrasing sound like music, even when occasionally the sense of it was obscure to himself and to his listeners. And he had fine hands with long sensitive fingers which he employed to give a visual emphasis to the rhythm of what he read or preached. In his sermons he had a Celtic eloquence, but he lacked the evangelical fire so typical of his race, perhaps because he was college trained. Consciously or unconsciously he was no humbug, however. He was a good man, kind-hearted, public-spirited, tolerant, unselfish. He had never spared himself either in his ministerial or social duties and wherever he had laboured he had been popular. He had indeed done an immense amount of good in his life without, to his knowledge, ever having brought a soul to salvation. He was not a Salvationist, however. His duties as a minister were prescribed, and he carried them out to the sheer best of his ability.

His last "parish" in a working-class district of a big Yorkshire town had been an extremely busy one. There had been a Boys' Welfare Club, a Mothers' Union, a soldiers' and war-workers' canteen. He had been a member of many secular organisations for social welfare. In all this his wife Gwen had been a great help to him, taking a part in all the activities of the chapel, teaching in Sunday School, running a company of Guides, as well as managing their home without a servant and nursing him through his illnesses. She was Welsh too, but again

Anglicised. They had married too late to have children of their own.

Both had been tired when they came to Bramblewick, but neither of them had regarded the new appointment as a rest. Certainly they had taken things easy for a while. They had been cautioned by the superintendent of the Burnharbour circuit, to which Bramblewick belonged, that he would find many differences between his new flock and the one he had left. At Bramblewick there was no poverty. The old village, except in the summer, was almost uninhabited. Most of the cottages were owned by people from York and Leeds or Bradford, who either came to them themselves for the holidays or let them furnished. There were no fishermen left. The retired sea-captains, with only one or two exceptions like Captain Christopher, lived in the "modern" part of Bramblewick, Up-Bank, in villas or semi-detached villas built of brick. They were not pretentious residences. They were not pretentious people. Indeed Mr Jones found it difficult to credit the superintendent's statement that at least five of these retired skippers had personal fortunes exceeding tens of thousands of pounds: that Captain Bartholomew Fosdyck, senior trustee of the Wesleyan Chapel, was worth more than a quarter of a million. But the superintendent, himself of Yorkshire birth, was a shrewd man. One of his most important jobs was the circuit finances. Collections represented only a small part of a religious body's income. In the sight of heaven all men were equal and the widow's mite was perhaps more significant than the rich man's five-pound note, but mites wouldn't provide training colleges and foreign missions and chapels, and chapel maintenance and repairs and new organs and ministers' stipends and manses. Its main income had to come from the wealthy in the shape of subscriptions, gifts and bequests.

In many ways, the superintendent had frankly pointed out to Mr Jones, the situation at Bramblewick was far from satisfactory. The membership of the chapel had shown a steady decline for the past ten years. One reason for this was undoubtedly that the fisherman population had gone. Another was that the chapel was in the old village, a stiff climb back for the people who lived "Up-Bank", whereas the Parish Church was near them and on the level. There was no doubt that the "Up-Bankers" (especially the womenfolk) had a feeling of snobbish disdain towards the old village. The Church could scarcely be said to be in a flourishing state, but its membership had increased as the Chapel membership had declined. It had built a new Church Room, the vicar had organised a Mothers' Union, and the Church had tended to become the centre of social activities in the parish. For some years now the Wesleyan circuit organisers had been considering the advisability of building a new chapel "Up-Bank". But here again they had been up against finance, and—bigger obstacle still— the die-hard conservatism of the local elders, especially that of Captain Bartholomew Fosdyck who, if he had so willed, could have built a new chapel out of his own pocket.

Mr Jones was thinking of his first candid discussion with the superintendent as he made his way this fine but chilly October morning to call on Captain Bartholomew Fosdyck. He remembered how the superintendent had summed up the discussion. They were, he had said, a hard, tight-fisted lot at Bramblewick. It was perhaps because they had made their money first in a hard, dangerous way. Or at least the nucleus of it. They had invested it wisely in shipping. The war had undoubtedly increased the value of their investments without their direct effort, but the district had made a fine contribution and sacrifices in its young serving men. Also in War Loan. It wasn't as though they hoarded their wealth. It was all invested, if not in shipping then in gilt-edged. It wasn't as though they lived extravagantly. So far as he could see the only pleasure they got out of it was a mere possessive pride, a sense of satisfaction of potential power. Their sin, if it could be called sin, was the negative one that, having such a potential power for charity, they used it so little, or so warily.

Mr Jones was not feeling happy. He had been a year in Bramblewick now and there were many things that made him wish he had not come at all. True that physically he had never felt better in his life. The clean sea and moorland air had been a perpetual tonic to his city-poisoned constitution. The place suited his wife, too. They both appreciated its natural beauty. The red pantiles of the crazily-built old village charmed them, so did the beach and the wooded streams that ran into the bay from the moorland hills. Superficially they got on quite well with the inhabitants, too. They were nearly all polite and apparently friendly, especially the tradesmen and the few folks down-bank. Yet with them all they both felt the existence of an impenetrable reserve. There was nothing hostile about it. It was, they felt, purely defensive, but it was hard, completely unyielding and in none was it more noticeable than in the character of

Captain Bartholomew Fosdyck. . .

The manse was in one of the newest of Bramblewick's rows of brick villas, built just before the outbreak of war by a local speculator. It was on the north side of the railway line joining the Burnharbour main road, and Mr Jones had to pass under the railway bridge where the main road met that from the station and took its name as Station Road as far as the Bank Top. There were avenues of villas leading from it to the left and he had turned into one of these. They were all semi-detached, bigger and better built than the manse but still quite modest. Captain Fosdyck's was in the middle of the avenue on the north side. He could recognise it easily by the gleaming white flag-pole in its front garden and the sight of it increased the gloom of his thoughts. Still fresh in his mind was the occasion on which he had had the temerity to broach to Captain Fosdyck the matter of the proposed new chapel. He had been encouraged to do so by the captain's own remark on the thinness of the congregation at the evening service from which they were returning up the Bank. It was a wild night with pelting rain. He had insisted on Gwen staying at home. He had said to the captain that people "Up-Bank" could scarcely be blamed for not coming to chapel on such a night, that really it would be an excellent thing if the proposed scheme for a new one could be set going before another winter. The captain had stopped and turned facing him and almost bellowed,

"Rubbish. Stuff and nonsense. If folks are going to stop going to God's house because of a puff o' wind and a drop o' rain let 'em have the damnation they deserve. What's wrong with awd chapel, eh? It was good enough for our fathers. Good enough for theirs. Good enough for John Wesley, too. And open air was good enough for him afore it was built. So long as it's Gospel and the Lord's Word, it doesn't matter where it's preached. There'll not be any flitting chapels in my time, Mr Jones. Get that straight."

Yes he had got it straight, and he had not much hope that he wasn't going to get it straight again about the stove for the Sunday School. If it had been a matter of his own comfort alone perhaps he'd have let the thing go, but this was Gwen's affair. She'd come back last Sunday afternoon shaking with cold and coughing and almost sick with the fumes. She'd had to send the children home after a very brief session. . . Involuntarily Mr Jones' fingers tightened on the handle of his umbrella as he approached the captain's house. Never had he felt so conscious of his own lack of inches and physical strength. He was saved the feared ordeal of walking up the garden path in sight of the front window and ringing the bell and waiting. For the captain was in the garden, polishing the window with a piece of chamois leather, and evidently he had caught the reflection of Mr Jones in it, for he turned round to greet him with a gruff but not unfriendly, "Now, Mr Jones". In spite of the cold the captain had his jacket off and his sleeves were rolled up showing the enormous muscles of his forearms which were like those of a professional boxer. He stood like a boxer too, with his head leaning slightly forward and his arms hanging loose. But Mr Jones did not think of him as being like a boxer at all, but like a thick gnarled oak tree in an exposed hedgerow, buffeted by storms, pruned and stunted, but growing ever thicker and resistant. He knew that the captain was well over the allotted span of human life. The fringe of whiskers that grew under his clean-shaved chin was white. His broad massive face was deeply-lined too, but there was no sign of senility in it. He had no teeth but this was not noticeable because he spoke through only half open lips and his lower jaws were so thick and heavy they pressed out what otherwise would have been the hollowness of his cheeks. His eyes were small but very bright. He had a long thick nose with a slight but cruel and domineering hook to it. A most unpleasant countenance, thought Mr Jones. A most unpleasant man. He could well believe the tale he had heard through Gwen that the captain had once been known as Bully Fosdyck and that, even after his conversion and while still sailing as ship's master, his reputation as a disciplinarian had not diminished. In addition to slave-driving his officers and men in their ordinary duties he had exacted from them a standard of moral behaviour conformable with his own. There was no swearing allowed on his ship, no drinking of course, and Divine Service was held as punctiliously as though on a man-of-war.

Mr Jones said, "Good morning, Captain Fosdyck," and hesitatingly opened the gate. The front garden was raised from the road and he had to climb three steps to reach its level. Instinctively, he left the gate open behind him. It was a small garden: a mere square of lawn with a narrow herbaceous border and some close-pruned roses under the window. It was prim and tidy. The flagpost was fixed in the centre. It was stepped in a tabernacle and the slack of the halyard was neatly fastened to a shiny brass cleat. There was no flag of course. Mr Jones stopped on the edge of the path, nervous and not knowing how to begin. But the captain solved that problem, for he said,

"And what's your business, Mr Jones? Chapel?"

Mr Jones coughed and laughed nervously.

"Not exactly, Captain Fosdyck. Not exactly. I wanted to have a word with you about another matter."

He noticed that the captain's right hand was doing a sort of conjuring trick with the cleaning leather. Without any apparent movement of his fingers it was disappearing underneath them and the last corner vanished completely when he said,

"Oh. Owt private? Do you want us to gan inside?"

It was the last thing Mr Jones wished to do and there was a comfort in the open gate so close behind him that gave him the courage to say aloud what was on his mind.

"Oh no, it's not private, Captain. It's the schoolroom stove. Mrs Jones, you know. The stove's broken, beyond repair I fear. Last Sunday she had to give it up after a prayer and one hymn. It smoked so badly. I was wondering whether the trustees would consider having a new one installed before the winter comes on. Whether you would care to bring the matter up at the next meeting?"

He stopped, aware that his voice had shaken more than it had done when he had preached his first public sermon thirty years ago; aware more than ever of the significance of his first Christian name. He felt indeed like a David before a Goliath and his eyes moved from Goliath's face to that hand from which the chamois leather became visible again but now as a sphere the size of a golf ball. It would not have surprised him if it had been the size of a marble and had actually turned to

58

stone. The captain said, slowly,

"Schoolroom stove! Schoolroom stove! What are you talking about, Mr Jones? There's nowt wrong with that stove that I know of saving a crack or two." And then he suddenly guffawed. "Last Sunday, eh? Why—did you notice which way the wind was blowing last Sunday?"

"No. I didn't, Captain Fosdyck."

"Nay, of course you wouldn't, not being a seafaring man. It was blowin' south-east by east, not over strong but strong enough. It only blows from that direction once in a while, but when it does t' schoolroom stove smokes and nowt will stop it next to pulling t' chapel roof off and building it t' other way round. That's your trouble, Mr Jones! It might be six months afore it blows south-east by east again."

Mr Jones was still nervous, but deep inside him something else that belonged to his Celtic inheritance was stirring, something too which belonged to the character of his biblical namesake. He said with a firmness that surprised himself,

"Yes, Captain, I've no doubt that is what made it smoke. But the stove itself is dangerous. It's nearly in bits. It's also rather too small for the size of the room. I've got to consider my wife's health although she's more concerned with the health of the children. I suggest we should have a new stove and also a bigger one."

The Captain had clenched his fist again on the ball of leather.

"A bigger one—a *bigger* one! And how much extra coal would it burn? That stove served when t' spot was a day school and when we had a Government grant. We don't get a grant now, Mr Jones. Chapel can't afford to be spending brass right and left for luxuries. Any idea what a new stove would cost?"

The thing that had been stirring in Mr Jones's breast suddenly rose up and possessed him. He didn't lose his temper but he lost all fear, all consciousness of a physical inferiority.

"I'm not asking for luxuries, Captain Fosdyck," he said. "I'm asking for a necessity. The chapel doesn't pay Mrs Jones for teaching the Sunday School. She does it because it's God's work, because she's fond of the little ones. But I'll not have her do that at the expense of her health. She'll have to give it up, I'm afraid, at least for the winter."

It was Captain Fosdyck's turn to be surprised and almost alarmed. Personally he did not think very much of Mr Jones. He thought he fancied himself a bit too much in the pulpit. His sermons were inclined to be flowery and above most folk's heads. Supremely confident in his own moral rectitude, equally confident (so that he never thought about it) that his life after death would be spent among the blessed, the Captain was nevertheless a firm believer in a physical hell, and he thought that a preacher should never let his congregation forget it. He'd never heard Mr Jones as much as mention the word in a sermon. . . Still there was a lot in his favour. The summer visitors had liked him. He'd actually filled the chapel three Sundays last August, morning and night. Biggest collection of the year. And there was his wife, too. She'd got up a concert with the Sunday School children and made over twelve pounds for the Chapel Fund, nearly all out of the visitors, too. He released his grip on the ball of leather, and he teased it out with his other hand, and gave it a shake, and he laughed.

"Now don't be over hasty, Mr Jones. You've got a right to think about your missus. I'd not like to see her give up t' school. I was having a look at that stove t'other day. What it wants is an iron band round it, and t' flue pipe wants patching a bit. It's a job for the smith. I'd ask him myself, but that chap an' me's not on speaking terms. Knaggs, they call him. An ignorant boastful chap. Thinks he knows everything, of course. But he's a good smith, I'll say that for him. If you're going down that way, call at the smiddy and see him. You needn't tell him I sent you. Get him to have a look at it. But see you get your price for the job if he'll do it. If he says it's beyond repair then we'll see if we can't get hold of another one second-hand. Nay, I wouldn't like your missus to give up t' Sunday School. That would be a victory for the devil. There's nowt else is there?"

Mr Jones had a sense of humour. He chuckled to himself as he walked briskly along the avenue towards the Station road, remembering how he had felt a few minutes before as he had walked in the opposite direction. There came to his mind the lines from Samuel: "And David put his hand in his bag and took thence a stone and slang it and smote the Philistine in his forehead, that the stone sank into his forehead and he fell upon his face to the earth". That story, read first to him by Uncle Glyn in all its gory detail, had always appealed to his imagination, the small conquering the big, the weak the strong. But as he turned into the road towards the bank top he began to wonder if after all his victory was so great, and he became despondent again. What good was he doing in a place like this? There was no poverty here, no crime, no great social problems of overcrowding and sweated labour and unemployment and sickness. The people were not all like Captain Fosdyck, but they were nearly all old and set. They believed in God, but just as much they believed in themselves, in their own infallible righteousness.

He paused at the top of the Bank, for what he and Gwen from the first time they had seen it had always called the "surprise view". It was so unexpected, such a complete contrast to the avenues and villas of modern Bramblewick. This morning it was lovelier than he had ever seen it before. The sea and land were veiled with a thin autumnal mist through which the sun shone with little heat yet with enough filtered light to make the massed roofs of the old village below him glow like a slow burning fire. Landward of the village in the narrow wooded valleys through which ran the twin tributaries of the beck, the leaves of oak and ash and beech made a more subdued burning with the grey green of fading pastures, the dull yellow of stubble and the dark brown of ploughed land reaching beyond and gradually merging into the uniform grey of the misty moorlands. The tide was down: the sea peaceful. On such a day as this, Mr Jones thought, in the industrial city where he had held his last ministry the mist would have been fog, trapping the smoke and fumes from innumerable factory chimneys: the air instead of tasting of brine would have tasted of sulphur and burnt gasoline, the pavements would have been greasy with mud, and he himself most likely would have been suffering from or in the process of starting one more of his innumerable types of cold or flu. To the discomfort of all this would have been added the eternal clamour of traffic, vans, tramcars, buses, people.

Here where he paused he could hear only three sounds, and all of them were pleasant, a flock of gulls wheeling over the edge of the cliff, horses and a cart coming up the bank, and a musical clanging: the sound of the smith's anvil from the smiddy at the bank bottom. No, he thought suddenly, he didn't want to go back to that, but he wished that the people here had some of the qualities his poor people had, that having health they could show their gratitude for it more, that they could appreciate this peace and beauty. The clanging of the anvil reminded him of his mission, and he carried on down the bank steps: broad slabs of freestone arranged in irregular flights and elevated above the rough cart road. He passed the horses and cart that had been down to the gas-house with coal, and he said "Good morning" to the carter who answered with a respectful but grumpy "Morning sir". Then he came to the smiddy on the left hand, where the road twisted down to the stone bridge over the beck into the heart of the village.

He had never made any personal contact with Knaggs the smith, but again he had learnt quite a lot about him through Gwen who had an excellent informant on local matters in Liza Watterson, a down-bank spinster who came to do her "rough" once a week. He knew that he declared himself to be a socialist and a disbeliever in God, that he was very self-opinionated but also an excellent workman, that the village had to tolerate him on this account. He also knew that he was a widower with a son called Edwin who was supposed to be very clever as he'd won a scholarship to the new secondary school at Burnharbour, and that he lived above the smiddy with his elderly spinster sister Betsy who, completely indifferent to his views on life and religion, was a regular member of the Church. Another Philistine, thought Mr Jones as he looked in through the open door: perhaps another Goliath, but having seen his face plenty of times, not such a formidable one as Captain Fosdyck.

He did not see his face now for he was at the forge, working the bellows with his left hand, his back to the doorway. But at a bench just inside the door was a boy wearing a school cap, but without his jacket, deeply concentrating on the task of drilling a hole in a small brass plate. The boy looked up at Mr Jones and smiled pleasantly. It was Edwin. Mr Jones returned the smile. He was a quick judge of character. He thought straight away that whatever the father was like, there was not much wrong with the son. He was handsome but in a manly way. He had a good forehead and nose, a full mouth with excellent teeth, and very bright intelligent eyes. Mr Jones spoke to him easily, without any conde-scension.

"Hallo. You're Edwin, aren't you? What are you making?" The boy grinned a little shyly and his cheeks flushed.

"Oh, it's nothing, sir. I'm trying to make a model steam engine as a matter of fact. One to go in a boat. Here's the boat."

He reached to a shelf above the bench and took down a model launch about a yard in length, carved out of a single piece of wood. Mr Jones looked at it with unfeigned admiration.

"My—that's fine. Have you made that yourself?"

The boy laughed.

"Yes, sir. But I'm afraid it's a bit rough. I don't think I've got it quite true either, but perhaps I'll get it right when I sandpaper it. It's going to be painted of course."

Mr Jones liked good manners in a boy when they were unaffected as Edwin's were. He liked his modesty too, which did not hide an intense eagerness. Surely, he thought, the father of such a boy could not be the intolerant braggart he was alleged to be. Before he had a chance to speak to Edwin again, the smith himself turned his face and stared deliberately at his visitor. He did not speak. He gave no sign of recognition. He went on blowing at the bellows, then he turned to the fire again, stopped blowing, grasped the cool end of the thick iron rod he had been heating with his left hand, brought it to the anvil and started to hammer the white-hot end into the shape of a hook. Fascinated, Mr Jones watched him. Again his sense of humour was in the ascendant. He did not believe in a personal devil, any more than he believed in a physical hell, but he thought there was something that could only be termed satanic in the smith's expression while he had been staring at him. There was something even more satanic in the way he looked now as he bent over the anvil with the light from the hot metal reddening his grimy cheeks and glinting in his eyes, and the sparks spouting up from each blow of his hammer in a fiery fountain, pelting his bared arms and even his face without apparently hurting him. But satanic was the word, and not evil. There was a curious difference in Mr Jones's mind between the two. Evil was something he abhorred. Greed, self-indulgence, meanness, were the things he meant by that. They were the sordid, the insidious enemies of virtue. But Satanism was an open militant force, something to inspire a Christian's militancy, to join honourable battle with and fight. He did not feel half so afraid of the smith as he had done of Captain Fosdyck. He did not dislike him. Quite definitely he liked his son, and would have continued speaking to him but for the noise of the hammering.

It stopped at last and the smith turned and laid the rod on the hearth; then he turned again and with a sardonic grin remarked,

"Morning. Sorry to have kept you waiting."

Mr Jones did not miss the mockery in his voice, the over-emphasised politeness. But it was quite unintentionally that with his first remark he touched the smith in his weakest spot. He might have been inspired. He laughed.

"Don't be sorry for that, Mr Knaggs. I've been having a look at that boat your boy's made. A fine bit of work."

He didn't overdo it. He was not thinking of the effect his words might have on the smith. He guessed the boy would resent anything suggestive of flattery. But he was quick to see that the smith was pleased, for his grin was less sardonic.

"Ah," he said, looking towards the bench. "*That!* Aye, he's made a middling good job of it. But he ought to be at school by rights, not doing that. School's closed for German measles."

Mr Jones shuddered slightly at the mention of an infectious disease and he looked at Edwin with an involuntary apprehension. But he'd had German measles, he remembered, and it was one of the things you didn't have twice, and he said addressing both of them,

"That's the Burnharbour County, isn't it?"

"Aye," the father answered. "It's his second year. Top of his form, too. Not bad for the son of a village blacksmith, eh?"

Again the mockery was in his voice. But again Mr Jones was cautious. It would have been easy for him to have turned the remark with a compliment to the smith himself. All he said was,

"It's very, very good. Excellent." He was aware that the smith was trying to size him up, that the first good impression he had made might only be transient. He decided on a quick and a direct approach. "I don't want to trouble you if you are very busy, Mr Knaggs, but if you could spare the time could you have a look at the stove in the chapel schoolroom and give an opinion on it? It's got a bad crack in it and it smokes badly. I'd like to know if it could be repaired."

The smith laughed.

"So that's it, eh? I thought maybe you'd come to ask me why I didn't come to chapel. But maybe you'll know what my opinion about chapels and churches is, and the folks that go to them?"

"I know you are not a member of the Wesleyan Chapel, Mr Knaggs," Mr Jones answered evenly, "or we would have met before."

The smith was silent for a moment. He still stared at Mr Jones. His expression was still sardonic, but obviously he was a little nonplussed. Suddenly he reached for his jacket and cap lying on the other end of the bench, and started to put them on.

"I'll come and look at it now," he said gruffly, and to his son, with a peculiar tenderness, "Put a bit more slack on that fire lad. I won't be long."

It wasn't far to the Chapel. Chapel Street was merely a rather wide cobbled alley turning left from the road just before the bridge and climbing up and along the ridge of the shale cliff which divided the gorge of the beck from the sea. Cottages were built on both the landward and seaward edges of this cliff but many of those originally on the seaward side had tumbled into the sea and the Chapel had only a space of a few feet between its back and the sheer seaward cliff face. In very stormy weather the windows looking on to the sea had to be shuttered against the spray of breaking waves which had been known to reach as high as the roof. . . Again, as they walked along Chapel Street, Mr Jones felt conscious of his stature. The smith was not so powerfully built as Captain Fosdyck, but he was much taller, and he held himself very straight. Mr Jones's sense of humour was still in the ascendant, however. Really, he thought, the two of them must have looked extremely funny walking along to the Chapel together, the village atheist and the little Wesleyan minister. He wondered if the smith himself was thinking the same thing, if he too was feeling self-conscious. If that was why this man, who was alleged to be such a great talker, was now silent? He had no doubt anyway that he had found a soft spot in his armour and he proceeded to take advantage of it.

"I like that boy of yours, Mr Knaggs. Did you say this was his second year at the County?"

The smith was looking straight ahead.

"Aye," he grunted.

"He won a scholarship, I heard?"

"Aye. From Burnharbour Council School. Came out first of about fifty lads that sat for it."

Mr Jones knew that since the closing of the Wesleyan Day School the few local boys had been obliged to go to the Burnharbour elementary school, although the local Church School for infants and girls was still open.

"I'm not surprised," he answered, conscious more than ever that he was taking a very good line. "He looks an extremely intelligent boy. I like his manners."

"I taught him his manners," Mr Knaggs said rather surprisingly. "He wouldn't learn them anywhere else in this spot."

Mr Jones's sense of humour nearly got the better of him. It was only by a supreme effort that he did not laugh aloud, and was able to say with outward gravity,

"Well, he does you credit. And what are you going to make of him when he leaves school?"

They were getting near the Chapel. Mr Jones felt in his pocket for the schoolroom key.

"When he leaves school," the smith replied, "it'll be for college or university. I reckon he'll get a scholarship for that, same as he did for the County School. It'll be his own choice then, but I reckon it'll be science of some sort. He'll have had a better chance than I had, anyway. This is where I got my schooling. Bramblewick Bay Wesleyan. *Bah!*"

The teacher of good manners spat contemptuously on the cobbles as Mr Jones inserted the key in the door. They had reached the Chapel front. A brick wall on the right of the alley was a fence against the precipice to the beck. Opposite to this the chapel itself rose to twice the height

69

of the adjoining cottages and was about twice the width. Two tall windows, not arched, but with their clear panes bordered with coloured lights, were set right and left of a carved stone tablet bearing the terse inscription,

WESLEYAN CHAPEL.   BUILT 1779

The original entrance had been on the seaward side, but the approaches to it had fallen over and now the only way into the chapel proper was up a flight of stone steps to a door leading to the gallery. The door that Mr Jones opened was on the street level, and he led the way along a dark narrow corridor which ran practically the whole depth of the building from front to back where it opened into a large room with three windows facing the sea. In spite of the windows, it was gloomy and icy cold, and the air still smelled of stale flue smoke. The guilty stove was on their right. But the smith did not look at it. He glanced round the room with an expression on his face that suggested he wanted to spit again.

"Aye. This is the spot. Hasn't changed much either except the master's desk being gone, and I see you've got some holy pictures on the walls instead of where we had maps."

Mr Jones felt a small twinge of indignation at this contemptuous reference to the decorations on the wall. He was glad that Gwen was not with him. When they had first been shown the room by Captain Fosdyck they had both been appalled by its dinginess. There was nothing whatever on the walls, which were painted a dirty grey, a shade darker where the maps that the smith referred to had once hung. She had suggested at once

70

that the walls should be repainted a light colour, but the captain had shaken his head. That paint was only ten years old. All it needed was washing. So Gwen had bought the pictures from a firm of religious publishers. They were German prints, poster size, illustrating incidents from the life of Christ. As works of art or piety they might not be up to much but the colours were bright and they certainly had made the place seem less gloomy. One of the pictures illustrated the miracle of the loaves and fishes. The smith grinned at it sardonically.

"Miracle!" he said. "Do you believe that ever happened, Mr Jones? Do you believe about Jairus' daughter, and turning water into wine, and walking on the sea and all that?"

"There are more things in heaven and earth, Horatio, than are dreamt of in your philosophy," Mr Jones retorted.

The smith turned on him, sneering.

"That's Shakespeare's Hamlet. I've read Shakespeare. I've read the Bible too from cover to cover. I haven't the advantage of your education, of course, but I've read a few books, and not the sort you'd give away for Sunday School prizes, either. I doubt if any of the old jossers who come to hear you preach on a Sunday have ever heard of 'em. Ingersoll and Emerson and Haekel and John Stuart Mill. And Darwin and Huxley and Lyell and Wallace; aye, and Karl Marx and Bernard Shaw."

Mr Jones at last was beginning to feel uncomfortable. True he had heard of all these scientists and philosophers and knew more or less what they had written or argued about but, with the exception of Shaw, he could not have said that he had read any of their books. Nor would he

71

have been familiar with the works of Shaw had not Gwen been a great theatre-goer, especially to repertory. The controversial aspects of religion had never been of great interest to him. He had always taken the fundamental truths of Christianity for granted. He had never felt it incumbent on him to defend that faith. He regarded himself as minister to his flock, his duty to guide and encourage and help them personally, to be as Christ-like as he humanly could. He still wasn't afraid of the smith but he wasn't going to let himself in for an argument. Was it simply to trail the tail of his coat that the man had so readily come along with him?

He laughed and said,

"I'd never judge a man's education by the school or college he went to, Mr Knaggs. I'd have to admit that so far as books and names like those go the preacher would be as ignorant as the congregation." And he added quickly, "That's the stove. You can still smell the smoke from last Sunday although I'm told it only smokes badly when the wind's a certain way."

The smith glanced at it. It was an old-fashioned slow-combustion stove with a visible cast-iron flue reaching almost to the ceiling before entering the wall. The body of the stove and the top were cracked in several places. The wall itself and the ceiling were blackened with soot.

"Aye," the smith said slowly. "I see it. And I can see you won't be drawn into talking. None of you professionals ever will because you know you'd be beaten. Still I suppose you've got to earn your living same as anyone else. And you'd soon get the sack if you told folks the plain truth about themselves. Same as the doctor. I don't blame you, but I only wish I had the chance to stand one night in your place and let those old jossers have it straight. Old Bully Fosdyck and Grainger Stevenson, and Matt Roberts, and old Abigail and Selina Lawther who got ten thousand quid apiece when old Captain Lawther died, and will still walk to Burnharbour and back rather than spend a bob on railway fare. Religion! I'd give 'em religion, the bloody humbugs. And Bully Fosdyck's the worst of lot — and the richest. Wasn't it him who asked you to come to me about this stove?"

Mr Jones grinned.

"It was as a matter of fact."

"I thought so. He wouldn't have the neck to come himself. But he'd sink his pride enough to give you the job if he thought he could save a bit of brass. That stove's junk. Has been this past twenty years. To my knowledge it's over forty years old. But you'll not get him to agree to a new one, I'll tell you that straight! And I'll tell you that if he'd asked me to mend it I'd have told him to go to hell. But I'm sorry for you and your missus having to put up with ignorant chaps like him. I'll do my best for you."

He took a flexible steel ruler from his pocket and measured the circumference of the body, then the height of the cracked piping. He jotted the measurements down on the back of a grimy envelope. Then he said, turning to the door,

"Right. That's all I want. I must be off back. I've got no time to waste this morning. And I reckon you'll be wanting to get back Up-Bank among the nobility. You'll not have many calls to make down here. . . But wait a minute. Doesn't Captain Tom Bransby's wife go to your

73

chapel? She used to sing in the choir I know. Their bairn anyway goes to Sunday School. But maybe you've already called on 'em."

"No, Mr Knaggs, I've just come down. Is anything wrong?"

"Oh you haven't heard then? I should have thought the whole village must have heard by now. There's been a fine old do. . . Come on I'll tell you as we go out. You'd better let me have key, by the way. I'll have to try those bands when I've made 'em."

The smith this time led the way along the corridor, talking over his shoulder.

"A fine old do there's been! Tom's been on the booze for weeks. You'll know about him having been in trouble and having lost his master's ticket. Well he came home late last night, and it seems he and his wife had a dust up. Anyway he must have gone for her and hit her pretty hard. The coastguard and Sam Bunny found them. She was unconscious on the floor. Tom was about collapsing, did collapse in fact. They had to get doctor for both of 'em and it seems that he's a sight worse than her, although she had to have a cut in her head stitched."

They had reached the street door. Mr Jones felt distressed.

"How dreadful," he said. "What about the little girl, Jane?"

The smith had stepped out. Mr Jones was closing the door.

"Seems she slept through it all. But Sam Bunny went for Polly Scaife, the postman's wife, and she's taken her. It'll be a court job, I reckon. It looks almost as though he tried to do her in, but he was tight of course. He's got

D.T.s now."

For the first time Mr Jones almost hated the smith. He was grinning again sardonically and seemed to be taking a malicious delight in the news he was giving. He locked the door and handed him the key.

"Thank you very much for taking on the job, Mr Knaggs. It's very good of you. I'll go round to the Bransbys at once."

He knew where the Bransbys' cottage was, and he was glad it was in the opposite direction to the smiddy. He quickly forgot the smith as he hurried along. He tried to remember all that Gwen had told him about the Bransbys. She of course had had the full story of the young captain's downfall from Liza; the Board of Trade inquiry; how when he'd come "home" he'd taken an "insurance book" and quickly lost it through drink; how he'd started betting on horses through a Burnharbour bookmaker, lost what he had left of his savings, and then had to sell up and move "down-Bank". For a year now the only money he had earned had been by doing odd jobs for local farmers including his father-in-law old Mark Moorsholm whose farm was near High Batts.

He knew Tom well enough by sight. He had felt a minister's interest in him, but found him quite unapproachable. His wife was no easier. She came to chapel every Sunday evening with Jane. She was always neatly and soberly dressed. She was very good-looking (really beautiful, Gwen thought) and far more intelligent-looking than any woman in the congregation. But her expression was always completely impassive even during the hymns in which she joined in a very pleasant contralto. He gathered that she had left the choir on her marriage without giving any reason for doing so, and that she had refused all invitations to go back. He had never felt that it was his duty to force himself upon people. But there was a strong bond of interest with the Bransbys in Jane. Gwen doted on her. Jane made up for all the discouragement she had received in the running of her Sunday School. And it wasn't just her unusual beauty. Gwen herself had a passion for poetry and elocution, and (although she kept it repressed within reasonable limits) for dramatic art and the theatre. She had been a day-schoolmistress before they had met and for years had delighted in producing school plays and other entertainments. She had found among the twenty or so children who attended Sunday School very much the same stolidity of temperament and reserve so typical of the older Bramblewick people, with Jane the one shining exception. The child had a lovely speaking voice. She seemed to have an instinct for the right pronunciation of words, a wonderful sense of rhythm whether it was poetry or prose, and she could act without the slightest affectation or self-consciousness. She'd been in a little sketch at the "visitors" concert and she'd brought the house down. Gwen, he felt, was going to be terribly distressed if things were as bad as the smith had suggested. . .

He had followed the continuation of Chapel Street, up a little beyond the Chapel, then down past the Mariners to the dock. The dock was deserted and he saw no one until he turned into the very alley where Tom lived and then he saw the police constable coming towards him. He was frightened. Obviously he was coming from the cottage. He stopped and said good

76

morning. He was "Church" but he was a pleasant sort of man and Mr Jones was used to chatting with him. He too guessed Mr Jones's errand. He spoke very quietly, nodding his head in the direction of the cottage.

"You're going to call are you, Mr Jones?"

Mr Jones spoke nervously,

"Yes, if it's all right. I've only just this moment heard what has happened. I hope it's not very serious."

He was relieved to see the constable grin.

"No, I don't think so, sir, least not from the point of view of the police. She's got a nasty cut but I reckon it was more of an accident than anything else. He'd had a few drinks I gather. More than a few maybe, but the chaps who saw him out of the Mariners declare he wasn't drunk. Anyway, she won't charge him, and that's what I had to come and find out. Like you, sir, I was only told about it. I wasn't sent for. But *he's* in a bad way. D.T.s. There's a neighbour in watching by his bedside. Another neighbour has taken the bairn. The doctor says he might get dangerous in fits but he's very weak. I don't suppose you can do him any good but I think if you could persuade his wife to go to a neighbour it would be a good thing. She says she won't leave him. She's very stubborn about it."

"Dear me. Dear me," said Mr Jones. "I'm very sorry about it. I'll certainly see what I can do. But I'm glad it's not going to be a case for the court."

"So am I, sir, to tell the truth. I'm very sorry for both of them."

There was no need for him to knock at the door. It was open and as he approached it he saw the postman's wife coming out to empty a bowl of dirty water in the gutter. Again, although they belonged to the Church, Mr Jones was on very cordial terms with Jonty and his wife. There was nothing reserved about her character. She was garrulous. Obviously she considered herself in charge, for she emptied the bowl and then held Mr Jones back from the doorway while she spoke to him in low and confidential tones.

"I'm real pleased you've come to call, sir. I'd rather it was you than t' bobby. But I soon got shut of *him*. No one asked him to come anyway! Fat lot of use *he* is, prowling round and askin' a lot of daft questions hours after doctor's been and things have been straightened up. I suppose you'll have heard all that's happened, Mr Jones?"

He guessed that she was very willing to impart full and dramatic details, and he said ruthlessly,

"Yes. Is it all right for me to see Mrs Bransby?"

Polly looked rather disappointed.

"Aye, sir. She's downstairs. She won't go to bed. Says she's all right. But don't take any notice of *him. Eee*—his language is fair awful now and again. But he's raving poor chap. He doesn't know what he's saying. It's a good job, isn't it, we've got t' little bairn out of t' way. I took her to school this morning and I'm going to take her home for dinner. Come your way's in, sir."

In his various city ministries Mr Jones had seen a great deal of the sordid aspects of life. He had known slums where families with as many as six children were living in a single room, where the stench alone was enough to make the caller vomit. He had seen children sleeping without blankets in winter time, unwashed, verminous, their bodies covered with sores. He had, in carrying out his duties as a minister, visited "homes" where the father had come in drunk at least once a week and amused himself beating up his wife. He had been insulted, and on more than one occasion physically assaulted for sticking up not for his religious faith, but for his belief in justice and humanity.

There was nothing sordid in the sight that met him as he entered the living-room of Tom Bransby's cottage. The smell was the wholesome one of soap and disinfectant. The room, bare though it was compared with most of the local cottages he had seen, was spotlessly clean and tidy. The fireside gleamed. Even the kettle was black-leaded and polished. Yet never had he felt more nervous, more lacking in self-confidence or for that matter more deeply distressed. Cruelty, tragedy seemed to him to be just the normal inevitable by-products of a crowded industrial community. Here in this quiet peaceful lovely village it seemed abnormal and incongruous that the same human conflicts and passions could exist. It was incongruous that the neatly-dressed good-looking woman who sat stiffly in an armchair by the fire should have her head bandaged and her face swollen and bruised from her chin upwards to one eye which was black and nearly closed. If it had been one of the dock labourers' wives of Shadwell he'd been calling on the morning after pay-night, there would have been other signs in the room of what had happened: a broken chair or crockery maybe; an empty bottle or two. The woman herself would have been whining or cursing: most likely cursing for probably she had been drinking too. Ella just smiled and said quite calmly,

"Good morning, Mr Jones. Won't you sit down?"

It was a queer smile for one side of her mouth was too swollen and stiff to move, and Mr Jones saw no friendliness in it. He said nervously,

"Thank you, I mustn't stay, Mrs Bransby. I just came in—to—er see if there was anything I could do. Any way in which I could help. I'm very sorry indeed to hear you've had trouble."

She smiled again.

"It *is* good of you, Mr Jones. And thank you very much for calling. I'm all right, thank you. I'm only a bit dizzy when I try to stand, so I'm sitting here, and Mrs Scaife is doing what's wanted. It's my husband who's so ill."

She said that without any change in her voice, but her eyes were elevated to the ceiling through which he could hear him moaning and babbling.

"Yes," he said. "I gathered that. But don't you think, Mrs Bransby, it would be a better thing if you were in bed yourself. I—er—I'm not concerned about what's happened, but I can see you've had a shock, Don't you think it would be a good thing to go to a neighbour's house and rest?"

"Just what the doctor and everyone else says to her," Polly put in. "There's nowt she can do while he's bad like that."

Mr Jones felt distinctly relieved to hear another voice behind him, but Ella said still quite calmly,

"No, I've got to stay here. I'm not going to leave him. And I'll be all right soon. Only of course I'm glad Mrs Scaife is going to look after Jane for a bit. He's very ill, you know. I'm sure he didn't mean to harm me. He was leaning against the door and I went to help him and he pushed me out of the way and I must have lost my balance and fallen against the fender. It was just an accident."

He knew that she was lying. He knew too that under her seeming politeness she was resenting his presence, wishing him to mind his own business and not interfere with hers. He felt baffled. He knew that all the time she was listening to the voice upstairs but he could not tell how deeply her heart was involved in what had happened, whether it was love for him that made her lie, that made her refuse to leave him, but he sensed that she had an immense pride which all this and what had gone before had tested but not broken. He laughed nervously.

"Of course it was an accident, Mrs Bransby. We're only trying to do our best, and I still think you ought to take things easy. My wife would gladly come down and help. Shall I go up and see your husband? Perhaps I could take a turn at sitting by him?"

"My husband's coming to give Sam a spell when he gets back from his rounds," Polly put in. "There's no harm in your going up, though. Bedroom's on first floor."

She pointed to the staircase doorway. Ella said nothing but turned her head to the fire. He did not want to go up, and for that reason felt it was his duty to do so. He stopped, however, when he reached the top of the stairs. The bedroom door was ajar. The room was very bare with only a small strip of cheap oilcloth on the floor. There was a chest of drawers, a small dressing-table and a corner wardrobe. The small double bed was in the centre and it almost blocked out the light from the tiny window. On the near side of it was a fire, and in front of this close to the bed sat Sam Bunny on a cane chair. Tom himself was lying on his back but as Mr Jones caught sight of him he had raised his head from the pillow and his hands were raised in front of him clawing at the air. It was not the first case of D.T.s Mr Jones had seen. It was, he knew, a form of temporary insanity. The patient "saw things": loathsome reptiles, devils, imagined himself being pursued. Tom's eyes now were glaring with terror and were focused on something close in front of him. The sweat was trickling from his brow, his mouth was working, but the sounds he made were to Mr Jones quite incoherent. He seemed to be trying to protect himself with his hands from the thing he saw. His terror was so real that Mr Jones could have imagined there was something there and he had a sense of relief when he heard Sam say in a slow, easy, comforting voice,

"Now it's all right, Tom. There's nowt to bother yoursen about. There's nowt going to harm you or get you. You're safe in your bunk and here's Sam Bunny who used to sail bo'sun with you, standing by. You're dreaming, that's what you're doing, Tom. You wouldn't get Sam Bunny sitting calm by the fire if there were any red devils scrambling about. Let your head go back on the pillow again and try and sleep."

He reached his arm across the bed and gently took one of Tom's hands and coaxed him down. He actually closed his eyes, and then Sam, turning slightly, saw Mr Jones and grinned in recognition. But he did not speak. He nodded to the bed, and Mr Jones saw that there was nothing he could do that this once shipmate and friend of the sick man could not do better. He tiptoed downstairs. Ella turned as he entered the room again, but she did not speak. Polly said,

"What did you make of him, Mr Jones?"

"It seems he's in very good hands."

"Aye. T' doctor said that all we could do for him at present was keep him warm and keep his strength up with broth and stuff like that and have someone he knew by him to comfort him when t' fits come. Sam's a very old friend of his. So is Jonty my husband. I think he'll get over it all right."

Still Ella did not speak. From upstairs the silence lasted.

Mr Jones spoke nervously.

"Well, if there's anything that I or Mrs Jones can do, Mrs Bransby, please count on us. Or if we can help with Jane. You know we are both very fond of her."

Ella smiled again.

"Thank you very much, Mr Jones. It *is* good of you. But I'll be all right by tomorrow and be able to get about my work. It is good of you to have called."

Polly came with him to the door. He guessed she wanted to talk with him, to go into dramatic details, to be as expansive as Ella had been close, but he firmly took his leave of her at the doorstep wishing her good morning, and asking her to let him know if there was anything he could do. But what could he do, he asked himself as he walked down the alley? Obviously one could not offer conventional spiritual comfort to a man suffering from D.T.s, appropriate though the treatment might sound. As obviously it was futile trying to invoke spiritual guidance with a woman so self-willed and independent as his wife who had shown subtly—but how effectively—that she would rather he minded his own business. Still more obviously he could not do what in a similar case in town he would have done automatically, gone to the nearest shop and ordered a parcel of invalid delicacies to be sent to the home, or better still get Gwen to call with it. He might be wrong, but the chances were that if he tried that proud woman would regard it as a deliberate insult.

He felt depressed, profoundly discouraged. He'd come face to face with tragedy. Behind the grim enough aspect of the physical quarrel, the woman's injury, the man's desperate sickness, was something much deeper and more important. A home was being broken. And, as always, the real sufferer was to be the child. What was going to happen to that child? Thank God she had not witnessed the actual quarrel, but would things be any better if the man did recover? It was not just a weakness for drink that had led to his downfall. Wasn't it true that he'd been a fine fellow before and during the war, that he and his family were just victims of that calamity? Ah—thought Mr Jones—here was something more important than chapel funds and tight-fisted trustees and argumentative truculent blacksmiths! Supposing that a man like Tom Bransby could be saved, not in the religious salvationist's meaning of the word, but saved as a man, a husband, a father, re-established as a decent member of society?

He had reached the end of the alley and he turned upwards for another alley that would lead him directly to the Bank and the way to home and to his waiting wife. Was it possible, he wondered? Could such a miracle be wrought? He walked quicker, and suddenly he experienced an extraordinary sense of elation. Had *he* the gift and the power to give back to that unfortunate man a lost faith in himself, new hope, new courage so that he could start life again, and win victory from defeat? He walked still faster, and he prayed earnestly to God to give him that power.

4

FOR THE FIRST TIME in twelve days Tom Bransby awakened from a night of unbroken tranquil sleep. For the first time for many years the sensation of awakening was not unpleasant. But at first he did not comprehend why. His thoughts were muddled. Like the brass knobs at the foot of the bed, the things on the dressing-table, he couldn't get them into focus, and they were mixed too with direct sensations, a pleasant hunger, an unfamiliar steadiness of pulse and nerve, the feeling of being physically well. The window blind was up and it was broad daylight. If he couldn't get things into visual focus he knew where he was and that there was nothing in the room to frighten him: no hissing snakes or flaming devils. Through the open window he heard a dull booming and he knew it was the sound of the surf on the scaurs, but although it told him the sea was rough with a gale blowing, it was a pleasant and an almost soothing sound. He could hear voices too, talking softly in the room below, one of them Ella's, but again they were normal and not unpleasing and he did not strain his ears to listen.

He was still drowsy. He gave up trying to identify the various objects in the room and closed his eyes and just listened to the booming of the surf, and then slowly there came to him the full realisation of what had happened to him yesterday evening when the minister had prayed with him for the forgiveness for his sins, and he had seen the Light and received the knowledge of salvation. . .

"Though your sins be as scarlet they shall be white as snow: though they be red like crimson they shall be as wool."

His sins had not been as scarlet, nor red like crimson, least not in the fair and kindly opinion of Mr Jones, who in the lengthening daylight intervals of semi-sanity in Tom's sickness had talked to him and made him talk. He had done this more in the manner of a physician than a priest. He was not a confessor, and he had not sought for confessions. He had probed, but not with a morbid curiosity. A man's inner mind was his own private affair. It was a mixture of good and evil tendencies, some instinctive and involuntary, others controllable by the will, or better still by character, and it was by character, by the way he behaved towards the rest of society that he should be judged. He had done this more skilfully than he knew, using his common sense as a Christian and not swayed by Freud or any of the other psychologists with whose work and theories he had only the slightest acquaintance. His first job had been to win the patient's confidence. Then to find out what defect in his character had led him into this sorry mess. He knew it was not a case for preaching or religious exhortation. Tom was a sick man, but more sick of mind than body. The doctor (he was a busy man who had to come by car from Burnharbour) had been content to diagnose acute alcoholism and had taken a cynical view of Tom's future. Good nursing and abstinence would pull him round, but the chances were he'd be on the booze again as soon as he was strong enough to walk to the nearest pub...

Tom was awake but he kept his eyes shut, and he listened to the booming of the sea. That sound had no terror now. It seemed to belong to the delicious joy that suffused him. He felt completely secure. Pleasantly he allowed his thoughts to wander back through the stages of his illness. He thought of his homecoming, his quarrel with Ella, of how he had struck her down and believed that he had killed her. He remembered Sam and the coastguard at the door, and then lying in bed and the things he had seen, the devils and the horrid reptiles. He remembered Sam Bunny holding his hand and trying to comfort him, telling him there was nothing there to be afraid of, and then he remembered being awake in daytime, free of his nightmare delusions, but weak and trembling and desperate with remorse about his wasted life, the harm he had done and the suffering he had caused to Ella and Jane. And then he remembered first the voice of Mr Jones, not so deep as Sam's yet very comforting, and then his face and the way he had smiled.

He had never had much time for parsons, nor for religion. Like most of the Bransbys he was brought up a Wesleyan. He'd gone to chapel and Sunday School, but when at the age of fourteen he'd left school and gone to sea as cabin boy on his father's ship, he'd never given religion another thought. Chapel and Sunday school had bored him. They'd only been a sort of discipline inflicted on him by his mother. The ministers in his time had been milk-and-water sort of chaps. But there had been a "local" (a Burnharbour grocer) called Jasper Laycock who believed in hell and damnation and his sermons were all variations on one simple theme: you kept the ten commandments and you went to heaven when you died or you broke them and lived your afterlife everlastingly in Hell. Jasper had been a little man with a big head and a long scrawny neck with a prominent and mobile Adam's apple. His head was bald, but he had a large drooping white moustache stained brown in the middle with tea. He had small glittering black eyes. He'd had a way of preaching very quietly for a while, almost whispering, then suddenly banging his fist down on the Bible and shouting at the top of his voice a fierce exhortation to his listeners to beware of the wrath to come, of the fires of Hell that waited for the evil-doer, the fires that glowed and flamed but never went out, that burnt and tortured but never consumed.

Jasper's hell had been real enough to Tom, and so had Satan. But the busy healthy life of his early days at sea, the companionship of men who seemed cheerfully indifferent to many of the ten commandments and to religion itself, even in the face of calamity and death, had blurred the vividness of Jasper's picture painting. He was well-behaved not because of what he'd learnt at chapel and Sunday School but because John Henry, his father, although kind was a strict disciplinarian, because he was keen and ambitious to learn the arts and crafts of seamanship, and above all because the main virtues of decent manhood were inherent in his blood. John Henry himself had treated him to his first drink. He had liked it and he had liked the sensation it had given him, but there had been no fear then that one day it might master him.

The voice of Mr Jones had soothed him before he had

become aware that it was the voice of a clergyman. The night's delirium had left him exhausted and he was only semi-conscious. The face he had seen was blurred, but it was smiling and kind and he was not certain after that first visit that it had not been a dream. But the next day Mr Jones had talked, not as a clergyman but as an interested friend. He'd said nothing about what had happened. He'd talked about himself, about Shadwell and London Docks, about sailors he'd met, and Tom had found himself talking, remembering his own first experiences of London, the time John Henry (the ship was in dry dock) had taken him to see the Tower, and Buckingham Palace, and the Zoo and Madame Tussaud's.

No, Mr Jones had not guessed how skilful he had been. He had gone back to Gwen from that first early visit to Tom feeling rather discouraged. The weather had changed. It was dull and windy and wet and the pull up the Bank had tired him. Gwen, however, had rushed to open the front door. Tea was ready, his house shoes were warming in front of a big fire, and guessing his mood she refused to let him talk until he was rested and refreshed. Although both her parents had been born in England, and she herself had never crossed the Western Border, Gwen was as characteristically Welsh as her husband. She was short, dark-haired, with a delicate complexion and large expressive dark-grey eyes. She had a full mouth and her teeth were big and still good. Long before she had met Dai, she had been engaged to marry a student in the same college where she had got her teacher's diploma. He had taken a job in Rhodesia, and it was their plan that she should join him later, and that they should marry and settle down in that country. He had died of dysentery a month after his arrival, and she had gone on teaching, finding in her contact with children an anodyne both to her broken heart and her frustrated maternal instincts. To her even Dai was a child in many ways. She could pet him, tease him, rag him about his good looks, even get really cross with him on occasions, but beneath all this she had a deep admiration and respect for him, and that was the strongest and most permanent foundation of their love. . . He'd told her at last what had happened, that he'd found Tom in a semi-conscious state, no longer raving but looking desperately weak and ill. He'd opened his eyes once but given no sign of intelligent recognition. As for his wife, she seemed quite recovered, but she'd been as reserved as before and as subtly resentful of his calling.

Gwen had laughed.

"What did you expect, Dai? Haven't you learnt yet that it isn't every woman falls in love with your handsome face straight away? What about Jane? Did you ask Mrs Bransby if she could come to tea tomorrow?"

Dai had laughed and, mimicking Ella,

"Yes. That will be all right, Mr Jones. It *is* so good of you to ask her. You *are* so kind."

That next day after seeing Tom he'd collected Jane at the school door (she was still staying with Polly) and he'd gone home feeling much more cheerful. All the way up the Bank Jane had chattered to him, holding his hand. Gwen had made a very special tea. After that she'd opened the piano and without the slightest sign of self-consciousness Jane had sung nursery rhymes, and Gwen had played action songs with her in which Dai himself had joined. Polly had come up for her at seven o'clock. Later, when they were alone, Dai reported progress. Tom was better. He had actually talked, listlessly perhaps, but intelligently. But he still hadn't got into the man's mind. He hadn't dared to refer to the trouble and again he'd had no sense of co-operation from the wife.

But it was from that day Tom himself was now measuring the dawning joy of his salvation. It was on that day he'd really looked at the minister's face, and felt not just a kindness in it but a love: the love for which his tortured mind craved. He had been aware of Ella from the first moments of semi-consciousness. But she had only recalled for him his shame for what he had done. He hadn't dared to look into her eyes. He had mumbled out his penitence to her. She'd said in her quiet way "Oh, don't worry, Tom. You didn't mean it." But he had known what she was really thinking. Mr Jones was different. He seemed to shine, to radiate a warmth. From then on that warmth had melted the hardness within him that Ella had never touched.

It was the first time that he had spoken at length to any one about his experiences during the war. He had never possessed the sailor's gift for yarning. Who wanted to hear anything about the war once it was over? Certainly not his wife. He'd told Mr Jones (this was the day after Jane had been to the Manse) the story of the sinking of his father's ship. How many times had he gone over every detail of it in his mind? How many times had he actually *lived* again through the horror of it. The very telling of it had been an immeasurable relief. It was not with the consciousness of a moral transgression that he had told Mr Jones of the beginning of his hate, his lust for revenge on the Germans. But he hadn't been trying to justify himself either. He'd just been trying to ease himself of all that had been pent up within him for so long. Nor had Mr Jones by a word or a look suggested that hatred and vengeance were in themselves sinful, although he could now see plain enough they were. All the same he had been leading up bit by bit to what had taken place in the room beneath him on that terrible night, and didn't that, and the sinking of his father's ship, and his ramming of the other one, and his boozing, and his gambling, and the way he had let himself go, all belong to the same picture?

It had taken the minister to show him beyond all doubt that it did. The Court of Inquiry would have laughed if he had told them that he had deliberately rammed that ship while mentally unbalanced because he hadn't had quite enough to drink. Mr Jones hadn't laughed. He'd said that it was a very understandable thing that a man who had gone through such a dreadful experience could conceive a passionate hatred for those he imagined were responsible. It was human enough to desire revenge, and he could understand that such a desire might become an obsession, and that the thwarting of it might lead to such a condition of mind as to make a man do something actually criminal, yes even manslaughter or murder. Yes, and he could believe too (although this was a matter on which only a doctor could speak with authority) that alcohol might have the effect of preventing such an act, giving the man a sense of mental stability, however false that might be.

Yes, Mr Jones had understood all right. And he'd

understood why after the inquiry he'd let himself go. He hadn't been making excuses. But the picture had to be clear. Drink had been the thing that had given him courage and faith in himself, while its effect lasted. But (and it hadn't needed Mr Jones to tell him this) it was like any other sort of drug: you had to take more and more of it for the thing to work. And that was where religion came in. The love of God was inexhaustible. It was like the light and warmth and power of the sun. It just went on for ever. The wonderful thing was that all you need do to have this love was to believe in it. And now he did *believe* in it.

He opened his eyes again. He looked about the room. For a moment he had a misgiving: that the joy he had felt belonged to a dream, that as soon as he regained complete wakefulness it would be dispelled. But he was reassured. He was really awake, and he still felt an extraordinary bliss. He heard Ella downstairs. His nostrils were assailed by the smell of frying bacon. The woman she had been talking to (it had sounded like Polly Scaife) had evidently gone. It was a good smell. It was good to feel hungry, instead of that terrible craving for the smell and taste of liquor. It was better still to feel that he need have no fear of Ella now. That he could look her straight in the face and accept her forgiveness for all the harm he had done her, to tell her that he and she and Jane were going to start a new life from now on.

And yet, as he heard her footsteps on the stairs, he involuntarily shut his eyes again. Involuntarily, like a naughty child making a noise after bedtime, he kept them closed when she entered the room, and pretended to be asleep, and he blinked hypocritically when she spoke to him, and he could not look at her direct.

"Hallo, Tom. I've brought you your breakfast. You seem to have had a good sleep. You're looking a lot better."

He would have liked to have told her how much and in what way he was really feeling better, but as he glanced at her, out of the tail of his eye, he was aware of the same old constraint. He had the feeling that if he started telling her what had happened to him she would listen quite attentively saying just the right things, excusing him for what he had done wrong, approving his new good intentions, but that all the time she would be seeing through him like an X-ray penetrates flesh, and somehow or other she would succeed in destroying the very source of his joy. He *was* afraid of her yet.

"I *am* feeling better," he said as she put the tray on a table at the bedside. "It's very good of you to bring my breakfast up like this, Ella."

She poured out his tea.

"Don't be silly, Tom. I've done you an egg. I'll do you another if you can manage it. You've got to eat all you can and get your strength back."

Why did she make him feel like this? Why was he still afraid of her? She seemed to bear him no ill-will for what had happened. Her voice was kind, she *was* kind, and yet he could feel more than he had ever done that she really hated and despised him.

He answered her evenly, taking another sly glance at her as he did so, noting that her cheek still showed traces of the bruise.

"Don't bother, Ella. There'll be as much as I can manage here. Where's Jane?"

He had not seen Jane since the night. Throughout the worst phases of his delirium and the alternating phases of acute melancholia he had preserved a peculiar streak of complete sanity about his child. He had never asked for her. When Ella had told him in his first calm moments that she had been staying with the Scaifes since he had been taken ill, he had not questioned her, but he had felt a secret satisfaction that she had been safely out of it all, and had neither seen nor heard him when he had been raving. He had a sudden longing for her now. He could not resist the guilty thought that it was she rather than his wife that he'd like to have at his bedside. Jane might not be able to understand what he wanted to say about his happiness, but he'd be able to say it and not be tongue-tied.

"She's at school of course," Ella said. "But she'll be popping in at dinner time. I thought she'd best be sleeping with Polly until you're quite better."

"Yes. She'd best be there. But I'd like to see her when she comes in if you think it will be all right. I'll have a shave of course. I don't want to frighten her with this beard."

He felt that she was looking at him, and he kept his eyes averted. He couldn't have been a pretty sight, he thought. If the hand that lay on the bedclothes in front of him was anything to judge by, his face must be like that of a man of sixty. It was white and so thin he could see the shape of every bone yet it felt as heavy as lead. She moved towards the door.

"All right. I'll bring Jane up when she comes. She *has* been pining for you. I'll bring you some hot water when you've had your breakfast, then you can tidy up. Shout if there's anything you want. There's plenty of eggs if you could manage another. Father sent a dozen down with Jonty."

He was relieved to hear her shut the door, to hear her steps on the stairs going down. He took a deep draught of tea, and hungrily started to eat. And with every mouthful his mind seemed to become more alert. He continued to think about his wife. He had never quite succeeded in understanding her. He had never been able to get over her air of superiority. She'd had that air even when she was a girl. She must have been about fourteen when he'd noticed her first. He'd seen her one day walking along the beach carrying a basket of butter which she'd have been taking to Thompson's the grocer. When the tide was down that was the shortest way to the village from Mark Moorsholm's farm. She'd been tall for her age and rather skinny, but even in the way she walked she had that air of superiority and haughtiness. Not that she had anything to give herself airs about, the place she came from. True that she was supposed to have Ellington blood in her on her mother's side. But she wouldn't know it then, and if she had done it was nothing to be proud of.

Funny, Tom thought, that in all the time he had known Ella she had never once mentioned that about her mother. There was no proof of course, but it was accepted as local history. The Ellingtons of Ellington Hall had been very liberal in spreading their blood about the Riding in their time. Ellington was a small inland market town but the family had originally owned many farms along the coast including what was now Mark Moorsholm's. Ella's mother had been an illegitimate child born to the daughter of another of the Ellington tenant farmers. The Squire of Ellington at that time had three grown-up sons. They were like himself, hard drinkers and gamblers, lovers of horses and women, and never over-scrupulous so far as the women were concerned. The story was that while it was undoubtedly an Ellington that fathered this particular child none knew which of them it was and according to some it was the Squire himself. A farmer husband was found for the mother. The daughter grew up and married Mark, dying herself in a second childbirth, the child itself being stillborn. And by that time the last of the legitimate Ellingtons was dead and the vast estate broken up, although it was said that there was scarcely a village in a fifty mile radius of the Hall that had not some living memento of the family.

Yes. That might have accounted for it. He had never known any of the ElJingtons, of course, but it was said that their women had been great beauties, driving in carriages and going to court; real aristocrats. And yet Ella had never tried to make out that she *was* superior to local folks, or anything but a farmer's daughter. She hadn't put on airs. It was just something about her that made him feel she was superior, and that she knew it, something he could never really get at. It may have been that, as much as her good looks, that had attracted him when she had been growing up and he had started to court her. She was not the first girl he had been interested in. But she was the first that he had really loved, and he had been "walking out" (during his spells ashore) for two years, before he'd had the courage to declare his love and ask her if she would marry him.

He poured himself out another cup of tea. He had to use both hands to lift the pot but he did it successfully. He had finished his egg, and felt quite capable of tackling another piece of toast. He was enjoying his breakfast and no mistake, and it was wonderful to feel so well and to be able to go on thinking about Ella in such a calm clear way.

With something like amusement he recalled what he had felt like when—as calmly as though he had asked her to tell him the time—she had answered that she did love him and that she would marry him; how he had looked at her, waiting for a sign of pleasure or desire in her eyes to show she meant what she said, and how not seeing it he had seized her in his arms and kissed her. She had not resisted him physically, but her lips had not moved, her body had remained limp and unyielding and a chill of fear had seized him. She did not love him. He did not love *her*. He had made a mistake in trying to court her at all.

This had happened two days before he was due back to join his ship. They had parted that night just as usual without even shaking hands, neither of them referring to what had taken place. As he had walked home he had decided that he would send her a letter from the first port of call, explaining what he felt and that he had made a mistake in asking her to marry him. But thinking this over next day he saw that it would be cowardly. He'd have to tell her straight out. Surely she'd see as clearly as he did that it was no good them going on together.

They'd met on the cliff edge below the farm. It was a calm warm evening in July and the air was heavily scented with new-mown hay. They had walked along in silence for a while. Ella was wearing a thin cotton dress and no hat. She was sunburnt and he remembered her stopping to pick some poppies from the side of the path, which she had held up to her breast, and that somehow those flowers had made her look more lovely than she had ever been to him before. But that had not weakened his resolve. In a way he had felt sorry for her. She had never said much to him of course, but he had known that she was very unhappy at home. Old Mark was a weak-minded sort of chap. Her stepmother was a hard domineering woman who had borne him no children and hated Ella. But that very fact should have made her a bit more responsive. He had offered her an escape and not a bad one either. He'd already got all his tickets and would have a ship of his own soon. But he had not been suffering from injured pride. After all, she had said she did love him and that she would marry him. It was just that she couldn't unbend herself, conquer this mysterious pride of hers, make him feel that she really *did* love him body and soul.

They'd come to a stile, and there was a gap in the cliff fence through which there was a clear view down to the beach and the sea. Ella had paused. It was the very place where he had proposed to her, and he wondered if she'd paused on purpose, that she herself was expecting him to say what he had made up his mind to say. She'd stood looking at the sea in silence, and—with a space between them—he'd said quite calmly,

"Well, I'm off on the seven train tomorrow morning, Ella."

She'd half turned, and again without any emotion said,

"Yes?"

He had gone on just as calmly, confident that she was going to make it easy for him.

"Aye. It's the Plate this time. I don't suppose I'll be back till after Christmas, and I may not be able to get home then, for we're on time charter."

She turned to look at the sea again, and he'd known that the thing he was going to say next was to be what would end it. But before he spoke he saw her shudder, and he heard her sob, and the next moment she'd flung her arms round his neck almost choking him, her body, trembling and warm through her cotton dress, was against his and she was kissing him passionately all over his face, sobbing, "Tom, I love you, I love you."

Yes he'd loved her, and she had loved him, but it was only in their embraces that he had ever felt she was completely his. Not that they hadn't got on well together up to the time of his downfall. Their marriage had been as successful as any other in Bramblewick where the husband was away for at least ten months out of the twelve. There had never been anyone else for either of them, but after Jane had come he had felt that her physical love had cooled. Only towards Jane herself had she shown a really passionate affection.

And now it seemed her love for him was completely dead. His love for her was dead too. The thought did not distress him. He buttered the last piece of toast, looked at his well-cleaned plate, and wondered whether he should shout for another egg. He decided not to. It would probably spoil his appetite for dinner. . . No it did not distress him that their love was dead. What was that love anyway but carnal? It was natural of course. If it wasn't for that there'd be no marriages and no children. For him there would have been no Jane. But compared with the love that glowed in him now it was like the flash of a match. The love of God, late though it had been in coming to him, would never languish. In His service it would grow and grow. From now on he would be the servant of God, keeping all His commandments. Mr Jones had said nothing about the commandments. All he had talked about was God's love, that great benevolent power that was anyone's for the mere asking. But that was only another way of saying what old Jasper Laycock had preached. No sinner could have this love. You had first to *believe*, and then you must live and obey according to the word, and you must *fear* too. Jasper had been no fool. . .

There was the sound of Ella's voice, then the voice of Sam Bunny. He heard her say "Yes, Sam. He's awake and looking a lot better. Go on up." He heard Sam's steps on the stairs. He felt no need now to pretend to be asleep. He smiled as his old shipmate opened the bedroom door and came in. He was unshaven, rather bleary-eyed, and as he came near the bed Tom caught a strong whiff of alcohol. It conjured up an instant vision of the bar room of the Mariners. It wouldn't be open yet. But there were ways and means. He himself had never wanted a drink out of hours and not been able to get it. . .

With a peculiar satisfaction he realised that neither the smell of alcohol nor the quick vision of the Mariners it had invoked had revived in him the vaguest craving for the stuff itself. Instead he felt stronger in his new-found faith. If Sam had been having an illegal drink (and this on top of what judging by his eyes had been a pretty stiff night) the more he was to be pitied for his weakness and folly. Sam, however, was looking anything but sorry for himself. He grinned broadly when he said,

"By gum, Tom, but you're looking better."

Tom looked at him squarely, and said with an insinuating calmness,

"Aye, Sam. I *am*."

"Ella said you'd had a good night. You look like a new man."

Tom tried to catch Sam's eyes, to hold them. He felt that his own were very clear and steady, and again very quietly and insinuatingly he said,

"I *am* a new man. I *am* a new man."

It might have been that the influence of Bramble-wick's famous local preacher was unconsciously asserting itself. In a manner that was characteristically Jasper Laycock's Tom waited as though to let those significant words sink in, looking hard at Sam all the time. But Sam had never been quick at the uptake. He said with good-natured sarcasm,

"What's done it, Tom? Us looking after you so well, or has the doctor been giving you some special physic? Don't tell me he's let you have a drop. Not of whisky?"

Tom smiled with supreme self-confidence. There was no resentment in his voice. He really felt sorry for Sam.

"Whisky," he echoed. "Do you know what I'd do if the doctor or anyone else offered me a drink? I'd throw it out of the window. . . Sit down, Sam. I'd like to have a talk with you."

Sam sat down in the chair in which he had kept vigil in turn with Jonty throughout the worst nights of Tom's illness. He was no longer smiling. He looked puzzled.

"I only mentioned whisky for a joke. It's whisky's

been to blame for this do. I know it's none of my business, Tom, but in my opinion you were taking a sight too much for any man. And not getting your meals proper either."

"You needn't tell me that," Tom cut in sharply. "I've just told you what I'd do if someone offered it to me."

Sam looked uncomfortable.

"I was never one for whisky myself. It was too dear for one thing."

"It would have been dear at any price. And the same for beer or any sort of strong drink." Tom suddenly reached out his right hand and clutched Sam's sleeve. "Listen to me, Sam. Listen to me."

For a moment it might have seemed to Sam that Tom was becoming delirious again. There had been one night when he had clutched him like that with both hands and wouldn't let go until the hallucination that was terrifying him had gone. But his face then had burnt with fever. His eyes had been like a madman's. Now his face, where there was no beard, was pale. His clutch was not spasmodic, and meeting his eyes Sam saw that they were steady and anything but mad. They looked as sane as they'd done when he'd been on the *Northgate's* bridge during the days and nights of their salvage of the Spanish steamer. He was neither mad nor very ill. Yet at the same time he was talking in a queer way, and instinctively Sam's attitude became conciliatory and soothing. He laughed.

"Righto, Tom. I'm listening. Whatever's done it, I'm glad you're feeling better."

From sheer weakness Tom was obliged to leave go his hand and let his head go back on the pillow, but he signed to Sam to come nearer to him. He spoke urgently but he kept his voice low. He didn't want Ella to hear.

"Sam, do you believe in God?"

Sam looked more uncomfortable.

"Why, of course. Everyone does except bloody know-alls like Will Knaggs."

"I wouldn't call him that. A man like Knaggs ought to be pitied. I've chucked swearing anyway. . . Do you believe in Heaven and Hell, Sam? Do you believe that when you die you stand for judgment before the Almighty, and that according to how you've behaved in this life you're rewarded or you're punished?"

"I've never thought much about it, Tom," Sam answered uneasily. "It says all that in the Bible, so I reckon it is so. You think about it when you're in chapel sometimes of course, and when you're burying a chap at sea. Aye, of course it'll be true."

"Only when you're in chapel, or when a shipmate goes to meet his Maker. Yes, I was like that, Sam. I never thought about it. I always thought I was good enough to do my job, without any other help. I got my tickets straight off. I got my ship, and I was as good a master as any."

"That's true enough, Tom, I'd never ask to sail with a better. I was thinking only just now how we towed that Spanish steamer into Brest. You know it's only bad luck that you're not sailing master now."

It was an attempt to steer the talk away into a safer course but Tom was not to be diverted.

"It's not bad luck. It was bad living that put me where I was. Drinking and swearing—blaspheming, joining in loose talk. Living without God. Never thinking about religion. Who do you think was standing by my side on the *Northgate's* bridge those days and nights we were making for Brest? Who stands by anyone when they're hard-pressed although they don't know it until the light comes. Isn't it God?"

Sam hesitated.

"Aye, aye. I suppose it is in a way. That's what it says in the Bible. But you were a good seaman, Tom. There's not one in a hundred skippers would have done what you did."

He stood up. He was feeling more and more uncomfortable. Religion was all right inside chapels or sailors' missions (handy spots for writing letters, or having a cheap meal or a doss if you were spent up), or as he'd said burials. But he'd never liked arguments about it, and he had more than a growing suspicion that Tom was getting at him. He was right, but it was too late to escape. Tom had the strength to seize him by his sleeve again.

"Sam, a wonderful thing has happened to me, and it can happen to anyone, to the biggest sinners. Do you remember that bit in the Bible which says though your sins be as scarlet they shall be white as snow? I'd forgotten, and I'd forgotten a lot of other things. It was the minister, Mr Jones who reminded me. He's a grand chap. If only other parsons were like him the world would be a different place. He sees straight through you, a parson like Mr Jones. He sees what's in your heart, and knows what's wrong. But he can put you on the right road, too. You used to go to chapel when you were a lad. Same as me. Do you remember Jasper Laycock?"

Sam looked interested.

"Him who used to make folks jump by suddenly

banging his fist down on the Bible? Aye, I do. Do you remember time he banged his hand down on his glass of water by mistake? I don't know how folks stopped laughing out loud."

Tom did not laugh. His expression became even more earnest.

"Aye, folks might have laughed at old Jasper. But he preached what was in his heart. He was a temperance man, too. If we'd paid heed to him, we'd have been different on that score, never mind anything else. Have you ever stopped to think of the harm strong drink does? That it's done to you as well as me?"

Sam did not answer, but he glanced involuntarily towards the staircase door. He'd had about enough of this. But Tom hung on to him.

"Think about it, Sam," he went on. "Think about it now. I'm not angry with you. I'm sorry for you. You've been pitying me. Now I'm pitying you. And I want to help you, same as Mr Jones has helped me. I've got a wife and a kid. You've got an old mother. Have you done the right thing by her, Sam, all the years you've been at sea, and never getting higher than a bosun's berth. And why? You know the answer as well as I do. It's been drink with you. Right from the first it's been drink. You could have got your second mate's ticket as easy as I did, if you'd studied. And what did you do? Your poor old mother saved up so that you could go to a navigation school, not once but a dozen times over. Instead of attending school you got into the pubs with bad companions. You just let yourself go, and you've gone on doing that ever since. I don't say you've made such a bad mess of things as I have. That ought to make things easier for you to change your ways. Give it up, Sam. Ask God to forgive your sins. Repent, and take the love that's waiting for you."

To Sam's relief, Tom was obliged to leave go of him again and sink back on the pillow. Instinctively he moved himself a little nearer the door. He was feeling vexed. Tom was right about him not having got on in the way most Bramblewick sailors had done. But he was damned if it was drink that had done it. It had never done him any harm. It was true that sometimes when he'd had too much he felt ill on waking the next day, but it only wanted another drink to put him right again. It never stopped him doing his job. He never drank on duty but for the ration of rum that was an official issue under special circumstances at sea in hard weather. It never made him quarrelsome. Quite the opposite. Whenever he went ashore at home or abroad it was his unvarying custom to have a drink at the first pub or wine shop that took his fancy. Whether it was beer or wine or spirits, he would sit staring at his first glass for a long time before sipping it. The anticipation was enough. Then he would start to drink very slowly enjoying first of all the astringent taste, then the glow of it moving like a slow fire from his stomach into his limbs and suffusing at last into what he regarded as his soul.

It was then that he felt completely benevolent towards the whole world and specifically towards any person, known or unknown, who happened to be within speaking distance. Usually they were male but it made no difference if they were female. He would ask them to join him in the next, and the next too, unless by that time he had found among the company a man of kindred goodwill and hospitality. He could not sing and he talked very little as a rule. But whether he was in company or not, his thoughts would inevitably at a certain stage of intoxication turn to his old mother, and his soul would be filled with a gentle love and longing for her. He would not remember her sharp tongue, and how she nagged and bullied him. She was a thin scraggy woman, with a sharp nose as well as a sharp voice. She was stingy. It was well known that she could make a bucket of coal last a week in wintertime. She rarely bought anything but bones from the butcher. When he was home she'd have old newspapers spread on the living-room floor to save wearing the oilcloth. He was not allowed to smoke in the house. She would nag and upbraid him about smoking as much as about drinking, both being a waste of brass. But he would not remember this when the nostalgia was on him. He would not remember that when he did get home his first desire was to be out of it and into the Mariners, to charge his soul again with sweet illusions.

He felt vexed with Tom. True enough that his mother had saved to enable him to make periodic attempts at getting his second mate's ticket. But only out of the money he had earned himself. True enough that instead of working hard at the nautical school he had spent a great deal of his time (and money) drinking. But Tom knew quite well that the reason was that he simply had no head for figures and book learning, without which it was impossible to pass the examination. And what right had Tom Bransby to preach to him anyway? But his anger faded as he looked Tom directly in the face. He was still ill. His eyes weren't like they were when he'd been delirious, but there was a queer look in them, and all this talk about religion was a clear sign that he wasn't himself. . . He hadn't answered him yet. He wished he could get away without answering, and his wish was granted for there was the sound of Ella coming up the stairs and instantly Tom's manner became furtive. He tried to reach Sam's arm again, and failing to do so, whispered hoarsely,

"Don t let on to her what we've been talking about."

He sank back on the pillow again. Readily taking his cue Sam said loudly, so that Ella could hear,

"Well, I'll be getting along, Tom."

He turned to open the door for Ella who was carrying a jug of hot water. She smiled her thanks, but as he passed her he took a last glance at Tom. He had turned his head on the pillow. It was as though he had neither heard Sam's farewell remark, nor Ella coming in.

An inquest was held on Tom Bransby in the Mariners that night. The same company was present: the coastguard, Long Jonty, Sam Bunny, Knaggs the smith, with Captain Christopher in his customary place in the chimney corner. The fire was bright with long leaping flames. The north-east gale roared in the chimney, and there was the deeper-pitched and constant roar of the sea as a background to their voices. Sam Bunny had drunk enough ale to mellow his vexation (that had been aggravated by another upbraiding from his mother) but he had not reached the state of benevolent glow. He had not felt himself to be under any constraint of privacy as to what had happened in Tom's bedroom, but he'd had the impression all the time he was recounting it that the smith was laughing up his sleeve, not only at Tom but at himself.

"Aye," he summed up. "He started going for me like a preacher. He said he'd been saved himself, and wanted to help to save me. He as much as said I ought to lay off ale altogether, and go and study for my tickets again."

Captain Christopher's eyes twinkled.

"Now, Sam," he said with gentle irony. "That wouldn't be a bad idea, you know. Think how pleased your mother would be."

Sam took a deep drink but said nothing.

"Did you say he'd given up swearing too?" the smith said sardonically.

"He hadn't last time I sat up with him," laughed Jonty. "There wasn't any preaching from him then, poor chap. Is he right in his head now?"

The coastguard said seriously,

"When I was on the West India Station we had a stoker we called Rummy. A great big fellow with a touch of the tarbrush in him, the rest of him Irish. Gentle as a lamb when he was sober but a terror when he was tight, and he wouldn't leave the rum alone. He got on the spree one night when we was at St. George in Grenada, laid out about half a dozen negroes in a pub and half killed one of the pickets that was sent to bring him aboard. Like Tom he got D.T.s and then he got religion. Decided he wanted to be a missionary, but he ended up in a lunatic asylum, religious mania."

"Why there was a woman here had that," the captain put in. "One of you would remember her. Betsy Graham. Crazy Betsy we used to call her. She lived in Emmerson's Yard. She'd lost her husband at sea soon after she was wed. She had dozens of cats, and when you went past her house you could always hear her praying or reading from the Bible out loud. In chapel when the preacher was praying and there was owt he said that she specially agreed about she'd shout out amen in a loud voice. Once she burst out crying in the middle of a sermon and started shouting 'Jesus save us' at the top of her voice. They had to take her out and they stopped her going to chapel after that. But with her it was the opposite way on to that stoker of your, Hutchings. She started boozing when she got very old, and stealing food from folks' houses. She ended up in Burnharbour Workhouse."

The smith, his hand on his half-empty glass, chuckled.

"It looks to me as though there's not much difference between boozing and religion."

The captain bridled.

"Aye, it would look like that to you. Owt's bad if you let it run away with you. If Tom Bransby's gone religious, why it's better than what he was doing before. For myself I think it might be the real saving of him, of his wife and bairn, too, and good luck to the parson who's done it. I didn't think much of that chap Jones when he first came here. But I reckon now there's never been a better."

Captain Christopher, although brought up Wesleyan, was not a member of the chapel. He went occasionally, but he also went occasionally to church. The sermons usually bored him but he liked to hear the Bible read, and he liked hymns and joining in the singing of them. He believed in God but he didn't worry as to whether there was a hell or heaven.

He was a widower. He'd had two sons. Both had gone to sea. The first had fallen down the hold of a ship and broken his neck. The second had died of malaria in Bombay. He had retired from the sea when this had happened to ease his wife's sorrow and loneliness. But she had died soon after and he'd felt no wish to go back. Like Sam Bunny, Captain Christopher had never regarded the making of money as the chief aim of his life. He was aware of his age. He had very little physical strength left. His wits he knew were getting dull. It did not worry him. The moderate amount of rum he drank every night gave him a temporary alertness of mind so that he could enjoy and contribute to the gossiping and discussions that went on in the Mariners and induced later a deep and undisturbed slumber, which was like a rehearsal of the death he did not fear. His anger against the smith had only been a flash, and there was only a suspicion of irony in his voice as he said,

"You'll have nowt against him anyway, Knaggs, seeing you've got him as a customer. Have you got the schoolroom stove mended for him, yet?"

But the smith was stung. He drained his glass and rattled it on the table.

"Parsons, religion, it's all humbug from start to finish. I only took that job on because I'm sorry for the chap and his missus, having to put up with a bloody old humbug like Bully Fosdyck. Let's see what religion will do for Tom Bransby. Let's see what happens when he's on his legs again and he remembers what a cosy spot the Mariners is on a winter night. . . I'd like to see Tom Bransby offered a glass of whisky and refuse. I bet he would. I bet he would."

The Rev. David Ivor Jones was thinking about Tom Bransby and wondering what religion was going to do for him as he sat bathing his feet in hot water in front of the fire that night while Gwen, at the table near him littered with the paraphernalia of dressmaking, was engaged in the task of constructing the headgear and coat of a dormouse for the sketch she was going to produce at the annual Wesleyan Bazaar Concert to be held just before Christmas. The sketch was *The Mad Hatter's Tea Party*, and she had adapted it herself from the book. The part of Alice was to be played by Jane.

Dai wasn't bathing his feet because he had a cold coming on. Indeed he hadn't had a cold for many months, and he'd been thinking as he'd walked up the Bank from seeing Tom that he had never, since he could remember, gone so long without having something the matter with him. He'd never felt as well. But no sooner had he sat down by the fire after tea than his feet had started to tickle with chilblains. He'd had them before (what hadn't he had?) and he knew the cure. It was a chemical you took internally that did something to your blood, but the snag was that you had to start taking it in summer, months before the regular chilblain season. Now he knew (by bitter experience) there was no cure for this season's affliction. There was, however, a temporary and most efficient palliative. The hot bath, hot as you could stand it. The bath itself would make them worse tomorrow, but he had felt that sufficient unto that day would be the evil thereof, and therefore he had yielded to it. The irritation had gone completely, enabling him to concentrate on this question of Tom Bransby, but the more he thought of it the less comfortable he felt in his mind. Yet he ought to have been feeling very happy, he told himself. There was more joy in heaven over one sinner that repenteth than over ninety-nine just persons. Likewise, there should be considerable joy in his heart to think that he had brought Tom Bransby to the knowledge and the love of Christ. That the drunkard had repented and had sworn off drink forever and apparently meant it. If there was such a thing as a soul being saved then surely this was it. Yet why this utter lack of satisfaction? Why was it that he felt he liked Tom less as a convert than as a sinner?

"Dai, why are you frowning so?" Gwen broke into his thoughts. "Are your poor toes still tickling? Shall I give you some more hot water?"

He laughed. Deep inside him he was in a way ashamed of his poor health. It was an unfair thing to impose on a woman. It was drawing more than what was any man's right on the love and devotion that should have belonged to her children. But it pleased him that his present trouble was a trivial one. He held up one foot (it was pink as salmon) and wiggled the toes.

"I'm all right. Every bit of tickling has gone. I'm right as rain, and they won't start again until tomorrow, and perhaps not then. The Lord giveth and the Lord taketh away, Gwen. He's taken away my monthly cold in the head, and I've had no indigestion since we came here. I can't complain if He tickles my toes, once in a while."

"You've had no colds because since you came here you've had the sense not to go getting your feet wet. And you might say it's my cooking that's improved your digestion. Now don't go sticking your feet so close to the fire when you get them dry. And that isn't why you were frowning." She reached over and gave him a towel, and as she did so she bent down and kissed his forehead.

"Stop worrying about that man, Dai. . . Whether he means it or not, about not drinking any more, and going straight and building up his life again, you've done something splendid with him, and I'm proud of you the way you've stuck at it. Never mind him or that queer wife he's got. Think of Jane coming to tea tomorrow. She's going to make a lovely Alice." She held up the headgear she was making and put it over her head. "How's this for the dormouse, Dai? Come on, let's have a rehearsal now. You be the Mad Hatter."

It was half-past ten. The Mariners was closed. The company had all gone their various ways. Ned Turnbull the lamp-lighter was near the reverse end of his round. But as he came to the lamp on the old coastguard station corner he had to wait while a wave like a great foaming hungry tongue reached up from the dark throat of the slipway and licked the edge of the breakwater wall and then, unappeased, gurgled slowly back again. He waded ankle deep through the foam it had left, climbed to the lamp and extinguished it. The roar of the sea drowned the sound of his footsteps as he made his way home.

As usual, old Mrs Bunny had waited for her son's return; as usual there was only a handful of fire in the grate and the only light was a guttering candle. As usual, from the first moment he had entered the room, she was at him with her sharp rasping voice, nagging him: where had he been all night? No there was no need for him to say: in the pub, drinking, wasting his money, drinking and smoking instead of saving and having another go for his second mate's ticket. . . Shortly Sam would be going back to sea. There would be no drinking on board ship and in the first few days of complete sobriety he would think clearly of his mother and this comfortless home and wonder why he ever came back to it. Time and distance would gradually take the sharp edge from reality so that when he drank at last on a remote shore the pleasant illusions were induced quicker. Tonight it had taken him a long time and more glasses of ale than usual to reach that state of bliss. He was indeed drunk, a fact which his mother had only too readily perceived. He was too drunk to answer her, even if he had wished to, and he did not. He just sat in the chair which she had put for him opposite to her own by the cold fireside, and he just smiled at her blissfully, thinking she wasn't such a bad old mother after all. . .

Tom Bransby also was looking happy, but in a different way. There was an oil reading lamp on the table alongside his bed. On the table, too, was a Bible, open at the first chapter of the Book of Isaiah. He was lying on his back asleep. He was clean-shaven. His face was still deathly pale. But the lines of illness, of suffering and anxiety were gone. It was a good face now, strong and dignified, and wholly masculine. He breathed deeply and regularly through his nostrils. His mouth was closed but his lips were relaxed as though at any moment they would break into a smile at a happy dream that was passing through his mind. . . Downstairs, his wife, Ella, sat at the kitchen table, mending a frock for Jane. Her eyes were soft as she looked at the garment. Her fingers seemed to grasp it lovingly, as though it was a living part of her own child. But occasionally she looked up from it to the ceiling as if Tom had called (she heard nothing but the sound of the sea and the wind in the chimney) and her eyes went hard and her lips and nostrils quivered. She might have been wishing him dead.

5

IT WAS DECEMBER, with the weather mild again, as so often happens on the coast before the real climax of winter comes with its hard frosts and gales and snow. But the days were short and it was still dark at half-past seven when Tom got up to go to work.

He had slept in the attic since he had got better and Jane had come back. This had been his own idea. Jane's cot had gone down to the bedroom. He had only a narrow camp bed to sleep on. He liked to be alone so that he could have a candle and read the Bible before he went to sleep, or as sometimes happened when he woke up and started thinking. His thoughts were not unpleasant as they usually had been in the old days, but they'd kept him awake if he didn't control them which was just what reading the Bible helped him to do.

He got into his trousers and shirt very quietly, made his bed then, still in his stocking feet and with the rest of his clothes under his arm, he took the candle and tiptoed downstairs. Ella didn't like him being the first up. She had protested that it was her job, always had been and always should be. But he had been strong-minded about it. Their love might be dead, but she had been a good wife to him. He had treated her very badly one way or another. He had repented and she had forgiven him, and now he was going to try and make up in as many practical ways as he could for what he'd done wrong. It was deeds that counted. Not words.

He lit the kitchen lamp and then very quietly cleaned out the grate, carefully sifting the cinders. He had put some kindling to dry in the oven and he soon had the fire going and the kettle on. He washed himself in the sink, leaving shaving to when he got home for tea. He completed dressing. Ella had mended his serge jacket, and he wore a sailor's guernsey with it. He had a boiler suit to take with him for working in. He made the tea, and he put some fat in the frying pan, and then a fillet of cooked fish that had been left over from last night's supper. He kept the teapot on the hob, so last thing when he went out he could take Ella a cup. She'd say again that he shouldn't, but she deserved it—all the nursing and fetching and carrying she had done for him, and no matter what she said she'd be glad enough to come downstairs and find the fire on and everything ready for getting her own and Jane's breakfast.

He had laid the table and when the fish was hot he sat down, bowed his head and silently asked a blessing. When he had done eating, he took his plate and cup and saucer to the sink, washed and dried them and put them away. He poured out a cup of tea and walked upstairs with it and gently opened the bedroom door. He couldn't help thinking as he put the tea and the candle down on the bedside table of how only a few weeks ago he had lain raving in that bed while Ella must have been wondering whether he was going to die or be taken to a lunatic asylum. And there was Jane too, his darling Jane, still peacefully asleep. Well, thank God for her sake that he had done neither, that he had seen the blessed Light in time. He would have liked to have gone to the cot and kissed her, but it was still too early for her to be awakened. He had no desire to kiss Ella, but he felt nothing but goodwill towards her and he touched her on the shoulder lightly. She woke up at once, and stared at him in a rather startled way. He whispered,

"Here's a cup of tea for you, Ella. It's just on eight o'clock. I've lit the fire. I'll be back somewhere round five."

He didn't wait for her to answer, but moved quietly out again and went downstairs. He put his boots on, went to a cupboard and took out a carpenter's bag of tools, which with a rope he swung over his shoulder like a haversack. He banked up the fire with the cinders, then turned the lamp out, and opened the street door, and closed it behind him. It was a fine morning, just starting to get light, and he walked with firm steps down the alley which on the night he had gone fishing down the landing had nearly beaten him. But he had ceased to think of that night, except as a sort of curtain of his past.

He reached the dock. The tide was out, the sea calm. He walked down the slipway, and as he cleared the seaward breast of the old coastguard station he had a full view of the bay sweeping southwards to the headland of High Batts. He stopped involuntarily. The sun was on the point of rising. Eastwards of the headland over the sea a bank of cloud, suspended in the windless and still dimly-starred sky, was edged with copper which as he watched turned crimson. Then it turned to gold and the sun rose up out of the sea, egg-shaped at first as though it had been squeezed up through a tough but elastic tegument, but quickly assuming a perfect spheroid as it floated clear.

Tom gazed at it with deep admiration. As a mariner he'd always had a special interest in sunrises and sunsets. At no time is the weather more eloquent of its mood or more likely to reveal its intent. . . In his wanderings about the oceans of the world he must have seen and closely observed many sunrises more striking than this one, especially in the tropics in the seasons of storms. But never, he thought, had he seen one that he liked as much. It was really beautiful; just like a picture, and as he continued down the slipway to the beach he thought that it was not only the sunrise that was like a beautiful picture, but the whole view about him: the half-bared scaurs and the sea on his left, the low clay cliffs brown as chocolate, and the south edge of the village on his right, the view ahead of him of beach and gradually rising cliffs culminating in High Batts, whose brow the sun was now crowning with golden light.

Why was everything so beautiful this morning? he asked himself as he walked steadily along the beach. Why was he so happy? Wasn't it because all this beauty was God's handiwork, because his heart was full of God's love? Wasn't it, too, because he was going straight, living a man's life again, working, doing his duty by his wife and child? Scarcely six weeks ago and at this time of the morning he'd have been in bed, dreaming his awful dreams, or perhaps lying awake with his tongue and throat parched, thinking of how soon he'd be able to get into the Mariners and have his first drink. Not that the work he was doing at present was bringing him in much money or that it was anything to be especially proud of, for a man who'd once been master of a

10,000-ton steamship. It was still only odd jobs same as he'd been doing before when he'd had the will to, or there had been no other way of raising the money for his drinking. But there was plenty of it to do, and he was keeping at it steady. He was getting his strength back, and it was giving him time to think and decide in what way he was really going to re-establish himself in the world again, to get Ella and Jane out of that cottage, maybe Up-Bank. To give Ella reason to be proud of him again, to give Jane a good education. He didn't want to be rich, God forbid. He didn't want to be like Captain Bartholomew Fosdyck. But he'd like to show Bramblewick, and in particular Will Knaggs (who he'd heard had been laughing at him having given up drink), that what had happened to him wasn't just humbug. He would too, in time.

Yes, the world was beautiful and he was happy and well. He'd got the whip hand of himself. He took a half glance at the landing scaurs, and thought how in the old days fishing was the one thing that had made him really forget his misery, provided of course he had some drink too. The time he must have wasted, not only standing and watching his rod, but in getting bait! There was no harm in fishing, of course, not in itself. But when it got hold of a man like it had done of him it was getting on for a vice. It wasn't as though he had fished for food: it was the pure selfish pleasure that attracted him, and he knew it was so, for even now looking at the scaurs he felt a certain urge to be down there getting bait instead of hurrying along to do the jobs that awaited him. It would be ideal for fishing at the turn of the tide tonight in his favourite place. It was in December that the really big fish came in. . .

Resolutely he walked on, feeling more and more pleased with himself. It was not a very big temptation, this. It wasn't like being tempted to drink again. But it was a temptation, and how easily he had resisted it. What a wonderful thing religion was.

He came to the end of the clay cliff and reached the first of the two becks which run through narrow wooded ravines into the bay. There was a cove here with a rough road leading up the side of the ravine past the Old Mill, into the country. The cove was a good place for finding driftwood and other flotsam and jetsam after high tide when the sea was rough. Even now, with the sea smooth, there was a chance of something having been left there on the night tide, but he only glanced at the line of dead weed at high-water mark and hurried on. Beachcombing, he reflected, was another pursuit which in the past had wasted a lot of his time. There was a fascination in it out of all proportion to the rewards it yielded. Wood was all right, either planks that could be used for carpentry, or rough stuff for burning. But the things he'd looked for were coins or jewellery (lost occasionally by summer visitors), bits of jet that could be sold for eighteen pence a pound to the Burnharbour jet ornament makers and changed ultimately into booze, bits of brass and copper that   might also be turned to money when he'd collected enough, and things that had no value at all except that they'd interest or amuse Jane: glass floats from trawl nets, corks, fossils, agates and cornelians, queer-shaped stones. It had not occurred to him, nor did it now in his mood of exaltation, that Jane would have preferred to have found these treasures (which she genuinely appreciated) for herself.

There was half a mile of steep shale cliff between the two becks. The foot of this, even at neap tides, was washed by the sea and there was no permanent beach until the cliff ended at the second ravine where there was another cove. It was here that a rough lane climbed up from the beach on the south side of the beck. There was a farm on the top, and the lane led from this farm to another farther along the cliff and thence gradually upwards to High Batts and the moor. There was a broken plank, and a fish box in the cove. He hid them both in the thicket of thorn and brambles, which came down almost to the water's edge, resisted the impulse to search the rest of the cove, and started up the lane, which grew steeper as it left the beck. But his wind was not so good as he thought, and half-way up he had to pause for a breather. The bank of the ravine hid the sun and High Batts. But looking back he had a clear view to the north. He could see the old village (now nearly two miles away) with the sunlight on its red roofs and glinting here and there on a window pane. He could see the villas of Up-Bank Bramblewick, including the one that had once been his own: The Hollies, now the home of another sea captain, Kit Harrison, a man three years younger than himself, who'd sailed with him for several voyages on the *Northgate*. He'd married a local girl, daughter of another sea captain, and already had two children. He was not immediately perturbed by his recognition of that familiar place. A mile or so north-east of the village, where the cliffs ran out to form the point of Low Batts, a large steamer had appeared, moving south. She was too distant for him to distinguish the exact colour or markings on her funnel, but he guessed from her lines, the position of her funnel, her masts and superstructure what company she belonged to. And as a wisp of steam came suddenly from her funnel, he guessed her name and the name of her master. The steam was from her horn, and in a few seconds the sound came: a long blast, the signal that a local ship always gave, inward or outward bound, when passing Bramblewick. She was the *Moor Cliff*, registered at Sunderland, but largely Bramblewick-owned, with Captain Bartholomew Fosdyck one of the principal shareholders, and her master Kit Harrison himself.

She was a fine ship, almost brand new, built to replace one of the four the company had lost during the war, and it might well have been that if Tom had stuck to the company, and that terrible thing hadn't happened, he'd have been on her bridge this very moment, looking through his binoculars at the Hollies for a sight of Ella and Jane, for the sheet Ella would have been hanging from the bedroom window, the flag hoisted on the mast in the front garden... There was a sheet hanging from the Hollies window now. It was too far to see if there was a flag, but undoubtedly it would be there, and one on Captain Fosdyck's flagpost too. It was the *Moor Cliff*, all right. Kit Harrison hadn't been home this voyage, but Sam Bunny had gone two days ago to the Tyne to join her. She'd be outward bound for the Plate.

He turned and started up the lane again, but not with quite the same vigour as before. He wished he hadn't seen that ship, or the sheet hanging from the Hollies' bedroom window. Not that he had anything against Kit Harrison, he told himself. He was a quiet, steady good-natured chap, a first-rate seaman. He'd been away when the Hollies was sold and the bid had been made by a relation, but on his next voyage home he'd approached Tom, and expressed his sympathy. Bought him a double whisky, too, and would undoubtedly have offered to lend him a five-pound note if he'd as much as dropped a hint. No, he had nothing against Kit. If it hadn't been him it would have been someone else. And he wasn't really wishing he was back at sea, but the sight of that fine ship certainly had bothered him. It would be no good if he did want to go back to sea, anyway. The term of his suspension was nearly up, but Lloyd's would watch out he never got command of a ship again, even if Bartholomew Fosdyck , or any other of the Bramblewick part-owners, gave him a chance. Give a dog a bad name and hang it. And yet he'd make a better ship's master, now, than ever before—a teetotaller and a converted man. He'd forgotten nothing he had learnt of the art and craft of seamanship. He'd be just as capable (probably more capable) of taking the *Moor Cliff* to the Plate and back as the man who was on her bridge at this moment signalling a message of farewell to his wife and children. If only he hadn't had to wait until all this had happened to him before seeing the Light. If only he had paid heed to the preaching of old Jasper Laycock. But God, he reflected, moves in a mysterious way, His wonders to perform. It was not for him to start questioning or complaining.

He heard the steamer blow again, but he did not turn to look at it. He had reached the top of the Bank and there was a hedge on the left side hiding the sea and on his right was the farm. His first job of the day was here repairing a binder. He resolutely turned into the yard and knocked at the farm-house door.

6

HE HAD some gates to mend at the next farm, which belonged to old Peter Jilson (Mark's nearest neighbour) and was called Brock Hill. It was one of the largest farms in the parish and had been one of the most prosperous. But Peter was a mean, ill-tempered, quarrelsome chap and after the war, when the boom in farming was ending, he'd fallen out with his two grown-up sons, Joe and George (he'd refused to pay them any wages), and they'd gone off to another parish to farm on their own. Brock Hill, like Mark's farm, had been allowed to go back, but not quite so badly. Tom did not dawdle over his jobs there, for there was no joy in working for a man whose main idea was to get as much done for the least brass, but it was nearly three o'clock, the sun was getting low and the sea and hills misty when he'd finished the gates and got paid for them and started across the fields towards the home of his father-in-law. He and Mark had had their quarrels and misunderstandings, but on the whole they had always got on fairly well together. Mark had made no difficulties about his courting of Ella. If anything he had encouraged it, for he had been completely dominated by his second wife, who wanted Ella out of the way. She had died three years ago. He was nearly seventy and, after his two unhappy experiences of matrimony, he had not been tempted to chance a third, and since her death he'd had an elderly married couple living with him: the man as farm-hand, the woman to housekeep and milk. Neither of them was satisfactory. Compared with his second wife (she'd had her virtues), the woman was a slut. The man was unintelligent and lazy. All that he was good at, Mark had confided to Tom, was catching rabbits, the sale of which he took in lieu of wages. The rest of the work he did was an unprofitable return for his board and lodgings.

In many ways Tom felt sorry for his father-in-law. The farm was his own. He'd made money on his sheep during the war, but his health was failing. The land and the buildings were being neglected for need of sufficient labour, he'd had a lot of bad luck with his stock and, at an age when most men would be retiring, he was having to work harder than ever to keep things going. Several times he had dropped a hint that he would have liked Ella back. Only last summer, when Tom had been helping him with the hay, he'd made a definite proposal that the whole family (he was very attached to Jane) should move into the farm. Tom happened to be sober, for the simple reason that he hadn't the price of a drink, and indeed was only haymaking with the hope of earning the price of several. The idea had not appealed to him. But he'd told Mark it did and that he'd talk it over with Ella when he got home. It might have been that Mark had considered the thing as good as settled. In a good humour (for if Ella came it would mean he could get rid of the other woman, and Tom, even with his boozing, would be more use than Charley her husband) he had readily agreed to giving Tom a pound advance on his earnings. Unfortunately, Tom had put half that sum on a horse with the Burnharbour bookmaker who had been in the Mariners the same night. More unfortunately, the horse had won at very long odds and he had taken no further part in that season's haymaking, although he'd had the grace later to pay back to Mark the unearned balance of the pound he had borrowed.

Mark had not mentioned his proposition again. Tom hadn't either. But he was thinking of it now as he approached the farm. Ella and Jane were not the only people he had let down. If he'd told Ella that night what her father had proposed instead of going straight to the Mariners, things might have turned out very different. If they'd all come here last summer it would have been a good thing for the old man anyway. Yet that wouldn't have stopped him drinking or brought him to salvation. Mark himself was not a teetotaller; anything but. There'd been Saturday nights at Bramblewick when he'd had so much that he'd had to be lifted into the saddle of his old mare, and only the sagacity of the mare herself had got him safe along the beach and the tortuous way home in the dark. He was an honest man, known for his square dealings. But he was not a church- or a chapel-goer. He was at times blasphemous and foul-mouthed. There might have been less temptation living up here, so far from Bramblewick, but there was a pub, the Hare and Hounds, on the moor road and likely as not Mark and he would have gone off drinking together. . . No, he had travelled the hardest and most dangerous way. There could not have been for him any short-cut to salvation. He'd had to travel deep into the shadow of the valley in order to climb up into the sunshine on the other side and anyway, he was a sailor (or had been once) and not a farmer or a farm labourer. The jobs he was doing now had little to do with farming so far as his skill was concerned. They were the jobs of a handyman: jobs that any man who'd lived on board ships could have done if he'd had the mind.

And yet next to the beach there was no part of the Bramblewick district he liked being in more than this. It always had been so since he was a boy. He could now see the farm itself. It stood in a slight depression halfway between the cliff (where it started to rise steeply to High Batts) and the edge of the moor. A tiny beck, its course marked by a few sallows and stunted oaks and rowan trees, passed near the farm. This beck, it was a mere trickle in summer time, had its source in the old alum quarry, a vast amphitheatre that had been carved out of the shoulder of High Batts moor generations ago. The alum shale had been burnt in kilns whose ruins were still standing. The debris from quarry and kilns had been dumped down the slopes of the hill towards the cultivated fields, making huge mounds that were now overgrown with whins and bramble and which, despite the skill of Mark's hired man in the winning of his wages, swarmed with rabbits.

Here as a small boy he had come brambling or bird's nesting, according to the season. Above the alum shale in the quarry there was a steep sandstone cliff, a favourite nesting-place for jackdaws and rock pigeons and kestrels. He'd had a catapult and once he had potted a rabbit and proudly taken it home to his mother. He daren't have gone near the farm then. To the village boys all farmers were natural enemies. But when he'd grown into a youth, and he was home from sea, he'd often come here with Harry, and he remembered that the first time he had met Mark it was in the whins below the quarry, and Mark had caught them in the very act of setting a rabbit snare and had been quite good-natured about it after a bit of cursing. And here, too, after their first passionate love-making, he and Ella had so often met and parted. He recognised up on his right hand a rowan tree growing among the whins under which they had often sat. It was bare now, but he could remember how sweet the flowers smelt in spring and how red were the berries in autumn; how once Ella had tried making a necklace of them, but had been beaten by the size and hardness of their stones. And here was the very stile where they used to say good-bye, for it was very rare during their courtship that he went to the house. He had disliked Ella's step-mother as much as Ella had done.

He climbed the stile (it was only a hundred yards from the farm), and just on the other side of the thorn edge was Mark himself, a gun under his arm, and with the other hand holding up the headless and partly de-feathered carcase of a goose. Each was surprised and for a moment the anger and disgust that were in the old man's face as he'd stood surveying the bird were directed at his son-in-law. He spoke with a broad accent.

"Why the hell did tha' come sudden like that? Tha' meade me jump."

Tom grinned. He had been startled himself.

"Sorry. I didn't expect to see you here. What's up?"

Mark held up the carcase of the bird. The blood was dripping from its neck. The body was still quivering. He was indignant, but not with Tom.

"What's up? Why a bloody fox of course. In broad

dayleet too. Ah was just cutting some hay when ah saw it. Ah went and fetched gun, but it was too sly for me. And that after getting into a chicken house last neet and killing a dozen layin' bods. That bastard Charley again! His wife's bad enough but he's a hundred times warse. Ah asked him last neet if he'd fastened bods up and of course he said he had. He'd never been near 'em. There waddn't be any foxes aboot if he did his job trapping them. But he sees nea brass in foxes, only in rabbits. And this is t' bod ah was fattening for Ella and Jane and thoo for Christmas. Tha'd best take it back wi' tha when tha gans. Did tha see a fox just noo ? It must have gone way thoo come."

If Tom winced at Mark's profanity, he gave no outward sign of it. He'd been up to the farm several times since his conversion but he'd been discouraged by his vain efforts to reform Sam Bunny (he'd heard that Sam had been blind drunk the night before he'd left to join the *Moor Cliff*) and he'd felt almost as diffident about discussing it with Mark as he did with Ella. He was sympathetic.

"I didn't see any sign of a fox. It's a bit of bad luck."

Mark spat with disgust. He'd been a good-looking man once, Tom remembered. He'd been not over tall, but lean and powerfully built and always when he rode down to "market" on a Saturday night he'd been smartly dressed with starched collar and black tie, and whipcord jacket and riding breeches with leggings, and shining brown boots. His back was bent now, his figure was podgy. He was bald but for a fringe of dirty white hair showing from under his shabby felt hat. He had no moustache but he hadn't shaved for several days, and he looked dirty and unkempt, and above everything worn and unhappy. He signed to Tom to hold the bird while he took the cartridges out of the gun. Then he shouldered the gun and turned towards the farm.

"Hod its head doon, and let it bleed. It's yah thing in favour of foxes, they nearly allus bite a bod's head off and lap t' blood, so it'll be ni warse when it's cooked. . . Bad luck, did tha say? There's been nowt else but bad luck on this farm since my second missus died and I was daft eneaf to get that chap and his wife to live it spot. There's neither of 'em any use except for filling their guts with my vittels. It waddn't be so bad if that bloody woman knew hoo to cook. She can take a young cabbage and make it si teaf tha'd think tha was chewing an awd sack. She either forgets to put any salt in t' pan when she's boiling spuds, or she puts in eneaf ti cure a side of bacon. I'll say this for my second missus—she had a sharpish tongue and she liked to be boss, but she could cook and she could milk and pitch hay, and keep t' spot clean and tidy. . . Look at everything. Whole spot's gahing to bits."

Mark made a sweeping gesture with his hand that seemed to indicate not only the farm but the entire universe, and his unmitigated pessimism towards it. Tom remained silent. He thought the old man was exaggerating in saying the whole farm was going to bits, but he knew that things were bad enough. It didn't take an expert to see that there was not a fence that was properly trimmed or, on the higher fields which bounded the moor, a wall without its gaps. The ditches were choked. Again in the higher fields, which had originally been reclaimed from the moor and were called intakes, bracken and sedges were gaining on the sown pasture grasses, and as for the farm buildings there was scarcely one that didn't need some sort of repair. Was Mark getting at him he wondered? He felt guilty. Even if he hadn't brought Ella and Jane to live here, things couldn't have got quite so bad if he'd come regularly. Just working on broken days (like this one was going to be) he'd done several important repairs.

He did not know what comment to make. But Mark apparently did not expect one. As they drew near to the front of the house he turned to Tom and said good-humouredly,

"Tha's looking a lot better in thi' sen, Tom. Tha's changed and ni mistake. Is tha still keeping off booze? I fetched a couple of bottles of ale from Hare and Hounds last night. Will tha split yan of 'em wi me, noo?"

It was Tom's habit to think visually. He had an instant picture of Mark pouring ale into a glass: saw the colour of it, the effervescence, the creamy froth. He'd had a meal at the first farm of boiled ham and it had been very salt, and he was thirsty. Beer had never given him the same passionate craving that spirits had done. But two months ago, if Mark had made such an offer there'd have been no hesitation in his acceptance. He said now with an equal lack of hesitation,

"No, thanks. I've stopped drinking for good. But I'd like a drink of water."

Mark smiled, but not in the same way as the blacksmith might have done.

"Why—there's plenty of that. . . I'm glad tha's come, Tom. There's about a dozen tiles come loose on t' roof and rain's gettin' in and fetched a bit o' ceiling down in t' big bedroom. Dis tha think tha could fix 'em afore it gets dark? I'll show tha."

The house faced the sea. It was substantially built of roughly dressed freestone that must have come from the cliff of the big quarry. There was a walled garden in front, but the hens had got in and it was a wilderness. Behind, the wall continued to the barn and cow-house and stables and pigsties, and there was a gate through it to the back of the house itself. The mending of that gate had been one of Tom's first jobs, and Mark complimented him upon it as he led the way through. The back door leading into the kitchen was open and on their approach a woman appeared at it. She was elderly, stout, slovenly. She had a cook's knife in her hand and her hands and arms were wet with blood, stuck with chicken's feathers. With blood on her dress, too, and a dirty cloth tied over her head she looked like a woman terrorist of the French Revolution. Physically, however, Mark Moorsholm's housekeeper was harmless and even in those matters which perpetually aroused his ire, she was good-intentioned. It was just that she had the mind of a child. Like a child, too, she was garrulous.

She addressed her master.

"Eh—has tha bin oot wi' thy gun? Hast ha bin shooting?" and then, noticing the goose, babbled on, "Whatever has tha getten there? Is it a goose? Eh—it isn't yan o' our geese is it? Why, its head's off. Where did tha get it, Captain Bransby? Has t'master told tha a fox got into a 'en-hoose last neet and killed a lot of 'ens? Ah'm just dressin' 'em. No need to waste' em. As ah said to maister, they'll fetch their price, them as we can't eat oursens. Why, it must have been a fox that's had that goose. Is t'others all reet? I heard a cackling and a goin's on just noo."

Mark apparently knew that it was no good trying to stem the torrent of questions by answering them. He moved resolutely for the door and she was obliged to back inside, and as he followed close on her he said,

"Mash a pot of tea, Martha."

Tom, not following, heard her say,

"Aye, ah will. Ah will. But fire's gone oot and ah'll et ti gan and get some kindlin'. Charley hasn't left me a bit. He'll be up i' quarry whins with his nets and ferret."

She was still talking when Mark came out again, having left his gun inside. He took the goose from Tom, hung it up on a nail and then said, without troubling to lower his voice,

"Listen tiv her. On and on like a beck in flood. And she's been all day dressin' them bods that my missus would have done in an 'oor. An' kitchen fire oot at this time of day and no kindlin'. Come on. Ah'll show tha where them tiles are loose, and then ah'll et ti get that fodder cut and get coo-house mucked out. Ah'll lay Charley won't be back till everything's done and he can sit doon comfortably tiv his tea."

The loose tiles were near the ridge of the house roof. Tom knew where the ladder was. It had been another of his jobs to put several new rungs in it and, as he set it up against the wall unassisted, for Mark had moved on to the stackyard, he noticed these rungs with satisfaction. He climbed the ladder and glanced at the tiles. Nothing difficult, he thought, only he'd need a roof ladder. Mark did not own one, but a plank would do with a few laths nailed on to it as rungs. He started whistling as he climbed down. Mark had depressed him saying that about the farm, and going on about Martha and Charley. But he felt better now. There was nothing like work to make a man happy: to have a job to do, and to be able to do it well. There was a shed close by. He found a long rough plank (it must have come from the beach at some time) and some smaller stuff. He moved to the back door where he had put down his tool bag. The sound of a running tap inside reminded him of his thirst and he stepped into the kitchen. Martha had gone out to look for kindling. The place was in a terrible mess. On the table were the carcases of the unfortunate hens: three of them still as the fox had left them, beheaded and gory. There was also the unwashed crockery from the last meal, and the table and flagged floor were strewn with feathers, which Martha had evidently tried to dispose of in the fireplace.

There was a cupboard close to the sink. He wanted a clean cup and he opened the door and saw on the shelf immediately in front of him two quart flagons of brown ale, one of them with a quarter of its contents gone. He smiled. The ale in the opened bottle had a head on it, a dear sign that it had very recently been touched. It must have been Mark, when he came into the kitchen to put his gun back, having a quick swig and perhaps not saying anything about it in deference to his own refusal. As though the sight of him drinking would have done that!

He picked up the bottle, held it to the light of the window, and examined it coolly. Harmless-looking stuff. But for the froth on it it would be hard to tell it from cold milkless tea. Yet funny, and terrible too, to think what harm it really could do; not just one drink in itself of course, nor yet one bottle, nor two for that matter, but what just one drink could lead to in starting or restarting a habit. Thank God he realised that now. Thank God he had the faith and the resolution to be able to hold it in his hand, and yet not have the slightest desire to drink, in spite of him being so thirsty. Not even the smell of drink, which only a few weeks ago would have been to him like the smell of raw meat to a famished cat, could worry him now. He would prove it.

He unscrewed the stopper. He felt the pressure of escaping gas round the rubber ring, heard the hiss of it. Then deliberately he put the bottle to his nostrils and inhaled deeply. And as he did so it was as though the sensation of thirst he had at the back of his throat became a violent scorching flame. He lowered the bottle to his lips. He felt the coldness of the glass, his tongue licked and tasted the bitter moisture on it. He held his head back and elevated the bottle. But before the liquor reached his mouth he heard heavy footsteps on the flags outside the kitchen door. He put the bottle back on to the shelf, swiftly replaced the stopper, seized a mug from the shelf above it, closed the cupboard door and leaned over to the tap. He filled the mug to the brim and gulped it down. Then he swung round as the doorway darkened.

It was Jonty Scaife, the postman. He came right in, without knocking. He saw Tom, but showed no surprise. He had a small bundle of letters in his hand and he sorted them and selected two.

"Where's Mark?" he said quite casually to Tom.

"In the stackyard, I think."

"Well there's nobbut a couple of bills for him. I don't suppose he's got owt to post. It's a fine day, Tom. Are you up helping t'awd man?" He put the two letters on the table and saw the hens. "Hallo, what's happened?"

Tom felt that his cheeks were burning, that his voice was trembling when he answered.

"A fox got into a hen-house last night. . . But I've just come. I'm just going to mend some loose tiles on the roof."

Ostentatiously, he moved forward and set the mug down on the table close to the letters so that Jonty could see that it contained water. Jonty laughed.

"Who'd be a farmer eh? I'm glad I'm not. Well, I'll be getting along."

He turned to go, but Tom followed him quickly and he at once picked up his tools and ostentatiously hurried to the plank and started to measure a strip of wood for the first rung. He heard Jonty close the gate, was certain that he was out of sight. Then like one who has escaped from the very jaws of death, he started to shake so that he could not hold the wood still and he had to lean up against the ladder. He was terrified: not that Jonty had seen him with the bottle (for it was clear he had not), but because only Jonty's coming had stopped him from drinking, from breaking his pledge, from doing just what the smith and probably most of Bramblewick, too, had said he would do at the first real chance. If Jonty had not come he'd have finished that bottle at one go. Likely as not he'd have had the other bottle, too, before Mark had come back. With the money he'd got in his pocket, he'd have been up to the Hare and Hounds, then. He'd have made a night of it and gone home tight and once again he'd have been the laughing stock and the disgrace of Bramblewick. And those two bottles were still there. Probably when he'd finished the roof and was ready to go home, Mark would again offer him a drink.

Would he? Tom suddenly sprung upright. He glanced across at the stackyard. He could just see Mark's shoulders moving under a fork full of hay. A little farther off he could hear Martha breaking sticks among the whins. He turned round and strode swiftly back to the house, into the kitchen. He opened the cupboard door, seized a bottle in each hand, and strode out again across the back yard, across it to the stackyard. There was no gate. Mark was just entering a calf-house on his right. He yelled to him to stop. The old man swung round and stared at his son-in-law in surprise. He did not speak. Tom walked right up to him and then stopped, holding the bottles out at arm's length as though they were indian clubs.

"Do you see these?" he demanded fiercely. "Do you see these?"

Mark looked scared. Tom's eyes were bright with anger.

"Aye. Of course ah do, Tom. What's up?"

"Do you see what they *are*?"

"Of course ah do. They're what ah fetched down from t' Hare and Hounds last neet. Ah offered tha a drink and tha refused, Tom. Dis tha want a drink, noo? Ah'm not objecting if that's what tha's 'intin' at. Tha can have both bloody bottles if tha wants. Ah've never objected to tha drinking, Tom. Even when tha had too much. It was never none of mah business."

"No you never *did* object. It never *was* your business. It never did trouble you that your own daughter's husband was a drunkard and a waster. And like a lot of others you'd not believe that a chap like me could change

139

and see how he'd done wrong and want to start afresh. Do you think it's a kid's game I'm playing, about being converted, and giving up boozing and swearing and trying to do right after all I've done wrong? Do you think I'm putting it on?"

Mark had to lean his load against the jambs of the door. He looked more puzzled than scared now. He couldn't see what Tom was getting at.

"Nay," he said. "Ah dean't think tha's puttin' owt on. Ah'm glad enough tha's got better of thi illness, and that tha's working again regular. Tha made a good job of yon gate. Tha mended yon ladder, and there was t' wagon shafts. Ah've bin glad to have tha. If there's owt—"

Tom cut him short.

"Glad to have me, eh? Glad that Ella and Jane have got plenty to eat again and there's money to buy clothes with? And yet almost the first thing you do when I get here today is offer me a drink. Try to set me boozing again. You asked that old woman of yours to mash a pot of tea, but you go in yourself and have a swig of beer and then leave the stuff handy for me to find it. Do you believe in God and the devil? Do you know that the devil is always setting traps for those that are trying to run straight? Aye, I'll tell you the truth. I went into the kitchen to get a drink of water, and I went to the cupboard for a cup and I saw these two bottles. And 1 thought I was strong enough to resist temptation. And I picked one up, and I took out the stopper and I smelt it, and before I knew what I was at I had the bottle to my lips, and I'd have drunk it too if Jonty Scaife hadn't come in. And if I'd done that I'd have been blind drunk tonight, and I might have given Ella a worse do than

I did last time. And it would have been the end of everything. How much did these two bottles cost you?"

"Why, ah think they're one and a tanner apiece."

Tom put one of them under his arm. He unscrewed the stopper of the other and let it pour on to the ground. When it was empty he did the same as with the first. Then he said with a deadly calm,

"I'll put you an extra day's work in for this. But if I'm going to do any more work at this spot, hide your beer where I can't see it. And if you want to use any bad language about what I've done or about anything else, wait till I'm out of hearing. I'll get on with that job now."

He turned and, his shoulders squared, and with quick even strides, walked back towards the house. Mark stared at him speechless until he reached the plank and started sawing, then he took the weight of the hay on to his shoulder again and was about to enter the calf house when he heard a voice behind him. It was Charley, coming into the stackyard from the quarry path and he must have overheard at least part of Tom's denunciation for he said, in a whining voice,

"What's up wi Tam? What's 'e bin making all t' noise aboot, Mr Moorsholm?"

Mark released himself from the load of hay and swung around on his hated manservant. He was not so old as his wife but he was dirtier and even more untidy, thin and scraggy, with thin blue lips and a long crooked nose that was perpetually wet, and his eyes small, mean and avaricious.

Mark shouted at him,

"What's up with *who*? Who gave *thoo* leave to call Captain Bransby Tom, thoo mucky useless good-for-nowt? What's thoo been doin' with thi' sen all day? Sitting an thi backside smoking thi pipe waitin' for a ferrit ti come oot and ower lazy to tak a spade and dig for it? Ah pay thoo to dea a bit o' work as well as play wi rabbits. Why dissn't tha catch that bloody fox? Did tha know it's getten a goose as well as bods it slaughtered last neet, all an account of thy bloody laziness? Dean't thoo start asking any questions aboot Captain Bransby. And listen here, yance an' for all. Dean't thoo mention ale within his hearing. And dean't thoo use any bloody bad language, thoo or thy missus. . . Noo get 'od of a fork and get that coo-house mucked oot. Thoo's a bloody seet warse than useless!"

Tom did not hear what his father-in-law was saying. He had already sawn a couple of slats. The water had quenched his physical thirst. He had wiped from his lips the faint taste of ale the bottle had left. And by having it out with Mark he felt he had wiped something equally unpleasant from his soul. It was as though he had had another of his bad dreams, that he was awake and he felt again that God was by his side.

7

THE WESLEYAN CHAPEL ANNUAL BAZAAR AND CONCERT was always held a week before Christmas. It was reckoned that folks were in more of a spending mood then, and that they could kill two birds with one stone by supporting the chapel and buying useful Christmas presents for friends and relations. Every female member of the chapel was supposed to make and give something for the Bazaar. The stalls were long narrow trestle tables arranged along the sides of the old schoolroom, with upright frames and crossbars on which the things for sale could be hung or draped. These things ranged from pin-cushions and pen-wipers to embroidered tablecloths, and layettes, floormats (made of rag clippings), men's socks, lace handkerchiefs, crocheted ties, gloves, and even ladies' underwear, although such garments were discreetly kept at the back of the stall out of sight.

Gwen Jones, naturally, was well experienced in organising bazaars. She had rightly regarded them as much as a social function as a way of raising funds for chapel or charitable purposes. She had always been full of bright ideas for side-shows and competitions, lucky dips and innocent raffles, and wouldn't have been above dressing up as a gipsy and telling fortunes at threepence a time if she'd been allowed a free hand. Dai, indeed, had always given her a pretty free hand, although when it had been a purely chapel function he'd had to draw the line at raffles and fortune-telling. But at Bramblewick there was no need for his restraining influence. Captain Bartholomew Fosdyck might be the senior, and virtually only, trustee of the chapel, but so far as its feminine activities went the bosses were his elderly nieces, the Misses Selina and Abigail Lawther, with the chapel organist and choir mistress, Miss Lucy Widdison, to give them, if they ever needed it, official support.

Miss Widdison was the only daughter of still another of Bramblewick's wealthy seafarers, but her father had had a paralytic stroke soon after his retirement from sea and never left his Up-Bank villa. She had no particular gifts as a musician. As a girl she had learnt to play the piano, and then a harmonium her father had brought from Hamburg one voyage. She had never been good-looking and she was now fifty. Her mother had died young and it was only natural that she should keep house for her father and not marry herself, for no Bramblewick man would keep a servant if he could help. Early on Gwen had pitted her own bright and cheerful personality against Miss Widdison's with less success than Dai had achieved in his conflict with Captain Fosdyck. She had dared to suggest that the choir took the hymns too slowly, pointing out as an example that "Onward Christian Soldiers" was a march, a really gay and inspiring tune. When she played and sang it herself she did indeed see soldiers marching, crusaders with flashing swords and spears and flying banners. But it was evident that what Miss Widdison saw (if she saw anything at all) was a funeral procession moving slowly and sombrely to the parish burial ground on a grey winter day. She had looked shocked at Gwen's suggestion, but also quite implacable.

"I am sorry, Mrs Jones. But we couldn't possibly play a hymn just like an ordinary tune. It wouldn't be respectful in the house of God."

This had been one of the several occasions when the Celt in Gwen had come near to boiling up into an explosion. She was not happy in Bramblewick, except for Jane Bransby and what it had done for Dai's health. For herself she would, a hundred times over, have been back in a city. Sometimes, daring to be mildly disloyal to her love for Dai, she thought of Africa and of the life she would have had there if her man had not died. She had a brother who was a missionary in Southern Rhodesia. His letters (they wrote to each other at frequent intervals) were very vivid and from them and the numerous snapshots he enclosed, and her own imagination, she had built up a picture of the place and the life there as a sort of paradise. The country was high and cool and healthy. The mission had a clinic, a day school and a kindergarten full of happy black children. If only Dai had been younger, stronger; if only at the time of his last illness they'd had the money to pay their passage out to Rhodesia and take at least that holiday which the brother had persistently offered them both.

But Gwen would always pull herself up with a jerk if her dreaming reached the bounds of a serious discontent. She hadn't boiled over with Miss Widdison. The poor woman was plain and narrow-minded and repressed, and she must have had a miserable life with no brothers and sisters and having to look after an invalid (and probably crotchety) father. She undoubtedly liked playing the organ and being mistress of the choir, and perhaps she really got quite as much joy and consolation from a mournfully-rendered Moody and Sankey hymn as Gwen herself would from Gilbert arid Sullivan. And since the impressive financial success of the visitors' concert, both Miss Widdison and the Lawther sisters had at least affected a respect for her organising ability. Most of the items in the present concert were to be given by the Sunday School children. In Sunday School affairs (possibly the stove before it had been mended had something to do with this), she had almost complete authority. She had run no risks of criticism or obstruction, however. She had held all practices and rehearsals at the Manse (thus saving chapel coal and gas) and it was not until the morning of the bazaar that she had started work on the construction of a "stage", although the plans of it had been in her mind for weeks.

Strictly orthodox Wesleyans do not hold with dancing or theatricals. Both are manifestations of the devil. The Church of England saw no great evil in either. But what was the Church of England with its incense and altars and crucifixes but Papacy in disguise? Bramblewick Wesleyans (those who were left of them) were orthodox all right. But they were also stupid, Gwen reasoned, not knowing what they really meant by dancing and theatricals, and the visitors' concert had proved that with discretion she could not only avoid their disapproval but even earn their approbation. But she did not refer to her stage as a stage, when she had asked Captain Fosdyck for the loan of a certain amount of light timber; she had wanted it, she had said tactfully, for decorating the concert platform. And instinctively she had used the same discretion with Tom Bransby who, through Dai, had very willingly volunteered to help her with the job.

Dai still felt anything but comfortable about Tom. He was not cynical. But he could not help feeling that the whole business was too good to be true. It had been so easy. What he mistrusted was the very completeness of Tom's conversion. From being the village drunkard and wastrel he was behaving almost like a saint. It was embarrassing for Tom, and the whole village (judging by the information that came by Gwen's "help") was giving Dai himself credit for the transformation, attributing to him the gifts almost of a faith-healer. Next thing, he had remarked ironically to his wife, it would be getting into the daily papers and they'd be starting pilgrimages to Bramblewick Wesleyan Chapel. There was one man, however, who remained completely unconvinced that the "cure" was real or permanent: Will Knaggs.

Strangely, Dai could not bring himself to share in the popular dislike of the smith. Instead he had to admit that in spite of his insolence and conceit he definitely enjoyed their frequent encounters. However wicked the man might be judged by religious standards, there could be no doubt of his honesty and courage. Dai admired a plain speaker. He was one himself when occasion demanded. The smiddy was on the only convenient road down to the old village. If Knaggs was at the forge he would hurry past unobserved and be glad of it. But if he was observed he'd be equally glad and he'd step inside the shop and talk and be talked at. It was banter mostly, with Dai giving as much as he took. He would never let himself in for a definite argument. To that oft-repeated and classic question of the Hyde Park Corner tub-thumping atheist, "Where did Cain get his wife from if Adam and Eve were the first people on earth?" Dai would adroitly give the Shakespearean rejoinder, and he had taken the wind out of his adversary's sails by saying that he was a firm believer in the Darwinian theory of evolution, and that such a belief was not incompatible with a belief in God and Christianity.

This had brought the rejoinder,

"You're a slippery one, Mr Jones. You're as hard to get hold of as an eel. I'd like to hear you telling old Selina and Abigail we're all descended from monkeys, although if anyone needed proof of it they'd needn't look further than Bramblewick Wesleyan, with old Bully Fosdyck and his thick neck and great hairy paws. Call him the missing link and you'd not be far wrong."

The comparison, Dai thought, was not inapt and indeed he privately relished many of the smith's pungent remarks about the members of his flock. But whenever Knaggs raised the subject of Tom Bransby he felt uneasy. The mockery he did not mind, either of himself or of Tom. What worried him was that behind the mockery he knew there was more than a measure of possible truth. . . Did Mr Jones really believe (the smith demanded) that a chap's whole character could change as sudden as that, and stay changed? There he was with a holy light shining in his eyes and looking as though butter wouldn't melt in his mouth. Getting up first in the morning and giving his wife her breakfast in bed. Always washed and shaved and with a collar and tie on, his boots polished, walking past the Mariners sniffing as though it was a midden. Did Mr Jones know that Tom had tried to persuade Sam Bunny to give up drinking and swearing, that he'd even tried it on with old Captain Christopher? Did Mr Jones really know Tom as he was before he'd nearly murdered his wife and then got D.T.s? Had he heard about the rest of the Bransbys and what boozers they all were? The leopard couldn't change its spots, and human nature was human nature. Of course there were such things as conversions. There was the Welsh Revival before the war. Chaps standing up in meetings and weeping and confessing their sins and shouting out they were saved. But what happened to them after? You didn't hear much about the Revivalists and "Oh that will be Glory for me" now. It was all hysterics, a sort of madness. Could Mr Jones honestly say that Tom Bransby was normal now? "The devil was sick, the devil a monk would be." Tom had been sick and he'd had a bad fright, too, about his missus, but how long would he last like he was now? Wasn't it some sort of religious mania he'd got? Wasn't he just getting drunk on religion, as before he had got drunk on whisky?

Dai hadn't tried to defend himself or Tom. He hadn't thought that Knaggs was being malicious, although in everything he said he sensed that almost satanic mockery of religion. Was he right? Was Tom "taking" religion as a dope? Certainly there was no hypocrisy about his conversion and the way he had behaved since he had become physically well and able to work. To suspect him even of mild insanity because he had become a regular worshipper at all chapel services, including the mid-week service (which Dai would gladly have dispensed with if Captain Fosdyck and the Misses Lawther and Widdison had not kept him up to the scratch) was to suggest that Dai was insane himself. Yet he would not have liked to have told Knaggs that Tom, only a few days ago, had said to him (with an earnestness that had been almost pathetic) that he wished to devote himself more fully to the work of God than just chapel-going. He'd like to learn how to pray aloud and lead in prayer, as Captain Fosdyck and certain others of the "elders" did on occasions, perhaps in time even to preach and tell publicly what religion had done for him. Dai had been scared and non-committal, but he had marked with what enthusiasm Tom had accepted his suggestion, that he might help with the carpentry for the concert "platform".

Gwen, too, noted this eagerness but she didn't bother to analyse it. It was the first time she'd had anything to do with Tom, and rather to her own surprise, she took an immediate liking to him. She had expected to find him nervous and shy, or just the opposite: self-satisfied, assertive and bumptious. He was none of these things. He was like a good-natured, well-mannered boy, perhaps a little over-anxious to make a good impression, but so eager to help. And she would not have been a woman if she had not noticed, too, his definitely masculine qualities, his square lean figure, the way he held himself when he stood or moved, the trick all sailors acquire and never lose of anticipating the pitch or roll of a ship's deck. His face was still lean and pale and deeply lined for his age, but she noted the firmness of his mouth and jaw and it was only the exceptional brightness of his eyes that made her think of what Dai had said, his vague fear that he might still be mentally unbalanced.

The bazaar was to be opened at two o'clock. It was now morning. The schoolroom was crowded with the chapel ladies dressing their stalls. Dai had to make a call on one of the invalid members of his flock and wouldn't be down until later, and Gwen was glad that Captain Fosdyck had not put in an early appearance. She felt a bit nervous. But Tom's first remark when she showed him the sketch of her "stage" encouraged her.

"It looks a treat," he said. "Jane's very excited about it you know, Mrs Jones. I know a little bit of what she's going to do. She was reciting it last night, about the dormouse and the mad hatter. You've been very good to that little girl of mine, you and Mr Jones. I think I can fix all this up for you easy enough, although Captain Fosdyck seems to have cut you close with the wood. Still I've got plenty of wood I've picked up on the shore. I've got some line, too, that will do for the curtains."

Gwen had behaved with extreme tact in handling Miss Widdison about the programme. The choir mistress was responsible for the grown-up items supplied by members of the choir and herself and friends. For these she needed only the piano and piano stool, and of course a table and chair for the chairman Captain Fosdyck. Gwen's most important tactical gain was to get the "grown-ups" to bat first, using only the front six feet of the platform. Her "stage" would go behind, with a depth of another six feet to the end wall of the schoolroom where, fortunately, there was a recess large enough to hold her young artistes. The curtains would be kept drawn during the first half of the concert. She was ambitious. At the visitors' concert she'd had to make do with screens and no special lighting. No electricity was available, of course. Nothing could be done with the schoolroom gas supply except that one of the lights (it was incandescent) happened to be so placed as to give a top illumination to her stage when shaded from the rest of the room. But she must have footlights, so she had borrowed six paraffin lamps and she explained to Tom how she needed a wide plank to be set on edge just at the edge of the platform to hide the wall lamps from the audience. She had got some sheets of tinfoil to tack to the inside of this to act as a reflector. He understood perfectly. The framework curtain would be covered with stout coloured paper, and Gwen had already made a pelmet of pleated tissue paper to go along the top.

Before the war the Wesleyan Bazaar had been a two-day event with a concert each night and a supper at the conclusion of the second one. Within a few minutes of the opening of the doors on the first afternoon the room would have been packed, and at the concerts many would have been turned away after the last possible standing space had been filled. It was not so now. Apart from the stall-holders there were not more than fifty people present when the time for the official opening was at hand. But, as Captain Fosdyck whispered to Mr Jones (they stood near the door waiting for the distinguished lady who was to perform the opening ceremony), "There's none but folks with brass. They're all here to spend, and that's main thing, Mr Jones, in a do like this. We're wise, too, to have the opening before the bairns come in from school. They'd only make a lot of noise. I hope Miss Bellingham's car hasn't broke down. She gave us five guineas last bazaar. It might be ten, this, for all her brass is in shipping and shipping's done very well in the war and since."

Captain Fosdyck had been consistently pleasant to Dai since the affair of the stove. Dai had just as consistently disliked him and he particularly disliked him at this moment as he stood with his back to the stove itself (the smith had made a grand job of it) watching the open doorway, in a brand-new suit of clothes, brand-new boots, a massive gold watch-chain looped across his ample waist, his face shiny and suddenly wreathed with an unctuous smile as the lady all were expecting appeared and paused at the threshold looking with modest hesitation at the elderly man who was selling admission tickets (sixpence for adults, children half-price) as though she was quite ready to pay for admission if asked.

Dai had not met Miss Bellingham, but he'd heard a lot about her. She lived in a large house on the outskirts of Burnharbour which she had inherited along with a considerable fortune from her shipowner father. But on top of this she'd had several other male relatives in the shipowning business, and as so often happens with already wealthy and not especially deserving persons, she had inherited other large sums and was reputed to be worth at least half a million. But her own father had been educated and so had she. She was a real lady, had a carriage and a motor car and many servants. She took an active and a charitable interest in local public affairs and during the war had supported hospitals, canteens and parcel funds and had easily headed the list for investments in War Bonds. She was tall and aristocratic-looking and she wore a fur coat, and again Dai felt wretchedly conscious of his lack of inches. But at the same time he had a feeling that he disliked Miss Bellingham considerably more than he disliked Captain Fosdyck and this gave him courage again and awaked, too, his ever ready sense of humour.

The captain had moved forward and made as good an effort at bowing as his thick-set body permitted. Miss Bellingham smiled graciously, and extended an ungloved and richly-jewelled hand to his, which Dai remembered had performed such a remarkable conjuring trick with the piece of chamois leather. He hoped the captain would be gentle.

"Good afternoon, Captain Fosdyck."

Her manner, Dai thought, was faintly condescending

and yet there was a subtle familiarity in it, as though she recognised under the captain's rugged exterior an essentially kindred spirit; the richest woman of the town greeting the richest man of the village, the lord greeting the squire; both for the moment oblivious to the elderly man (he was a retired baker) who kept the door. But the captain was embarrassed, and his embarrassment had a peculiar effect on his speech—usually so blunt and, despite its Yorkshire inflection and the hardness of the vowels, grammatical.

"Good afternoon, Miss Bellingham. We are very pleased to see you. And I most sincerely 'ope" (it was the first time Dai had known him to drop an aitch) "you are in the best of 'ealth. We are hall" (the unnecessary one surprised him even more) "ready for the hopening to begin."

Dai had to bite his lips to stop himself smiling, but the next moment the captain had seized him by the arm and he was being introduced to the great lady as the new minister who " 'Ad halready made 'imself most popular in the district". The lady reached out her hand and smiled graciously. She was very pleased to make his acquaintance and he said that he was very pleased to make her acquaintance, and that it was very very kind of her to come and open the bazaar. Next the captain gave a sign to Miss Bellingham, and he led the way forward between the waiting patrons of the bazaar (some sitting on chairs and forms, others standing by the stalls) towards the platform: the captain first, the lady next, Dai last of all. Every one stared as the procession advanced, and once more Dai had to compress his lips for his eyes suddenly met Gwen's (she was standing quite close to the platform) and he saw in them a twinkle of mischievous understanding.

Later that night in the privacy of their home, Dai was to tell his wife how, during that brief ambulation from the doorway to the steps of the platform, two extra-ordinary things had flashed through his mind. First, while walking close to Miss Bellingham, so close that he seemed enveloped in her perfume that trailed behind her like the smoke of a steamer, he had experienced a sudden impulse to reach up his hands and snatch the fur coat from her body and give her a good smack. Next he had an impulse, it was when his eyes had met Gwen's, to push both Miss Bellingham and Captain Fosdyck out of the way, to rush forward and mount the platform and declaim from the twenty-first chapter of the book of St. Matthew, "And Jesus went into the temple of God, and cast out all them that sold and bought in the temple, and overthrew the tables of the money changers and the seats of them that sold doves", and shout at the top of his voice that the Wesleyan Bazaar was not open but shut.

No man can help his thoughts nor his impulses good or bad. He can only be judged by his behaviour and Miss Bellingham reached the platform unharmed, preceded by Captain Fosdyck and followed by Dai himself. And at once he became the minister with a clear instinctive duty to perform. Miss Widdison was already seated at the piano. The captain and Miss Bellingham stood by their chairs each side of the table. Dai raised his hand. The assembly was hushed. Then Miss Widdison played the opening bars of the Old Hundredth, paused and began again and the assembly sang the first verse of the hymn,

"Praise God from Whom all blessings flow,
Praise Him all creatures here below.
Praise Him above ye heavenly Host,
Praise Father, Son and Holy Ghost."

Every one stood or sat at ease again, including Dai whose duty was done. But the captain's sitting down was a mere formality. He promptly stood up again and the assembly, by a moderately hearty clapping of hands, showed that they understood that the real proceedings were under way. The captain beamed, cleared his throat, hooked the thumb of his left hand on one of the loops of his gold chain and started to speak, bluffly, with no immediate sign of nervousness, and no confusion with his aspirates:

"Now friends. You all know me as a man of few words and used to getting sharp to the point. Another year's gone by, and here's t' Wesleyan Bazaar again. There's no need for me to tell any of you what a bazaar's for. It's to make money, and to make money for a good cause, Chapel. There'll be no need for me to tell you, either, things haven't been so good since the war. There's no fishermen left in Bramblewick now. A lot of our young men have been killed or drowned. Chapel congregation has got smaller. But that's only more reason why them that's left should put their hands deeper in their pockets. As you'll notice when you look at the stalls we've still got a lot of good helpers. There's plenty of good things to buy and there's no rules to stop any one putting down two shillings for a thing that's marked one shilling and eleven pence ha'penny and not picking up their change."

He had made a joke and there was laughter and applause. Miss Bellingham smiled, too, Dai observed. She was sitting on the captain's right, looking very calm and collected. The captain cleared his throat again and went on,

"No, I'm not going to pretend that things are going over well with the Wesleyan Chapel. It's not my job to preach, and this isn't the spot or time for preaching anyway. But I'll say this, it will be a bad day for this spot and for this country when folks forget chapel and religion. War's been a bad thing in more ways than one. It's caused a lot of looseness, especially among young folk, pleasure-seeking, the pictures, Sabbath breaking, self-indulgence, unthriftiness, aye—and Socialism. There's only one cure for that. To turn back to God and religion."

The captain paused again, but his listeners were very quiet now and serious. Dai also felt serious, his sense of humour well in abeyance. He was thinking of what the captain had said about war being a bad thing for the young, and of the remark he had made while they had been waiting for Miss Bellingham that shipping had done very well in the war and even better since, and that perhaps Miss Bellingham would make it ten guineas this time instead of five. He was thinking, too, of the repairing of the stove, his refusal to have the schoolroom painted, the fight Gwen had had to get the Sunday School going. But the captain's voice bore in on his thoughts and he noticed at once that it was lacking in its early self-assurance. He was even stammering.

"Well as—er—as—as I said before, I—I'm a man of

few words. I have—I have a pleasant duty to perform."
He half-turned towards Miss Bellingham, and as though
she had exercised some peculiar spell on him, his aitches
from that moment came and went by the board. "There
his no need," he went on turning to the assembly again,
"for me to hintroduce to you the lady who his sitting hon
my right. Hevery one in this district knows her and 'er
family. You never pick hup a copy of the *Burnharbour
Guardian* but what you see Miss Bellingham's name's in
it. Halways, if I may say so, doing something for hothers,
and just the same in peace as in war. I 'ave great
pleasure in calling on Miss Bellingham to hopen. . . hour
. . . bazaar."

The captain sat down. Miss Bellingham got up. There
was polite applause. She began her speech. She was a
practised public speaker with a clear cultured voice. She
was very unhappy to hear the chairman's statement that
things were not so good with their own chapel. What a
dreadful thing the war had been. We must not in any
way underrate what had been done by our gallant
soldiers and sailors, so many of whom had made the
great sacrifice, but at the same time it would be foolish
not to realise the great moral and social problems the war
had created and left. She was glad that the chairman
had mentioned among the evils that only religion could
successfully fight that of Socialism, by which of course he
meant Bolshevism and all that stood for. She believed. . .

What she believed was obviously of great interest to
herself and to a certain number of her listeners including
Captain Fosdyck, but it was of little interest to Dai, for a
vague but ominous sensation of discomfort in the heels
and toes of both his feet had suddenly become an almost

intolerable irritation. The chilblains were on him again. He felt as if he could have torn off his boots and plunged the offending members, not into hot, but into boiling water; it seemed to him that every word the lady uttered exacerbated his suffering. But at last, having enlarged on the perils of Bolshevism (and its implication of Atheism and Anti-Christianity) and suggested without saying it what a good thing it was that England was still ruled by Conservatives and Christians, that Capitalism was next to Godliness, if not Godliness itself, she had come round adroitly to the topic of Christmas and the season of goodwill; to the buying of presents and the praiseworthy purpose of the Wesleyan Bazaar, and in a few more well-chosen words she declared the bazaar open.

She was a busy woman with other engagements to fulfil and after making some purchases at the stalls she had to hurry away. Captain Fosdyck accompanied her to the street door. He came up to Dai immediately on his return. His chilblains were more tolerable now that he was on his feet and moving among the people at the stalls. The captain drew him to one side and said in a hoarse indignant whisper,

"What do you think, Mr Jones? What do you *think*? Richest woman twixt Humber and Tees and she's gone off and never given us a cheque at all, never mentioned it, and I doubt if she spent more than a quid at the stalls."

"Dear me," said Dai. "Dear me."

"And after what she said on the platform. We'll think twice before asking her to open bazaar again. We'll be badly down on this year's takings. I reckon we'd best take a collection at the concert. We don't as a rule, but if t' concert's as good as the one Mrs Jones got up in summer folks won't mind paying a bit extra, although it's a pity we didn't think of it before and made an extra charge to come in. It's too late now, of course."

The captain's pessimism was unjustified. When evening came the room began to fill with people, and he was delighted.

"There's folks here," he remarked to Dai in one of his many confidential whispers, "who've never been at our bazaar before. Church folk. There's Captain and Mrs Zachariah Moorsholm. He's a cousin of Mark Moorsholm, Tom Bransby's wife's father. He's a sidesman at the church. There's Jonty Scaife and his wife, and Betsy Knaggs, and Will Knaggs' lad, Edwin. She's church in spite of her brother being what he is. There's the railway signal man and his wife. They're neither church nor chapel, but their bairns come to Sunday School, don't they? I reckon it's what the bairns are going to do in the concert that's attracting folks like them. We should have charged to come in, yet maybe some of 'em will patronise t' stalls before concert starts. We'll start a bit late so as to give 'em a chance."

There was no need for a late start, however. The captain's pious hope was realised. Five minutes before the advertised time the stalls were bare and had been partly dismantled to make room for chairs and forms, which were eagerly taken. Even the standing room at the back of the school soon was filled and still more people were trying to squeeze in through the doorway, now guarded semi-officially, by the police constable. Dai had forgotten his chilblains. He was feeling excited. The whole atmosphere there had changed since the afternoon. He had the feeling that the people who were here now had really come to enjoy themselves. He was thrilled on Gwen's account, thinking it was *her* part of the concert they had come to see. He had no vanity and not a shred of jealousy in his character. Whatever triumph was achieved he wished it to be wholly hers: the deserved reward for her courage, her unstinted devotion to the true happiness and spiritual welfare of her Sunday School children in the face of so much discouragement and apathy.

He had no active part to play in the evening's proceedings. He had taken upon himself to act as a sort of usher on the single side aisle of the room, which had to be kept as a clear gangway between the platform and the entrance door. He could move about, and he could see all that was going on from one end of the room to the other. The two first rows of chairs and forms were reserved for the performers, children and "grown-ups". Gwen was there with her "gang", as she called them. She was in her best party frock, a darkish red with cream lace collar and cuffs, which to Dai made her look more than usually lovely. She was smiling and her eyes looked excited and happy as she bent forward to speak to Jane Bransby and another little girl Jane was holding by the hand, giving them probably a short rehearsal. She was wonderful with children, Dai thought. It wasn't just a "way". She had the gift of communicating to them, of recreating in them her own lovable character.

Involuntarily, he looked from her to Tom Bransby, who, very smart in his well-sponged blue serge suit with white shirt and black tie, was standing by the wall at the far end of the front row. And as involuntarily Dai thought of that phrase the smith had used, "Looking

161

as though butter wouldn't melt in his mouth", but immediately rejected it as unjust. He certainly looked supremely happy. But mightn't that be because he too had come under Gwen's benign influence? He was standing there to help with the curtains, which he himself had rigged up for Gwen. His wife was sitting well up towards the platform not far from Jonty and Polly Scaife. Her expression was quite impassive, as it was in chapel, but Dai could see that she was watching Gwen and her own daughter. Behind her was Captain Christopher sitting bold upright, his hands clasped on his stick, and nearer to Dai was Betsy Knaggs, the blacksmith's semi-crippled sister, and Edwin, who caught Dai's glance and smiled. But there was no sign of Knaggs himself, and now Captain Fosdyck climbed up on to the platform and held up his hand for silence.

He was a good chairman and obviously much happier with the bridge of the ship to himself. He beamed, and as soon as there was tolerable quiet he said,

"Now friends. As I've said once before today, I'm a man of few words. You're here to listen to a concert, not to me, so I'll waste no time. I am calling on our dear friend, Miss Lucy Widdison, to start things off by playing us a piece on the piano."

Not a single aitch missing, Dai noted, and not a single unnecessary one. Miss Widdison, who was wearing a brown skirt with a pale-green blouse, stepped on to the platform and walked to the piano. Her face was flushed, but she looked as determined as a seasoned soldier moving into battle and she carried her bundle of music like a weapon. She was followed by a lanky, pale-faced girl with gold-rimmed spectacles and long plaits tied

162

with yellow ribbon who dutifully took up her position on Miss Widdison's side as she sat down and placed her music on the piano. Dai shuddered slightly when he heard the deep slow ominous opening chords of the Rachmaninoff Prelude in C Sharp Minor. It was one of his pet aversions and it was a particularly unsuitable composition for the school piano, the soft pedal of which was out of order. He imagined, too, that the captain was not going to like it very much. He had taken out his handkerchief and was doing with it the same trick he had done with the chamois leather. It had disappeared inside his hand before a dozen bars had been played. Yet it was clear that Miss Widdison, despite the grim set of her face, was enjoying herself. The girl (it was her niece, and she was giving her weekly lessons both on piano and organ) seemed very proud of the way she followed the music and turned the pages just at the right moment and when it ended the audience clapped loudly and more than one voice shouted "Encore". But Captain Fosdyck, unfolding his fingers and letting the handkerchief spring out, was on his feet instantly.

"Now friends. We've all enjoyed Miss Widdison's piece, but we've a long programme and we mustn't have any encores." He took a card from his pocket, studied it and then declared, "We're now going to be treated to a duet by our friends from Barnby Dale, Mr and Mrs George Lightfoot, entitled *The Keys of Heaven*".

Barnby Dale was a small village five miles inland over the moor. It had a tiny Wesleyan Chapel, but no resident minister. Dai had to take the service there once a month and he recognised the couple who now ascended the platform as the proprietors of the only village shop. The man was thin, pale, partly bald, but with a heavy brown moustache and bad teeth. His wife was short and plump with a red face and spectacles. Miss Widdison and her niece had remained at the piano. Mr and Mrs Lightfoot stood facing each other while Miss Widdison played the air. Then Mr Lightfoot started to sing the first verse in which he offered the lady opposite to him (to be addressed throughout the song as "madam") the Keys of Heaven if she would walk and talk with him, and by inference become his bride.

He had a pleasant baritone voice, but it was completely devoid of feeling and the audience could not have been surprised when "madam", having echoed his proposal, ended her verse with *"no she wouldn't talk, no she wouldn't walk, no she wouldn't talk and walk with him"*. In his second verse he made the offer of a blue silk gown. Madam refused *"to talk and walk"*. He increased the offer to a coach and six *"six black horses as black as pitch"*, but she still refused. Up till this point both performers had stood perfectly static, staring woodenly at each other. But now there was action. Mr Lightfoot put his hand on his left breast, Mrs Lightfoot lowered her eyes as effectively as her spectacles would permit. In a soft tremulo he offered her not the keys of heaven, nor a blue gown, nor a coach and six, but the keys of his heart, and *"they would marry until death did them part"*. She lifted her eyes, reached out her hand to his then, turning to face the audience, they ended the last verse by singing in harmony that they *would* walk and talk together, and everyone seemed delighted, including Captain Fosdyck who, however, had squashed his programme up this time instead of his handkerchief. But he had straightened it out again before the happy couple had got to their seats, and he lost no time in announcing the next item, which was a song by Miss Clarissa Widdison (the pale lanky girl at the piano), Miss Widdison's niece. It was *Annie Laurie*.

Clarissa was nervous and would not leave her auntie's side. Her voice was not strong and the piano was too loud. But she got through it all right and Dai thought he had best not look at the captain's hands again, only he was glad that he had been so firm about encores. The next item was a humorous monologue given by a Burnharbour lady friend which was not, in Dai's opinion, very humorous, and this was followed by a female quartette drawn from the choir (there were no male members left) singing *Sweet and Low*, which would have been very good had Miss Widdison been able to use the soft pedal in the really emotional passages. . . And so it went on for nearly an hour, with no performer rising to the level even of a family sing-song, yet everyone appearing to be happy. Was it just the Christmas atmosphere? Was it just that they were all non-critical and easy to please? How would they react to something that was really good and really beautiful?

Dai began to feel nervous. He had noticed that Gwen and her "gang" had disappeared behind a screen, which hid the entrance to her back-stage dressing-room. He had more than a rough idea of what she and her "gang" were going to do. He had been present at most of the rehearsals at the Manse. He had actually helped Gwen in the construction of various flats and cut-outs and backcloths, but had never seen them assembled. She had been busy for weeks making costumes out of taffeta and tinsel, but all had been confusion in his mind as to their exact purpose, with the exception of The Mad Hatter's Tea Party sketch. It was her affair and he'd wanted it to be so up to the end. He was beginning to get stage fright himself and he prayed that nothing would go wrong, that none of the children would forget their parts and dry up, that the whole thing would be the huge success it deserved.

Mr Lightfoot was now singing what the captain had announced as the last item in the first part of the concert, *Little Grey Home in the West*. His wife had given a rendering of *Because* earlier in the programme. It ended in applause and there was another round of clapping when Miss Widdison and her niece, their duties ended, followed Mr Lightfoot from the platform. Then Captain Fosdyck asked for silence.

"Well, friends, that's the end of the first part of our concert. As you'll know from the bills that have been out next part's to be given by the Sunday School children, under their teacher, Mrs Jones. You'll all have been noticing there's a different carry on up here to what we've had at other bazaar concerts." He pointed to the curtain behind him. "You may have noticed there were a lot of bairns sitting on t' front row when this concert started and that most of them have disappeared. Well, you folks who own them needn't worry. They haven't been kidnapped. You'll see them again soon if you keep your eyes on the curtain." The audience saw the joke and there was laughter, but the captain went on quickly. "But you'll have to wait a minute or so before you do. And that time needn't be wasted. This has been a smaller bazaar than we've ever had before, even in wartime. Our takings will be down. So we'll have a collection. And we'll have it now, and seeing it's Christmas time let's have it a silver one."

He descended from the platform. The applause was less enthusiastic and it quickly died into a buzz of conversation in which there were pools of embarrassed silence as the collecting boxes were passed along each row. The captain came up to Dai and whispered,

"A wise thing to take it now, Mr Jones, and surprise folks. I understand Mrs Jones wants the lights turning low when she starts. Will you take the middle one? But wait till all t' boxes are safe."

Things were happening near the platform. Gwen had appeared. Tom Bransby had stepped up on to it. The chairman's table and chair had been moved, the piano moved more to one side, and now Tom was lighting the lamps that were concealed by the plank at the edge of the platform. Gwen spoke to him when he had done and Dai saw him smile happily, but rather self-consciously like a schoolboy just placed at the top of his class. Gwen sat down at the piano. Tom took up his position in the corner behind it where his curtain halyards hung. The collection was finished. The captain took charge of the boxes. Then he signed to Gwen and she signed back to him. All the gas lamps except the shaded one that shone on the curtain were turned low. There was a hush of expectancy and then Gwen started to play the lovely tune of *Good King Wenceslas*. She played the tune to the end, then paused and started again and the children still out of sight began to sing and very slowly the double curtains were drawn back.

Dai felt a lump in his throat. He very nearly wept, for

he thought he had never seen anything so lovely. The audience, too, seemed to share his emotions. There was a sound as though everyone was catching their breath. Only a couple of bed sheets spread on the floor and sprinkled with tinsel for snow; a large sheet of stiffened cardboard cut out in the shape of a stunted pine, decked with cotton wool and more sparkling tinsel; a backcloth showing the edge of a wood and a snowy hill against a dark-blue sky and, in the sky, stars and a white full moon. There was the perfect illusion for the setting of the carol. Three wide steps led from the left entrance suggesting that just out of sight was the King's home. The King himself (Dai knew it was the eight-year-old son of the railway signalman, but he did not think of it then) stood with one foot on the lowermost step. He wore a red ermine-trimmed cloak (Gwen had made it from an old blanket and the ermine was cotton wool), a Saxon crown and a broad sword with a gilded hilt. The unseen choir of children sang,

> "*Good King Wenceslas looked out,*
> *On the feast of Stephen;*
> *When the snow lay round about,*
> *Deep and crisp and even;*
> *Brightly shone the moon that night,*
> *Though the frost was cruel;*
> *When a poor man came in sight,*
> *Gathering winter fuel.*"

The poor man came in sight. He (it was Tommy Harrison, whose father had bought The Hollies) was in rags and tatters, round-shouldered and tottering as he searched the ground for sticks. The King looked at him, then over his shoulder, and sang alone,

> *"Hither, page, and stand by me,*
> *If thou know'st it telling,*
> *Yonder peasant, who is he,*
> *Where and what his dwelling?"*

Then down the steps came Jane as the page, with a blue cloak and fur cap and thonged sandals, and sang,

> *"Sire, he lives a good league hence,*
> *Underneath the mountain,*
> *Right against the forest fence,*
> *By Saint Agnes' fountain."*

Dai had read somewhere that critics had protested at the substitution of this nineteenth-century version of the legend of King Wenceslas for a traditional spring carol, that the poem itself had been referred to as doggerel. It may have been doggerel, but it was romantic and for him it belonged as inevitably to Christmas as trees and Charles Dickens, and "stockings" and happy children's parties at Uncle Glyn's. And just to see Jane Bransby, and hear her sweet voice, was enough. Not that she stole the thunder. All three children were equally good in their way and that was Gwen's triumph. But Jane's way was different. He had never seen a child with such charm, such   unaffected grace and poise. . . The King sang,

> *"Bring me flesh and bring me wine,*
> *Bring me pine logs hither.*

Thou and I shall see him dine
When we bear them thither."

The invisible chorus ended the verse while the page brought sticks and a bundle of food and the two moved off, following the poor man. Then they halted and the page sang,

"Sire, the night is darker now
And the wind blows stronger;
Fails my heart I know not how,
I can go no longer."

The King sang,

"Mark my footsteps good, my page,
Tread thou in them boldly:
Thou shalt find the winter's rage
Freeze thy blood less coldly."

And as the two walked slowly across the little stage the chorus sang,

"In his master's steps he trod
Where the snow lay dinted.
Heat was in the very sod
Which the saint had printed.

Therefore Christian men be sure,
Wealth or rank possessing,
You who now will bless the poor,
Shall yourselves find blessing."

Tom Bransby drew the curtains. There was a moment's dead silence. And then for the first time that evening the audience really let itself go with wild applause. . .

The Mad Hatter's Tea Party was the last item of the concert. There had been recitations, dialogues, part-songs, carols, by various members of the "gang" performed in front of the curtain while the "sets" for the tableaux were being changed. Gwen had resisted the temptation to allow her "star" to do more than her share. She realised the perils of jealousy and vanity. In the second tableau she had given Jane no part at all. It was a fantasy of spring. Four of the smaller children had pretended to be snowdrop buds, lying huddled and still and almost invisible on the ground whose mantle of snow had been changed to the green of a lawn with appropriate surrounds. She had played *The Rustle of Spring*. Jane would have made an ideal Pan to dance piping round the dormant buds until they rose with upstretched arms (shrouded in green cotton) and finally revealed white hoods that suggested the petals of snowdrops and joined Pan in his dance. She'd had to give that part to another of the signalman's girls who had a squeaky voice and could neither sing nor recite and had been pathetically thrilled to find herself a tolerable success at something. She had not, however, dared to give anyone else but Jane the part of the Good Fairy in the third tableau, *The Sleeping Beauty*, for it was only possible to do the awakening scene in the wood, and that had meant a recited prologue describing how the Princess's parents had long ago offended the Wicked

171

Fairy who had put the evil curse on their darling girl; how she had pricked her finger on the Wicked Fairy's spinning wheel and fallen into a trance, and what the Good Fairy had done to circumvent the Wicked one. Who should recite this but the Good Fairy herself, before the curtain went up for the finale? Jane had done it to perfection, yet the dramatic interest was in the Princess herself, who had nothing to do but be kissed, wake up and smile at Prince Valiant and say, "Is it you, dear Prince? I have waited for you such a long time."

Yet there could have been no other choice than Jane for Alice. In a simple cotton frock and her fair hair parted in the middle and combed straight down her shoulders she *was* Alice from the moment the curtains were drawn and she was seen surveying rather petulantly that extraordinary tea table with places laid for so many guests, but with only three of them occupied, and these crowded together at one corner: the March Hare and the Hatter, the Dormouse fast asleep between them and being used as a cushion for their elbows.

"No room. No room," they cried at Alice.

"There's *plenty* of room," said Alice indignantly, and she sat down in a large armchair at one end of the table.

"Have some wine," the March Hare said in encouraging tones.

"I don't see any wine."

"There isn't any."

"Then it wasn't very civil of you to offer it."

"It wasn't very civil of you to sit down without being invited."

"I didn't know it was *your* table. It's laid for a great many more than three."

"Your hair wants cutting," said the Hatter. . .

Until this moment the audience had watched and listened in complete silence. Perhaps, Dai thought, they were overcome by the sheer novelty and incongruity of what they saw; the long table with its empty places; the four recognisable village children, one with a great top-hat on his head, another with a hat shaped like a mouse's head complete with long whiskers, another with the "head" of a hare, and Jane Bransby just ordinary. They were mostly elderly chapel-goers. They'd had their education in the village school. Probably not more than a score of them had read *Alice in Wonderland*. They had not realised at first whether it was meant to be funny or just a fairy tale like *The Sleeping Beauty*. But with the Hatter's remark they saw that it was funny and Alice had to wait until the laughter died down before she could answer, indignantly,

"You should learn not to make personal remarks. It's very *rude*."

After that there were no more doubts.

"Why is a raven like a writing desk?" demanded the March Hare.

"I believe I can guess that."

"Do you mean that you think you can find out the answer to it?" said the March Hare.

"Exactly so."

"Then you should say what you mean."

"I do. At least—at least I mean what I say, that's the same thing, you know."

"Not the same thing a bit," said the Hatter. "Why, you might just as well say that 'I see what I eat' is the same thing as 'I eat what I see.' "

"You might just as well say," added the March Hare, "that 'I like what I get' is the same as 'I get what I like.' "

And then the Dormouse (played by the youngest of the signalman's family) made his first contribution to the conversation with, "You might just as well say that 'I breathe when I sleep' is the same thing as 'I sleep when I breathe.' "

"It is the same thing with you," said the Hatter.

The audience roared with laughter. To Dai this spontaneous appreciation was as exciting as the play itself. He looked about him: saw Miss Widdison, and the Lawther sisters, Captain Christopher and Miss Betsy Knaggs and Edwin; they were all laughing. He looked at Captain Fosdyck, and Jonty and his little wife, at Ella Bransby, at the people he knew and the people he knew only by sight. With one or two exceptions he had disliked them all. They were so hard, so frigid, so dour and gloomy. Now he felt an extraordinary friendliness towards them, even towards Captain Fosdyck himself who was almost helpless with laughter. Was it the magic of Charles Dodgson's art that was doing it, touching some unsuspected spring of potential joy in their souls? What a gift it was, to be able to make people laugh kindly, to make them really merry, to deaden even temporarily what was ugly and drab. He could not see Ella Bransby's face but he knew that for the time being at least she was completely obsessed with the play. Tom, leaning over the top of the piano, looked enraptured, and from him Dai glanced at Gwen and he felt a deeper pride and love for her. He had no jealousy. It was she as much as the long-dead creator of *Alice in Wonderland* who was doing this thing; creating from book and children and audiences too another goodness which, he felt, was worth all the sermons he had ever preached.

The play went on. There was the fooling with the Hatter's watch. The Dormouse went to sleep again. The Hatter poured some hot tea on his nose to wake him up. (Captain Fosdyck sounded as though he might have an apoplectic fit.) Then there was the discourse on Time leading to the Hatter's rendering of the song,

> *"Twinkle, twinkle, little bat,*
> *How I wonder what you're at.*
> *Up above the world you fly,*
> *Like a tea-tray in the sky."*

with the Dormouse joining in sleepily, "Twinkle, twinkle, twinkle, twinkle" until he had to be pinched to make him stop. Then there was the March Hare voting that Alice should tell a story and, as she didn't know one, the Dormouse being wakened up again and starting, "Once upon a time there were three little sisters and their names were Elsie, Lacie and Tilly; and they lived at the bottom of a well," and more fooling about wells and treacle until the Hatter remarked, "I want a clean cup. Let's all move one place up."

They moved up, the only one benefiting by the change being the Hatter, a fact that was well conveyed to the almost hysterical audience by the way Alice surveyed her plate on which the March Hare had spilt his milk. And so on until at last the behaviour of the Hatter, March Hare, and Dormouse too became too much for Alice and she got up and walked away from the table with the remark,

"It's the stupidest tea-party I ever was at in all my life."

The play was over, but Tom Bransby himself was so overcome with mirth, watching the Hatter and the March Hare trying to push the Dormouse into the teapot, that he forgot he had to pull the curtain and Gwen had to remind him by touching his arm. The clapping and the laughter went on after the curtain was drawn and it was not until Captain Fosdyck got up on to the platform and shouted, "Quiet please" many times that there was quiet, and Dai saw that there were still tears in his own eyes when he spoke and that he was quite short of breath.

"Friends, friends. That's the end of our concert. And you'll not need me to tell you it's been one of the best concerts there's ever been in this spot."

There was renewed clapping and cheers, which gave the captain time for breath.

"Well," he went on, "there's no more to be said except to thank everyone who's helped to make it a success. Those that belong our own chapel, those who have come from away to help us, especially our friends from Barnby Dale." The applause started again, but the captain evidently thought that Mr and Mrs Lightfoot had got their due and he held up his hand and went on. "But we've got an extra special word of thanks to give to the lady who's organised the second part of our concert and taught these little bairns the things we've been treated to and made us all laugh so much. Let's give Mrs Jones, and the bairns, too, a real good clap."

Again Dai was nearly overcome with emotion as the audience clapped and cheered and Gwen stood up from the piano seat and smiled her thanks. At last the captain raised his hand.

"I've got one more word," he said, "before I ask Mrs Jones to play *God Save the King*, and the *Doxology*. T' bazaar's finished. As I said before our takings will be down on other years. We're not going to have another collection. But those who feel they'd like to give a bit extra, after enjoying themselves so much, well, there's nowt to stop 'em, and I'll say straight out that I'm putting down a five-pound note. And now let's sing."

The audience stood. *The King* and the *Doxology* were sung, the lights were turned up and there was a general move towards the door. Dai spoke to Edwin Knaggs as he passed.

"Did you like it, Edwin?"

The boy smiled and answered in his quiet self-assured way,

"Yes *rather*, Mr Jones. Especially the last bit. Wasn't it funny? I wish father had seen it."

Dai gave him an affectionate slap on the shoulder and moved on towards the platform. He saw Ella Bransby still in her seat and evidently waiting for Jane. She stood up when he approached her. She was dressed in a well-fitting brown tweed coat and skirt and Dai couldn't help thinking that she looked infinitely more ladylike than the fur-clad lady from Burnharbour. She smiled agreeably, but as before she made him feel vaguely ill at ease as though her very agreeableness were enforced and insincere. He asked her if she liked the concert. She had, very much indeed. She thought it had all been beautiful, especially "Good King Wenceslas" and it was wonderful the way Mrs Jones had done it all.

"And what did you think of Jane?"

It was only then that Dai felt that she was really being sincere. She actually flushed and he couldn't mistake the almost passionate pride in her voice.

"Jane was very good, wasn't she, Mr Jones? But I knew she would be. She always was so different from other children. But of course," she added quickly, "it's Mrs Jones who's done it all. I'm waiting to take Jane home. And for my husband."

Was there a different quality in her voice when she said that last word? Dai caught sight of Tom and Gwen talking together near the far end of the platform.

There were other parents waiting for their children. He seized readily on the excuse to get away.

"Your husband's over there. I'll tell him you're waiting, Mrs Bransby."

He made his way forward, discreetly avoiding Captain Fosdyck who was holdng forth to Mr and Mrs Lightfoot of Barnby Dale. Gwen turned, laughing, to him. "I was just telling Captain Bransby how marvellously his curtain worked."

Tom was beaming.

"Not when it came to the end. I forgot all about it, I was so taken up with those two trying to put the Dormouse into the teapot. If Mrs Jones hadn't nudged me we'd have all been laughing at it yet."

"So you really enjoyed it, in spite of my wife giving you all the work?"

"Enjoyed it? I should think I did. Captain Fosdyck's right. There's never been a concert like it in this place before. It's been a real treat for everyone."

"And what did you think of your own daughter?"

Tom looked a little self-conscious.

"Well, Mr Jones, it's hardly for me to say, but she seemed to speak up clearer than an of the other bairns. She always was good at singing and reciting. But there again, it's what Mrs Jones has taught her."

"I've taught her next to nothing," Gwen said with a sudden earnestness. And as she spoke Dai had a sudden premonition of calamity, but he was just as powerless to forestall it. "I've taught her nothing, really. It's an instinct with her. Jane is a born actress. It's there in her bones and blood, and in her mind. She's got the voice and the looks and the feeling for it. Mark my words, Captain Bransby, she's going to be great. You'll see her name one day in headlines."

If Gwen had seen what Dai had seen in Tom Bransby's face she might have stopped in time. But she was looking more at Dai than at him and it was only when he interrupted that she saw the horror and dismay in it.

"My daughter an *actress*, Mrs Jones? My daughter going on the stage? Living *that* sort of life? God forbid. God forbid. I know what the stage is like. I know what the stage is for. Just another of Satan's devices for leading men and women into sin."

Gwen looked helplessly from Tom to her husband. Gallantly, but with even less discretion, he went to her assistance.

"Captain Bransby—Tom! My wife doesn't mean anything like that. The real stage is noble, edifying. The finest poetry, the finest music has been written for and performed on the stage. Surely you don't think that my wife means that Jane should become a music-hall actress! Why, think of what you've seen tonight, on the little stage you've helped my wife to make. Think how happy we've all been. How we've laughed. Surely you don't think there was anything evil in *Good King Wenceslas* and *The Sleeping Beauty* and *The Mad Hatter's Tea Party*. Why, you just said how much you'd enjoyed it, how it had made you laugh."

Tom glanced at the stage. Then he turned again to Dai with a deeper horror in his face. His voice was low, but vibrant and in his eyes was a fanatical gleam.

"I don't want to have words with you, Mr Jones. You've done more for me than any living man. You've shown me the way to salvation. And I know that Mrs Jones means well by Jane. I *know* I've enjoyed it tonight. I *know* I've laughed. I *know* there's been no evil *meant*. But I never thought of it being a stage, with having only little girls playing. I never thought of it being theatricals. I want that little girl of mine to grow up pure and good, to walk in the way of the Lord. I'd not like to have her having anything more to do with this sort of thing. And if I thought she was going to grow up to be an actress then I'd pray to the Lord to strike her dumb tonight. It's time she was home and in bed, and there's my wife waiting, so I'll wish you both good night."

He walked away. Gwen had turned her face to the empty stage. Dai seized her arm and squeezed it and whispered,

"It's all right, Gwen. He's just overwrought. The whole thing has been a terrific success. I'm terribly proud of you."

She turned to him, smiling, but there were tears in her eyes and she whispered brokenly,

"Yes, Dai, I understand. . . Here's Captain Fosdyck

coming. Pretend it hasn't happened. Only Jane, poor little Jane. . ."

Captain Fosdyck was advancing towards them, grinning, with his great paw outstretched to shake Gwen's hand.

BOOK TWO

THE VOICE OF THE TURTLE

1

IT WAS EASTERTIDE and a warm sunny morning. The wind was light, blowing off the land and scarcely stirring the level surface of the bay. The tide was ebbing, starting to bare the first of the scaurs. Edwin Knaggs, striding south along the beach, felt the warmth of the sun on his cheeks. He took deep breaths of the clean sea air in which was mingled the scent of earth and grass and trees, the pungent savour of spring, and he was exuberant, for this was what he had been dreaming of for weeks.

Not that he had been unhappy. Everything in his life so far had gone well and according to plan. True that this had been chiefly his father's plan, but he'd had no reason to challenge it. He had, as his father had boasted he would do, won a scholarship from the County School to a northern university. He had entered for a degree in science, had passed his "inter" with the same ease with which he had passed his matric, and was sitting for his final in the coming term. He had also entered for one of the travelling scholarships offered by the university to students in natural science and was modestly confident of winning it.

He was happy at the university. He liked the work and he liked the play. He had inherited his father's health and physique, although he was an inch or two taller and of slenderer build. As at school he had done well at games and athletics. The work that interested him most was zoology, with geology a close second. Of the careers that he might follow ultimately the one that appealed to him most was that of a government naturalist. That too was the one that his father approved of strongest. He might, his father had declared (and only half-jokingly), become a second Charles Darwin and write another *Voyage of the Beagle*. Darwin, in the smith's opinion, was the greatest Englishman in history!

So Edwin's exuberance was not reaction. If he had been day-dreaming of Bramblewick for weeks it was because spring had been in the air even of the land-locked city of Donbridge, where even the modern university buildings were begrimed with the soot from the woollen mills and engineering works that hemmed them in to the valley of a sluggish and polluted river. And because to him spring meant Bramblewick, and here it was: the beach, the cliffs, the baring scaurs, the glittering blue sea, the spring air, the soft spring wind with its earthy odours, the sunshine on his face, and a day of delight before him.

He wore the conventional tweed sports jacket and grey flannel trousers of the university student, but with waterproof ankle boots instead of brogues and fancy socks. The jacket was brown and he had a white flannel shirt with an open collar. He wore no hat. He had his father's black hair and it was wavy and long but not affectedly so. Except for the hair, however, and a general swarthiness, there was little in common in their faces. Although Edwin's nose was full there was no suspicion of satanic hook. His eyebrows were not bushy and their curve was not exaggerated like his father's were. His eyes were grey with long dark lashes, his mouth full, humorous and kind. Indeed, although there was no war between them, they were opposites. To the father who could take a bar of iron, heat it, and mould it into any shape that suited his purpose, who could watch the sun rising from the sea, or hear the song of a thrush utterly unmoved, the universe was made up of things, real and abstract, living and dead, but all explicable by physical science. To the son, who had been nurtured on this uncompromising materialism, who had found little to confute it in the laboratory and lecture theatre discourses of his university professors (much to his father's satisfaction at finding his theories were not out of date) there were far more things in heaven and earth than were dreamt of in any philosophy, never mind his father's. They could not be defined. He did not wish to define them. But they were here, in the colour of the sea and the cliffs and fields and moors, in their shapes and the patterns they made. He had been aware of them when in the city he had gone to concerts and heard great music, and when looking at certain pictures and reading certain poems. The truth was that Edwin possessed something whose existence was denied by his father's philosophy: a soul. And although he did not know it yet, it was an artist's soul.

It was a spring tide and ebbing fast, but he kept well up to the foot of the cliff away from the drying scaurs so as not to be distracted from the planned objective of his expedition. He was bound for High Batts and the great scaur which ran out from its foot for nearly a quarter of a mile when the tide was dead low. Here were meadows of tangles and wrack, weedy pools and rock fissures, the homes and hiding-places of a great variety of marine animals. Marine biology was the branch of zoology which from the first had interested him the most, chiefly because it was concerned mostly with living things. It was necessary to understand the structure and inner workings of an animal to comprehend its habits, but the dissection of a dead worm or frog or dogfish was dull compared with the observation of the living animal in its own natural habitat. His special interest was in their form and colour, the way these were adapted to the colour and form of the plants, rocks and sand among which they lived. It was a subject that had interested naturalists of all time and he did not expect to make any startling discoveries about it. He did not particularly wish to. It was just that it delighted him.

He crossed Browe Beck, the second of the two becks, and the one from which the steep lane led up to the farm where Tom Bransby had once called to mend a binder. The beck followed the course of an ancient geological fault which had been scoured out by glacial action at a later but still very ancient period. At the south side for a few hundred yards the cliff consisted of boulder clay and for nearly a mile the beach was shingle that had been washed out of the clay. The shingle was still wet, and the sun shone brightly on it. It seemed to be made of jewels!

It was here, Edwin remembered, that his father had given him his first lesson in glacial geology. He had explained how there had been two monstrous glaciers pressing south from Scandinavia and from northern England and Scotland. The one from Scandinavia had followed what was now the bed of the North Sea and had contested the easterly spread of the other along the English coast. The proof of this was in the pebbles and ice-worn boulders that were in the clay which had been left when the glaciers melted and now formed the beach. They were fragments from rocks which were definitely Scandinavian and North England and Scottish in their origin. The commonest of the boulders was a beautifully crystalline pinkish granite called "Shap", which came from Westmoreland, but there were granites, basalts, and porphyries from Norway and the Western Highlands all mixed up together.

Again it had been the material facts and what they proved that had interested the smith. It hadn't mattered to him if it was a bit of dark basalt or an exquisitely marbled and tinted porphyry he was handling so long as he could identify it and deduce its origin. It had been the beauty of the pebbles that had fascinated the son and it was so now. They were of every conceivable colour from the pure and translucent white of quartz and the lovely bronze green of malachite to the marbled red of jasper. There were carnelians and agates. He had scarcely crossed the beck when he caught a red glint in the shingle. It was a carnelian about the size of a pea, coral red but translucent so that when he held it to the sky it was like a flame. He resisted the strong temptation to loiter and look more closely for more, but as he walked on he could not keep his eyes averted from the shingle and soon he had a handful of coloured pebbles. At last he had the resolution to give it up. The scaurs at this part of the bay ran parallel to the beach in long even terraces. The nearest one was broken by a long pool, but the one next to it seawards was now bare and he put the pebbles in his pocket and left the shingle for good.

He could now enjoy the view ahead without distraction, for it was hard scaur with no weed and only a few limpets living on it. He had long since passed the boulder clay. The shale cliff from the beach rose gradually to the south, but it curved in to form a small secondary bay immediately north of High Batts. The scaur he was on followed the curve into the bay. On this side High Batts itself was not precipitous. The real cliff faced east and was still invisible. Actually the headland owed its existence to another geological fault. The liassic shales which composed the cliff and the sea bed, too, to the north had been thrust upwards several hundred feet so that on the line of fracture the lias had been brought level with a formation that really belonged above it. This consisted chiefly of beds of hard sandstone more resistant to the glaciers that had scooped out the bay and the vale between the bay and moors. The east cliff was nearly all sandstone and fell almost sheer from a height of six hundred feet. But on the side which Edwin faced there were rough pastures and thickets of whin half-way down and the cliff below this was broken. A pathway, steep in parts, zigzagged down it to the shore at the point of the headland. It was the only means of access to the shore south of the lane that led to the farms from the beck.

In bad weather the little bay was anything but a haven. It was exposed to the north and the east and the flood-tide, especially with a backing northerly wind, would drive fiercely into it, making a maelstrom of broken water. Now it was peaceful but there was a wildness and grandeur in its aspect that suggested the peace only of a sleeping monster. The shingle had ended. Instead of an even beach fringing the cliff foot there were boulders and masses of fallen rock through which he had to pick his way. The bay was in shadow, too, and almost chilly, but once across it he was in the sun again and it seemed warmer than before. And now he had nearly reached his destination. The cliff and the scaurs were curving east. The going for a while was easier and then there was another pile of huge sandstone blocks which reached from the cliff foot for a considerable distance seawards. Where they ended the great High Batts scaur began.

The tide was not low yet. The top of the scaur was bare but the area which he wished to explore on the north side of it was still under water. Close by the rocks was a deep creek which led to the open sea. He stopped, looked round him and found a convenient sandstone block whose top had already been dried by the sun and he took off his rucksack and unpacked a towel. He started to undress. As he did so he glanced up the cliff and for a moment hesitated, for close to where the footpath started down from the edge of the pasture land he observed what looked like a human figure moving, and moving down. But it was against the sun and very distant, and when he shaded his eyes with one hand he could not see it at all, although he could see several sheep almost in the same place. It was not modesty that had made him hesitate, but an involuntary resentment. Half the charm of this place to him was in its solitude and selfishly he did not wish to share it with a crowd of Easter holiday picnickers, of which one might have been the vanguard. There was a railway "halt" at the summit of High Batts.

But he decided that it must have been one of the sheep he had seen, and anyway the path was out of sight the rest of the way and the point where it reached the shore was well south of the scaur. He stripped and moved to the creek. He had a good body, lean and muscular, with a smooth white skin. He stood poised for a moment, hands on his hips, looking at the water. It was deep and crystal clear. The rock on each side was grown with brown tangles, but there was clean sand at the bottom and a safe fairway. It was his first bathe of the year and he knew the water would be cold. He took a deep breath, raised his hands and dived, with his eyes open and not too steeply, and he went down to the sand, skimmed it with his hands and swam on under water for a few strokes, turning then so that he could look up and see the sunlight on the water's rippled surface as through a pane of green corrugated glass. He felt the silky fronds of the tangles stroking his flesh as he ascended. He saw with his last underwater glance a red starfish and a purple sea-urchin among the tangle stems, distorted and enlarged by refraction so that they looked like fantastic tropical fruits. Then his head broke the surface. He expelled the air from his lungs and took a deep breath as he struck out seawards.

He was wise enough not to overdo it. The water was intensely cold. A few strokes and he turned and swam back and hauled himself out on to the scaur where his towel lay. Rubbing himself vigorously he moved back to the rock. He rubbed until his skin was red and tingling, then he put on his shirt and trousers and swung himself up on to the rock into the full blaze of the sun. It was a glorious sensation, the tingling and mild smart of his skin, the smell of brine and the taste of it on his lips, the warmth of the sunshine on his face and his chilled hands and feet. But what thrilled him more was the experience of that dive, the vivid memory of what he had seen in those few seconds of immersion, the whiteness of the sun-dappled sand, the green light in the water, the brown waving tangles, the red starfish and the purple sea-urchin.

He unpacked his rucksack, which contained sandwiches, a billycan, a bottle of milk for tea, a large drawing book and a box of watercolour paints. He glanced through the used pages of the book. Mostly they were pencil drawings of zoological dissections, the skull of a frog, the complete skeleton of a dogfish, the nervous system of an earthworm and of a cockroach. He had a natural gift for drawing. Undoubtedly it came from his father, who from the first had impressed upon him the importance of making a drawing of anything he was going to make, from a kite to a model steam engine. He had never thought of it as an artistic gift. His father would have been the last person to encourage such an idea. What he meant by drawing was making an accurate representation on paper of any object: natural size or to scale. That was precisely what these zoological drawings were. Their virtue was in their accuracy and the same virtue was apparent in the coloured drawings which were not of dissections, but of living animals: a frog, a swimming crab, a number of butterflies and caterpillars. They had earned the special commendation of the zoology professor. They were, he had said (he had spoken as a scientist, of course), technically on a level with the work of the best illustrators of scientific text books. They were not however, in Edwin's meaning of the word, pictures. He had merely drawn and painted what he had seen, producing to the best of his skill a facsimile of his subject. He did not underestimate, nor did he overestimate that skill. The point was that none of these drawings, not even the one of a purple Emperor butterfly so realistic that it might have been the specimen itself that had alighted on the page, gave him the slightest thrill, whereas without even closing his eyes he could see what he had seen in the water, not just the patch of sand nor the rock nor the tangles nor the starfish nor the sea-urchin, but the whole experience, re-live it, re-feel it, and that the emotion that he felt was unlike anything he had ever felt before. It was a passionate urge to make a picture, to express in line and paint not what he had seen, but what he had felt.

He found a clean page and, without stopping to think, drew pencil lines upon it. They were single lines, free and boldly curving, each made with a single unhesitating stroke. Some were in the vertical plane, some in the horizontal, some oblique. Vaguely they suggested the outlines of the underwater walls of the creek, the tangles and the level bottom of sand. He was drawing with the book laid flat on the rock. Popping the pencil between his lips he now held the book with both hands at arm's length and studied the drawing intently, then he put it down again and drew halfway up on the right-hand side the rough outlines of two sea-urchins, one higher than the other and about half its size. Near the bottom of the paper and between two receding lines that suggested the borders of the sand he drew a five-pointed star: its limbs thicker than the starfish he had seen, a caricature and not a portrait.

He studied the drawing for a while. Then with a rubber he reduced the weight of the penciling until the lines were almost invisible. He opened the paint-box, rummaged among the things from his rucksack for a cup and a small can of water and started to mix a thin grey green wash. He laid it on with a wide camel hair brush over the whole paper, letting it soak in thoroughly, then brushing off the surplus. He held it up in the sunshine to dry a little, gazing at it all the time with a look of intense concentration. Shortly he tested the paper with a finger, laid it down again and charged a smaller brush with pure ultramarine. He applied this between two of the curving vertical lines on the right-hand side and helped the colour to spread on the still damp paper with a brush charged with water only. Then here and there he added dabs of light red and a little sepia, helping these to spread too and blend with the blue to form a tint that varied from purple to the paler and warmer grey of a dove's breast.

He had left untouched the paper enclosed by the lines that suggested the shapes of the tangles and the two urchins. It was the rock he had painted and he gave only a small dab of ultramarine and burnt sienna to the rock on the opposite side, and this low down like a shadow. He thinned it upwards, making it lighter in tone, with more water. He added some yellow ochre to the wash and then a little rose madder and let it all spread and blend with the original grey green wash until it became a glowing grey that made a perfect contrast with the darker rock on the right, suggesting that it was sunlight. He washed his brushes and looked in his box to select the next colour.

The spring tide was ebbing. The collecting grounds to the north of the scaur were bare. But Edwin Knaggs was oblivious to everything except the picture he was making. He did not know if it was good. All he did know was that the thing was alive, that he was creating something that was not just a reproduction of the forms and colours he had seen. Had he so wished he could have made an accurate coloured drawing of a stem and frond of tangle, or of the starfish or the sea-urchin just from memory for he had drawn and painted all these many times before. He was not concerned now with drawing or painting things as they were. The grey green wash had been suggested by, but did not literally represent, the water. There was little resemblance to the actual sunken walls of the creek in the shape and colour of what he had done. When he had painted the tangles he did not worry whether they looked like real tangles or not. He made them a golden brown with streaks of emerald green on them. He painted one of the sea-urchins pink and the other half pink and half purple. That left him with the sandy bottom and the starfish still the grey green of the original wash. He wetted the "sand" with pure water then dabbed some yellow ochre on to it. On to this he dabbed some burnt sienna, keeping it all very thin and light, but still warm in tone and working it carefully to the outline of the star and then he had to wait impatiently—he was getting to the climax—for this to reach a safe enough stage of dryness.

Was it good? He still didn't know for sure. The colours he had put on gave him intense pleasure. They were all grey, but they were luminous and warm and he felt that he had balanced them well, that their harmony was nearly complete. To make it complete one thing was needed, it was the thing he remembered most vividly from his dive: the starfish, a splash of pure primary colour to set as it were the keystone to the design. He took a clean brush and charged it with vermilion. He tried a stroke of it on the opposite page. It was much brighter than the starfish had been. He hesitated. Should he tone it down? But the starfish itself was not drawn to life but to fit the pattern. He dabbed it on as it was, in the centre of the pentagon, charged his brush again and deftly coaxed the pigment to the tips of the five arms. He rinsed the brush, squeezed it out and picked up a spot of blue and darkened the under edge of just two of the arms. He put the brush down, picked up the book and again held the drawing at arm's length and, for one moment, he experienced something like the emotion a woman must feel when she looks at her first baby for the first time.

He gasped with pleasure. The vermilion was right. It was the keystone that locked the whole thing together. And the whole thing was good. He was sure of it now. It glowed with life, it was beautiful. It did succeed in recreating, in crystallising his experience. The pleasure he felt, however, was purely objective. There was no vanity of self-satisfaction in it. He became cooler. It was a picture, but not a big or important one. It was an experiment, a sketch, a beginning. Why shouldn't he try a real landscape?

He looked about him. It was nearly low tide. Beyond the farthest scaurs the floating fronds of the great tangle beds were now visible. It was an exceptionally low tide, too: a unique opportunity for finding the animals which had been the main objective of his expedition. He did not think of them. Instead he was observing, as he had never done before, the shape and colour of the sandstone blocks that were piled along the foot of the cliff and outwards to the scaur. They were not rounded like the glacial boulders. They were huge and rugged. They were stratified with alternate bands of hard and softer stone and they were sculptured by the sea and weather into fantastic shapes. Their colours were as rich and varied as the tints of a sunlit autumn wood: deep velvety browns, lighter browns, bronze and copper reds, streaks of gold and silver and soft purplish shadows that were shot with turquoise where the light was reflected upwards from the shallow pools the sea had left among them. He concentrated his gaze upon the block that was nearest to the one on which he sat. It was about a dozen yards away. It was the biggest of a group of several which it dominated like the main figure in a sculptural group, and the smallest was more than the height of a man; it was more exciting than the creek.

The picture was not quite dry but the pages were perforated and without another glance at it he ripped it out of the book and laid it aside. He picked up his pencil. He looked at the sandstones again, and then at the virgin page and back at the stones. And his confidence began to waver. The stones were immense. They seemed to him now to have the size and grandeur of mountains. The sheet of paper seemed like a postage stamp. In his imagination he saw the picture as it might be. It was something like a picture he had seen in a gallery or an exhibition somewhere. It might have been by Cezanne or Gaugin, but it was big and, of course, on canvas and in oils and although he could not recall the details of the subject there were rocks or mountains in it and he could recall how extraordinarily vivid the actual painting had been. He could remember the very brush marks.

He had never used oil paint except for painting boats or other things he had made, but then he had never tried to paint a picture before the one he had just done. He felt vexed, frustrated, and he looked at his water colour again and he didn't like it half so much as he had done at first. Then again he looked towards the group of sandstones and, as he did so, he was startled to hear a girl's voice, reciting loud and clear as though on a stage, coming from behind the biggest of the stones,

> *"Now the great winds shoreward blow;*
> *Now the salt tides seaward flow;*
> *Now the wild white horses play,*
> *Champ and chafe and toss in the spray."*

Edwin covered his painting with the book, and swung down from his stone on the side facing the group of stones which still completely hid the owner of the voice. After a brief pause it continued to declaim,

> *"Sand-strewn caverns, cool and deep,*
> *Where the winds are all asleep;*
> *Where the spent lights quiver and gleam;*
> *Where the salt weed sways in the stream;*

Where the sea-beasts rang'd all round
Feed in the ooze of—"

And then, from behind the biggest of the sandstone blocks, the reciter appeared, saw Edwin, stopped with her mouth agape, staring at him with a surprise and embarrassment equal to his own. He did not for a moment recognise her as Jane Bransby. He saw a girl with sandals on her feet and long skinny bare legs and a short tweed skirt and a sleeveless cotton blouse. She wore no hat, and her hair was untidy, with one side of it plaited and tied with a red ribbon, the other loose and half falling across her forehead and cheeks which were scarlet. It was Jane, however, who was the first to recover. She smiled a little nervously, but quite agreeably, and Edwin took his cue from that.

"Hallo. You gave me quite a surprise coming round the rock like that. But—but—I suppose I gave you a surprise too."

She laughed.

"Yes. A bit. I didn't expect anyone to be here. I was talking to myself."

"Talking? You were reciting! And I know that poem, too. It's *The Forsaken Merman*. And, by Jove, I know who you are, now. You're Jane Bransby. You were Alice in Wonderland, years ago at the Wesleyan Bazaar!"

Jane came forward slowly and Edwin, accepting the gesture, moved towards her. But she stopped with a shallow pool between them. She had a frond of bright green seaweed in her hand and that hand was swaying gently. She looked at Edwin with frank interest. She was still more self-possessed than he was and there was a faintly mocking note in her voice.

"What a good memory you've got! I know what your name is. I go to the same school that you used to go to. Your name's printed on the Honour's Board in the Hall, and you got a university scholarship. You must be awfully clever!"

Edwin blushed.

"Oh, I don't think I'm clever. What about you? You were marvellous in that play. I can remember how everyone clapped and shouted. And I liked the way you were reciting that poem. It's one of my favourites, by the way. We learnt it at school. Fancy our having been to the same school. What are you doing along here? Oh, but of course you live near High Batts now. No wonder I haven't seen you when I've been home. I—"

He stopped, aware that he was talking too much. But he was feeling less embarrassed and Jane, brushing back the hair from her forehead with her free hand, gave him an encouraging smile.

"Yes, our farm's just at the top of the cliff. I'm supposed to be making a collection of seaweeds. It's a holiday task for science. But I don't like science very much. I like history and English, especially English and poetry and plays, especially Shakespeare. I don't mind getting seaweeds and pressing them, but I don't want to know their Latin names and things like that. Same with flowers. I like beautiful things. And I like being down here on the shore."

"So do I," said Edwin fervently. "So do I! And I like it along here better than any other part of the bay. . . Isn't it funny that we should meet! It was just like a play the way you came from behind that rock, reciting! Look here, I know quite a lot about seaweeds. Shall I help you with your collection? There's some lovely ones you get at low-water mark on a spring tide ebb like this. How many sorts have you got?"

Jane, although her sandals were already wet, lightly sprang across the shallow pool that separated them; she held up the piece of green weed.

"Only this one so far and of course you find it *everywhere.* Still it is pretty, isn't it, when it's fresh and wet, but it will look silly when it's pressed and dry in a book!"

It was one of the commonest of the seashore algae. It consisted of a single broad irregularly-shaped frond, silky and translucent and almost jade in its tint.

"One of the *Chlorophyceae,*" laughed Edwin. "I don't know its exact name, but it doesn't matter, does it? The main thing is it's nice to look at."

"Of course! That's what *I* think. Do you collect seaweeds?"

"No. I'm interested in marine animals, but you've got to know something about weeds because so many animals either feed on weeds or use them to hide in."

"You've been painting, though, haven't you?" Jane was looking at Edwin's things on the stone behind him. "Are you an artist, too?"

Edwin took a quick glance back at the stone and his sketchbook, saw that his picture was hidden.

"An artist? Good lord, no. I just make drawings of animals and things and sometimes tint them. Come on, the tide will be flowing soon! Doesn't that poem start 'Come dear children let us away, down and away below?' "

"Yes. And I love the bit about the whales:

> *"Where great whales come sailing by*
> *Sail and sail with unshut eye*
> *Round the world for ever and aye.*

"Aren't you going to take your painting things with you? I'd like to see you paint something. Have you got anything you have done in that book?"

Edwin was already leading the way to low water.

"No," he said firmly. "Nothing worth looking at. But let's find some real animals as well as seaweeds. Do you know anything about sea animals?"

"Well, I know what anemones are, and crabs and starfish!"

"Ever seen a sea-slug?"

"No. I don't like slugs!"

"Ah—just you wait. You'll change your mind if I can find an *Eolis rufibranchialis* or a *Dendronotus aborescens*."

Jane laughed.

> *"Nobody knows from whence I came,*
> *But Rumpelstiltskin is my name!*

"They must be beautiful with names like that! They sound like fairies."

"They *are* like fairies. Some of them. You wait."

They were seawards of the sandstone rocks, walking on flat shale, but with the north edge of the High Batts scaur making a miniature cliff to the right of them. The fucus and green algae of the mid-tide shore had given way to patches of a thick stunted brown weed, that looked as though it had been cropped, and formed a springy carpet under their feet, but there were pools and in one of them, which was shallow, lay several large flat stones like flags.

"Here's a likely spot," said Edwin. "Stand by and see what happens when I lift one of those. Not too near. It may come right over and drench you."

He put his fingers under the edge of the nearest stone, heaved it up and balanced it by the opposite edge, like the lid of a manhole. There was a splashing and a scurrying and Jane shrieked,

"There's a fish—there's a fish!"

"Watch where it goes. Mark the place!"

Edwin had to shift his balance and let the stone go over on to its back. Then he sprang to Jane's side. She was pointing excitedly to a patch of longish weed at the edge of the pool.

"It went in *there!*"

Gently, Edwin parted the fronds of the weed with his fingers.

"There it is. Only a blenny!"

"I can't see anything, but a piece of weed!"

Edwin touched the "piece of weed" with his fingers. It darted away and disappeared in another patch. He laughed.

"Camouflage! Protective coloration. Pretending to be something that you're not. There are fish that do it better than the common blenny, though. Let's see what's on the underneath part of the stone. Have you ever looked under a stone like that?"

"No, of course I haven't. How do you think I could lift one that size?"

"Oh, it's easy enough when you learn the knack of it. Look, it's swarming with things!"

He crouched down to look at it and Jane did likewise. They were on opposite sides and their heads were nearly touching. He had not exaggerated. There was scarcely a square inch of the stone that had not something living on it. There were several bright red anemones, although their tentacles were withdrawn. There were reddish brown and purple starfish and a brittle-star, which had already cast one of its legs, the leg itself jerking violently so as to distract attention from the body. There was a spider crab which had tiny fronds of seaweed growing on its back like a miniature rock garden, there were tube-building worms, there was a creature that looked like a flattened earwig, only with its back covered with iridescent scales, and Edwin, pointing to it said,

"That's *Polynoe*. A sort of worm. And you ought to see it at night for it's got little phosphorescent spots on its sides and it looks just like a boat decorated with fairy lamps for a regatta!"

"How wonderful!"

"Ah—but not so wonderful as *Eolis rufibranchialis*, and here he is! At least I think so!"

With a pair of forceps he removed from the stone what looked like a small blob of grey translucent jelly. He popped it into a glass tube he had filled with seawater and he held it up for Jane to see. For a moment it remained a shapeless blob at the bottom of the tube. Then it began to move slowly, to elongate and unfold like a Japanese paper water flower, only it took the shape of a snail with a finely tapering stern, two pairs of waving twirling "horns" and, growing from its back, a series of tentacle-like pappilae, bright red in colour with an ivory ring near their tips. It moved slowly up the tube as Edwin tilted it.

"It's *rufibranchialis* all right. You can tell by the colour. I won't say it's the most beautiful of the sea-slugs, but it's one of them and it's one of the commonest, too."

Jane clapped her hands with excitement.

"It's lovely—lovely! It's just like a lovely flower. Do let's go on finding things. Is that why you've come here today—to study things like sea-slugs? I'm not interfering in your work, am I?"

"Lord no! I'm on holiday like you, only I'm not even doing this as a holiday task. I'm just keen on it, that's all, and being here on such a marvellous day, and it's grand having someone who's interested. Come on. Let's hurry down to low-water mark before the tide turns. Oh, dear—it's turned already. That's what happens with these big spring ebbs. But never mind. There'll be plenty of things to find. Let's turn over another stone!"

The tide *had* turned and was flowing fast. As a marine zoologist Edwin might have felt disappointed and vexed, for the spring equinoctial tides, when as on this occasion they coincide with calm weather, are the best of the year for collecting. He had no sense of disappointment. He felt blissfully happy. It was as though the delicious physical tingling produced by his dip had permeated his soul. He was not consciously aware that Jane was the direct cause. At twenty, and with his good looks and charm, he was not without feminine experience. Will Knaggs, the smith (a student of Edward Carpenter and Havelock Ellis), had naturally seen to it that his son should go out into the world equipped with a full knowledge of the biological (and pathological) aspects of sex. As to its tender and romantic aspects he had gone through the customary emotional stages associated with the adolescence and early post-adolescence of the male. His first love, at the age of fifteen, had been for a girl in a confectioner's shop in Burnharbour. She had golden hair and big grey eyes and a beautiful mouth with perfect teeth and seductive lips. But it was a love that had been wholly unreciprocated and it had come to a bitter climax when, one early-closing day in summer, he had seen her walking arm in arm with a youth who served behind the counter of the grocer's shop next door: a smart Alick who wore suede shoes and very baggy Oxford bags and a striped blazer.

There had been no lack of reciprocity in his second love affair. Her name was Angela and he had picked her up on the beach during the Whitsuntide holidays. She, too, was a shop assistant from Bradford and she had a strong West Riding accent. She said "were" for "was" and everything she liked was "reight champion". But she was dark and pretty and, although only sixteen, she had a well-developed figure. She'd only had a board school education and would not even have heard of Edward Carpenter or Havelock Ellis. She was a well-informed young lady all the same and a competent instructress, and he not too stupid or reluctant a pupil in the art of kissing.

He had a rigid code of honour towards the opposite sex which his father had not specifically taught him. Perhaps he had acquired it from the good books he had read, Dickens in particular. He was strongly masculine but not lustful. He was not a philanderer. There had been many other affairs, none of which so far as he knew had hurt or done any harm to the willing participants in them. And, not through cautiousness, but because it had just not happened, he had never been involved in an overwhelming passion.

Consciously, Jane was not interesting the male in him. She was only a kid, he felt, and a long way from physical maturity. She was thin to the point of skinniness. He had hardly seen her face because of the unruly strands of hair that kept falling across it. She was dressed almost like a ragamuffin and, from the days of the confectioner's girl, he'd had an eye for feminine clothes. Her voice was charming, but he remembered that from the Wesleyan Bazaar concert. There was indeed something of Alice about her now, something quite fantastic. Regardless that he was wearing only ankle boots he waded over the top of them into a pool, and tilted up another large flat stone. Jane followed him and saw the creature that was hiding under it as quickly as he did. She shrieked.

"An octopus! A *real* octopus! Do be careful. Will it bite?"

The pool was fairly deep and the stone had partly bridged a deeper crevice in it, a miniature of the creek into which Edwin had dived. It was fringed with short tangles and there was a patch of greyish sand at the bottom of it. The sudden lifting of the stone had caught the octopus completely off its guard, for it was actually on the sand and its darkish brown body was conspicuous against it. But almost instantly it started to change colour, from brown to a mottled grey, lighter and lighter, until it matched the sand. Then arching its body it spread out its arms and began to move towards the nearest tangle frond. As the tip of its foremost leg touched the weed that leg began to turn brown.

"It's blushing!" Jane cried. "Look, it's almost invisible again. *Ooh*—but it does look horrible. Fancy meeting a really big one when you were bathing. Aren't they a wee bit dangerous, even small ones like that?"

Edwin laughed.

"Dangerous? Wait. I'll show you. That chameleon trick may work with a big cod, but not with a marine biologist."

He straddled the creek and with his sleeve rolled up made a dexterous jab into the tangle. Jane shrieked again and moved back in horror as he held the thing out to her with its arms writhing round his hand and sucking on to his skin.

"It's all right! It's all right!" he laughed. "It's quite harmless. Look. . ."

He took the tip of one of the arms that was half-coiled round his wrist and peeled it off, showing the rows of sucking discs with which it had adhered. The whole animal, although pulsating, was flabby now, its colours changing green, grey, red, brown and nearly white in a vain effort to match its novel background. Jane dared to touch it with a finger but recoiled involuntarily.

"Ooh—It's *horrible*. I don't know how you can go on holding it. Are you going to take it home with you?"

"I wish I could, but I haven't got an aquarium at present. They make grand pets. They are very brainy too. Their favourite food is small crabs and, if they can find a dead fish, they'll put it just in front of where they are hiding and wait for the crabs to come along and be caught by the bait. We'll have to let it go."

He lowered his hand into the pool. Immediately the octopus relaxed its hold. But now it did not creep away. Its body suddenly elongated, with its eight legs drawn together, and streamlined as it ejected water from its siphon. It shot backwards towards the deepest end of the pool and as it went it emitted from the siphon a "cloud" of dark-brown ink: its final weapon of self-defence! Jane's cry of admiration was mixed with relief.

"I *do* think it's clever. But I don't think I'd like to keep an octopus for a pet. . . Are you going to be a marine biologist or whatever you call it when you've finished at university? Is that what you're training to be?"

Edwin was still gazing at the cloud of camouflage "smoke" into which the octopus had disappeared, but vaguely he had his eyes on another patch of tangle the lifting of the stone had disclosed.

"Yes, I think so. A biologist of some sort, anyway. But I'm hoping to get a travelling scholarship first and see the world before settling down to a permanent job. What are you going to be, anyway?"

He glanced at her then, and as he did so she pulled the loose strands of hair from her face again and patted them back with her wet hand to make them stay. She was looking straight at him and he noticed her eyes for the first time. He was surprised by the seriousness of their expression; by the vehemence in her voice when she answered,

"I'm going to be an actress, if I'm not prevented!"

"An actress? How exciting! You know you were darned good in that *Alice in Wonderland* play. I thought you were marvellous!"

Jane ignored the compliment. Clearly she thought he was not taking her seriously. She had to push her hair up again. Her eyes flashed.

"Oh, that was only a children's play. It would have been an awful flop too if Mrs Jones hadn't been producing it. I mean real plays, Shakespeare, Bernard Shaw. I know I'm not beautiful. But that isn't everything. I don't want to be a film actress. I want to go on the real stage!"

"But—but—you sound quite cross about it. Why shouldn't you if you want to?"

"Because my daddy thinks the stage is wicked. He hates anything like that. Surely you know all about my daddy being so religious? I *hate* religion. I don't hate my daddy, but I do hate him being religious and against everything that young people like doing, like dancing and going to the pictures and having fun. Your father knows all about my daddy, if you don't!"

It was a challenge which Edwin parried skilfully, for he sensed a rather delicate situation. He laughed.

"No one would say my father was religious, least not in that way. But you know he's not quite so bad as he's painted. Yes I do know your father by sight, but that's all. You lose touch with local people when you're away more than half the year. You live at Moor Farm now, don't you, just above the cliff?"

"Yes. But thank goodness I got a scholarship and go to Burnharbour every day."

"Don't you like farming?"

" Yes I do, in a way. I like animals. I even like milking, but that's only a waste of time—isn't it?—if you want to do something really important. How would *you* like to be a blacksmith?"

Her indignation was cooling, or she too was sensing that things had become too personal.

"I don't mean anything spiteful against your father," she added quickly. "I know I shouldn't talk so openly about what I feel. I do love my daddy—and I don't want to do anything that upsets him. And you must think I'm blowing my own trumpet about wanting to be an actress, or perhaps you think it's just schoolgirl's nonsense."

"Now that *is* nonsense if you like! I *don't* think you're blowing your own trumpet and I wouldn't blame you if you did! I dislike people who are dumb about themselves. I'm terribly interested. I think it's awful when parents decide on what careers their sons or daughters shall or shall not follow. Like the big business man who makes his eldest son go into the firm with the idea of succeeding him when he retires or dies, or the mother who tries to stop her daughter marrying a particular man. Very often it's because she's in love with the man herself, or at any rate jealous of her daughter's happiness. I say that everyone has the right to choose for himself or herself, although you can't blame parents for advising and trying to use their influence for what they believe to be right, even if it's wrong! Of course I'm lucky, and it's easier too for a son. If I'd wanted to be a blacksmith dad wouldn't have stopped me. In fact, he'd have willingly taught me all he knew. But he's always been open-minded, the same about religion. I won't say he hasn't made his own views clear about the Bible and the Church. And I won't say he'd be thrilled if I suddenly chucked science for theology and decided to become a clergyman. But I don't think he'd tell me not to darken his door again or that he was going to cut me off with a shilling, although again I don't think he'd come to hear me preach. . . I say, you've got me quite excited about it. I do want to hear more about this ambition of yours. Do let us go on talking about it. I would like to help you."

It had been Jane's turn to look surprised and almost bewildered by Edwin's outburst.

"That is kind of you," she said very meekly, and then suddenly practical, "but we'll have to move, won't we? The tide's coming in fast. Look, it's coming into the pool."

Edwin was still standing ankle deep near the edge of the deep part of the pool, Jane a pace or two distant on the dry scaur. As he moved to join her his eyes once more were attracted to that patch of tangle stirring now by the tide entering the pool from the seaward end.

"By Jove!" he cried. "I thought I'd seen something moving there! A *lobster*!"

He waded towards it, keeping to the edge of the miniature creek. He crouched down and put one hand in the water stealthily, as though he were tickling a trout. All Jane could see at first were two thin red stalks waving gently between the fronds of weed and, before she had time to connect these stalks with the animal itself, Edwin had grabbed it behind its claws and all in one quick movement whipped it out on to the dry scaur. Again Jane shrieked with mixed admiration and terror for he had thrown it with its claws open almost at her feet. But he collared it again neatly and held it up triumphantly.

"I thought I couldn't have been mistaken! All the time we've been talking I've been watching that bit of weed out of the tail of my eye!"

"You must have wonderful eyesight. And ugh—l

don't know how you dare get hold of it with your bare hands like that."

She was still regarding the gaping claws with apprehension.

"Oh, it's easy enough once you've got the knack. It's not a very big one. I should say it's about half an inch under legal size, but we're not going to bother about that. Don't think because I had my eyes on it I wasn't interested in what we were talking about, though. I am terribly interested. We must go on talking about it. I'll tell you what. I've got quite a lot of grub in my rucksack and a billycan for making tea. Let's get up to high-water mark and scrounge round for driftwood and make a fire. Golly—if we could find an old tin we could boil this lobster and eat it. Would you like to do that?"

"I'd love to. I love making fires and having picnics, but you mustn't think about giving me any of your food, although I wouldn't mind trying a bit of the lobster. Only what about the tide and your getting back home?"

"Don't worry about that. And I've got tons of grub. That's my Aunt Betsy. She thinks it terrible not to have a proper midday dinner, roast beef and Yorkshire pudding and with an apple pie or something else to fill you up. But what about you? What time do you have meals at home? Do your people worry if you're not back on time?"

"Mother doesn't. Daddy would if he thought I was going to the pictures at Burnharbour as I have done once or twice, pretending I'd missed the school train. He doesn't worry if I'm just out for a walk or down here on the shore. He's leading manure for the potatoes today. I expect I'll have to help him sow potatoes tomorrow if it keeps fine. I suppose you go to the theatre just when you want to. I've never even seen a real play yet. I've only read them and even then, when I get them from the school or the town library, I've got to put brown-paper covers on them and pretend they're just ordinary school books. I can only read in the train or in bed, when I know that daddy is asleep and I dare light a candle."

They were walking up the scaur now towards the cliff foot and the rocks where Edwin had left his belongings. The sun still shone from a clear blue sky but, as so often happens at the turn of the tide on a fine day, a light sea wind had risen, easterly and chilly. Edwin was glad to get his jacket on. He noticed his drawing-book. He'd forgotten about the painting he had made, and he had a sudden resurgence of happiness. Was it as good as he had thought? What an amazing day! He had just been wondering if he could do another picture when Jane had come round the rock reciting *The Forsaken Merman*. That seemed ages and ages ago. He itched to look at it again, but that would mean he'd have to let Jane see it, and he felt curiously shy at doing so. He thrust the book deep in his rucksack then glanced a little guiltily over his shoulder at her. She was waiting for him and, as he looked, she pushed back the unruly strands of hair from her face again and smiled very confidently, and with an extraordinary friendliness, suggesting that she was quite used to waiting for him like this, that she was accustomed to all his habits. He smiled back, and couldn't help saying,

"Isn't it funny, that only about twenty minutes ago I scarcely knew of your existence and you came round that rock just like a character out of a play, and here we are and I feel I've known you for years and years and of course I have in a way. Did you say you've never seen a real stage play?"

"Never. But I've imagined I have. I never read a play without seeing it actually acted on a stage. Oh, it must be wonderful to go to a theatre whenever you like."

"Who was it set you thinking about the stage?"

They were moving now, picking their way between the great fallen blocks of sandstone to the cliff foot, Edwin still carrying the lobster in his hand, Jane warily keeping clear of its claws.

"It was Mrs Jones, the Wesleyan minister's wife. She used to tell me about the plays she'd seen when they lived in town before they came to Bramblewick. And she used to do bits out of them. Oh, she was clever and such a nice kind woman."

"They've left Bramblewick, of course?"

"Yes. Soon after that Christmas concert. And they're in Rhodesia now. Mr Jones is a sort of missionary, only more of a teacher than a clergyman. And Mrs Jones is teaching too, helping her brother who is a real missionary. She writes to me regularly and I had a lovely long letter from her only yesterday. I've got it with me now. I'll let you see it if you like. . . Look, there's a nice piece of wood for our fire."

She leapt on to one of the rocks, and from that to another, then bent down and tugged at a short length of sea-splintered boxwood jammed in a crevice and held it up as triumphantly as Edwin had held his lobster.

"Fine!" he cried. "And there's nothing wrong with your eyesight either! We can kindle the fire with heather and it will smell marvellously. Let's make it close under the cliff, out of the wind!"

"I know the very place. It's out of the wind, yet it's not shaded from the sun. Do you build a proper fireplace when you make a picnic fire, or do you just make it anyhow, on the ground? It's ages since I made one. There's not much fun doing things like that by yourself!"

People who are liking each other make statements and ask questions and don't wait for answers or comments, and both of them were looking for wood, jumping from rock to rock and now approaching a narrow beach where the bigger rocks gave way to roughish shingle strewn with the debris of the winter high tides. There was nothing to attract the interest of a professional beachcomber among this debris. There was no driftwood of any size, but there was plenty of smaller stuff and Edwin spotted an old tin can that looked big enough for his lobster.

The cliff was not steep here. Its face had been excavated by the old alum shale-workers and there was a scree of shale on which, in patches, rough grass and ling found root, with a few clumps of stunted whins higher up. The path from High Batts came down this scree, but before it reached the beach it branched in many directions like a river emerging through a delta. But there was protection from the wind and the shingle was almost warm with the sun. Edwin dropped the lobster and his rucksack, took off his jacket again and gave a practical answer to one of Jane's questions by expertly building a gipsy fireplace with slabs of sandstone while Jane herself continued the search for wood. When he had done he picked up the tin can, tried it across the walls of his fireplace to see if it would fit then, satisfied that it would, he yelled to Jane who was at the far end of the beach,

"Hey! There's no fresh water on here, is there?"

"Only water that trickles out of the shale and it's bitter with alum. Haven't you brought any water?"

There was a mock indignation in her voice.

"Only for making tea. I naturally didn't think I'd have to cook a lobster. Never mind, we'll do it in sea-water. How are you getting on?"

"Fine. I've got nearly an armful already when I pick them up. Look at this!"

She held up a piece of a tree branch that had evidently washed down one of the becks of the bay when in spate, and she stood poised with it while again she brushed back her hair with her other hand, and for the first time Edwin knew that she was beautiful. His appreciation was aesthetic, however, and almost completely impersonal. She affected him in the same way, but in a greater degree, as the forms and colours of the rock pool had done when he had dived. He could not, in that moment, have said *why* he knew that she was beautiful. He was not looking at her features for she was too distant for him to see the details of her face and already he had noticed her eyes and nose and mouth without being deeply stirred. It was something undefinable, but everything about her had suddenly become aesthetically right: her tousled hair with the sun glinting on it, the broad shape of her face, her drab untidy clothes, her long thin straight brown legs, her poise with that one bare arm holding up the branch, the other hand pressing back her hair. In the immediate foreground was the shingle, its rounded pebbles predominantly ash-grey in tone, but with odd bits of dark blue lias and rust-red ironstone among them, and mixed too with the reds and ochres of decayed and withered wrack. Behind her were the sculptured sandstone rocks, brown and yellow and red, and beyond these again the big scaur, its highest ridge ivory white with the limestone shells of innumerable barnacles, curved out into the deep blue of the sea.

He was standing up with the old tin can in his hand. He had a sudden wild desire to fling the can away, to seize his drawing book and paint box and do what he had done with the rock pool. But he knew instantly that whatever success he had made of his first attempt at a picture this would defeat him. The little beach and the sandstone rocks and the sea were enough to frustrate him without that human figure standing there and making the whole vision perfect with her intrinsic beauty. He felt angry. For the first time in his adult life he experienced a profound dissatisfaction with himself. Everything in his life so far had gone according to plan. He'd had to work hard of course, stick at subjects he didn't like (mathematics was one of them), had had to stay indoors swotting for days and nights on end in spring and summer when he craved to be out – and in the country too, not in a filthy city. Yet everything had come easy in this process of qualifying himself for a career which, if not definitely indicated yet, would be lucrative and agreeable. The thought struck him: supposing that instead of specialising on science from the start he had specialised on drawing and painting? That instead of going to university he had gone to an art college (there were scholarships to such places)? Had he in the terms he had spent at school or university ever experienced such a desire to solve a problem, to win a distinction as he had at this moment to create a picture? Was he really so keen on a scientific career as he had always imagined? Had he discovered at last, and when it was too late, what he really wanted to do and be?

He was still looking towards Jane but comprehending the whole of that entrancing pattern of form and colour, and it was Jane herself who as suddenly brought him to earth. She shouted,

"Will that old tin do or shall I look for another?"

"It's just right," he shouted back. "So long as it doesn't leak. I'm going to fill it with water."

He strode down to the nearest pool, filled the can and when he got back Jane was at the fireplace with her armful of sticks.

"What a wonderful fireplace you've built!"

He was completely in the present again, his anger and dissatisfaction gone. He dared to look at Jane and there she was just a rather pleasant-looking kid, decidedly original and interesting and charming, but not beautiful by his practical standards of female beauty. And this picnic was going to be fun.

"Do you think so? Well, it is a bit of a curse when you get your billycan boiling and it upsets and puts the fire out just because you've been impatient. Come on let's get the fire lit. My aunt would have a shock if she knew how hungry I was. What a grand lot of sticks you've got. All we need now is some ling for kindling."

They climbed up the scree together for the ling. Soon they had the fire blazing and both cans fixed across its hottest part. Edwin wasn't squeamish and he didn't believe that animals like lobsters had a consciousness of pain, but he thought it best to take no chances and kill instantly by dropping it into boiling water. Jane was kneeling in front of the fire feeding it with sticks. Edwin sat down and took from his pocket a packet of cigarettes.

"Have one—or haven't you learnt to smoke yet?"

Jane smiled, a little self-consciously.

"I have tried, but I don't like smoking. Besides Mrs Jones always warned me against smoking because of it harming your voice. Not because it was wrong. She wasn't like that."

Edwin lit his cigarette.

"I don't remember her very well. I knew she was keen on music and plays, like most Welsh people. I know I liked him. He wasn't a bit like most parsons. He and my father used to have terrific arguments, but to tell the truth father admitted that Jones usually got the better of him and it's not often father will admit anything like that. He was always nice to me in spite of my never going to chapel or Sunday School. I bet you were sorry when they left."

"I cried every night for weeks. I loved Mrs Jones. But my daddy didn't like her because he thought she was encouraging me to be an actress. I'll tell you a secret if you like. You know old Jonty Scaife, the country postman? We've always been great friends and whenever there's a letter for me from Africa, he never brings it to the house but gives it to me on the sly."

"Good old Jonty! He's a great chap. Of course I know him and his funny little wife, Polly. But I should hate to have to keep things dark like that. I am sorry for you, you know. But I do believe that if you want something very very much, you get it in the end."

"*Do* you? How funny. That's just what she says in her last letter. Would you like to read it?"

She had a patch pocket on her skirt and she took from it a crumpled envelope. She handed it to Edwin with a vague hesitation. Obviously it was very precious to her. He also looked at it with hesitation, mechanically reading the name and address on it, noting the Rhodesian stamp, reluctant to pry. But she encouraged him.

"Go on. Read it. It's not very private. It's in answer to one I wrote to her just after Christmas, but they hadn't got then to where they are now, and my letter must have been forwarded on."

He took out the letter. It was written on flimsy "foreign correspondence" paper with ruled lines which, however, the writer had ignored. But it was a bold masculine hand. The address was a P.O. box number at a township in Rhodesia. Edwin glanced at the first paragraph and, then still self-conscious, he handed it to Jane.

"Come on. You read it aloud. I'd like that much better."

"All right then." Jane laughed.

"And before you start I'll shove the lobster in or the water will boil away!"

He dropped it in (it was already comatose) and put a flat stone over the tin for a lid.

"Righto. And I'm damned interested, too."

"Well, the first part isn't very interesting, but I suppose I'd better read it all, and it starts 'My darling Jane. What a lovely letter from you.' She means of course the one I wrote after Christmas. 'I read it aloud to Dai' (that's Mr Jones) 'and he said that if ever you decide *not* to be an actress you'll be able to earn your living as a writer. Your descriptions of the storm and the snowdrifts and how you went out with your father to rescue the poor sheep really made us shiver, and Dai said his toes were actually tickling with chilblains, this with the thermometer standing at ninety degrees in the shade. Of course, he hasn't had a thing the matter with him since we first came to Africa. I don't think you'd know him if you saw him. His face is the colour of mahogany and his hair is distinctly fashionable, pure platinum blonde. Also, he never wears his clergyman clothes out here even on a Sunday. He wears shorts and a shirt with an open neck, like the other white men. I don't think that old Captain Fosdyck would approve!' "

Edwin laughed.

"I like that! And I wonder what my father would say about it. I'm glad the place suits him. I did like him, you know, and I think my father did in his heart."

"I don't think anyone could *help* liking him!" Jane said, emphatically. "Just listen to what she says. 'He is so happy here and the natives, especially the black children, almost worship him. I've had to tell him that if he's not careful they'll really believe he is God, and that would make him too conceited. It's a most beautiful place where we live. The house is a big bungalow, built on the side of a hill. It's nearly covered with wisteria and passion flowers and there's a big garden, too, with English roses as well as hundreds of African flowers that I can't name. And from the wide veranda (it's called a stoep) where we have all our meals we can look down to the river, where the trees are huge and dark-leaved like English holly, and beyond this are miles and miles of veld, dotted with acacias and mimosa thorns with here and there a queer fat tree called a boboab, which looks exactly like an overgrown beetroot. And the mountains beyond the veld are a wonderful blue as though they're half-dissolved in the sky.'

"Doesn't it sound *lovely*!" Jane had to comment.

"It does. It gives me quite a wanderlust. And by Jove she writes well, doesn't she? *Do* go on."

" 'The native village is lower down the hill than the mission, near the river but high enough to be safe from the floods which they say are very heavy when the rains come. As soon as darkness comes (always about six o'clock) we can see the village fires, and almost every night the natives dance round them to the beat of drums and some weird wooden horns. It's not much like an English dance, of course, but the music they make is real music with the most fascinating and complicated rhythm. I try to imitate it on my piano, but it's quite hopeless. And their dances too are really dramatic. They are a sort of mumming with the men dressed up to represent animals or spirits and I am sure there is always a story behind what they are doing, that they are acting a sort of play. But I shall know better when I have learnt to speak their language, which is a very difficult one. The missionaries who first came to this place tried to teach the natives that dancing was wicked, especially as the girls are naked down to their waist, and the men usually have a lot of beer to drink. They make this from the sap of bamboos that grow on the mountains and it tastes just like cider. They tried to make the girls wear cotton dresses buttoned right up to the neck, but thank goodness the fashion never caught on.' "

"Thank goodness it didn't!" Edwin interrupted. "I feel as hotly as my father does about missionaries when I hear of how they just try to force their own ideas about behaviour on the natives. Only I do believe that some missionaries do a lot of good. She sounds very sane about everything. Go on. Sorry I interrupted."

"That's all right. I like to know what you think about it. But I'm afraid there isn't any more about the place they're living in and the natives and things like that. She says next that she's going to write in her next letter pages and pages about all the queer animals and insects and the school. But she's getting back to my letter to her again now. In it I told her all the Bramblewick news I thought might interest her and Mr Jones. Especially about the meeting that was held to decide if the Wesleyans should build a new chapel up the bank and close the old one. The Sunday School has been closed since the Joneses went, of course. She says, 'Dai did laugh when I read to him what you said about the chapel meeting. We could both of us see old Captain Fosdyck standing up and saying that what was good enough for John Wesley should be good enough for anyone else. That's what he said to Dai. And to think that if he wanted to he could build a new chapel himself and still have plenty to spare. And do you really think that he is leaving all his money to the Wesleyans when he dies? The old villain. Perhaps you are right. That he thinks he will impress St. Peter more by paying up the lot for a place in heaven. One thing is certain: he can't take it with him.' "

"I say! Sorry to break in again, but *do* you think that's what Bully Fosdyck's going to do?"

"Oh no. I just said that for fun. Everyone thinks he'll just leave it to his nieces, old Selina and Abigail, in spite of them being so rich already. Only they're keen on the new chapel, although they daren't go against him at the meeting."

"But hasn't he got a son somewhere abroad? I seemed to remember some yarn about that!"

"Yes. I've heard mother talking about it. But he's supposed to be dead. He was called Zachariah. They quarrelled years and years ago, before I was born. I think he was an apprentice on board his father's ship and they had a row because he got drunk. Captain Fosdyck gave him a thrashing and at the next port Zachariah deserted. The last time he was heard of alive was in Melbourne, I think, and the story was that he'd married a black woman. But I'm sure he's dead. He was a very bad character from all accounts and that's perhaps one reason why Captain Fosdyck has to be so religious!"

"Oh," said Edwin thoughtfully. "There may be something in that. You seem to have your head screwed on the right way. . . Go on reading. I promise I won't interrupt again."

Jane laughed.

"But I don't mind a bit! It shows you're interested, anyway."

"You bet I'm interested. Please go on."

It took Jane a moment to find the place and again she had to adjust her hair. He was watching her. She was still kneeling in front of the fire. Her face was now in profile. It was a good face, he thought. The more he looked at it the more he liked it in what he still believed was a strictly impersonal way. He admired the shape of her ear, and the way her hair (this was the tidy side) curved behind it. He liked the shape of her head and her neck and the line of the jaw and the profile of her just slightly tilted nose.

She had full lips and they were very red. There was a small mole on her cheek, but it was not a serious blemish on an otherwise perfect skin. She was beautiful, but it was an elusive beauty and much of it he felt was in the way she held herself and moved, and in her expression which seemed to change with every modulation of her really enchanting voice. Yes, with that voice and face and with what her figure promised to be, with that undoubted charm and intelligence she might well become an actress, perhaps even a great one. It was an exciting thought. He felt a greater urge to encourage and help. She was smiling now as she began to read again:

" 'Poor Jane!' she goes on. 'You must have felt sad about the Christmas bazaar, and we don't blame you a bit for not wanting to go, and we think it was very brave and unselfish that you did just to please Miss Widdison and the new minister who, by the way, sounds a much more suitable person for the post than the Reverend Dai. Fancy Mr and Mrs Lightfoot singing *Madam will you Walk* again. It did bring it all back and made us feel so sad, not only for you but for the children of the village who might have been taking part in the concert if the Sunday School hadn't shut up shop. But perhaps if the new chapel does happen they'll start another Sunday School "up-bank" and cut the Church out. Still, you wouldn't be a Sunday scholar now even if we had stayed at Bramblewick, would you? I am so pleased that you are going to the County School, even if things are not going just as you would like. It is so difficult for me to tell you in a letter what I really feel about it all. I do admire your father so much. It was splendid the way he gave up drinking and pulled himself together. It's wonderful that without any training for it he's made your farm a success with all the odds against him, although your mother must have been a great help to him. One must have a respect for anyone who stands up for their ideals.' "

Jane stopped. She wasn't smiling now. Edwin saw her bite her lip and he said quickly,

"She must be a grand person, Mrs Jones. It must be awful for you having lost a friend like that. Look, is it upsetting you reading it?"

She turned with a quick smile, but he noticed that there were tears in her eyes.

"No. It's all right. And it's just lovely having someone to read it to. I've got two friends at school, but I couldn't tell them about it. They'd just think I was silly. The only letters that would interest them would be letters from boyfriends. They just wouldn't understand. And mother's queer too, in a way. I know it sounds awful, but I believe she was jealous of Mrs Jones. She's not like daddy by the way. I won't say that she wants me to be an actress. But she wants me to be something different from any other girl round here. I think really she'd like to see me become a real lady and marry a squire's son or something like that. She doesn't mind what she does on the farm, even cleaning out the pigsties. But she hates me doing any dirty work, although I don't mind a bit. If it hadn't been for her I'd have never gone to the County School. Daddy wanted me to stay at home... Oh *blast* my hair!"

They both laughed as she adjusted it once more. The tension was relieved.

"All right then, I'll go on, after 'ideals'. It sounds like a dictation lesson, doesn't it? She goes on, 'But having said that, I must say that you have a right to your own life. It's going to be very hard for you to establish that right. You'll have to fight, but try not to hurt the people who love you, even if they are really opposing you. I am certain that there is nothing in life that's worthwhile that hasn't got to be fought for. You too have your ideals, and you are justified in getting respect for them. It must have been galling for you having to refuse to play Rosalind in your school presentation of *As Tou Like It*, and just because you knew it would anger your father and perhaps lead to a scene at home. I am certain you would have done it to perfection. But don't let that discourage you. It's something to be at a school where they do take a practical interest in dramatics. It didn't surprise me that you have won the poetry-reading prize for the third time. It would have surprised me very much if you hadn't. The matric is a bore, but it's necessary and many of the subjects will be invaluable to you later on. I don't think that brains are the first essential for success on the stage, even the legitimate stage. The first thing is feeling. But you have to interpret the poetry and the prose and the beauty that other artists have created and you can't do that without an all-round intelligence, which even the dullest school subjects help you to develop. Of course, you don't *want* to be a school teacher. But unless Captain Fosdyck dies and leaves all his 'brass' to you, or Dai finds a gold reef when he's digging the vegetable garden (he says that's the thing that makes him dig) 'school teaching' is your most practical way out. It's your easiest way to college, and college means a town. Both mean freedom and independence of the sort you need. If you win a scholarship it may mean certain obligations. You may *have* to teach a certain number of years, or pay back the fees. But you shouldn't worry about that. There'll be theatres, professional and amateur, dramatic societies, probably at the college and certainly in the town. There will be libraries. You'll meet people. And you'll find what you want. You'll go to it just as surely as a homing pigeon finds its way to its cote. I am certain that you've only got to want a thing badly enough, and consistently, for it to happen. Look at me. Always wanting to live in South Africa, and here I am. So stick to it, Jane. Even history and science and the other things you hate. And don't feel too vexed with your daddy, because he does mean well although don't, for goodness' sake, leave this letter lying about. I feel all hot and cold at the thought of what he'd say if he read it. And now I must close or I'll miss the mailbag, which goes off by car every Friday. So until next time, goodbye and God bless you. Love from us both. Gwen.' . . . and that's the end."

She did not look at Edwin, but at the fire, and she self-consciously picked up a stick and pushed it under the can. He too was silent for a short while. Then he said, with enthusiasm,

"By Jove! That's a grand letter. Thank you for reading it to me."

She turned her face to him. She was blushing, and for once her voice lacked its characteristic self-assurance. She actually stammered,

"Oh—I—it is—I'm awfully pleased. I feel perhaps I shouldn't have shown it to *anyone*. You don't feel that I've done anything nasty?"

"Rubbish! And anyway, so far as I'm concerned, mum's the word. I'm jolly glad you have read it to me.

What sense she's got! She's right about that being your best way to get what you want. Town's the only place for you. It would be a teachers' training college, wouldn't it? There's one at Donbridge, a sort of branch of the university, although it's away from the main buildings. Of course there's the Donbridge Thespians Dramatic Society. Donbridge has a jolly fine repertory theatre too, as well as the ordinary theatres. There's a philharmonic hall, too, where they give orchestral concerts and recitals with first-class conductors and artists."

Jane took a deep breath.

"Oh it must be wonderful!"

"Are you keen on music?"

"Of course. But I never get the chance to listen to any. Daddy won't even have a wireless. I'd love to be able to go to things like that, but it's the theatre that excites me most. Oh dear, I should want to go to the theatre every night. Do go on telling me about it. What plays have you seen? What sort do you like best? Do you like modern ones or do you prefer Shakespeare?"

Edwin got up and with his handkerchief removed the lobster can from the fire. He put on the billycan in its place and he went on talking.

"I prefer modern plays myself, especially Shaw and Noel Coward and Somerset Maugham. But I like Shakespeare and I like Ibsen and Chekhov. The last Chekhov I saw was *Uncle Vanya*. I wouldn't have missed that for anything."

"I haven't read that one. But I've read *The Cherry Orchard* and *The Seagull*, and I've read *Ghosts* and *The Master Builder* by Ibsen. I don't say I altogether understand them, but then I don't understand a lot of Shakespeare's plays, but that doesn't make any difference to seeing them played in my imagination and pretending I'm playing the parts. Do you belong to the Dramatic Society?"

He had tipped the can onto the shingle and shaken out the lobster, steaming hot and now bright red. He laughed,

"No, I've never had any leanings towards that side of the stage. I hated even having to read aloud at school. But I've never deliberately missed the chance of seeing a play. There was a London company doing a Shaw season this winter and I saw every play they did!"

"Oh! You've no idea how I envy you. To do just what you want to do. To be just what you want to be. To have no one to interfere with you and say you must do this and do that because it's what *they* want!"

Edwin was surprised to hear himself say almost with heat,

"And how the devil do you know I'm going to be just what I want to be?"

It was Jane's turn to be surprised.

"Why, you said only a few minutes ago that you were going to be some sort of a biologist, and that's what you want to do, isn't it? You didn't talk as though *your* father was objecting. In fact you said he'd have let you become a blacksmith if you wanted to. What do you want to be if you don't want to be a scientist?"

Edwin was aware that his own cheeks were tingling. Meeting her eyes he felt that they were looking straight through him, reading his thoughts.

"Well, I'm damned! If anyone an hour ago had asked me that question, I mean anyone who knew me, I'd have

229

just thought they were joking. Almost ever since I can remember I've wanted to be a scientist of some sort. I suppose my father did put it into my head, but I don't think he did so deliberately. It is true that he would have helped me to be a blacksmith if I'd yearned for that. But something strange has happened to me today. It was happening before you came round that rock. It's probably all quite idiotic—in fact it is definitely idiotic. But I believe I've discovered that what I really want to be, more than anything in the world, is a painter!"

"You mean an artist and paint pictures! How exciting. How thrilling. And why shouldn't you be one if you want to?"

Edwin had to laugh.

"That's just what I said to you when you told me you were going to be an actress unless someone stopped you."

"Yes. How funny! But I've always wanted to be an actress. I haven't suddenly decided. Weren't you painting when I came round that rock? The first thing I noticed was your paint box. I wish you'd show me what you were doing. I expect it was very good."

Edwin again glanced involuntarily at his rucksack, but he ignored the request.

"Why *not* be a painter?" he asked ironically. "Why *not*? Because I've spent all my life learning to be something else and learning it thoroughly too. I'm a biologist, concerned only with material facts and the scientific explanation of them. Even paints are chemicals. Even colours in nature are just the physical reaction of various substances to the light of the sun. Look at that big block of sandstone." He waved his hand dramatically to the rock nearest to the shingle. "How does it affect you?'

Jane looked at the rock a little puzzled.

"What do you mean, how does it affect me?"

"Does it excite you, like poetry does, or something in a play or music?"

"No. But it's a lovely colour, particularly with the sea behind it."

"Yes, and the shingle in front of it, and with that heap of yellow weed catching the sun, and with the shadow it throws on that pool on to its own reflection. And its shape too, it looks as though it had been carved! I must have been on here and climbed over those rocks hundreds and hundreds of times. My father used to bring me on here getting fossils when I was only a kid. I could tell you just why that sandstone is banded and mottled and coloured as it is. I could draw you quite a good picture of what a thin section of that seaweed would look like under a microscope and what has happened to its cell structure to make it yellow instead of brown. But it's only today that I've seen that the rocks here are beautiful and, that with everything else, the pools and the scaur and the sea and the sky. . . they make—well—a picture, something to paint."

"Is *that* what you were painting then?" Jane persisted.

"No. I *had* tried to paint a picture of something else, the first I've ever tried to do. The first I've ever wanted to do. I thought it was good, then I sort of became aware of the rocks and the whole of what we're looking at now and I just knew I couldn't do it. It was beyond me. But I also felt that—well—if I'd learnt to paint instead of learning how to dissect dogfish and frogs and cockroaches and make coloured maps of their nervous systems and alimentary canals, I might have been able to get at least something of what I feel about this beauty down on paper. It's too late now, of course."

Jane laughed.

"Why, you talk as though you were an old man! Why is it too late? Remember what you said to me, and what Mrs Jones said in her letter, about being able to do anything if you wanted hard enough and you stuck at it!"

Edwin laughed now.

"You know, you're really brilliant the way you turn things round. And it is true. I'm sure you can if you want and you stick at it. But I don't know for absolute certainty that I do want to give up science. It may be just a sort of sudden craze. It probably is. It may be something to do with the sea air, with spring, with the sunshine, the change of this from Donbridge. And, by Jove, it may be just hunger. Come on. The billy's nearly boiling. Let's make the tea and have something to eat. We'll have to wait for the lobster to cool, but there's plenty of sandwiches. And we'll stop talking about me and painting. It's utterly mad, anyway. We'll talk about plays and you!"

He started to empty his rucksack, all but his drawing-book and painting apparatus, which he thrust well to the bottom of it. Jane had stood up.

"Can I help?"

He handed her a parcel.

"Yes. Here's the food. And I've got the tea. That flat stone there will do for a table. I hope you like your tea strong. This is fun, isn't it? Do you ever, when something very unusual happens, say to yourself, I'm going to remember this until the end of my life?"

She started to undo the parcel. She spoke thought-fully.

"I don't know. I don't think I ever do it deliberately. But there are plenty of things I think I shall remember always. And some of them aren't very nice, either. I shan't ever forget the day we moved down from our house on the North Cliff to that cottage in old Bramblewick, when daddy was drunk, and he nearly had a fight with one of the men who was helping. I shan't forget the night he was taken ill, and he came up to my room to kiss me goodnight. And going to stay with the Scaifes next day, and then overhearing Polly telling a neighbour about what had happened to mother. I was just terrified. And then I remember when the message came that Granddad Moorsholm, my mother's daddy, was dead, and the funeral. I do seem to remember the gloomiest things best. But I remember plenty of nice things too. I remember going on a picnic with Mrs Jones to Matty Brewster's Wood, where the daffodils grow. Daddy had shown me the place once, but he hated going there because he used to take his young brother Harry there before the war. Harry was lost with my Granddad Bransby when his ship was blown up with a mine. Well, the daffodils were out and it was a warm spring day like this and we sat down among them and Mrs Jones recited that poem of Wordsworth about the daffodils, you know, *'Ten thousand saw I at a glance, nodding their heads in sprightly dance'*. Isn't it funny how a smell or a sound, like someone whistling a tune, will bring things back? What brings that day back, though, is when I read or hear that bit out of *A Midsummer Night's Dream*, *'I know a bank whereon the wild thyme grows, where oxlips and nodding violets grow'*, which is rather funny as I'm sure there's no thyme in Matty Brewster's Wood, although there's plenty of violets and honeysuckle in summer. But that's one of my favourite bits out of Shakespeare. I don't think I'll forget this day."

"I shan't either. That's why I asked you. I'll remember it because it's all a bit mad, and you get sick of things being sane. . . Here we are!" He had put the tea into the billy and, holding the handle with his handkerchief, lifted it from the fire. "You have the mug. It's a good job Aunt Betsy packed one. I can use the lid, but I'll wait till it's brewed a bit. Milk first? There's plenty of sugar. I'll have a sandwich while I'm waiting for the tea. Don't you love the smell of heather in the fire?"

"It's all lovely!"

She knelt by the rock table on which she had spread the sandwiches and buns and cake. He squatted on the shingle between her and the fire and they started their meal. . . . Yes, he thought, he would remember this day, every minute of it: the walk along the shore from Bramblewick, the agates and the carnelians, the dip, his first picture, his joy and his discouragement, Jane coming round the rock reciting *The Forsaken Merman*, the blenny, the sea-slug, the octopus, the lobster, his discovery of Jane's elusive beauty, the reading of the letter, and now this picnic, with the sun shining on the beach and on the wind-flecked sea, the smell of brine mingled with the sweet strong scent of the fire. He saw no danger in the situation. He was not falling in love with Jane; he still regarded her impersonally, as though she was just a part of the whole spirit of the day and inseparable from it.

And, having little masculine vanity, it did not occur to him to wonder what she might be thinking of him as she knelt there, munching her sandwich, sipping her tea, giving him occasional smiling glances.

They were both hungry. The food was good and they didn't say much while they ate and drank. Shortly Edwin got up, fetched the lobster, broke off the claws and removed the shell from the flesh of the rest. He cracked the bigger claw and put it down in front of Jane. She protested, and in the end he tossed a coin for it, and she was delighted when she lost and he had to surrender the smaller claw to her. By now the tide had almost surrounded the Big Scaur and was lapping among the rocks where Edwin had first stopped. Glancing seawards he made a discovery. Along the horizon a thin grey streak had appeared between the blue of sea and sky and there was a darker shadow on the sea at a point where the streak thickened almost into the shape of a cloud.

"Hallo," he said. "It looks like goodbye to the sun very soon. There's a sea roak drifting in with the wind. It usually does happen when you get a fine day here at this time of the year. I hate fog, although it's not so bad when it's just fog, and not smoke and sulphur as you get in Donbridge sometimes. But it will take the colour out of everything and make it gloomy. What a pity."

"Oh, I don't mind. It can't spoil our picnic now." She had just finished the picking of the tip of her claw. "I have enjoyed this lobster. But really I'm quite full, and I do feel awful about eating so much of your food. Could I have just a drop more tea? I am making a pig of myself."

"Nonsense. And you've got to have that other cheesecake."

235

"Really I just couldn't. You take it."

"No. I'm going to have a fag."

He poured out some tea for her, then he took out his cigarette case.

"You're sure you won't have one?"

She hesitated.

"Well, perhaps I will for once. I don't suppose I'll like it, but one can't do me any harm, can it?"

She took one and smiled mischievously as she put it near to her lips and held it, poised.

"I suppose all the girls at the university smoke! Do tell me more about Donbridge. I don't think I'd like the factories and the traffic and there being so many people, but you can't expect everything to be nice, and what a lot of nice things there must be!"

Edwin had pulled a smouldering stick from the fire, and still squatting on the shingle he turned and held it out to her. She put the cigarette between her lips, then bent her head forward to the glowing end, tried to draw, and then giggled and drew back. Edwin laughed.

"Come on, that's no good. You've got to draw. And mind, don't swallow. Just hold the smoke in your mouth and breathe it out. Fancy my having to teach you. Try again!"

She laughed outright, and then with an exaggerated seriousness she gripped the cigarette tightly between her lips and again leaned forward to the stick. And it was then that he saw a sudden expression of terror in her eyes. For a fraction of a second he thought the stick had burnt her and he whipped it back. Simultaneously, however, she whipped the cigarette from her mouth. He realised that her eyes were focused not on himself but past his shoulder, behind him, and he heard the sound of someone approaching. He half-turned his head and saw Tom Bransby close up to the cliff foot, not more than twenty paces away, striding towards them.

His first mental reaction was purely primitive. It was that of a boy with pockets bulging with stolen apples, swarming down a tree into the arms of the owner of them. He was frightened. He felt the hair on the nape of his neck bristling, his stomach muscles contract as though he had been struck a blow. But the sensation passed. His fear became a protective one for Jane, and never had he experienced such a desperate need of swift and clear thinking and self-possession. He had only half-turned. He had not committed himself to the act of recognition. He could pretend for another fraction of a second that he was unaware of Captain Bransby's approach. He turned to look at Jane and his eyes went automatically to the cigarette, which she still held in her hand. He daren't speak, daren't tell her to drop it. But either her hand was temporarily paralysed or she had realised that to try to hide it would have only emphasised her guilt. She stood up, still holding it, and he heard her say in a shaky voice,

"Hallo, Daddy."

It was Edwin's cue. He turned, looked at Tom with affected surprise, and got up. As he did so Tom stopped within a few feet of the fire. It was the first time that Edwin had met him face to face. He hoped in that moment that he would never have to do it again, for never had he seen such hate in a man's expression. He knew the story of Tom Bransby's conversion. He had a clear memory of him as he had been before the miracle had happened; could picture him, never drunk, but walking unsteadily down one of the village streets with a dazed look in his eyes, or wandering about the beach or scaurs shabby and unkempt, carrying his fishing rod or a bait tin, or a bundle of driftwood. He could picture him as he had been the night of the bazaar concert (a picture more deeply engraved in his memory because of his father's ironic comments when he and his aunt had returned home) a transformed man, clean and tidily dressed and, as his father had said, a face shining with holy light. He'd been clean-shaven then and still a little haggard from his illness. Now he wore a moustache, slightly greyed, his cheeks were fuller, but the main lines in them deeper and permanently marked, his skin tanned. He was dressed in rough farmer's clothes, with corduroy trousers, a tweed jacket and heavy hob-nailed boots. He looked tough and formidable, with the thick knotted bullock stick in his right hand.

Not that Edwin had any physical fear for himself. He had a dislike for physical violence, of any sort of quarrelling. But he had learnt boxing as part of his school and university training in athletics. If there were going to be violence he could defend himself. But that was a horrible prospect, more horrible because on the face of things the older man's still unspoken anger was justified. Edwin's fear was for Jane. He was surprised to hear her say, still in a shaky voice yet with an extraordinary dignity,

"This is Mr Edwin Knaggs, Daddy. He came on here collecting sea animals at low tide. And I was collecting seaweeds for school and he helped me. And then he asked me to share his picnic."

She was superb, Edwin thought. She gave him the sudden hope that the threatening storm might be averted. He looked straight at Tom and said,

"Good afternoon, Captain Bransby."

But Tom ignored the salute. He made no movement except an involuntary swallowing gesture, as though to stop his rage choking him. Then glaring at them both he said,

"How long's this been going on?"

"What do you mean, Daddy?"

His voice rose.

"*You* know what I mean. How long have you and him been doing this? I want no lying."

"There's nothing to lie about, Daddy. I've never spoken to Mr Knaggs until today, least not since we were children."

Again Tom made that swallowing gesture. Then he glared at Edwin.

"What's the game?"

"I don't know what you mean, Captain Bransby."

"Don't you? Don't you? You look as though you don't. Innocent, aren't you, like all your sort when you're found out and stopped at your dirty games. What are you doing on here in this lonely spot, sharing a picnic with a young girl like mine? What were you doing just when I came round the corner of the cliff and surprised you at it? What's that girl of mine got in her hand that was in her mouth half a minute ago?"

Involuntarily, Edwin glanced at Jane and the cigarette, and even then he felt a thrill of admiration for her as she held it up like an exhibit at a court trial. Her cheeks were scarlet but her dignity was unaltered.

"Oh, Daddy—I was only doing it for fun. And it was my fault. I persuaded Mr Knaggs to give it to me. It was only for fun."

It was Edwin who had to make a desperate effort to control his anger now. Certainly the circumstantial evidence was strong enough to justify any parent's suspicions that theirs was not a chance meeting, that he and Jane were indeed having a flirtation. To a father of Captain Bransby's puritanical mind smoking for a girl of Jane's age, and his own daughter, too, was something to be shocked about to say the least. But to have Jane blamed for it, to have her take the blame was outrageous. Yet outwardly he remained calm and he too preserved his dignity.

"You're wrong, Captain Bransby, in thinking anything wrong has happened, or could have happened. Your daughter has told you the truth, except about the cigarette, and I'll admit straight away that I can understand you're feeling a bit angry about that, if you object to girls smoking. Many girls do these days. I suppose it's happened because of the war. In any case—"

Tom exploded.

"Are you trying to tell me that what she was doing was right? Are you trying to make out that these women who smoke are respectable? I know you and the home you've come from. I know your father, a mocking atheist and anti-Christ. Like father like son. You'll be another scoffer. If you didn't come on special to meet my daughter, what right has one of your sort to make up to a young girl like her and offer her food, never mind tobacco?"

It was only Jane's presence, the knowledge that she

was suffering tortures of embarrassment, that kept Edwin's anger under control. He answered still steadily,

"You're putting a wrong meaning on things. It's natural enough that I should speak to Jane, seeing that we nearly bumped into each other round one of those big rocks. And as she was collecting seaweed and I was looking for marine animals, it was natural that we should talk about our jobs. I can see no harm in asking her to share my tea and grub. As for the cigarette I offered her one as I would to anyone I was with. And the first time she refused. I'll admit that it was silly of me and perhaps wrong, seeing that she had never smoked before, to persuade her again. The fault was not hers anyway but mine. And I'm just sorry that you should be so hurt about it."

Jane suddenly rushed over to her father, and took him by the arm. Her face had gone deadly pale.

"Oh, Daddy—Daddy," she implored, and she was nearly crying. "Do believe it's true. All except about the cigarette, and I *did* ask for one the second time. But it was only for fun. I didn't really light it. I promise I'll never do it again. But don't go on being angry."

Her physical contact, and what she said, may have mollified his anger towards herself. He shook her off, but not roughly.

"You're only a child," he said to her. "You're too young to understand what this sort of thing means. Get your ways home. . . but *you're* not a child!" he blazed at Edwin again. "I've no doubt you've had plenty of practice. And like your father you've got a glib enough tongue. I'll tell you straight, if I'd found you laying hands on that girl of mine, I'd have put this stick across your

241

back. I'd have thrashed you black and blue, although maybe you're more to be pitied than blamed, the way you've been brought up. I want to hear no more from you, only understand this, if you try this on again with my girl look out for yourself. She's been brought up in a religious home. She's pure and I'll not have her contaminated by someone smart like you. Don't you dare to speak to her again. . . . Now get your ways home, Jane, at once."

Edwin said nothing. He had a powerful sense of justice and fair play. He was stung. No one had ever spoken to him like this before. But he knew that he was dealing with a man who, temporarily at least, was not far from being insane and utterly incapable of being reasoned with. Jane had turned to go, and in the last agonised glance she gave him, he knew that his silence was not being mistaken for cowardice. Without speaking again Tom turned too, striding after her as she took the high water track along which he had appeared. It led round a bluff of the under-cliff to one of the several ways into which the main cliff path separated before reaching the shore. He did not overtake her and she did not look back either at him or at Edwin. The last he saw of her was when she reached the bluff, walking erect, and with her left hand raised in that familiar gesture, holding back her hair. And it was at that moment—as though the curtain had fallen on the play which had begun when she had come round the rock reciting—the advance waves of the fog driven swifter by the increasing sea wind reached the shore and, swirling upwards against the ramparts of the cliff, shut out the sky and the sun. He stared at the bluff round which Tom himself had now vanished. Then his gaze shifted to the still smouldering fire, with the billy resting cock-eyed in the embers, to the flat stone on which Jane had spread the food, to the unwanted cheesecake and the splinters of the lobster's claw. It seemed incredible that only a few minutes ago she had been kneeling there chattering and smiling while she ate and drank. He imagined suddenly that he could hear her voice. He listened intently, but all that he could hear was the gentle splashing of the incoming tide among the now almost invisible rocks and the desolate cry of a gull from the sea. He felt that he had never been so miserable in his life.

2

IT WAS nearly seven o'clock and, with the fog, completely dark. Will Knaggs was in his study in an easy-chair by the fire with a book in his hand, trying to concentrate, but glancing repeatedly at the clock and all the time listening for the sound of his son opening the street door. He was late and that was unusual for Edwin. A few minutes ago Aunt Betsy had shouted up from the kitchen that the fish was nearly done and whatever could have happened to the lad? She'd give him a scolding if it got dried and spoilt through having to be kept on the oven top. And it was a bit of lemon sole too—his favourite! . . . He knew she would shout again—why the devil should women make such a fuss?—when she heard the clock strike seven, and he put the book down and started watching the minute hand as it crept upwards. . .

Nothing bad could have happened, of course. The fog was thick, judging by the steamer horns blowing in the bay, but if anyone could look after himself along Bramblewick beach it was Edwin. If the spring flood had caught him on High Batts he could have come along the cliff tops, or he might have waited till the ebb and that would make him late. Still, he hoped he was not going to be very late. He wished he could hear the door open and Edwin's cheery "Hallo everybody", that they could get supper over and then get settled down here for the rest of the evening. Another fortnight and the lad would be away again. There was little enough time for all the things they had to talk about.

It was a big square low-ceilinged room. Aunt Betsy sometimes referred to it ironically as "the holy of holies". It had been one of her chief worries when Edwin was in the explorer stage of childhood to keep him out of it. But to Edwin it was "the museum" and it had been a red-letter day in his more advanced boyhood when his father had formally given him the freedom of it, putting him on trust not to damage any of the collections of butterflies or stuffed birds or fossils; to handle all the books carefully and always put them back exactly where he found them. Museum it certainly was, but it was also the living-room of a student. There were loaded bookshelves along three walls of it, with a revolving bookcase just on the left side of the easy-chair, and a radio cabinet close at hand. On top of the shelves were mahogany cabinets with innumerable drawers. Here were the butterflies and moths, marine and freshwater shells, fossils, flint implements. Between the cabinets on the walls were glass cases containing stuffed birds, fish, and bigger insects. And on the wide mantelshelf, placed centrally like a cross on the altar of a church, between two heavy brass candlesticks, was a plaster bust of Charles Darwin, whose benevolent bearded face bore a strong resemblance to that of Jehovah in the Sistine ceiling painting of Michelangelo.

Sitting there in his chair, surrounded by so many symbols of an intellectual life, it would have been difficult to picture the smith in the setting of the Mariners Tavern. But for a long time he had ceased to be a regular evening guest at the Mariners—not from any ethical reasons. He hadn't caught what he would have called Tom Bransby's disease; he hadn't gone teetotal. But drinking to him had always been a social affair, and society to him meant talking, holding forth, argument—and that necessitated the company of other men who, if not convivial or even congenial, must be at least tolerably intelligent. Captain Christopher, who undoubtedly had possessed that quality (although he had always been a hard man to draw into an argument), had long since gone to the Old Churchyard on the brow of the hill that overlooks Bramblewick Bay from the north, his name added to that of his two sailor sons (who had died "out foreign") and his wife on a modest headstone next door but one to that which marked the grave of old Jake Bransby. Hutchins, Chief Officer of Coastguards, had been pensioned from the service, and with his cantankerous daughter had gone back to live in his native Essex. Mrs Bunny was still alive and Sam came home at regular intervals, but the passing years had done nothing to sharpen his never particularly bright intelligence, and it was the same with Jonty Scaife, whose own official retirement was imminent and who, by the time he had drunk his second pint of beer, would sink into a sort of stupor that might have been pleasant for himself, but was exasperating for someone holding forth on such a topic as, for example, Nazism.

The smith too was showing certain physical signs of his advancing age. His once black hair and moustache were tinged with grey; his years of stooping over the anvil had now permanently rounded his shoulders, and some of the satanic gleam had gone from his eyes. He may have mellowed a little, lost some of his arrogance and churlishness, but his mind was as alert as ever. He read voraciously. One evening every week he would catch the five o'clock bus to Burnharbour and stay until dosing time in the public reading room, poring over the scientific and political weekly and monthly journals and reviews, making notes of anything that especially interested him, and always landing home with at least one volume from the reference library. He listened to all serious talks on the radio, including those on religion, and even to religious services if Betsy was out (for he was very fond of her and respected her stolid fidelity to the church and would not have liked to think that he listened only to mock). He did not belong to any political party. He took the daily labour newspaper, but he also read the conservative and liberal and independent dailies and always read the leaders in each, so that (with the radio) he had a well-balanced, if not necessarily accurate, picture of what was going on in his own country and in the outside world. He wasn't happy about what was going on either at home or abroad. After the six o'clock news tonight he had listened to a talk by a political commentator, which had worried him very much indeed. It was one of the things he wanted to talk about with Edwin after supper. The speaker had been discreet, as most radio commentators were, but he'd as much as said that in his opinion Hitler was more dangerous than even the Kaiser had been and that it was time that the British took their blinkers off.

The clock struck seven and, as he had expected, there came a shout up the stairs,

"Is that clock right, Will?"

He shouted back,

"Aye, of course! I set it by the wireless."

"Then whatever can have happened to Edwin!"

"He'll be all right. He must have waited for the tide to ebb."

He picked up the book again, but again he could not concentrate. His mind was on Edwin, and what the man had been saying. . .

It was now the middle "thirties". *Mein Kampf* had been published. Hindenburg was dead. Hitler had assumed supreme and uncontrolled authority in Germany, and the war of nerves had begun. The smith had not been able to get hold of a copy of *Mein Kampf*, but he had read extracts from it and studied comments, many of which suggested that Hitler was merely a showman and a gigantic bluffer: that he was out to get what he could for Germany by shouting a lot and pretending that the country was recreating its army and air force and war factories, but that if it came to a threat of real war he'd fizzle out like a damp firework. Other commentators (including the one he had heard tonight) shared the opposite view. The danger was real and the most alarming aspect of it was our own national complacence. Britain herself should be rearming. Where was the truth of it all? Might not this be another form of propaganda to persuade the British taxpayer to accept a bigger burden in order to pull our almost moribund heavy industries out of the slump? All of these industries had been in a bad way for years. Shipping and shipbuilding (a thing the smith knew something about as, during the war, he had worked in a Teesside yard) were almost at a standstill. Three-quarters at least of our Merchant Navy was laid up. Almost every shipyard in the north-east was empty. The building of the giant Cunard *Queen Mary* on the Clyde had been suspended and all her workers were on the dole. A big rearmament programme would soon set our blast furnaces and steel mills and shipyards going again. It would be a magic cure for unemployment, and the big bosses, the capitalists, would be able to smile again at their shareholder meetings!

It was hard to get at the truth, but the smith never saw a picture of Adolf Hitler in the papers without experiencing a certain misgiving that he would not have admitted was fear. It wasn't often a week went by without him seeing such a picture. The man was "news" and mostly they were "news" photographs: Hitler at a conference of Nazi chiefs; Hitler presenting prizes at a sports gathering; Hitler receiving a bouquet of flowers from a little girl at the opening of a Youth Festival; Hitler with his mouth wide open, caught by an ultra-rapid snapshot during one of his mass harangues. It was not, the smith thought, a vicious or a cruel face. There was none of the Kaiser's haughty swank about it. His moustache was ridiculous. It looked as though it was stuck on to his lip with elastic and that it would see-saw when he talked like that of a music-hall comedian. He did not feel that behind that forehead was an exceptional intellect like Shaw's, or Napoleon's or Darwin's. It was not the face of a genius, good or bad. But it was—and the photo where he was spouting showed it best of all—the face of a fanatic or a man possessed of a single dominating idea to sway other people to his own way of thinking and action. He was a preacher, a revivalist. He looked as though he had just the same sort of power as those Welsh revivalists had when they drove their audiences into a state of religious frenzy with their preaching and their hymn-singing. The optimists might be right about him. That there should be another war with Germany was against all reason, but religion was against all reason in his opinion. And more wars had been fought in the name of religion than for any other cause, and among the bloodiest in the name of Judaism and Christianity. Nazism, like Bolshevism, was just another religion if you took the word to mean a system of faith and worship. Hitler might be a bluffer, but he was a fanatic, capable of bluffing himself and the German people with his extravagant notions of their superiority. It might lead to war, and to a war to which the last one would seem like a brawl in a pub. AND IF IT CAME EDWIN WOULD BE IN IT. . .

He glanced at the clock (it was five minutes past seven) and down at his book again. It was one of his favourite works of Robert Ingersoll, the American anti-cleric. But he could not read. He wasn't worried about Edwin being late, but about what the future held for him—a future which, but for what was happening in Germany, had seemed to hold no possibility of failure. There was nothing that lad couldn't do if he set his mind to it. It wasn't beyond him to become one of the greatest scientists of his time, and he was not just going by what he as a father felt. His schoolmasters, his professors—all had prophesied for him a brilliant career, and everything was going in his favour. Some parents were envious of their son's success. He himself would have liked Edwin's opportunities, and if he'd had them he wouldn't now be a blacksmith. But he wasn't jealous. He was just proud and thankful to see in him the product of a rational, common-sense upbringing, free of all religious humbug. Cant, humbug, stupidity—that's what was wrong with modern civilisation. Undoubtedly, religion had played its part in human evolution. Anything that taught people to behave themselves was good. But, as Shaw had shown in his *Black Girl in Her Search for God*, religions became out of date as evolution advanced. Shaw of course argued that there was something else. He seemed indeed to argue that there was an afterlife in which man might attain perfection. The smith could not accept that. Life was a continuous thing. But there was only one life for the individual. Man had only invented the myth of personal survival from personal fear of death and an exaggerated sense of his own importance, or—and the thought seemed to rise from his stomach like a nauseating spasm—AS A DOPE AGAINST THE AGONY OF LOSING SOMEONE YOU LOVED. . .

He felt a cold sweat on his temples. He clenched his fists till the knuckles were white and he muttered, half aloud, staring at the empty chair opposite to him where after supper his son would be sitting,

"If there's a war. If Edwin's killed. . ."

And it was then that he heard the sound of footsteps in the passage below the window, the sound of the sneck and the street door opening, and Edwin's voice,

"Hallo! Sorry I'm so late, Aunty. Forgive me, won't you?" and almost instantly Aunt Betsy's voice up the stairs, pretending to be vexed,

"Here he is, Will. Get your ways down for supper or it won't be worth eating," and to Edwin, "Eee—you have worried me. But I'll forgive you if you look sharp, but you can change your shoes first. You look wet through. Where have you been?" And again up the stairs, "Have you gone to sleep, Will? Edwin's back and supper's ready. Are you coming? You know I've got a church meeting tonight."

Will Knaggs had got to his feet. Very deliberately he placed the book he had been trying to read back in the bookcase. Then he braced himself and licked his lips, which had gone dry, and he made himself laugh aloud and shout,

"You and your meetings! You'd do better to stay at home and read a good book. Glad you're back, Edwin. I'm coming."

He turned down the gas and moved to the door. But he was still shaking inside him and he was muttering to himself,

"It won't—it can't happen. . . If it does Edwin won't be in it. I'll warn him. I'll have it out with him tonight."

3

IT WAS perhaps a tribute to the smith's success as a parent that Edwin rarely felt self-conscious with him. Their relationship had developed into that of old friends with Edwin showing an instinctive, but not an exaggerated, deference due to his father's age and experience, and the smith, aware of his son's potentially greater mental gifts, shedding all the arrogance and self-assertiveness that had made him so unpopular in the village. Since he had grown up Edwin had never felt the need to cloak his personal life. Certainly he had not told his father the details of any of his mild love affairs, for that would have been a breach of loyalty to the ladies concerned, but he would have said more about them if his father had shown a livelier interest. He had no sense of guilt about them. Certainly he had no sense of guilt about this afternoon's happenings but, during the melancholy hours that had elapsed since he had watched Tom Bransby and Jane disappear into the fog (he had allowed them an hour's start before following their route up the cliff) he had decided to keep silent about the whole business. It went against the grain to do this. Invariably, when he got back from an expedition his father would be eager to know what he had found, to see and examine his specimens and discuss them. He had no specimens. He had instead a mixed bag of experiences, undoubtedly to be reckoned among the happiest and most dismal in his life. They were all intimately

connected with each other and could not be disintegrat-
ed. He knew from the moment his father entered the
room that he was going to lie to him, negatively anyway.
But in that moment he knew, by instinct, that his father
was troubled too. Not that there was any anger
or disapproval in his expression. He said again, "I'm
glad you're back, Edwin," but Edwin knew there was
something wrong, that something (and it was not just his
being late for supper) had upset him and that his added
"And how did you get on?" was perfunctory and not the
usual eager invitation to him to start a recital of his day's
doings. Dutifully, he had sat down and was taking off
his wet boots. And he answered perfunctorily, with a
half lie,

"Oh, not so bad. It was a good ebb. I saw a few
nudibranchs, but nothing rare. I found a small octopus.
Oh, and I had a grand swim!"

Aunt Betsy, carrying the hot plates to the table,
looked—or pretended to look—shocked.

"What! Do you mean to say you took off all your
clothes and went bathing this time of year? I wonder
what you'll do next! And staying out late without
a proper meal, with a fog on and an east wind. Enough
to give you double pneumonia. Now hurry and get
something hot inside you. And don't say you've brought
a live octopus home with you like you did that adder
and left it for me to find in the coalhouse when I went to
fill the scuttle. *Eee!* you're almost as daft as your father!"

As Edwin moved to sit at the table he put his arm
round her shoulder and gave her a hug.

"It's all right, Aunty. I didn't bring it home!"

He had a deep affection for his aunt. She was two

years older than his father. Like him, she was dark and, as so often happens with people with a bodily deformity, she had a very beautiful face. It was the sort of face Edwin often thought that the Italian masters had all sought to portray in their paintings of the Madonna: noble, serene, benevolent, and above everything spiritual. She had a lovely voice too. He had, as a boy (and this without his father's instigation) hated going to church. He had gone because it had given her such pleasure, and one of the compensations for the boredom of the service was being close to Aunt Betsy, dressed in her lavender-scented best Sunday black silk, with her gold jewellery, hearing her sing—especially the straight hymns when she really let herself go. She wasn't hump-backed, but she had been born with a form of spinal curvature, and one of her legs was shorter than the other so that she had to wear boots with a false sole and she walked with a limp. . . He was used to her fussing and he liked it and was glad of it now as a temporary distraction. It gave him a chance to look obliquely at his father and he was relieved to see him grinning and apparently at ease again as he took his chair and lifted the cover from the dish which Aunt Betsy had placed alongside the hot plates.

"Burnt to a cinder!" he said ironically. "I don't think! Your auntie's not a bad cook. Only she makes too much fuss. . . Pity you didn't fetch that octopus. I've often had an idea I'd like to taste one. I've read somewhere that they're reckoned a great delicacy in Italy like snails and frogs in France."

"Don't be disgusting," Aunt Betsy admonished. "Are you sure that shirt of yours is dry, Edwin?"

"Of course it is. I didn't bathe with my clothes on. Sit down, Aunty, and have some food yourself. By Jove— it's lemon sole, isn't it?"

"She made a special trip to Burnharbour to get it for you, lad. You ought to feel honoured."

"Well we don't see that much of him we can't afford to spoil him a bit while he's home. There's some mince pies to follow, but I fear they'll have gone a bit dry with keeping on the oven top."

The smith never talked much at meals. His study was the place for that and he always had a very healthy appetite. Yet again Edwin got the impression that he was preoccupied with something other than the meal when he said almost casually,

"It was a good ebb then."

"Yes, but I've known bigger."

"Aye. It doesn't follow that you get the lowest ebb at the equinox. You'd come the cliff way back?"

"Yes. I had to, but the tide's ebbing now again."

"I'm glad you're safe home," Aunt Betsy put in. "Those cliffs aren't at all safe when it gets dark with a fog. Pass your plate for some more chips, Edwin. What about you, Will? There's plenty of everything. Are you sure that clock was right? I mustn't be late for the meeting."

Yes, his father was troubled, or he wouldn't have let that last remark pass without a gentle gibe! He didn't want any more fish. He toyed with the mince pie when it came. And Edwin observed his relief when supper was over, and Aunt Betsy, firmly refusing their help, started clearing the things. She too could be ironic.

"You two get away into your own room. I know you'll be wanting to talk scientific and get all the problems of the world put straight. As though science could do that. Wasn't that man you were listening to on the wireless saying there was going to be another war? What rubbish! But I could only hear bits of it when the frying pan wasn't sizzling. Don't forget to look to the kitchen fire while I'm out. I know you'll expect some supper when I come back. Now off you go both of you out of my way. . ."

Edwin gave her a quick hug, and thanked her for the meal, which in spite of his own mental preoccupation he had enjoyed, and he followed his father up the stairs. He waited on the threshold of the study while his father turned up the gas, feeling a little nervous, wondering what was coming, and the thought crossed his mind: had he, somehow or other, found out what had happened at High Batts this afternoon? Did he know about the scene with Tom Bransby? But that was impossible unless he had been watching them with field-glasses, and he would never do that: not spy deliberately. Besides he was not angry. He was only worried; a fact that became more obvious as the gas went up and he turned and said almost furtively,

"Shut the door, Edwin. Ah—I'm glad we're by ourselves at last. Get sat down in your chair. There's your fags on the mantelshelf. We'll have a bottle of ale later on, but I want to talk first. Did you hear what your aunty said just now? About the chap talking on the wireless, saying there might be another war. It's a thing I've been going to ask you ever since you came back from Donbridge, but there's been so many other things that have been more interesting to you and me. I want to have your opinion. You're living among the brains. You must be closer in touch with what's really going on than me in this spot. I read all I can lay hands on. But one paper says one thing and another paper the opposite, and you never know where you are. And tonight there was this chap talking about Hitler. What do you make of it?"

Edwin was relieved. After all it seemed that the worry was not a personal one. But he was still puzzled. He lit a cigarette. His father had sat down now, and was staring at him with a quite unusual intensity.

"Do you mean what do I think about Hitler?"

"Aye. Do you think he's just a gasbag? Or do you think he means business? What are they saying about him at the university?"

Edwin laughed.

"Why honestly I don't know. I don't think anyone thinks there's going to be another war. It would be silly anyway seeing that we haven't recovered from the last one, which we were supposed to have won. But I've never been interested in that sort of thing. I don't take history or economics. They'd bore me."

"But you've got an Officers' Training Corps at the university. I read about that in the paper. They had them in universities before the last war, and those who were in them were called up when the army was mobilised, and given commissions. And I'll bet three-quarters of them were slaughtered before the war ended— slaughtered or maimed for life. Officers stood less chance than the Tommies in the trenches. The Germans used to have special sharp-shooters to pick 'em off. I've heard Jonty Scaife say they lost every one of the young officers in his battalion in one week when they were up in the line. . . I've never asked you before, Edwin, but you're not in the Officers' Training Corps, are you?"

It was dawning on Edwin what his father was getting at, but he hadn't yet realised how deeply was his concern.

"No, of course I'm not, or I'd have told you. I was asked to join my first term, but it just didn't appeal, learning how to form fours, and musket drill, and marching. Another thing—they go into camp in summer vacation. I shouldn't have liked giving up even a weekend at home. And I'm sure I wouldn't like to be a soldier."

The smith looked less worried.

"Ah—I should think not. I should think not. Soldiering's only for those who have a natural liking for it, or for those who have no brains at all. It's a mug's game for anyone like you. Mind, when it comes to it, and your own country's in danger, it's up to every man to do his bit. But it doesn't follow he does his bit best by fighting in the line. I was tempted to join up in '14, in spite of just being married to your poor mother. I wanted to be in khaki or navy blue like most other young men. I remember seeing Jonty in his soldier's uniform again, instead of his postman's rigout, and some of Bramblewick's ships' officers, who never wore any sort of uniform at their ordinary job, appearing in Naval Reserve togs with gold braid round their sleeves, one of 'em even a lieutenant-commander. I won't say they swanked, but I'll admit I envied them, for no one knew then what the war was going to be really like. In fact that August there was a rumour that the whole German Navy had been sunk in its first engagement and that the Kaiser had already asked for peace terms. But it was excitement and I wanted to be in it. I thought it might be a chance of travelling abroad, if only to Germany. The chap at the Burnharbour recruiting office told me, as I was in a trade of my own and married, I'd better think it over before taking the King's shilling and, as I've often told you—and I'm not ashamed of it—I'd shut up the shop and was up on the Tees in a shipbuilding yard by the time conscription came in, and I wouldn't have been allowed to go then if I'd wanted to. I was a foreman and ships were being needed more than ever for the war. I was more use doing that than being in the trenches."

It flashed through Edwin's mind that as a boy he'd sometimes felt secretly ashamed that his father had not been in the Army or Navy. Other boys had boasted about the medals their fathers had won. No less than five local ships' officers had been awarded Distinguished Service Crosses for fighting U-boats, and convoy work. The War Memorial in the Parish Church bore the names of more than fifty local men who had lost their lives at sea or in the fighting on land. Some of the boys had taunted him about his father being only a munition worker, and he'd had more than one fight defending the family honour. He had never thought that his father was a coward or a shirker. And he knew now that he was not saying all this to defend himself. He wished, however, that the conversation would take a less personal turn. He said,

"I know that, Father. But anyway you needn't bother about me and the OTC. Besides, this is my last term. And I don't believe there's going to be another war between us and Germany. We have quite a lot of German students at Donbridge. We have two in zoology, both very decent chaps, and but for their accents you couldn't tell them from Englishmen. Surely the last war has taught the world that war just doesn't pay. It leaves the victors as badly off as the losers, if not worse off. And another war would be worse than the last because of the aeroplanes and the progress made in science since then."

"Aye, I know that," the smith said slowly. "If there's another war it will make the last one look like the battle of Hastings. It'll all be tanks and aeroplanes and gas and maybe disease germs. It'll all be scientific. There'll be no trenches. Infantry and rifles will be as out of date as bowmen and bows and arrows. I think H. G. Wells is a bit of an exaggerator, but things he prophesied before the last war came true, and I won't say he's not right about what may come unless science is put to its right uses. I'm bothered. I'll admit it. I don't trust this chap Hitler. He's too much like one of them religious revivalists. We haven't treated the Germans altogether right since the war ended. It's a bloody muck-up on the Continent, and I don't know what to make of Russia either. . . I'm bothered about you, Edwin. You're all I've got. I've been ambitious for you. But I've never tried to push you into anything just to please myself. You've had a free choice. I've done my best to help you choose what you want to be. But I'll not say I'm not proud and satisfied you've chosen to be a biologist, like that grand chap there on the mantelshelf. You'll get your degree this summer. You'll get that scholarship all right. I want to see you at the top of the tree. One of the world's greatest scientists. I don't want you to go as cannon fodder."

For a moment Edwin felt incapable of looking directly at his father. In his mind he was back in the cove at High Batts, looking at Jane kneeling before the fire, telling her—almost shouting at her—that he didn't want to be a biologist but a painter! He had never held such a high ambition for himself as his father had done. Even he had never expressed his hopes in words like these before. It gave him a shock. It was absurd, of course, that he should even think of chucking his career and taking up painting. But he knew too that he would have to paint again, that science was no longer the single goal of his life. And he knew that, if his father could read his thoughts in that moment, he would be staggered. For the second time that day he felt the desperate need for swift and clear thinking, for supreme tact. His father must not be given as much as an inkling of what had happened at High Batts. But in avoiding the head-on collision he skidded badly. He said, with only half his mind behind it, and laughingly,

"Don't you worry, Father, I've no ambition to be cannon fodder. If there were another war I'd want to be in the air, not fighting in the mud. Do you remember that model glider you helped me to make when I was a school kid? There's a chap at the university, an engineer student, who's quite crazy about model aircraft and has dozens he's made himself, and we've got quite pally. But he's also a member of a real glider club. They have meetings at a place up in the Pennines. He took me out there behind his motorbike one day and I actually had a short trip with him in a dual-control glider. It wasn't a good day. There wasn't enough wind and we didn't climb more than a couple of hundred feet, but the sensation was grand, far more exciting than sailing a boat, and the thrilling thing is there's absolutely no sound. I remember you once explaining to me how a seagull flies above a cliff face (we were on the cliff at Low Batts, I think), how it sort of sits on the wind or the upward current of air and scarcely has to move its wings at all, and that's just what it was like in a glider."

He knew before he had finished that he was getting into difficulties. He was not surprised to hear a real reproach in his father's voice when he said,

"You never told me you'd been flying, Edwin."

He had to half-lie again.

"No. But I meant to. And I'd have written and told you at the time, but then I thought auntie might have been worried. Not that there was any danger, of course."

The smith was ironic.

"Nay, there never was any danger in flying. . . It's all right," he added quickly. "I'm not vexed. You're grown up. You have a right to do what you like and it would be against all my principles to try and stop you doing a thing just because it was dangerous. When I saw you climb up your first real tree right up to the top I was anxious all right, but I knew I'd have been daft to try and stop you doing it. It must have been, as you say, a grand sensation flying in a glider. I remember explaining that about the gulls. It used to puzzle me how they could stay in the air, almost motionless, then swoop down and turn and climb again without a stroke of their wings. I'll admit I often wished I could do it myself. I was born a generation too soon. You're in the real age of science, Edwin. Only I'm half-wondering if after all it's going to be such an improvement. You haven't joined that glider club, have you?"

Too obviously he was trying to make the remark

sound casual. Edwin was on his guard now.

"No, I've only made that one trip. The place is a long way out. They've got very few machines and a big membership, and even my pal considers himself lucky if he gets one flip a month."

"Then what made you say you'd want to fly if there was another war? Do you think that flying would be any safer than being an ordinary soldier?"

"I was just joking. There won't be another war."

For a moment the smith just stared in silence at his son. Then he said ponderously,

"I hope you're right, Edwin. I hope you're right. I'm sorry if I got a bit gloomy about things. I shouldn't have listened to that chap on the wireless. I've got my heart set on you making a big name for yourself. Another war would finish that no matter what else happened. You're too healthy a chap not to be called up. I'm glad you're not in the Training Corps, anyway, and I won't say I'm not pleased you haven't taken too strongly to this gliding business. That's what the Germans are supposed to be doing—teaching their lads to fly in gliders so that they'll be able to fly real planes quicker. But there you are! It's maybe all talk and propaganda. I think I heard your aunty go out just now. I've got a couple of bottles of ale in the pantry. We'll have a drink and talk about summat else than war. I'd like to see one of those gliders. But more than anything I'd like to see that flying machine that can go straight up and down and hover."

Edwin had got up.

"I'll get the beer, Father. I heard Aunt Betsy go out so that's all right. Yes, you mean the autogyro. . ."

He was relieved. The danger for the time being at any

rate was passed. Autogyros would be a safe enough subject to talk about when he got back and the beer itself would make a diversion. There was only a short flight of stairs to the kitchen and he left the study door open. But as he reached the kitchen he heard hurried steps on the cobbles outside. There was a loud knock on the street door, and at the same time it opened and he was startled to see the local constable, who spoke urgently,

"Now, Edwin, is your father at home?"

Before he could answer the smith shouted down the stairs,

"Aye? What is it?"

"I want you to come quick and open the door of the Wesleyan Chapel schoolroom. We've an idea that summat bad's happened to old Captain Fosdyck. He was seen going in there about four o'clock—carrying a rope. Door's locked from inside and key's in it. . . but we don't want to smash it down if we can get it opened without. He may be all right, but what would he want to lock the door behind him for?"

The smith had appeared and he was looking vexed.

"Why?" he demanded. "Because it's the only way to keep that door shut from inside. Sneck won't work and never would. That old skinflint would never pay to have a new one fitted! What do you think he's done—hanged himself?" he added sarcastically. "You'll find he's gone to sleep trying to read his Bible."

He had suddenly become the surly arrogant tub-thumper of the Mariners, but the policeman was unperturbed.

"I hope it is so. But he had an engagement to meet the Wesleyan Superintendent at six o'clock this evening.

He'd come over special from Burnharbour to meet him, and the captain was never one to forget an engagement. Besides, he always has his tea at five o'clock. He's nearly ninety, you know. He may have had a seizure. And what would he want that rope for?"

The smith was already putting on his coat.

"He'll have been at some job or other," he said. "Mending summat. Trying to save a few bob that might go to a workman. You ought to know what he is by now."

He took a small toolkit from a drawer in the kitchen dresser and said to Edwin,

"Are you coming? It would be a pity to miss the excitement."

They hurried down the road and turned into Chapel Street, none of them speaking, their footfalls sounding loud in the silence of the deserted and still fog-bound village. The light from the occasional street lamps was haloed and curtailed by the fog so that the cottages had no visible roofs, and their oddly-shaped walls seemed unsubstantial, like scenery in a play. Again Edwin had the sensation that he was in a sort of *Alice in Wonderland* fantasy, only now it was a morbid one. The sensation grew stronger as they reached the chapel and he saw, in the light of the gas lamp that was actually fixed on the chapel wall, a small group of men and women standing in front of the schoolroom door: all silent and expectant like a funeral party waiting for the coffin to emerge from a house and the procession start.

But among them, as a sure evidence of reality, he recognised the tall figure of Jonty Scaife, and the short podgy one of his wife (who seemed to have a special instinct for being on the spot "when owt was up"). His father and the police constable were realistic enough in the way they tackled the door. The constable shone his torch on the keyhole. The smith inserted the head of a pair of fine pliers, seized the key end, gave it a gentle twist and the door opened inwards on its own accord. There was a stir among the onlookers, but the constable, taking official charge, said sternly,

"Now keep back there. This isn't a peepshow. We don't want any ladies. There's maybe summat happened in there that won't be pleasant to look at."

He shone his torch up the long corridor, then he said,

"Come on, Will, we'll go first. Come on, you men."

Gladly Edwin would have stayed outside. He had no relish for the macabre, and it made him feel no better when, following close upon her husband, Polly said indignantly,

"Did you ever hear such daftness? As though women aren't as good as men. It's always a woman has to lay a body out, and it's usually me, too, in this spot. It was me the bobby sent for when them dead sailors washed up in the war, and they must have been dead a fortnight. *Eee* one of 'em had no head. . ."

But he felt he could not desert his father, and he followed on down the corridor. As he reached the schoolroom his father was just lighting the gas. Instantly it became apparent to everyone that, dead or alive, the captain was not present in that room which had been the scene of so many of his social and devotional activities. But for the forms and trestle tables neatly piled at the end where Gwen Jones had built her stage it was empty, and the constable's voice echoed as though in an empty church when he said,

"Well, he's not here. Can he have got into the chapel from here?"

Polly Scaife made her presence known by answering him.

"Nay. He could have done once, but he had t' door stopped-up after some of t' Sunday School bairns got into t' vestry and started larkin' wi' t' collecting boxes. But he couldn't have gone out and locked t' street door from inside, could he? . . . and look—isn't that his jacket lying on the window-shelf? It takes a woman to see things in spite of 'em not being wanted."

The constable moved across to the farthest of the three windows, which in daytime looked out on the once day-school playground and the sea. He held up the jacket that was lying there and someone said,

"Aye, that's his all right!"

But the smith with just a glance at the jacket had moved on to the door beyond that window: a door which as an old day scholar he must have remembered well. He said grimly,

"This is where he must have gone. . . Aye, the door's unlocked. Bring your torch. And I've already an idea what he's been at. . . We'll see when we get outside."

The door opened on a narrow passage with a flight of stone steps rising to the level of the playground. The playground reached the length of the school and chapel buildings, but it was less than fifteen feet from the building to the sheer edge of cliff from which it was protected by a tall fence of stout planks. Repeatedly, in the long history of the now obsolete day school, this fence had been shifted inwards as the cliff face had shot away. On more than one occasion in stormy wet weather the fence itself had gone into the sea. Edwin was not the last to reach the playground, but by the time he had done so there were at least five persons (including the undauntable Polly and her husband) standing by his father and the constable. All were looking towards the fence which despite the fog was lit by the incandescent gas lamp shining through the schoolroom windows. And as he moved forward he saw that where they were looking several of the vertical planks had been torn away, leaving one splintered and jagged post. The planks on each side of the gap were leaning outwards to the cliff edge and the invisible sea. The constable was shining his torch through the gap, his father peering forward, and now he took the torch from the constable, stepped warily through the gap and moved from sight beyond it. The constable shouted, anxiously,

"Be careful there."

But his warning was unnecessary. The smith had moved back through the gap and he now said very quietly,

"He's gone. It's as clear as daylight what's happened. Cliff's been shooting away. There were some stakes driven into the clay down to the shale just in front of the fence to make a sort of staith. He must have been trying to repair them. I reckon he'd have the rope round his waist and tied to the fence in case he slipped. Well, he must have slipped or gone dizzy. And the fence must have given way. Are you going to have a look?"

He handed the torch back to the constable, who very gingerly moved through the gap and very quickly back again. But he continued to direct the light of his torch through the gap, and the onlookers, including Edwin, had crowded round.

"You're right," he said. "You can see the marks on the clay where he must have slid. It's a fifty-foot drop to the bottom, isn't it?"

"It's more than that," put in Jonty, "and it's a straight drop."

"It would be no use trying to get down with a rope. Anyway, the tide's not down yet. You can hear it. What about a boat?"

"Less use still," said the smith. "There's some big stones just below here. Some of 'em will almost be dry with the tide ebbing. By the time a boat was launched there wouldn't be enough water to float it. Besides, he didn't go over just now. He must have gone hours ago, with the tide high and only starting to ebb."

"And t' tide would be running strong to norrard," put in another of the male onlookers, a retired seafarer. "Unless he washed straight out to sea I reckon we'll find him along Lower Batts scaur when t' tide's down, but it'll be hard finding him in this fog. We'll need every lantern there is in Bramblewick."

"Aye—we will," said Polly, "and lucky if he's found at all until the tenth day, when a drownded body floats."

The constable was still directing his torch through the gap, its beam throwing a circular pattern on the wall of fog that hid all that lay below the edge of the cliff over which Captain Fosdyck had unquestionably fallen to his death. . . It occurred to Edwin in the brief ensuing silence that no word or sign of sorrow had come from any of the onlookers. He had never known his father calmer, more matter of fact, or more efficient. The constable seemed to be depending entirely on his judgment; to be waiting now for him to speak. And he did speak, very quietly, almost solemnly, almost humbly without a trace of sarcasm or arrogance.

"Aye—he's gone. He must be dead. If he wasn't killed when he hit the water he'd sink like a stone, a man of his weight, and he'd be drowned. I'll say this for him. He had guts. There's not many chaps of his age would have climbed over this fence to do a job like that, even if it was daft, and only to save the chapel a few bob" . . . and suddenly his manner became brisk again, efficient. "What's to be done now—eh?" he said to the constable. "We'll be able to get round under the cliff in a few minutes, from the slipway. If there's a crowd of us we can cover all the scaurs to Low Batts as the tide ebbs. I expect you'll want to let the coastguards know. We'll go and get lanterns and get as many chaps as we can find."

"Aye." The constable agreed quickly. "I'll give the coastguards a ring. And I'll have to report it to the Superintendent of Police at Burnharbour. . . We'll leave all this as it is and get those doors locked. Come on now all of you, there's been enough sight-seeing."

There was a movement back to the schoolroom door and Edwin found himself at his father's side again.

"It's a bloody nuisance, this," he said. "It's going to mess up our evening. No need for you to come unless you like. Chances are we won't find him anyway, but I've sort of got to go."

"Of course I'm coming," Edwin answered, and he couldn't help adding, for it had moved him very deeply, given him an extraordinary thrill of pride, "I'm glad you said that about the captain, Father. Gosh—he must have had guts."

The smith grunted.

"He was a mean old bastard. I hated the sight of him. He was no use to anyone. No one will be sorry he's gone. . . but it's queer. Seeing how he'd been killed like that. . ." And he added enigmatically, quiet again and subdued, "I don't like thinking about death, Edwin. Even when it's someone you hate like him."

4

IT WAS ten o'clock; Jane had gone to bed. Tom Bransby was sitting at the kitchen table (bare and scrubbed immaculately clean) with a large family Bible in front of him, ready soon to read the "daily lesson". His wife sat by the fireside knitting.

It was several months ago that Tom had started a task which he had felt was incumbent on all good Christians to perform: the reading of the entire Bible from Genesis to Revelation. Usually Jane was present during the reading. Often he would ask her to do it herself. But he had never compelled her to be present. And tonight she had a headache. She'd seemed tired and as she'd been so contrite and penitent about what had happened he had himself got her candle for her, filled her hot water bottle (with the fog it was a coldish night) and kissed her affectionately on the forehead as she had gone upstairs. She was a good girl, he knew. What wrong she had done in being on the beach with Knaggs' son she had done in girlish innocence. And she had spoken the truth. He had known that by the look in her eyes. She couldn't look *him* in the face and tell a lie. And he knew that she'd been speaking the truth when she had promised him that she would never speak to, or have anything to do with, that chap again. He had forgiven her, of course. She would know what he had meant with that kiss and the hug he had given her.

He had not opened the Bible yet, but he had a marker in the place where he had left off yesterday. From where he sat he could not see his wife's face, for her chair was turned towards the dying fire. He could hear the steady click of her needles, knew she was waiting for him to start, and he delayed deliberately for this was always a solemn moment. Once he had opened the Book it would be as though he were in the presence of God, just as in chapel before the service began. He wanted to feel that when he began there was nothing un-Christian in his thoughts, that he was indeed *good*: that in this day he had done nothing he ought not to have done, or left undone anything he ought to have done.

Not that he had any serious misgivings on either score. He knew that according to the best of his ability he was leading a good life and working hard, making the farm a success. The room they were in at present was one evidence of this. How different it had looked that day when the fox had slain the poultry, and he had come in here to get a drink of water, and had found old Mark's two bottles of ale in the cupboard. Apart from the dirt and the untidiness of the place as it had been then under the mismanagement of that old woman, half the flags on the floor had been broken or displaced, much of the plaster on walls and ceiling gone, the sink had been merely a cement trough, the water pumped from a well that would dry up completely in hot weather and was anything but sanitary when full. The floor now was level concrete. Doing his own plumbing (he had learnt the art of "wiping a joint" and other mysteries of the trade from a book) he had laid water on to the house and the farm buildings from a sweet and ample spring; he had replaced the old open-hearthed fire with a second-hand but modern cooking range with a back boiler, fixed a new sink with hot and cold taps, and had even installed a bath in one of the small upstairs rooms.

Everything about the kitchen was shipshape. He had built a dresser from planks he'd found on the beach. It was hung now with shining crockery. He had rigged up an airing rail with a neatly spliced raising and lowering rope secured to a brass cleat (another treasure from the beach). He had re-plastered the walls and distempered them cream, and all woodwork was done with glossy oil paint, again like a ship. It was the same with the whole house, the same with the whole farm, every building of which was now in first-class repair, every fence and gate trim and in working order, and almost every rood of arable land in good heart.

True that all this had been achieved with his wife's willing and skilful co-operation. Born and bred on the farm, and with generations of farmer's blood in her veins (never mind that of the Ellingtons), it was natural that she at first should know more about the job, especially the livestock (although with that, as with the land, they'd had the ready advice and help of their neighbours, Joe and George Jilson, who had inherited Brock Hill when old Peter died a year before Mark, and had already done wonders in repairing the old man's neglect). True too that the farm was hers, that none of this would have been possible had it not come to her, with its live and dead stock (such as they were) when old Mark had died. But equally true that without him working tooth and nail at the job, learning from Joe and George how to manage a horse, to plough and sow and reap and mow—all within the first year—her legacy, with the heavy mortgage that had been on the farm along with Mark's many debts, would not have amounted to very much. Besides, when he thought of his achievement he naturally included Ella as a part of himself.

She was a grand wife. Theirs was a perfect partnership. By now he had almost forgotten that thing about her that used to trouble him in the bad days and for some time after his conversion: her pride, her air of superiority, the feeling she had given him that her kindness and tolerance were a mockery. How he had misjudged her! That devotion of hers had never been put on. For a fraction of the suffering he had caused her many a woman had broken from her man forever. She had stuck by him, never losing her faith, never forgetful of the vows she had made when they were married. Their physical love had died at that time and had never reawakened, but something had replaced it that was deeper, purer and enduring.

Yes, it was a Christian home they had made together. Under God he was the master of it, yet he and Ella were as one. They never quarrelled. They very rarely disagreed. If they did, it was give and take, with himself always listening fairly to her point of view. It was Jane who had been the chief cause of what disagreements there had been. He had been strongly against her going to the County School. He had felt that she would have been much better at home helping her mother in the kitchen and with the animals. These modem schools were apt to put all sorts of ideas into a child's head. They might be all right for boys who were going into businesses or professions where scholastic certificates were essential. But a woman's place was the home, and she wouldn't find a better example to model her life on than her own mother. . . He had given way, reluctantly, reserving his right as a father to put a stop to the whole thing if he became convinced that it was doing Jane harm. That right Ella undoubtedly realised. Although she had said so little, he knew she had been as shocked as he had been when, in Jane's presence, he had told her what had happened on the beach. By then his own anger was completely under control. He had spoken gravely, but quite calmly, and he believed fairly. He might have pointed out that it would not have happened at all if Jane had not gone down to the beach looking for seaweed for her school lessons. But Ella must have realised that without telling. She had said nothing but to agree with him that Jane had done wrong to talk to Edwin Knaggs at all. About the smoking, the look on her face was enough to tell him that she shared his horror. He might have punished her. If he had done so, he knew that Ella would have approved, but he felt that he had her approval just the same in the attitude he had taken, which was the Christian one, to point out the evil and let Jane's conscience find the cure. "If thine enemy hunger, feed him; if he thirst give him drink, for in doing so thou shalt heap coals of fire on his head. Be not overcome with evil but overcome evil with good."

Perhaps in the end it would prove a good thing that Jane had gone down to the beach, as it had been a good thing that he had found the bottles of ale that day.

Tom put his hand—scrubbed as clean as the table top after his day's labour in the potato field—on the family Bible. Even this, strictly speaking, belonged to his wife. It had been her father's, although she could never remember him using it for anything but to keep important letters or documents in (such as his gun licence). He opened it at the marked place, the second chapter of The Song of Solomon. As he did so he remembered Chapter 1, which he had read yesterday evening, had puzzled him for it hadn't seemed really religious like Ecclesiastes and the Book of Proverbs, which had preceded it. If it hadn't been for the chapter heading which explained that it was "The mutual love of Christ and his Church", he would have been more puzzled still, and even so he couldn't see why the Church and Christ should be likened to a man and woman in love with each other. But there it was, and it was not his place to start questioning the Holy Scriptures, but he thought he had better start by reading what it said at the beginning of Chapter 2.

He cleared his throat and said,

"We've come to the second chapter of the Song of Solomon. The last chapter ended, *'The beams of our house are cedar, and our rafters of fir'*. The whole of this seems to be a sort of parable, as I explained yesterday, and it says again at the start of Chapter 2, *'Mutual love of Christ and his Church. Her hope and her calling. Christ's care of her. Her profession, faith and hope.'* And now it starts."

He paused, not because he expected any comment

from his wife, but because he sensed a distinction between what he had read and the Word itself. And then he really started:

"I am the rose of Sharon, and the lily of the valleys.

"As the lily among thorns, so is my love among the daughters.

"As the apple tree among the trees of the wood, so is my beloved among the sons. I sat down under his shadow with great delight, and his fruit was sweet to my taste.

"He brought me to the banqueting house, and his banner over me was love.

"Stay me with flagons, comfort me with apples: for I am sick of love.

"His left hand is under my head, and his right hand doth embrace me.

"I charge you, O ye daughters of Jerusalem, by the roes, and by the hinds of the field, that ye stir not up, nor awake my love, till he please.

"The voice of my beloved! behold, he cometh leaping upon the mountains, skipping upon the hills.

"My beloved is like a roe or a young hart: behold, he standeth behind our wall, he looketh forth at the windows, shewing himself through the lattice.

"My beloved spake, and said unto me, Rise up, my love, my fair one, and come away.

"For, lo, the winter is past, the rain is over and gone;

"The flowers appear on the earth; the time of the singing of birds is come, and the voice of the turtle is heard in our land;

"The fig tree putteth forth her green figs, and the vines with the tender grape give a good smell. Arise, my love, my fair one, and come away.

"Oh my dove, that art in the clefts of the rock, in the secret places of the stairs, let me see thy countenance, let me hear thy voice; for sweet is thy voice, and thy countenance is comely.

"Take us the foxes, the little foxes, that spoil the vines: for our vines have tender grapes.

"My beloved is mine, and I am his: he feedeth among the lilies.

"Until the day break, and the shadows flee away, turn my beloved, and be thou like a roe or a young hart upon the mountains of Bether."

Tom stopped. It was the end of the chapter, and although he often read considerably more than one chapter, he said "Amen" and closed the book and glanced at the clock on the mantelshelf.

He'd had a long and strenuous day (he'd been up to light the fire at five) and he was very tired and sleepy. He was not a good reader. As a boy he had been to no other school but the old Boys' Wesleyan, and it had been the custom there to make reading only a sort of continuous spelling lesson, and whether it was poetry or prose no heed was paid to elocution. A boy got full marks or escaped chastisement if he pronounced his words in "straight" English and not broad Yorkshire, and paused when it came to a comma, raised his voice at a question mark, dropped it at a semicolon and a full stop. . . He had read the chapter in this way, slowly, monotonously, without feeling for rhythm or sense, as though it had been a bill of lading he had been checking with a stevedore. Indeed, the whole reading had been a mechanical process. He did not understand it and he had not tried to, but he had performed an act of devotion that was at least sincere.

He waited a moment or two in complete silence as a congregation would do at the end of the preacher's benediction before starting to go out. Then he said, in his ordinary voice,

"Well, I'll get to bed. I can hardly keep my eyes open. What about Bessie. D'ye think she'll calve tonight?"

"It's more than likely. I'll have another look at her soon."

He was putting the Bible away in the dresser drawer. He did not look at her and she had not looked at him or paused in her knitting.

"I don't like you to be sitting up all night, Ella. You must be as tired as I am. I'll take on your watch at midnight if only you'll wake me."

"Oh—it's all right, Tom. I don't mind a bit, and Bessie's used to me. And if there's no sign at midnight I'll go to bed. Don't you worry."

"All right. Goodnight, Ella."

"Goodnight, Tom."

She did turn as she spoke, but he was already moving to the stairs, and she turned to the fire again. She heard him mounting the stairs, then entering his bedroom on the north side of the house. Her own was on the south side, Jane's in the attic. She heard him moving about and, very soon, the creaking of the bed as he got into it. . . Until that moment she had stayed as he had left her, looking like the woman he imagined her to be: the good wife knitting by the fireside, dutiful and meek. He did look at her quite often, especially in the evenings, and when she had changed and tidied herself he sometimes thought that she made quite a picture, particularly when she was sitting alongside Jane, and that it was wonderful how alike they were and how Ella never seemed to change and grow old. She still hadn't a grey hair in her head and her cheeks were always such a bonny colour. But he had never told her so. And since he had decided that he had been wrong in thinking she had once despised him, he had never wondered whether her thoughts on any particular occasion were at variance with what she said and did. His belief, his trust in her, were as absolute as his belief and trust in himself and in God. He could look straight into her eyes at any time now and know that, as he could with Jane. But he only saw in her eyes what she, with a well-guarded female mind and soul of her own, intended him to see, and only once, that night on the cliff when he had planned to break off their engagement and she had suddenly flung herself into his arms, had he seen what was in them now as her ears informed her that he was in bed. As she had sat listening to him, as she had spoken to him when he had done, her face had been almost expressionless. There had been no flicker of interest in her eyes as she had wished him goodnight. Suddenly she was alert, her eyes bright, and she was breathing quickly. She stopped knitting, but she still held the work in her hands and she remained physically rigid as she stared at the staircase doorway through which he had gone, stared as a cat stares at a mouse, soundless, not moving, lest it should see or hear and escape. The bed had creaked, as Tom had lain down on it. There was no more sound. He had been a good sleeper since he had become a farmer. She got up from her chair and put her knitting on the table. Then she moved over to the dresser, took out the Bible, placed it on the table exactly where it had been when he had been reading it, and sat down in his chair. She opened it at the marked place and started to read what he had read: "*I am the rose of Sharon, and the lily of the valleys*". As she read the colour mounted in her cheeks, her breath came quicker, her lips quivered and were parted, but no sound escaped them until she came to the tenth verse and then, in a passionate whisper, she read,

" *My beloved spake, and said to me, Rise up my love, my fair one and come away. For lo, the winter is past, the rain is over and gone. The flowers appear on the earth; the time of the singing of the birds is come, and the voice of the turtle is heard in our land. The fig tree putteth forth her green figs, and the vines with the tender grapes give a good smell. Arise, my love, my fair one, and come away.*"

She took a deep breath and closed the book. She got up and stealthily put it back in the drawer. She moved to the foot of the stairs and for a moment stood listening. Then from a shelf near the fireplace she took a stable lantern and lit it with a spill. She changed her house shoes for gumboots. She took a thick tweed coat from behind the door to the yard, and a scarf that she tied gipsy fashion over her head. She turned the table lamp low, picked up the lantern and quietly opened the door and stepped out into the yard. The fog was still thick, but even without the lantern she could have found her way along the cemented causeway which Tom had laid from the yard to the cow-house. In Mark's time, except in the driest weather, this would have meant negotiating at least three permanent puddles and there would have been barely room to step between the cow-house door and the manure heap. At least one-half of the double door would have had a broken hinge and would have been tied up with binder twine. Tom had shifted the manure heap to the far end of the cow-house, handier for leading to the fields, and had fixed a chute for "mucking out". The door opened smoothly on well-oiled hinges when she unfastened the neat wood latch. Immediately her nostrils were assailed by the warm air within, charged with the smell of sweet hay and the pleasant tang of well-kept cattle. It was almost as though the friendly creatures were breathing in her face, and there was a stirring among them and a low contented mooing as she raised the lantern and looked along the heads of the stalls.

Here again, in the timbering and the ties and the cement fodder troughs, in the lime-washed walls and ceiling, was evidence of her husband's skilled craftsmanship. He had practically rebuilt the entire place on a plan he had found in a farmer's journal, but with almost everything he had done there was the unmistakable touch of the seafarer. To him the stalls were always bulkheads. There were racks for pitchforks and gripes, wood pegs for halters and chains, shelves on the walls for various gear so that everything could be handily stowed as on a ship. And even the rope ties for the cows had sailors' knots and splices and toggles in them. . . But the animals were her almost exclusive charge. He could milk; but only the quieter of the cows. Bessie was the oldest of the herd (she was due with her seventh calf) and from the first she had never let him go near her, let alone touch her udders. She was standing and she gave a low moo when Ella approached her, who examined her expertly, then laid her hand on her flank, felt the shape of the calf, felt its independent movement. Nothing was going to happen this side of midnight, and most likely not then.

She hung the lantern on a peg that Tom had conveniently fixed for that purpose although, unless she needed his assistance with a difficult calving, he never came into the cow-house at night. She fetched an armful of hay and put it in Bessie's trough. The other cows mooed jealously. Then she moved to the end wall of the house where, between two tool-racks and high up, was a cupboard with the word "Poison" painted on it in red. This was the store place for veterinary medicines. Tom had a horror of poisons. In the old days a bottle of carbolic acid, or even a packet containing strychnine (for poisoning foxes) would have been merely left by Mark on a window ledge, and Tom had insisted that Ella should keep all her cattle medicines in this cupboard and carry the key herself. She unlocked it. There were two shelves containing bottles, bandages and dressings. She reached her hand well behind the upper shelf and took out a small tin box bearing a chemist's label—Worm Powders. She opened this and took from it a packet of cigarettes. She took a cigarette, put it between her lips, returned the packet to the box and the box to the cupboard and locked the door. Then she moved back to the lantern, raised the chimney, lit the cigarette and stood for a moment inhaling and exhaling the smoke through her nostrils with an expression of intense pleasure as though she were quenching a long endured thirst with a delicious drink.

Nothing in her expression or manner had suggested that she was doing anything treacherous or wrong, or that she realised the ironic humour of the situation. Her actions had all been deliberate, not furtive, and perhaps she had forgotten how her husband had once hidden his flask of whisky under the loose flag in the washhouse of their Bramblewick cottage. If, when she had lit the cigarette and felt the sapid fumes on her palate, she had thought of Jane and her thwarted sin, the thought could not have disturbed her in the way her husband had imagined his account of that incident had done. . . Yet the hand that held the cigarette was trembling. There was a growing excitement in her eyes that had nothing to do with the cigarette, and suddenly she became rigid again, alert, listening, her eyes focused on the door which she had shut behind her when she had come in.

She heard, together with the sound of the cows moving at their ties and Bessie munching her hay, the call of an owl, the blowing of a steamer's horn well out from the fog-bound shore, and now the sound of a train puffing up the gradient to High Batts. It was the last train from Burnharbour, due at High Batts halt at half-past ten. It was rarely late, and before the coming of radio it had been a time signal for the coast. She put the cigarette between her lips and with both hands turned the stable lantern low. She took an electric torch from her coat pocket, moved to the door and opened it. She stood for a moment at the threshold looking in the direction of the house, now recognisable by a dim and fog-haloed light well above the level of the ground. It was from the attic skylight and it hadn't been visible when she had left the house. As usual Jane must have waited until she was certain her father was asleep. Ella knew her daughter's habits, and Jane knew that she knew them. It was one of several small conspiracies they shared in the interests of domestic peace. With a woman's and a mother's intuition Ella might have known now that Jane hadn't just lit her candle so that she could read. She might have known or she might have guessed that she had been deeply hurt, that her humility, her seeming penitence towards her father when he had enlarged on her behaviour had been assumed, acted, again in the interests of peace. She might indeed have guessed that Jane had fallen in love with the boy she had so innocently talked to and picnicked with on the shore, that at this moment she might be crying her eyes out for the joy that had been snatched away from her almost as soon as it had come. But again Ella, with her experience as a wife married to a man she no longer loved, might have been thinking that the biggest sin is to be found out, and that Jane would have to learn her lesson the same as she'd had to. She fastened the door and she did not look at the light again. She turned to her right, away from the house, along the length of the cow house and she flashed her torch on the stone stile that was at its end and the boundary of the yard wall. She climbed over it and was on the path that led through the home pasture to the cliff fields and Browe Beck.

She walked at a steady pace, flashing the torch occasionally, for the growth of spring grass had obliterated the path in places. It was bright emerald in the light of the torch, and it glittered with droplets of water from the fog. The air was still. The smoke from her cigarette dulled but it did not kill the strong smell of fecund earth. She heard the owl again, and the steamer and the sound of the invisible train growing less as it reached the deep cutting immediately above the farm, just before the tunnel. It had whistled and entered the tunnel and the last sound of it had died when she reached the boundary fence and flashed her torch on the stile where Tom had surprised old Mark with the slaughtered goose. The stile had been broken then. Tom had replaced it with the two halves of an iron and teak companion ladder from a steamer that had been wrecked at High Batts two winters ago. It was one of his most successful jobs. The thorn fence was trimmed, but it grew on the top of a tall earth bank and there was a gully on the other side.

She put the torch in her pocket. She reached out her hand for the iron rail of the ladder, took the first step up and stopped as she heard a sound from the other side. It was not a voice, and only she who for a week had waited and yearned for this moment would have recognised it as the sound of a man breathing. She did not speak. Perhaps because her heart was thumping too hard. She dropped her half-smoked cigarette. She moved up to the topmost step and looking down saw him, his face and hands light against the dark of the ground, his hands reaching up to her. And he spoke: a deep steady, self-assured voice.

"Ella. You're on time. Train's just whistled for the tunnel. Come on down."

And she moved down into his arms.

5

NEXT DAY, which was the Friday of Easter week, the *Burnharbour Weekly Guardian* contained a stop-press report of what it called, MYSTERY OF WELL-KNOWN BRAMBLEWICK RESIDENT. It said,

A gloom was cast over the village of Bramblewick last evening when it became known that one of its best known and highly respected residents, Captain Bartholomew Fosdyck, was missing from his home. Unfortunately there is every reason to believe that the gentleman has lost his life in the most tragic circumstances. Captain Fosdyck, who in spite of his great age (he was 88 on his last birthday) was a man of great vigour, left his home on the Esplanade in the middle of the afternoon on a visit to the Wesleyan Chapel, of which for many years he has been the senior trustee. The Captain is a widower, and he was expected by his housekeeper, Mrs. M. Kettlewell, to be back for his customary high tea at half-past five. Adjoining the Chapel, which is built on the edge of the steep north cliff in the old part of the village, is the Wesleyan Schoolroom, which for the past few years has been used only for meetings and semi-secular functions connected with the Chapel. The Captain was last seen entering the door which leads to this schoolroom at about 3 p.m. The tide was up and a thick fog had blown in from the sea. The Captain, like most seafarers, had always been a man of most regular habits, and after waiting until half-past six Mrs. Kettlewell, fearing that an accident might have befallen her employer, decided to send a message to the police station in the old village, as a result of which the police constable, P.C. Bennison, proceeded to the Chapel and found that the school-door was locked from the inside. Owing to the fog it was now dark. P.C. Bennison at once sought the expert help of Mr. W. Knaggs, the local black-smith who resides close by. The lock was quickly turned, and together with several other residents of the village (the alarm having now been spread) the constable proceeded into the schoolroom, which is on the cliff side of the village. Here the apprehensions of the searchers were increased by the finding of the Captain's jacket, and by the fact that a door leading to the old school playground, which actually over-looks the cliff, was unlocked. Proceeding into the play-ground, the searchers were shocked to find that a portion of the fence guarding it against the edge of the cliff had been broken and carried away. Closer examination of the gap thus left and the narrow area of slippery clay separating it from the actual edge of the cliff showed marks such as anyone would make suddenly losing their foothold and sliding down. It was known that the Captain had been carrying a rope when he entered the school, and it was assumed that he had been engaged repairing the fence and had used the rope as a lifeguard, securing it to the fence itself. The fence however could not have been strong enough to stand his weight when he slipped.

A search party was organised to search the beach below and north of the cliff as the tide receded. But the tides are now spring, and if as conjectured the unfortunate gentleman fell over in the afternoon his body may have been carried far out to sea. Up to the time of our going to press however, no intimation has been received that the body has been found, although police and coastguards and friends of the unfortunate gentleman are maintaining a constant vigil.

By the time the next issue of the *Guardian* was published the fate of Captain Bartholomew Fosdyck was no longer a mystery, and the paper devoted two of its columns to the inquest and the funeral including a portrait of the Captain, framed in heavy black. The columns were headed,

TRAGIC DEATH OF ONE OF BRAMBLEWICK'S BEST-KNOWN RESIDENTS

GAVE HIS LIFE FOR THE CHAPEL HE LOVED

The worst fears as to the fate of Captain Bartholomew Fosdyck of Bramblewick were confirmed early on Monday morning when two Burnharbour fishermen, John Dryden and Henry Langham, hauling their lobster pots just north of Low Batts point found the warp entangled with a rope which had secured to it some broken planks and palings which had been dragged under with the force of the tide current. Then as they hauled they saw the body of what undoubtedly was that of the deceased gentleman fast round the waist with the other end of the tangled rope. With difficulty, the body was cleared of the lobster pot warp and then as it was found impossible to lift it into the coble, the fishermen decided to tow it into Bramblewick Landing. A coastguard having observed the approaching boat through his glasses informed the police and summoned helpers. A stretcher was obtained

289

from the Rocket Brigade station, and finally the body was carried reverently through the old village, up the Bank to the late Captain's home. Once more the villagers of Bramblewick who had sadly watched the procession, had came face to face with a tragedy of the sea. Once more the sea had given up its dead. . . .

The inquest (held on the following day) was reported in detail. The two fishermen who had found the body had been closely questioned by the coroner about the rope, as to the manner in which it had been secured to the body. Medical evidence had been given by the local physician, Dr Whittel, who declared without hesitation his opinion that death had been due to suffocation by drowning. He had known the deceased quite well, although he could scarcely have regarded him as a patient for in spite of his advanced age he had always seemed to enjoy remarkably good health. In fact the physical state of the body was more like that of a man only in his middle age. Mrs Kettlewell, who also had given formal evidence of identification, had described the events of the day leading up to the time when she had decided to inform the police as to her employer's non-return, and she had confirmed what the doctor had said about his robustness. She had also said, in reply to a question from the coroner, that he had been in his customary high spirits when he had left the house. Next had come the evidence of Police Constable Bennison, who had described the opening of the schoolroom door, the finding of the jacket, the broken fence, the marks of slipping feet on the clay. In his summing up the coroner had gone over all this evidence, pointing out to the jury the significance of the way the rope had been tied, precluding any suggestion of suicide, and suggesting that what had probably happened was that the unfortunate man, while engaged on a voluntary task which he himself had regarded as dangerous, had slipped and fallen over the cliff edge into the sea, having made the fatal mistake of trusting to the strength of the fence to hold him with the rope in case this very thing had happened. The verdict was that of accidental drowning. . . .

Then came a report of the funeral:

> The funeral took place on Thursday, and an unusually large number of people were present to pay their last respects to the dead. As was fitting, the first part of the ceremony was held in the old Wesleyan Chapel, which was filled to capacity. The Superintendent of the Burnharbour Circuit, the Rev. Cuthbert Symington, M.A., D.D., officiated, assisted by the Resident Minister, the Rev. Arthur James R. Bright. The organist was Miss Widdison and all members of the choir were present.
>
> In a brief, but deeply moving address, the Rev. Symington said that although he had himself only spent a few years in the Circuit he had come to regard the late Captain as a personal friend, and he felt that he could not sum up his character better than by using the phrase "A true Christian gentleman." No one among those who were now gathered in this historical building on this sad and solemn occasion could have any doubt that the chapel itself had suffered an irreparable loss, or that the Captain had not been the very heart and soul of the local Wesleyan movement. He had, the Captain had told him himself, first attended the chapel as a little boy, and like so many who in later

life became the staunchest of Christians, his youthful course had apparently set him away from its early influences. During his early days at sea, he had, as he would always readily admit, fallen into many of the snares with which the way of the young sailor is set, and he had finally come to God in the hard way, through suffering and remorse, and final repentance. He had learnt the folly of sin and the wisdom of walking in the way of the Lord. He had risen high in his own profession and had been the Captain of many ships before going into ownership. Hard work, clean living, thrift, strict teetotalism, prayer and worship had been the watchwords of his later life, and yet there had never been a better example of the happiness and content that salvation brings to a man than in his ever ready humour, his cheerful smile. In the social life connected with the chapel, in their concerts and soirees and at no time more so than at the Annual Bazaar, the Captain had always been the moving spirit, but behind all this spontaneous gaiety had been the faithful servant of God into whose solemn presence his soul had passed. Although his death had come as such a great shock to all who knew and admired him, it might well be said that he had given his life for the ancient chapel he had loved so well, for one of the things that had always given him concern was the erosion of the cliff which at some distant date might indeed threaten the foundations of the chapel proper. And what more fitting epitaph could be spoken than that?

The 24th Psalm, *"The earth is the Lord's, and the fulness thereof"* was read by the Rev. Bright, and during the course of the service, the choir led the large congregation in the singing of the late Captain's two favourite hymns, *Eternal Father* and *Lead Kindly Light*.

All blinds were drawn, and flags were flying at half-mast

as the cortege proceeded up the Bank and wended its way through the New Town to the Old Churchyard where so many of the late Captain's shipmates lie buried. The coffin draped with the Red Ensign was borne from the hearse to the grave side by six retired or serving officers of the Mercantile Marine, each one of whom had sailed under the deceased Captain's command during the latter's active seafaring career, and the large concourse of people stood in silence to witness the last sad rites conducted by Rev. Symington. Apart from the principal mourners, Miss Selina and Miss Abigail Lowther (nieces), there were present the representatives and members of the district clergy of all denominations, of the Rural and Urban Councils of Burnharbour (where deceased was as well known and highly respected as in his own village), of the Mercantile Marine Service Association (originally The Imperial Merchant Service Guild of which deceased had been a member for more than fifty years) of H.M. Coastguards, the Police, The Royal National Lifeboat Institution (of which deceased had been local secretary for many years), Lloyds, The Shipwrecked Mariners Society, The Mission to Seamen, and all the district Friendly Societies and Lodges. And among. . .

There followed in alphabetical order a list of private mourners and donors of floral tributes, which took up half a column, and the report ended with the name of the local undertaker who had been responsible for the "arrangements".

It would have been indecorous if the report had contained any reference to the late captain's wealth and, as the editorial policy of the *Guardian* had always been one of strict neutrality in all controversial matters, an avoidance of anything even faintly savouring of tittle-tattle, no reference in its news columns was made in succeeding issues to what was soon an undeniable and immensely newsworthy (although unofficially unsupported) fact: that in spite of his astuteness as a business man the captain had left no valid will, had indeed died intestate. There were plenty of rumours, some of them clearly malicious. There was one that Mrs Kettlewell, who had been the captain's housekeeper for many years and might have expected at least a modest legacy on his death, had found a will and, reading nothing in it to her own interest, had destroyed it out of spite. She'd had the house to herself long enough to have done this, having refused entrance to Miss Selina and Miss Abigail. She had done so because she had recently heard Captain Fosdyck saying that his nieces had been trying to persuade him to agree to building a new chapel and closing the old one, and he had a feeling against them, and they a feeling against him. They were, however, the apparent "next-of-kins", and their claim to entry had been upheld by a rather bewildered police constable before a higher authority had taken charge and sealed up the entire house. The honesty of the Misses Lowther was scarcely to be questioned. Certainly, if they had found a will during their permitted search they would have disclosed it, no matter what its contents. They had found none, but it was rumoured that they had found among their uncle's papers several drafts of wills in his own handwriting, and in lead pencil, and that in one of them it seemed as though he had intended to leave all his property to the Wesleyan Church, but with a condition that none of it should go towards the building of a new chapel at Bramblewick. This rumour (and no one could say for certain that either of the ladies had made any definite statement in support of it) had given rise to another founded on the well-known fact that the captain had always hated lawyers; that he had tried to make a will himself to cheat the lawyers out of their fee, and had been beaten at the job. As he'd been healthy enough, probably confident of living at least another ten years, he hadn't thought of a will as being so urgent. . .

Naturally, the *Guardian* could not demean itself by referring even in the vaguest terms to the existence of such a controversy. In due course its advertising columns contained the usual notice requiring anyone who had claims against the estate of Captain Bartholomew Fosdyck deceased to make them within a specified date to a local firm of lawyers who were acting on behalf of the Solicitors to the Crown, and another more significant notice: that information was required as to the present whereabouts (if living) of Zachariah Fosdyck (or issue) only son of Captain Bartholomew Fosdyck, last heard of as residing in the City of Melbourne, Victoria in the year 1902 or thereabouts.

This notice, in a slightly different form, appeared in the principal British daily newspapers and also in the principal Australian newspapers in which most likely it would have been sent by cable through their London offices for good news should travel fast. But it was an astute freelance Yorkshire-born Melbourne journalist named Smethers (commissioned by a big London newspaper group) who first got on to the trail of the prodigal son, and scenting a sensational scoop he too travelled fast. He was familiar with the waterfronts of all the main Australian ports. He discovered that a seaman known as Zachy Foster (or some name like it) had stayed intermittently at a sailors' lodging house in Melbourne early in the century. He was remembered as a good seaman afloat, but as a quarrelsome drunkard ashore, that he had consorted with a married coloured lady known as Lily, and that at times he had been in trouble with the police for drunkenness and disorderly behaviour. Lily, unfortunately, was dead. But the "old-timer" from whom Smethers got this information told him also that Zachy had finally shipped on a schooner owned by a Swede that was bound for Brisbane to engage in the Pacific Island trade.

Smethers flew to Brisbane. There the trail grew warmer. The name of a schooner owned by a Swede was remembered. The Swede's name was Gus Ohlson and a man known as Zachy (he had a broad Yorkshire accent) had sailed with him regularly for several years. Then Gus had sold his ship and bought a boatbuilding and repair business at a coast settlement in Northern Queensland. He had a beautiful daughter called Gerd, and Zachy, somewhat of a reformed character by then, had married her in Brisbane two months before the birth of their first child, a daughter. Zachy it was thought was going into partnership with the old man. They had all left for the North together. Smethers got confirmation of the marriage and the birth of the first child, Anna, at the Registry Office. The man's name was given as Zachariah Fosdyck, a British subject. He knew now that there were at least three possible "next-of-kins" to be trailed, probably many more.

By plane, car and finally by hired motor-boat he reached the settlement in Northern Queensland to which they were supposed to have gone more than a quarter of a century ago. It was a small straggling place at the mouth of a muddy river. The world economic slump had hit Australia as badly as any other country and here things had been aggravated by drought. Most of the frame and tin houses in the settlement were deserted and many of them derelict. There was only one human being on the broken-down jetty to which Smether's boatman made fast, and he was an idiot youth who just grinned in answer to the questions Smethers asked. But not far from the pier was a tumbled-down shed and a boat slip, and near to it a bungalow that looked less derelict than the others. There were chickens and goats and washing was hanging on a railing outside. As Smethers moved towards it past the shed he noticed on the door of the shed a sun-blistered and almost faded legend, G. Ohlson, Boat Builder and Repairer, and (as he said with truth in his published story) his heart was beating wildly with excitement as he approached the entrance of the house itself and heard a woman's voice within and the voices of several children. The door was open. From the threshold he looked straight into what was the living room. He saw the children sitting round a table: three girls ranging from seven to three, and one toddler boy, all of them clean but poorly clad and rather skinny and under-nourished. They all had flaxen hair and the little girls in particular, despite their skinniness, were strikingly beautiful. The woman also had been beautiful, but her hair was white and she was terribly thin and looked wretchedly worried and unhappy.

Smethers wished her good day and then, confident that he had come to the end of the trail and that he had not been anticipated, he asked her if her name was Fosdyck. She looked startled and at first angry. In a curious mixture of broken English with a pronounced Yorkshire accent she asked him what business it was of his. He told her what he was, that he was looking for a certain Zachariah Fosdyck or any relations of his, and that if he found them he would be in the happy position of conveying some very good news to them.

She nearly dropped the saucepan of stewed fish that she had been about to serve to the children.

"My name now Johnson. I marry twice but both my husband is dead. My first husband was Zach Fosdyck. He was drowned. These children are his grandchildren. Their mother is my girl Anna who marry anodder sailor boy, and he too died of fever one year ago in South America. My daughter go to work on a farm up country because no work or money here. Tell me quick what you have to say. I am the widow of Zachy Fosdick sure thing. I haf all the papers that belong him from time long ago when he first went to sea. He was drowned here ten year ago when liddle boat he built capsized. He buried here in churchyard long with my fadder. These children are his grandchildren, and there are no udder relative but my Anna their mother. . ."

It was a scoop. The great British national which had commissioned Smethers gave nearly three columns of its 24-page issue to his first cabled report. They trusted their man. Taking a chance that there might be some legal hitch later in establishing the claim of the family to Bartholomew Fosdyck's fortune, they cabled back to him to spare no expense in shepherding the family to the nearest city and to a reputable firm of lawyers. And it would have been unnecessary for them to ask him to tie up the widow for the exclusive rights of her life story with Zach which later (written as only a good journalist like Smethers would know how) appeared in instalments (with photographs of persons and places, including Zach Fosdyck's grave) in the company's Sunday version of their daily paper.

It may be imagined that this story was followed with particular interest by many of the inhabitants of that fairly large coastal and rural area in which *The Burnharbour Guardian* circulated once a week, bringing its factual and dignified reports of local events: meetings of the Urban and Rural District' Councils; the Police Court; Church and Chapel activities; concerts and dances and whist drives; agricultural, horticultural and poultry shows; political meetings (always reported with meticulous neutrality); funerals, marriages; with notes on sports, gardening, the local fish and general market, the movements of locally-owned steamships. It might be imagined that the *Guardian* would have had at least something to say on a matter that was of such obvious local as well as national interest. But the serialised story, like the original "news" story in the *Daily* ——, was exclusive and of course copyright. It was sensational, undoubtedly garnished, and certainly not the sort of thing that respectable people would appreciate, particularly in its spicy references to Zachariah's life during the Melbourne period. It even mentioned Lily. It was laced too with some references to Captain Bartholomew Fosdyck (a reporter had been sent up to Bramblewick to get local atmosphere and pick up any relevant material); it retold the story of the captain's death that had been given only a paragraph in the 24-page issue of the *Daily* —— at the time; it alluded with a skilful avoidance of slander to the various rumours that had been going round, including the one about the captain's dislike for lawyers and that it might have been because of that he had made no will.

All this the publishers of the *Guardian* may have felt (they were themselves of an old coast family) must have caused annoyance and embarrassment to the relatives and many friends of the late captain, especially to those connected with the Wesleyan Chapel. So the whole affair was discreetly ignored. And (it may have been discretion again) no mention was made of the name of Captain Bartholomew in the report that appeared in the Guardian of the meeting that was held at Bramblewick a few weeks later to consider a project for a new Wesleyan Chapel to replace the one in the old village. The project was not to have an entirely new building, but to purchase a mansion that was situated near to the railway station and the new Parish Church, which had been empty for some years and was now on the market at a reasonable price. An architect's plan showed, how with little alteration to the main structure, the building could be converted from its secular purpose to that of a spacious well-lit chapel with another smaller annexe that could be used as a Sunday School room. There would be a new organ, plain but comfortable seating for the congregation, and central heating. For many years past it had been felt that the old chapel had outlived its purpose. The population of the village had tended to move to the newer part of the township, and it was emphasised by several speakers that the project, if agreed upon, would put new heart into the local Wesleyan movement, and above all attract the younger generation. A resolution that the project be accepted and that a Building Committee should be elected was carried unanimously. It was agreed also that a Building Fund should be opened at once, and before the meeting closed it was announced (and at that moment, although the *Guardian* didn't say it, their uncle might well have turned in his grave) that Miss Selina and Miss Abigail had each subscribed one hundred guineas to the Fund. . .

BOOK THREE

DEAD RECKONING

1

IT WAS afternoon of a day in December in the first winter of Hitler's war. Tom Bransby was down on the seaward side of home pasture clearing a ditch that had got plugged-up where it ran under the coastguard's path along the cliff edge. He'd been on the job about an hour, but he hadn't got at the obstruction yet, and he'd stopped to rub the numbness out of wet hands, and to look about him sailor-fashion at the sea and the land and the sky.

It was a fine afternoon. A transparent mist lay upon the hills and sea. There was a touch of frost in the air now that the reddened sun was lowering. But there was no wind, no real cloud in the sky; the sea was green-grey and smooth and, unless the very quiet of the elements and the flush of red berries that hung on the hedgerow thorns like drops of blood were portents, there was nothing to suggest to his expert eye a change of weather, to herald the approach of the frosts and tempests and heavy falls of snow that were to make that winter one of the worst in living memory.

Nor was there in the scene, unless again the very

quiet of it was a portent, anything to suggest to him that the storms of war now raging on the eastern borders of Hitler's Germany and in remote Finland were brewing to sweep north and south and west and east again until they raged over the entire globe. There were no trenches or gun emplacements or wire entanglements along the cliff edge or along the shore; no soldiers, no sounds of planes, no ships of war within sight upon the calm sea. Growing out of the mist that veiled the distant headland of Low Batts three dark smudges, close together and moving south, were the only signs of shipping, and these he recognised by their shape and size were peaceful trawlers on their way from their fishing grounds to Grimsby or Hull.

Tom Bransby had no radio. He read no papers. From the day that war had been declared he had seen what his clear duty as a Christian was to be in what followed. He had been through one war from the start to the end of it. He hadn't done that by choice or for "King and Country" like the boys who joined up at the recruiting offices, but simply because he was a ship's officer and it was his job. In the course of performing that job he had been torpedoed twice. He had been mined and had seen his father and young brother murdered. He had sworn vengeance: an eye for an eye, a tooth for a tooth. He had by God's grace been thwarted of that vengeance in deed, but the lust to take it, the lust to kill at least one German for the death of father and brother, had been one of the sins for which he'd prayed for forgiveness when he'd surrendered himself to God. He hadn't done that without forgiving his enemy too, and now with his country at war with Germany again, Germans out to kill Britishers,

Britishers out to kill Germans, he for one was not going back on his faith. He was a pacifist and, come what may, he'd stay one.

He hadn't believed that there would be another war between England and Germany. He'd thought that after the last one both sides must have seen that wars didn't pay, whether you lost or won. Even now he didn't believe that this one would come to real war like the last. In the last war this coast had been one of the hottest spots for the German U-boats. Before the Navy had got the whiphand over them dozens of ships, in convoy or sailing alone, had been sunk within sight of Bramble-wick. Two U-boats had actually been destroyed by depth charges in the very bay where they'd been waiting for a convoy. Since this war had started there hadn't been a sign of a U-boat along the coast. They had done damage elsewhere, of course. If he didn't read the papers or listen in there was always Jonty or one of the Jilsons to bring the news and, making all allowances for exaggeration and for the news coming second-hand, some of it must be true. There had been the sinking of the liner *Athenia* without warning on the second day of the war. The aircraft carrier *Courageous* had been torpedoed with a loss of five hundred men. A U-boat had got into Scapa Flow and sunk the *Royal Oak*, again with a heavy loss of life. The German Air Force had laid magnetic mines in the Humber and Thames estuaries. Many ships had been sunk by them including a big Dutch liner, the *Simon Bolivar*, and women and children had been included in the heavy casualties. Three Burnharbour-owned steamers had been torpedoed in the Atlantic, but without loss of life, and another one was reported to have been captured by a German surface raider. Against this the Navy was supposed to have sunk several U-boats and there was news that Hitler's pocket battleship *Admiral Graf Spee* had been heavily damaged by British warships and driven into Montevideo. Yet nothing seemed to be happening on land in France. There had been no sign of the great fleets of German bombers in fear of which the children of London and Hull and other cities had been evacuated to the country. Everyone had been given gas masks and leaflets saying what to do in an air raid, but Jonty himself had been scornful about this and the enrolling of local men as special constables and air raid wardens and coastguard auxiliaries. It was his opinion that once the Germans had settled things with the Poles and got what they wanted from Czechoslovakia, and the Russians got what they wanted from Finland, things would be settled somehow without having a real war with France and England, for that would only bring America in and they'd bound to be beaten in the end. Italy was doing her best to keep out of it, anyway. And the Japs were only bluffing about America. Why, he'd read in one paper that about ninety per cent of all Japs had to wear spectacles because of their weak sight and they were useless when it came to flying aeroplanes and shooting.

But Tom usually was too busy to listen to Jonty's theories, to listen even to his budget of news. One thing he knew the Government was right about: the necessity to grow more food, and nothing in that conflicted with his conscience. Ships too were carrying food. Doubtless some of those already sunk had been carrying wheat from America. But as likely they'd be carrying munitions of war. He'd heard from Jonty, and it hadn't surprised him, that all merchant ships were being armed. Their officers and crews would be expected to fight, to do their utmost to destroy the enemy, as he had prayed he might do after his father and brother had been killed.

He'd been distressed to hear that British ships had been sunk and seamen lost, more distressed to hear of women and children being killed or drowned or suffocated in burning oil as had happened in the *Simon Bolivar*. But that hadn't altered his attitude to war. . . He was a farmer. If the war did get worse, and it came to an all-out struggle between this country and the Germans, the Germans' biggest hope of beating us would be the sea blockade, what they'd tried to do in the last war and nearly succeeded: to sink our food and supply ships, to starve us out. They couldn't do that if every British farmer did his bit, and a bit more!

Like most farms in the district, his was essentially a grazing farm, its "selling crop" normally milk and young stock, with the wool and lambs from the moorland sheep. The Government experts held (and his neighbours Joe and George Jilson agreed) that the productivity of even the best grass farms could be increased by tillage, by ploughing up permanent pastures and sowing oats, either alone or with an undercrop of clover and grass, starting a system of crop rotation, mostly for fodder, with the main object an increase of milk. Barley, roots, beans, rape or kale and potatoes could come in rotation, but wheat was not recommended as the land was too light. It meant more labour, a greater outlay, but a bigger return in cash in the end. The Government too would give a grant of £1 an acre for all old grassland broken up and cropped, and a subsidy of £2 per acre for potatoes, the crop either to be sold or used as fodder for pigs or other stock. There had been four acres of rough stony grazing at the top part of the farm that hadn't been touched with the plough in Mark's time. There were clumps of whins and brambles and even heather growing on it. With adze and spade and pickaxe he had rooted up the whins and brambles. He had dug out the stones. Then (with the help of the Jilsons and their tractor only for the steepest bits) he had ploughed it all, fenced it with sheep netting and given it a heavy dressing of clod lime. It would get some slag or superphosphate in the spring when he'd broadcast it with oats direct on to the furrows, barrow it and roll it. It would mean, if he got a heavy crop, a big job at harvest time, but Jane would be home from Donbridge then (where she was now teaching in school) and with the three of them, and a little help from the Jilsons, they should manage it all right. A good crop would mean he'd be able to keep at least another couple of milkers, for there'd still be his hay and mangolds and spuds.

He had rubbed the numbness from his fingers and he knelt down at the side of the ditch and with a long pole started jabbing again at the invisible obstruction in the culvert. It was a grand job farming, he reflected. He was very proud of those four acres he had ploughed up. In his mind's eye he could see them as they'd look in summer, turning yellow and the wind waving through them. True it was a small thing compared with what the Jilsons had done. But then they were experts. They'd got their tractor too, Joe driving it and working every day, save Sunday, from light to dark. They were decent chaps. He liked them both, but particularly George, the elder one who was a childless widower only a year or two older than himself. Joe was forty-five, unmarried but he was engaged to a schoolmistress in the parish where they'd lived after the quarrel with old Peter, only she wouldn't marry him until she reached retiring age and got her pension. He went to see her every Sunday on his motorbike. They had a widowed sister Emily keeping house for them. The farmhouse was a good two miles distant and they kept very much to themselves, being so busy anyway, but Tom felt he couldn't have asked for better neighbours. Ella too got on with them well, although she'd hated both the brothers when she was a girl because they were rough and used to shout at her, and her father and Peter had often run foul of each other about fences and straying sheep.

Tom Bransby indeed was happy. It was not a particularly pleasant job he was doing, but it was necessary for there were several wet patches in the pasture and a lot of moss among the grass, and he intended to lay some tiles down to the main ditch. The war wasn't going to trouble him. He was doing his duty to the best of his ability, and according to his conscience as a Christian. So was Ella. And as for Jane he'd have much rather she'd been at home, but teaching was an honourable profession; she was doing well at it by all she said in her letters and far better for her to be doing that than aping a man by wearing uniform and being in the Waacs or the Waafs or Wrens and such like. She was a good girl. She had joined the Wesleyan Chapel in the district of Donbridge in which she lodged (with some very respectable people) and she actually taught in Sunday School. She'd been a great help to her mother during the last summer holidays, and even when she was dressed up for going into Burnharbour shopping she never used powder on her face, or lipstick, and she seemed quite indifferent to the youths who stared at her, although he couldn't blind himself to the fact that she must now be considered a very good-looking girl; better looking, indeed, than Ella had been at her age. . . It was a good thing that she'd shown no more interest in theatricals. He'd been wise in putting his foot down firmly about that when she was a child. . .

The obstruction at last showed signs of yielding. He gave the pole an extra hard jab and the muddy water that had gathered at the mouth of the culvert gurgled and began to drain away. Another job done! And now he must get the pigs fed and hay and bedding cut for the cows and the poultry shut up before a fox took a goose or a hen for his supper. And he must have a last look at the four acres before it got dark. The sun was nearly set. It was deep red through the mist which was thickening now along the slopes of the hills. It looked as though it might come a hard frost tonight. He pulled out the pole and looked round for his spade, preparing to go. Then he was startled by a voice, and looking round he saw just approaching him along the path the figure of a man in a reefer coat and coastguard's hat, and he saw it was Will Knaggs.

"Now, Tom!"

He had not spoken to Will Knaggs since the days before his illness and conversion. He hadn't seen him at close range for many years. He had heard from Jonty that he had become an auxiliary coastguard. And he was startled more by the apparent pleasantness in his voice than by seeing his old enemy in coastguard's uniform, and he answered without thinking,

"Now, Will."

He had stopped and there was only the wire fence between them.

"It's a coldish day. What are you at? Cleaning out your ditches?"

Tom was nonplussed. There was no sarcasm in the smith's voice, none of the old truculent mockery. He answered politely,

"Aye. There's been a block-up here, under the path, but I've loosened it now. . . It looks like a frost tonight."

And then he looked the smith directly in the face and saw something that surprised him more. It was a different face to the one he remembered and had always hated. It wasn't just age. It wasn't just that his hair and moustache had greyed; all the lines were deeper. It wasn't that it looked kinder. It was just that there was no fight or fire in it, no swagger, no bossiness or superiority. He looked ill too: his eyes were bloodshot as though he hadn't slept for days. He looked worried and tormented. It was clear he wanted someone to talk to and not, as in the old days, argue with.

"It's a long time since I've been on here," he went on. "I've been mostly on the Low Batts patrol since I took on this job, or taking day watch at the station watch-house, giving the regulars a spell. And of course I'd have been on the shore on this way today if the tide hadn't been up. You seem to have settled down all right to farming, Tom. You've made this spot look different to what it used to be!"

Was some of the old mockery creeping into his voice?

Tom was on his guard.

"Aye," he said. "Maybe."

The smith went on.

"I noticed as I came along that Joe and George Jilson have been ploughing up a lot of old land. And you've been doing a bit haven't you, up on the bank there? Well, it's my opinion we'll need every acre there is in this country to pull us through what's ahead. Every acre! Germans are claiming they've put down more than fifty thousand tons of British shipping this week. And even when we get to blows with their ships it seems we can't sink 'em. There's the *Graf Spee* got into a neutral port in spite of three of our ships doing their best at it. You'll have heard about the *Moor Cliff*?"

Tom caught his breath. He knew now that the smith wasn't mocking.

"The *Moor Cliff*? Nay, I've heard nothing. What's happened?"

"She's down. Kit Harrison and Sam Bunny with her. In a convoy, too. It's mostly out in mid-Atlantic where the trouble is, they say. The Germans seem to have a lot of big U-boats that can stay at sea for weeks. They're attacking by night, too. They must have got some new way of aiming their torpedoes. And I reckon we haven't seen even the start of the trouble yet. This war's going to be a hundred times worse than the last. We've let that chap Hitler take us in. He may be mad, but he's cunning all right. Once he's finished with Poland he'll turn west for certain, and it wouldn't surprise me if he had the Russians on his side by then."

Tom had gone pale. He broke in, quietly,

"Is it official the *Moor Cliff's* gone?"

311

"Aye. There were telegrams came both for Kit's missus and old Mrs Bunny this morning. But the doctor who's attending Mrs Bunny was against her having it. She's been a bit queer in her head since the war started. Thinks poor Sam is at Shields sitting for his second mate's ticket and she's been expecting a wire from him to say he's passed. Both of Kit's lads are at sea, by the way. It'll be worse for her than for Sam's mother. Mrs Bunny's over ninety, anyway. I tell you those are lucky who haven't got sons. You're lucky just having a daughter, although I doubt if any of us will be safe when the Germans make a start with their bombs and gas. And there's that lad of mine, Edwin. I thought he'd have been out of it, being in a job in Canada. But he started learning to fly out there as soon as war was declared, and now he's joined the Air Force and he'll be over here about Christmas, ready to be in it as soon as the Germans begin their real offensive."

No, there was no rancour or mockery about him now. He was a changed man, and it was as clear as daylight what had done it. Whatever his failings, there was no doubt he was fond of his son. He was bound to be worried. And of course he had no religion to fall back on for comfort. . . It was very bad news about Kit and Sam. It was a long time since he'd seen either of them for since he'd started farming it was rare that he went to Bramblewick. The chapel he attended was in a village a couple of miles south of High Batts. But several times, since he had watched the *Moor Cliff* steaming south on her first voyage with Kit as her master (and Sam her bos'un), she'd passed Bramblewick and signalled in the usual way. He'd once really envied Kit having that berth and living in The Hollies. And now he'd gone, and Sam too; gone like his own father and Harry had gone, although perhaps their death had been quicker and more merciful. . . He said slowly,

"It's a bad do about Kit Harrison and Sam Bunny. I didn't think myself it would come to U-boats and torpedoing again. The Germans tried that in the last war and we ended by sinking U-boats faster than they could build them. They may have got bigger boats. And better sights, and other patent things, but I reckon our side will match them. It's a bad thing is war, anyway. It doesn't do anyone any good. And it needn't happen if everyone, Germans too, just refused to be made into soldiers and sailors and airmen."

The smith laughed, but not mockingly.

"You sound like a CO!"

"Maybe I am a CO. I'm against war, anyway, and fighting and trying to kill my fellow creatures, no matter what nation they belong to or what colour for that matter. What about Edwin? You don't sound as though you want him to be in it. Wouldn't you rather he was a CO as you call it and stayed at his job, whatever it is?"

The smith was silent for a while. There was the sound of a distant aeroplane, and, perhaps suddenly mindful of his official duty, he half-turned to look north across the bay whence the sound came. Tom looked too, but there was nothing in sight except the three trawlers, now less than a mile away and maintaining their southerly course, and the smith turned again and said (and he seemed to be talking half to himself),

"He could have done that without calling himself a CO. He'd got a job under the Canadian Government as

313

research scientist at one of the biggest salmon-packing ports in British Columbia. You'll agree that fish is food, almost as important as meat. He's an artist too. He paints pictures and he's had a lot of praise about them from folks that know. And his career was just starting. He'd have made a big name for himself both in science and painting and made brass, too. And he chucks everything to try and get himself killed. Can you see that plane?" (He spoke as with a sudden irritation, as though it had been the buzzing of a wasp at the back of his neck.) "I can't! I suppose it's a Coastal Command Anson or one of those Lockheeds the Yanks have sold us. Maybe there's a convoy coming down from the north!"

The sun had gone. The mist had thickened and, but for the trawlers and the vague outline of Low Batts head, it would have been impossible to distinguish between sea and air. Silent now, both men gazed north. The sound grew louder and it seemed to be coming actually from the fishing craft. Then, some distance astern of the rearmost one, there was a dazzling flash on the surface of the sea: a geyser of water topped with billowing black smoke and then the noise of an explosion which reverberated in the cliffs like thunder. Before the sound had died there was another flash astern of the rear ship, but appreciably nearer to it. And the ship itself had changed-its course. It was swinging round in an arc. The other two were doing the same, one to port and the other to starboard, and it looked almost as all three were swinging to encircle the spot where the explosions still left their mark on the sea. The smith spoke excitedly.

"What is it, a U-boat? Are they minesweepers, those ships? Aren't those depth charges? They seem to be circling round as though they'd got something trapped. Is that plane spotting for them?"

Tom did not answer immediately. Gripping the rail of the fence with both hands (as though it had been the rail of the bridge of a ship) he was staring at the ships whose wakes now looked like three gigantic ostrich feathers laid on the grey sea. Then there was another flash, not astern, but actually ahead of one of them. Another loud explosion and he said, quietly, but very distinctly,

"They're bombs, not depth charges. That plane's attacking them. We can't see it, but I reckon they can, or they can see the bombs coming down, and they're dodging them. . . See that? If that chap hadn't put his helm hard over, that would have got him!"

There had been a third explosion close to the same ship but this time on its starboard beam, and she had turned to port. She began to roll to the wave it made but seemed unharmed.

"They're not sweepers," Tom went on. "They'd have guns if they were and they'd be firing back. They're ordinary fishermen."

There were three more flashes in rapid succession, but all wide of any mark. Then the sound of the invisible plane grew less, almost died, then grew louder on the seaward side of the craft which, with smoke billowing from their funnels and at full speed, were continuing to twist and turn. Still to seaward, the plane seemed to be moving south. It almost died again then began to grow louder as it approached, not from the sea, but from the land. The two men saw it coming low over the misty crest of High Batts cliff and it seemed to be diving straight towards them, to be actually lower than the crest of the hill, its twin engines making a deafening roar. It was black and hideous, bearing on its wings and tail the insignia of Nazism and the German Air Force. Almost directly overhead it banked and turned directly for the ships now scarcely half a mile distant from the shore.

The smith muttered,

"It's having another go at 'em!"

As he spoke they both saw a number of dark objects drop from the belly of the plane. A second later it swerved to starboard, banking steeply, showing the width of its wings. Tail-on again and aiming out to sea it almost instantly became invisible in the mist. The sound of its engines grew less. They had died to no more than a low droning when the first of the bombs exploded. There were six in all. They were easy to count, for there was half a second's interval between each, and although they fell in a straight line that line was oblique to their viewpoint on the cliff. The ships had scattered, and they had formed a triangle, or at least they must have done to the bomb-aimer, although from ashore they seemed to be almost in line with the middle one not so very distant seawards from the other two. It was between these two and well clear of both that the first flash came. And then, like the splashes of a flat stone flung by a boy to scull across a pond, the other five followed, each flash nearer the third ship which was at that moment turning to come broadside on. They saw four of those bombs explode on the water. The flash of the fifth was on the ship just abaft the funnel. The flash was white, but the geyser that followed it was not water but red and yellow flame in the intense illumination of which they saw the vessel's funnel and shattered deck-house rise and shoot upwards like rocks ejected from an erupting volcano. And almost instantly there was no light at all, nothing upon the sea where the ship had been but a heavy smudge of smoke.

Again it was the smith who spoke, and his voice was shaking.

"God! She's blown up. She's *gone!*"

Tom did not answer. He stood as he was, with his hands tightly grasping the rail of the fence, staring seawards. The noise of the explosions still echoed across the sea like the rumblings of a thunderstorm that had passed. The sound of the plane had died. The smith turned on him.

"She's blown up!" he said more urgently. "Didn't you see it—that bomb hit her fair and square?"

Tom did not move, but he answered with a strange calmness as though half in a trance,

"Aye. She's gone. Blown to bits. It's hard to see now with all that smoke, but the other chaps are steaming to where she was."

"Do you think the plane will come back and have a go at them?"

"I think she's gone, but they'll have to risk that. Some of her crew may have been blown clear. I was blown yards when my father's ship was blown up and him and my young brother were lost. But that was a mine and she was a big steamer. I should think that bomb landed in the engine room. I should say that every man on board her was killed straight off."

"Killed? You mean bloody well murdered!"

Tom did not reply. He was still staring seawards. But the smoke from the bombs, from the funnels of the surviving ships and from the one that had been hit combined with the mist and growing dusk made detailed observation of what was happening impossible. The ships themselves steaming into the thickest area of smoke had disappeared from sight. The smith said, more soberly,

"I suppose there's nothing we can do?"

At last Tom moved. He left go of the rail, glanced over his shoulder towards the farm then down at his spade. Then he said as calmly as before,

"No. We can do nothing. We've got no boat here. And anyway their mates will be picking up any that's escaped. I'd best be getting home. The missus will be worrying, hearing those bombs. She doesn't know where I am. I've got a lot to do too, and it's getting towards dark."

Puzzled, the smith looked at him, seemed about to make an angry remark, and then think better of it. He shrugged his shoulders and said,

"Aye. And I'd best be getting along too. I reckon the station will want a report of what's happened, although they must have seen it for themselves. Well, so long, Tom!"

"So long!"

The smith hurried off. Tom bent down to pick up his spade.

He turned once more to look across the bay at the smoke. Suddenly he put his other hand to the spade handle and he raised it, gripping it hard with both hands as he had done the rail, and he muttered something between his clenched teeth that might have been an imprecation. Then he heard the voice of his wife far up the field shouting for him anxiously. He shouted to her,

"All right, Ella," and without another glance at the sea he started up the field for home.

2

IN SPITE of the many disagreeable aspects of war, the killing and the maiming, the cost and the waste, its proved futility as a means of bringing real peace between nations, there can be little doubt that it has also many attractions and that to a healthy youth or young man (young enough at least to have no active experience of the war preceding it) service in the armed forces of his country in time of war, or impending war, is not a distasteful proposition.

Especially is this so in a nation where the actual theatre or theatres of operations, or impending operations, is the terrain of another nation, geographically remote, so that during the period of his training as a soldier, sailor or airman he makes no direct personal contact with the soldiers, sailors or airmen of the enemy whom later on he will do his best to kill or maim with bullet, shell or bomb; that he does not see the villages, towns and cities, the factories, hospitals, churches, the rich farmlands that he will help to ravage and destroy; the homes and the children who will be killed, maimed, frightened, starved.

The pill is well coated for the would-be warrior. First his nation when it goes to war is certain of the justice of its cause. Consequently the enemy side is wrong. Not only does he receive legal absolution in advance for any harm he may do the enemy with the weapons he will be trained to use, but he is assured that by doing such harm he is performing a high duty to his own country and to God. The inducement of an ultimate heavenly reward (particularly assured for him who dies in the field) may not be as strong as it was in the days of the religious crusades, nor love of king and country as strong as in the days of the Elizabethan wars, but even then an inducement—a motive just as powerful—was man's inherent love of adventure and excitement, of a gamble with his own life the stake. War is the greatest of all adventures!

Edwin Knaggs was thinking rather gloomily about the subject of war and his own relations to it as he stood that cold snowy foggy February Saturday afternoon in the crowded corridor of a halted train on the outskirts of the city of Donbridge, and he was wondering if it was going to be such an adventure after all. True that it was not merely the excitement of it that had attracted him in the first instance to learn to fly, to qualify himself for quick entry into the British Royal Air Force. Neither had he, consciously at least, just been caught by the germ of war fever, that contagious ferment which Hitler and Goebbels and Mussolini had disseminated so skilfully and with such success in their own countries, now tainting all winds of the globe. He had not been carried away by patriotic propaganda. He had a deep and sincere affection for his own country. He had decided, as soon as he had known that war was certain, that England was in possible danger of sea and air invasion, that he must go back to it just as he would have to jump into a river to a drowning child. Yet he had not made that decision without experiencing an intense exhilaration, a sense of starting on a huge adventure: a state of mind and spirit that had grown stronger with the discovery that he liked flying better than he had guessed, that he was a natural airman. He had taken to it like a duck to water, had passed all his tests in record time and might, had he so wished, have "stayed on" in Canada, joining the Royal Canadian Air Force or the Empire Training Scheme already being organised. But he'd wanted to get to threatened England, to the ultimate adventure. Already things had happened there in the air. The Royal Air Force had attacked German warships at Heligoland and Kiel. The German Air Force had attacked and damaged British warships in the Shetlands and the Firth of Forth. They were attacking merchant ships. They were laying mines in British estuaries. No bombs had been dropped on land yet by either side, but at any moment the real thing might start, and he wanted to be in it, and the quicker he went, he had felt then, the better. . .

But he wasn't feeling like that now as he stared through the steamy window at the walls of a factory opposite to which the train, already an hour late, had been halted more than thirty minutes as he watched the melting snowflakes, murky from the fog-trapped factory smoke overhead, spinning down into the dark water of the Donbridge canal which divided factory wall from rail embankment. He was wishing bitterly that there was no war, that he was back in Canada at his job and his painting which five months ago had suddenly become of no significance whatever. And even this, the crowded and belated train, the depressing aspect through the window, was less disagreeable than the Air Force Training Depot from which he was taking a weekend leave, where for the last fortnight all aircraft had been grounded owing to the fog and snow, where apart from lectures there had been nothing to do but have meals and sit about in a crowded and yet inadequately heated lounge listening to the conversation of young men with whom, apart from aviation, he had no interest in common. They were good chaps, the whole crowd of them. They were keen as mustard on their job. They were, to use their own phrase (and one he particularly detested), "browned off" by the weather, as indeed he was himself. But oh how they bored him with their slang, their insatiable appetite for swing music and crooning (the radio in the lounge was never silent except when the gramophone was playing), their seemingly complete indifference to the arts, to real music, painting, drama, literature.

"Browned off!" He loathed the phrase, and yet how admirably by its very etymological vagueness it conveyed his own present state of mind, reminding him of another, but more explicit, phrase that was in current use, although coined in America: "the phoney war". Was it really going to prove a phoney war so far as England was concerned? Things had turned out so differently from what he had expected. He had "come across" in a crack Atlantic liner unescorted and without incident. He had found England "blacked out", but un-invaded. London, where he had gone to present his papers and credentials for entry into the Air Force, had recovered from its early scares of raids. Many of the evacuated children had come back and, but for the blackout and the barrage balloons and shelters and gas masks and the preponderance of uniforms among the crowds, most things were as usual. The officials at the Air Ministry who had interviewed him had not seemed imbued with any great sense of urgency. Yet they must have been impressed with the documents he presented (there was one from a very high personage in the Canadian Government) for, after a fortnight of flying tests at a depot on Salisbury plain, he had been gazetted as a Flying Officer and posted to his present depot; not as he had imagined and hoped for advanced and final instruction in air gunnery and bombing, but as an instructor himself in routine flying. It seemed that he had the rare gift not only of natural airmanship, but of being able to impart his skill and self confidence to others. It was not what he had wanted to do at all. He'd wanted, or at least he'd thought he'd wanted, to be "in it" with the least possible delay. And to make things worse he had no sooner arrived at the depot than the snow had come, blizzard upon blizzard with short thaws between them with fog and slush that quickly froze again, and cold such as he had never experienced in Canada, for it was humid and seemed to penetrate the very bones. Even now, despite that he was wearing a thick greatcoat, that he was hemmed in on both sides by human beings (mostly service-men and -women bound like himself on weekend leave), he felt half-frozen and yet half-stifled with the steam-heated and tobacco-ladened air, depressed by the view, irritated by the whistling, the crooning, the disjointed and inane snatches of male and female conversation that came from his equally "browned off" fellow travellers. It annoyed him too that as an officer he held a first-class ticket, that all the first-class compartments were filled at least partly by third-class passengers, and it annoyed him again that he, hating all forms of snobbery, should feel such annoyance. . .

But, when the engine whistled as at last it did, his spirits began to rise. The train was moving, the soldiers were hoisting their kits on to their backs and even their whistling and crooning seemed less tuneless and dismal. Farther up the corridor a group of land girls were singing lustily and almost musically the most popular ditty of the day, *"South of the Border"*, and involuntarily he started humming it himself. In a few minutes now, unless another signal barred the way, he'd be in Donbridge for the first time since his student days. He'd made no plans. If the coastline hadn't been blocked with snow he'd have spent the weekend at home. He'd had a wide circle of friends in Donbridge in the old days, however. He was almost bound to meet with someone he knew. There was his old friend Professor Tomlinson the zoologist. The university would be closed but he could ring him up at his private address in the suburbs, perhaps go out and see him. He would at least be able to give information about other friends. Failing that there was the repertory theatre. He was too late for a matinee, but not to book for the evening performance. And it would be something to have two nights in a decent hotel, hot baths and good food, and a change from the atmosphere of that dismal RAF depot. . .

But he found the station as crowded as the train had been, chiefly with service-men and -women arriving or departing on leave. All the telephone kiosks were engaged with a queue for each. He remembered that opposite the station's main entrance, across Bridge Street (the city's main thoroughfare), was the General Post Office. There wouldn't be such a crowd there. He would phone the County Hotel first and make certain of his room. Then have a word with his old professor.

In the high archway of the station entrance he hesitated, however. Later he was to remember that hesitation and every detail of what happened during the following brief, but dramatic, period of time, and often he was to wonder what would have happened if he had obeyed the impulse to go back and wait his turn at the station kiosks. It had seemed then the most sensible thing to do for the snow had turned to heavy rain. Between the piles of snow that had been ploughed or shovelled to each side of the street the road itself was a puddle of dirty slush through which the traffic was splashing as through the ford of a brook. He was not fastidious, but he was wearing light shoes and it looked as though he couldn't have crossed the road without filling them.

Perhaps it was the sudden gap in the stream of traffic that decided him, that between the pavement and the opposite island which was clear of snow the way was open, a physically simpler proposition than the way back to the kiosks in the crowded station. Perhaps again some deep subconscious force made up his mind for him. He looked at the island with its shaded traffic lights already on because of the foggy overcast, at the entrance to the post office almost dead opposite, and keeping on tiptoes he made a dash for it, reached the island, saw that the way was still clear and continued the crossing. Then with more leisurely strides, for there was no slush on the pavement and the rain itself did not worry him, he walked to the flight of wide stone steps that led up an archway almost as large as that of the railway station into the post office. And he was to remember that as he set foot on the first of those steps he heard the clock in Donbridge City Hall, some distance up the street, start to strike the hour of three.

There was a lobby at the top of the steps. Straight ahead were doors marked private. The public room was on the right, with double swing doors that were fastened back. There was no one in the lobby when he reached it. It chanced too that there was no one coming immediately behind him, and that, of the moderately large number of people who were doing business in the room, only one person who was actually coming out: a girl of medium build and slender graceful figure, dressed in a well-cut tweed overcoat with a bright silk scarf at the neck and wearing a soft dark brown felt hat. She was advancing straight towards him. He saw her face full on. He observed the shape of her throat and chin, her full lips whose shape was not disguised with paint, the rather short nose, the wide set and unusually large cool grey eyes which in that moment were staring blankly into his own. And then—and they were not more than six feet apart—they both stopped. Her blank stare changed to one of astonished delight, her lips parted in a smile of recognition and they said, simultaneously,

"Jane!"

"Edwin!"

Speech momentarily failed them then. They just stood staring at each other. Then a sudden influx of post office customers compelled them to move to one side of the fairway, and when they stopped again she had the presence of mind to reach out her hand in a conventional gesture and say,

"I *am* pleased to see you. I heard you were in England and in the Air Force, but I never dreamt of meeting you like this!"

He took her hand.

"I just can't believe it. I thought when I saw you first there was something familiar about you. You haven't changed much except—"

He hesitated, and she smiled and said,

"That I've got my hair up and haven't got bare legs! I don't think you've changed much either, but of course you do look different in a uniform. You're looking very well. Do you like being in the Air Force?"

He had released her hand. They stood close together, but no closer than the passing traffic necessitated. They were behaving, according to the conventions, as two acquaintances meeting unexpectedly after many years, asking the conventional questions, giving the conventional answers, and they were both still a little dazed from the surprise of their meeting.

"Like it? I've never been so bored in my life as I have been the last few weeks!"

"Are you stationed near Donbridge?"

"At Belton Wood only twenty miles away. But it's taken me two and a half hours to get here today. I like flying. But there hasn't been any since the first heavy snow came. I did intend going up to Bramblewick this weekend, but the coast line is blocked. Do you live in Donbridge?"

"Yes, least out at Mountwood Park. I've been here for a long time. I was at the Teachers' Training College. Then I had a spell teaching, then went back to Coll for a special course, and then to the school where I am at present. It's near Mountwood Park. It's Council but it's specially for children from the slums, with no proper homes, whose parents won't evacuate them into the real country or who have fetched them back after the first scare."

He had sensed a complete lack of any enthusiasm in her voice as she had made this statement. He recalled too that when he had first caught sight of her moving towards him, before he had recognised her or she him, her expression had not been a happy one. He said,

"It sounds interesting. Do you like it?"

"Yes, for some things." (And then she did smile again.) "We produced a play at Christmas, *The Mad Hatter's Tea Party*—the thing we did at Bramblewick years ago when I played Alice. Funny, but I did it from the very copy Mrs Jones had given me, with her notes in it. Of course I didn't make half such a good job of the production as she made of ours, but it was good fun, and I had a grand girl for Alice, although I just couldn't break her of her Donbridge accent!"

"I remember that play. How marvellous you were in it! I remember that letter of hers you read to me too. So you took her advice about being a teacher! But what about being an actress, the thing you really wanted to do?"

She laughed, but not happily, and there was a restrained bitterness in her voice when she said,

"Oh—*that*! It *might* have happened but for the war. I joined the Thespians as soon as I came to Donbridge. I had only very small parts for a long time. Then last spring one or two quite decent ones and I was given the part of Liza Doolittle in *Pygmalion* for our opening play in September. I thought if I really made a success of it the people at the Donbridge Rep might notice it and give me a chance. But the Government requisitioned the Thespians' theatre for a store when war came. The Donbridge Repertory Players had to give up because of half their men joining up for service, and their theatre is now a cinema!"

"Oh lord—how awful! I mean about you. You must feel dreadful about it. . . Look here—there's no point in our standing in this draughty place, is there? Can't we go somewhere and have tea and talk? It's just the biggest piece of luck my meeting you. And to think that if I hadn't rushed over here to telephone I'd have missed you. What are you doing? Have you got any engagements for the rest of the day?"

She was smiling again.

"No, I've just been in town shopping, getting some knitting wool to send to mother. I popped in here to post it. I think I'd have caught a bus then for where I live. I hate Saturdays in Donbridge, and it's awful when the blackout comes, but it would be nice to go and have tea. What about the Grand Cinema Cafe? It's just a few yards down Bridge Street and it won't be crowded at this time of day. What about your phone call, though?"

He had forgotten about Professor Tomlinson.

"Oh, that doesn't matter! I only wanted to ring up and book a room at a pub. I can do that any time. The street's horribly slushy. I'd better get a taxi!"

She laughed and pointed to her feet, clad in rubber overshoes.

"Don't be silly! It's only a minute's walk and *I* don't mind the weather!"

"Come on, then!"

It was still raining and now there was a wind that was in their faces as they turned left from the post office entrance. But the scene, which only a few minutes ago he had thought so forbidding, now looked gay and inspiring. It was practically dusk, but a long time yet from official blackout. The shop windows were lit. There were lights in the buses and tramcars which showered twinkling reflections on the pavement and the road. Even the piles of melting snow looked less repulsive. He had taken her arm lightly, but confidently, and couldn't resist giving it a squeeze when he said,

"This *is* luck, you know. I just can't believe it. Only I do hope you're not getting wet!"

She did not return his squeeze, but she looked at him, smiling, and said,

"I like the feel of rain on my face, and the wind too. I suppose that's through having been brought up in the country. Canada must be wonderful. *You* haven't told me anything about yourself. *You* seem to have done the things you wanted to do, or haven't you? What about painting? Do you remember you said you wanted to be that, more than a scientist?"

"Yes, I do. But I wanted to be both. And now, having been both, I'm neither, but at this particular moment I don't care. Yes I'll tell you all about Canada and painting, least not all, but as much as you'll be able to stand. Only don't ask me about life in the Royal Air Force. And don't tell me, Jane, that you have a passion for crooning!"

"I hate it. . . Here's the Grand!"

They walked into the brilliantly illuminated and lavishly-decorated foyer. There was a broad marble stairway with gilt handrails leading upwards on the left with a neon sign saying Café, but they stopped to look at the cinema display placards. The most prominent ones were for next week's big attraction, and it was on a smaller one with a strip pasted on it TO-DAY that they saw that the feature film showing was Ginger Rogers' *Fifth Avenue Girl*.

"Jane—have you seen it?"

"No. Have you? I've heard it's very good!"

"It's *grand*! Shall we go when we've had tea?"

"But *have* you seen it?"

"Yes, I saw it in Canada, but I shouldn't mind seeing it a dozen times. Do you like Ginger Rogers?"

"Yes. I like her better as an actress even than when she was dancing with Fred Astaire. But I'm sure you won't want to see it again. You're only saying so—"

But he had already moved over to the box-office. He joined her triumphantly.

"It *is* my lucky day. Only two seats left for the next house at four-thirty, and I've got them!"

She looked at him severely.

"Look Edwin," (she hesitated slightly in pronouncing his Christian name). "You're not to do this sort of thing. You've got to let me pay my share!"

He seized her arm again and this time held it a little tighter and nudged her towards the staircase.

"Oh yeah?" he mocked, "and spoil my lucky day? I only hope you'll like it. *I* think Ginger's better as a straight actress, although I always liked her with Fred. Do you remember that ironic duet of theirs, *A Fine Romance*. . . ?"

The cafe was warm, softly lit and not crowded. They found a corner table. They took off their coats. She was wearing under hers a well-cut Harris coat and skirt, with a Fair Isle jersey.

"I do like the things you wear!"

He wasn't trying to flirt with her. He was just happy and liking her very much, and being honest about it. She too was obviously happy. She made the inevitable feminine rejoinder,

"Do you? They're very ancient."

But she was looking with interest at his pilot's wings, and as he hung up their coats, along with his haversack and service gas-mask, she could not have helped noticing that two smartly-dressed and made-up girls sitting a few tables away also were looking at him, suspending their own conversation, and perhaps temporarily their own friendship, while each made her own swift feminine reconnaissance. A pretty waitress with blonde hair and dazzling teeth was in attendance the moment he sat down, although the two girls, having been in first, had by queue ethics a clear priority, and again Jane must have observed how the waitress was bringing all her charms to bear on him.

"You said I mustn't ask you about the Royal Air Force," she said when the waitress had gone. "So I mustn't say I like your uniform and what you've got on it!"

He laughed, holding out a packet of cigarettes he had taken from his greatcoat pocket.

"No don't. Let's forget about the war. Have a cigarette?"

She took one. He had done it unthinkingly, but as he held out the lighter to her (just as he had held out the glowing stick from their fire to her once, and he had seen the sudden terror in her eyes as she had caught sight of her father) their eyes met and he remembered, and knew that she was remembering, not without pain. She drew at the cigarette and said coolly and with just a tinge of irony,

"You see I have learnt how!"

There was a measured silence between them. Then he said, feeling his way, anxious to avoid touching a possibly sore place,

"It was a lovely day, wasn't it?"

"Apart from the end, yes."

"Do you remember the lobster, and how we cooked it in the old tin?"

She looked happy again.

"Yes, and didn't it taste good! And I remember the octopus and the sea-slug, but I can't remember the long name you gave it, but it reminded me of Rumpelstiltskin."

"I've forgotten it myself. But I shall not forget how you came round that rock reciting *The Forsaken Merman*."

"I must have been horribly conceited. A horrible little prig!"

"What nonsense! You were perfectly natural. I was the prig, rattling off those long Latin names. . . I'm awfully sorry that things haven't gone the way you hoped. But you haven't given it up, have you? I mean the idea of the stage, professionally? You've got an extraordinarily beautiful speaking voice. You've got the face and the figure too. You were doubtful about the face, I remember. But I wasn't. And I'm certainly not now. I'm not a portrait painter. But I do know something about it. And I don't think I have ever deliberately missed seeing a stage play in my life, so I know that side too! You're still keen, aren't you?"

Her cheeks, which had been rather pale, had flushed. She knew he was serious, and she was serious herself, and now there was no bitterness in her voice, only a certain resignation.

"It is nice of you to say all that. And encouraging. Of course I'm still keen. But it's all so difficult. It's not only the Thespians and the Rep closing. It's, well, everything. Don't think I'm just grousing. I'm lucky, really. I've got quite an interesting job, well paid too. I *do* like being with children. I've got a very good friend too, Muriel Heston. I would like you to meet her. She's a professional pianist, the widow of a doctor who died about ten years ago, but left her quite well off. She has a large house out at Mountwood and she's given me a room of my own there, and I help her with the housekeeping. She's on the committee of the Thespians. That's how I met her first, and she's interested in all the arts. She was as keen on my going on the stage as Gwen Jones was. I'm certain I'd have got my chance with the Rep but for the war coming. . . And that's it. The war has upset everything. I just don't know what to do. Daddy's pestering me to go home. He's ploughed up a lot more land, and mother says he's so worried about my being in a city that may be bombed and although she doesn't say so I know they are both overworked and that I ought to go and help them. Anyway, I feel, and Muriel agrees with me, that it's no good my thinking about the stage until the war is over. And I feel I want to be doing something more important like nursing or joining one of the women's services. It isn't as though I was a good teacher. I'm only good at the things I liked myself at school, and of course doing plays. . . Oh dear—I'm sick of talking about myself. Do

334

tell me about your painting."

"I don't know what there is to tell, except that we seem to be in the same boat. Does your father know you've been trying to get on the stage?"

"Good gracious, no! He'd have a fit! Even when I had those small parts with the Thespians I had to have another name put down in the programme in case something might appear in the papers and he might get to know. I'm a terrible liar. He even thinks I teach in Sunday School and that Mrs Heston is a shining light in the district Wesleyan Chapel! Actually, I think she's a Fabian. Really, I live a double life!"

"So do I, or rather I *did!* Painting and science, and I never dared to let my father know it was painting that counted most. Queer that it started that day we first met!"

"I remember how excited you got about it. How you raved about the colours of the rocks and the sea. But you wouldn't let me see what you'd painted!"

"No. I wasn't certain then. I was scared, too. I had to sit for that scholarship as well as get my degree. Not just because of father. Don't think that! But because I hadn't enough faith in myself. I did my duty by the scholarship, anyway. I painted, or rather started to learn to paint, only in my spare time. Research at the marine biological stations at Roscoff, Monaco, Naples—Dr Jekyll. Painting and drawing at Paris, Florence, Rome—Mr Hyde, except that *my* Mr Hyde was a harmless sort of chap. Then the Bermudas and the States and Canada. I shouldn't know where to start if I were to tell you the whole story."

"But what sort of things do you paint?"

"Landscapes, seascapes, figures, but not portraits. Mountains and rocks and trees and clouds and the sea, the things I love. Nature, if you like. Nothing without sunshine. Oils for choice!"

"Are you good? I believe you are!"

"I might have been. I suppose I might be yet. But I can't forget what an old artist I knew in Florence told me. He was a Dutchman, a painter. He'd got cancer and he was drinking hard, but gosh he could paint. Quite a genius, only he had a fierce hate of humanity at large. He'd never exhibit his work, never sell it, either. He must be dead by now. He told me I'd never produce a real work of art until I'd known real unhappiness. That my painting was just clever, slick, even sentimental. He charged me with being too healthy, too happy, too damned successful!"

"But how silly! The poor man must have been envious."

"No. I think he was right in a way. I do believe that some of the loveliest and greatest things do come out of suffering and misery and ugliness. I don't say an artist should make a cult of misery and pain like the Indian fakirs, but he's got to have experience of every side of life, plus, of course, that something that makes him an artist. He mustn't just go on feasting on beauty. . . Mind, that was before Canada. I did feel I was getting somewhere just before the war started, and without any suffering, either, unless you could call black flies and mosquitoes suffering. That was last summer. I was playing Dr Jekyll and Mr Hyde again but quite conscientiously, surveying the sources of one of the chief salmon rivers way up among the coast mountains, but painting too in my legitimate spare time. It was magnificent country, not so awe-inspiring as the real Rockies, but the colours and the shapes just took your breath away. I was beginning to think that I was at least getting away from that slickness, painting with *real* feeling and sincerity. But when I got back from that trip everyone was talking about Hitler and the war, and it's queer, but when I looked at the things I'd done I loathed them and—"

He stopped, and laughed apologetically.

"Oh damn it, I'm getting much too serious!"

"You're not. It's all fascinating. Do go on. I wish I could see what you'd done. I feel sure that old man must have been wrong about you. I think the inspiration of any sort of art should be happiness and not misery."

"Do you, Jane ?"

"Yes, I *do*! I think it should come out of love. I mean out of loving things like the sea and woods and rocks you say you paint. Did you bring any of your pictures to England with you?"

"Only a few to show my father. I naturally chose the ones I thought he'd like, or at any rate not actively dislike. And they were water colours. He did try to like them, I think, but really he's not interested in anything in that line. It was a rather trying weekend. The war has got him down more than anyone I know. He's become nervy. Insists on listening to every news bulletin up till midnight, including the German broadcasts in English. He and Aunt Betsy came almost to a real row because he wanted it on during Sunday dinner. He doesn't like my being in the Air Force."

"Well, naturally he'd be worried. I know that I would be worried if my daddy was in it this time. . . oh, I think that war is horrible!"

He was surprised at a sudden vehemence in her

voice. He laughed a little self-consciously.

"I do agree with you. We shouldn't have started talking about it. But somehow or other you can't escape it. Anyway, here's blondie with tea. And Ginger should help! Tell me what other films you've seen her in, Jane!"

"No. You go on telling me about painting and Canada."

They talked, as only two people of strong mutual tastes and interests but divergent experiences can; all the early restraints of their first meeting gone, frankly enjoying each other's company. They were both healthy, broad-minded, intelligent human beings, with well-stocked minds and an inexhaustible potential of things to tell and discuss, both personal and abstract, and they were in no hurry for at an early stage Jane had disclosed that she had no plans for tomorrow in spite of the illusions her father might have as to pious occupations on the Sabbath. . .

In the cinema there was no need for them to talk at all. He had made no error in thinking that she would appreciate *Fifth Avenue Girl*. The play itself was not a masterpiece. But the situations were well contrived, the dialogue had real wit and Miss Rogers herself, a superb comedy actress, got the best out of her part, proving at least that her genius was not indissolubly welded to that of her famous one-time partner. They agreed not to spoil the effect by staying on for the "news" which (they had seen from the programme) contained the latest pictures from the Finnish battlegrounds. It was a quarter to six when they emerged into the foyer where the head of the queue for the second and last house was waiting. They stopped, a little dazzled by the lights.

"I did love it! I think Ginger Rogers really thrilling. Thank you so much for taking me!"

"I thought you'd like it! And now what? Don't you dare to tell me that you're going to pack off home. Do you feel hungry? Shall we go and have dinner somewhere, or is it too early?"

She was looking at him, happily.

"It isn't six o'clock yet! Are *you* hungry?"

"Not yet, but I shall be eventually!"

"How hungry, do you think? Will you need an enormous meal? Are you terribly fussy about what you eat?"

He began to suspect a gentle mocking.

"Of course I'm not. Do I look it? You can't say I'm fat!"

"No. But you might be fussy. Men can be, you know, about meals. I was just going to make a suggestion. . . I hope you won't think it's improper!"

He caught at that final remark, saw that there was a twinkle in her eyes.

"You sound most excitedly wicked, Jane. Come on, let's have it!"

"Well, just that you come and have a meal at home with me. Only it's my duty of course to warn you that my friend Muriel, whom I really want you to meet, for she's so nice, won't be there because she's away for the weekend in Manchester playing at a concert. There's no one else in the house except a fat and silly old spaniel called Bones who's supposed to be a protection against burglars, but would be more likely to sit up and beg if he saw one coming through the window. If Muriel had been home there would perhaps have been a really good supper. She *is* a good cook. As it is I've got some eggs—

mother sent me a dozen this morning, and some fresh butter and cream. I believe there's some tomatoes in the fridge, and two lettuces. I believe we've got some ham too. . . are you shocked?"

Her eyes were still twinkling, but in a flash he recognised behind the play her absolute candour. He laughed.

"Shocked? I'm simply staggered. And from a Sunday School teacher, too! What a grand idea. Thank you, Jane. I'd love to come. How do we get there?"

"There's a bus for Mountwood Park every half-hour. We might get one at ten to six. They start opposite the station."

"Come on then, let's hurry!"

There was a wide staircase leading down from the foyer, with the queue on one side, and leading out into the almost complete dark of the street. He took her arm.

"I'd forgotten the blackout. And it looks as though it's snowing again. My lamp's in my haversack. Have you got one?"

"Yes. In my handbag. Just a minute."

They halted at street level, but still in the shelter of the cinema's entrance, while Jane searched for the lamp, but before she found it a taxi drew up at the kerb to discharge a party for the show. Ignoring her protests, he rushed forward and accosted the driver over the shoulder of the male of the party who was settling the fare. The driver ignored him until the transaction was complete and he had flagged up his meter. Then he asked dourly where did he want to be. . . Mountwood Park? It was over four miles that, and all uphill, and it was starting to snow again, likely to come another blizzard. Couldn't he and the lady take a bus? In a great hurry was he? Aye, so was everybody. What address was it? . . . Dr Heston's Greystone House. Aye, he knew it, but he didn't know if he'd be able to find it a night like this on top of the blackout. If it got much worse, and it looked as though he might get stuck up Mountwood Bank, they'd have to get out and walk the rest. He wasn't going to risk spending the night in a snowdrift. . .

The snow was getting worse, but they didn't know how much worse until, nearly thirty minutes later, the taxi stopped and the driver shouted through the communication window,

"Is this it?"

He was shining his torch across what might have been a pavement to what undoubtedly was a square stone pillar at one side of a carriage drive, but Jane had to open the door and gaze intently at the pillar before she could say for certain "Yes," which she qualified with an expression of fervent gratitude to the driver. To this Edwin added his own particular thanks, along with a substantial multiplication of the fare.

"Do you think you'll get back all right?"

The driver was less dour.

"Aye. It'll be downhill. But ah doubt if there'll be many more cars come up this way t' neet. Nor buses. It's going to be worse than ever."

The taxi had halted in what normally would have been the middle of the road. The ploughs had not been able to clear more than one traffic lane in the previous heavy falls. They stepped out and, as the taxi turned, robbing them of its protection, they were struck by a gust of wind and a flurry of snow that temporarily blinded them. They clung on to each other. Then Jane succeeded in getting the beam of her torch on to the stone pillar and they struggled towards it over the wall of old snow that had been piled up by the ploughs. But she was laughing when they reached it, and the edge of a drift which extended beyond the pillar to the front of a large house.

"There it is!"

It is a fact that snow and violent winds which can cause such discomfort and harm to mankind can also, under certain circumstances, produce a lifting of the human spirit, a sense of exhilaration and joy. The drift was deep. The wind was eddying through the entrance of the drive, piling the snow deeper. But arm-in-arm they plunged forward into it, laughing at their efforts to keep upright, at the way it was plastering their faces, getting into their eyes and mouths. They were like a couple of hilarious school children and they were still laughing when they reached the porch. He had to hold the lamp while she searched her bag for the latchkey, and he had to scrape the snow from the door to find the keyhole. Already they had heard the friendly barking of a dog within. Yet their hilarity became thankful relief when they stepped inside and slammed the outer door against snow and storm and the first thing Edwin said was,

"Gosh—what a warm house!"

"Warm? Wait till you get really inside. Central heating and a fire too, I hope. I left it banked up. All right, Bones! Don't be impatient! I think we'd best go straight into the kitchen and take off our coats and put them on the airing rail. Are your feet wet? Mine are frozen. Here's silly old Bones!"

She had switched on a shaded light, and opened

a second door leading into the hall. Bones had been waiting there and he greeted them both with undiscriminating affection. The house was old, but modernised with tolerable taste, as Edwin observed from the distempered walls and the few elegant pieces of furniture that caught his eye as he followed Jane through the hall. But what pleased him most was the warmth, that indescribable sense of entering a comfortable, kindly home. He bent down and tickled Bones behind the ear as he too followed the leader, and the look the dog gave him from its big expressive spaniel eyes increased his sense of domestic felicity. They entered the kitchen. Jane had switched on the light and had immediately dashed to the window and drawn the heavy curtains.

"It's not air-raids," she laughed, "it's air-raid wardens and the police. Muriel's terribly careless. She's been fined twice already for not drawing the blinds at night. I do wish she was here for you to meet her. She's a lovely woman. Are your feet wet? Do get your coat off. Wasn't it fun struggling through that snow? It's ages since I've laughed so much. Do you like the kitchen?"

She had taken off her hat. There were still flakes of snow melting on her face. She looked excited and happy and with her mind only half on what she was saying. His own thoughts flashed back to that day on the beach, and looking at her it was as though he were watching her put up her hands to those unruly strands of hair to hold them from her face. But she was taking off her coat and he now did the same, and she lowered the airing rail, and while he was hoisting it up for her with their coats on it, he answered some of her questions. No his feet weren't very wet, but if she didn't mind he'd put on some slippers he had in his haversack while his shoes were drying, and that he thought the kitchen was just grand, and that oughtn't she to change her stockings which looked really wet with the flakes of snow melting on them?

He liked the way she was playing hostess to him.

"I'll go and change my stockings. But let me take you into the lounge first and you can change there and see that the fire's all right. Are you very hungry? Shall I get supper now? Or shall we wait?"

"Just whatever you wish. Only I feel so gorgeously warm myself I can't bear the thought of you being cold. Hurry up and change anyway!"

"All right. I will when I've shown you the lounge. Only there's one more thing."

She stood and looked him straight in the face, not smiling, but serious.

"I've been thinking about it all the way in the taxi, wondering if it would shock you, but I don't care if it does! If Muriel *was* here she wouldn't dream of letting you go back to Donbridge on a night like this and stay at a hotel. And she'd laugh at me if I told her *I'd* let you because of the conventions. We've always got at least two guestrooms aired. It isn't very often one of them isn't occupied for a weekend. She's got scores of friends, mostly musical. I'd feel awful if you *did* go. We have known one another a long time, haven't we? *Are* you shocked this time?"

He answered easily, sensing again her absolute candour.

"I'm not, Jane. Of course I'll stay. I don't think, as a matter of fact, you could make me go now I've got the wavelength of this central heating."

"You *are* nice, Edwin."

"You're nice, Jane. And we speak each other's language, don't we?"

"I think we do. . . Listen to the wind howling outside. I do hope our taximan has got home all right. Come on. I'll have to dash in and draw the curtains before I switch on the light. The lounge windows look out on the road. . . Oh heavens! And I left the fire on! Someone was fined only last week because their fire had burnt up and was showing!"

They were being perfectly honest with each other. So far as the conventions of the society to which they belonged were reasonable (and most of them, they would agree, were) they were themselves conventional. They were young but intelligent adults. They would have been apostate to their own code of behaviour had they shrunk from doing something they considered simple common sense, which another generation would have deemed, in Jane's ironically-inflected word, improper.

The fire, to Jane's relief, was only glowing. She drew the curtains, switched on the light, and said to Edwin as she passed him on the threshold of the room,

"I won't be long changing. Do make a big fire. Everything's safe now. There's some logs in that box on the right."

She was hurrying upstairs. As he walked slowly into the room he was aware more strongly than before of that atmosphere of complete felicity. It was not that it satisfied his strong and practised æsthetic sense. Although large, there were far too many things in it. There was a grand piano (in ebony) that occupied

345

awkwardly a large proportion of the floor space opposite him near the wall with the curtained window. There was an antique Queen Anne secretaire on the wall on his left and packed bookshelves right and left of it. In front of the fireplace on his right was a monstrous Chesterfield with chintz cover, two more similarly covered chairs, a leather-covered pouffe, and a wooden African stool. He saw the box for the logs. Behind it was a large mahogany radiogram with a cabinet for records. There were other chairs and a mahogany table, and on the floor several Kelim rugs on top of a faded but good Axminster carpet, and in front of the large Georgian fireplace a thick sheepskin rug on which Bones had already settled himself. But everything in the room he perceived was for use as the things in his father's "holy of holies" were, and many of the things were of intrinsic beauty, and thinking suddenly of the officers' lounge as it would be at this moment, it seemed perfection.

He took a couple of logs from the box and put them on the fire and raked out the ashes. Bones gave him an approving look and wagged his tail. He had brought his haversack in with him. He sat down on the Chesterfield and changed his shoes. His socks were not wet after all, but his feet were cold, and he pulled the Chesterfield nearer to the fire and sat down again with his feet reaching out to the fender on each side of the now sleeping Bones. The logs were dry and tarry and were already blazing. He stared at the flames and thought again of that day when he and Jane had been at their driftwood fire and they'd talked of the things they were going to do with their lives. He could see her kneeling on the shingle while she read the letter from her friend encouraging her to go on the stage, but warning her of the difficulties that lay ahead. He could see her excited eyes and hear her laughter and remember the exact tone of her voice. He could see her leaping from rock to rock looking for driftwood, and how she had stood holding that piece up for him to see, with one hand pressing back her hair, and with the blue of the sunlit sea behind her away to the horizon before the fog came. . . And now, just as vividly, he could see her as she had advanced towards him in the post office, grown up and beautiful, and with a knowledge of the world, wearing until that instant of recognition the mask of indifference that modern civilisation requires of an attractive woman if she is to move peacefully among its crowds; but with the mask dropped, still the Jane he had met and parted from that day. He had never believed that he had fallen in love with her then. But he had never forgotten. He had realised that trying to see her again or writing to her would have made things more unpleasant between her and her half-crazy father. He had never thought that she had fallen in love with him. They had parted and now it was as though that day and this day were one, and that now he was as happy as he had been then up to the time her father had come and ended everything.

Or was he happier? Had he ever in his life been so happy as he had been from the moment they had met, scarcely more than three hours ago, and they had walked through the rain and the glittering street to the cinema, and sat talking there, and then watching the film, sharing its delight? He knew suddenly that he was completely in love with her, that he would never of his own free will be able to part with her again. He was the happiest man on earth! And then, as suddenly, he had a complete reversal of emotion. Was she in love with him? Had she, since they had met, given him the slightest indication that she was, that she regarded him as anything but a friend, the sharer of one youthful experience of long ago? Wasn't her very candour, the way she had suggested his coming home with her and now spending the night in this snowbound house, a clear sign that she regarded him and their friendship in the sensible conventionally unconventional modern way, as he himself until now had thought it? He heard her coming. He felt his heart thumping and he knew that it was with fear. He stood up, watching the door, not knowing what he was going to say to her. It opened and she came in, closing the door and standing with her hand still on the knob. She had changed into a frock. It was made of heavy silk, claret red in colour, with cream lace at the collar and cuffs. The sleeves were full and the skirt flared. She was smiling at him, frankly posing as any woman would, having done her best to make herself attractive. But with his own courage and self-confidence at low ebb he thought it was just that and no more. She said, quite frankly,

"Do you like it?"

He said, with outward and sincere enthusiasm,

"You look marvellous!"

He saw the pleasure in her eyes (but no more than that) and having won her tribute she generously diminished it.

"I am glad you like it. Gwen Jones sent me the material last Christmas and I made it from a pattern I found in a woman's magazine, and Muriel gave me the lace."

He said (gathering some courage by the mere act of speech),

"It's a terrific success. You're terribly clever. And you look marvellous!"

She laughed. She was moving now, quickly, smoothly round the back of the Chesterfield towards a cupboard close to the piano.

"Oh I'm not clever a bit. But I'm glad you like it. What a lovely fire you've made. Do tell me about supper. That's going to be the real test. Would you like an omelette or straight ham and eggs?"

He had turned to watch her, his back now to the fire. She had reached the cupboard. . . She looked calm, completely self-possessed. He felt that he could not have imagined anyone looking more beautiful than she did in that dress, more desirable, or more completely remote. She was opening the cupboard door. He said,

"I just don't care. I leave it to you. But do let me help you, whatever it is!"

"No. That's my job. You're to sit here by the fire. Do you know how to work the radiogram? You told me you were dying to hear some music. You can have just what you like. Beethoven—we've got mostly the symphonies, concertos and sonatas. Tchaikovsky—there's the *Swan Lake* and the piano concerto. Bach, Mozart, Sibelius, Grieg, even jazz. Even Ginger and Fred Astaire in selections from *Top Hat*. You can play while I'm getting supper. But I thought first, seeing that I've already led you astray, you might like a drink! Only sherry, I'm afraid. It's Muriel's, of course, but I've no scruples about that, the number of drinks I've refused to have in the past!"

He knew, or he thought he knew, that she was just being friendly, just enjoying playing hostess to him. He answered in her own idiom,

"You're a real vamp! Thank you, I'd love a drink. And it's going to be fine having that music. Let me help you!"

He moved towards her and suddenly all his courage and self-confidence came back. She was holding a tray with one hand, reaching inside the cupboard for some glasses with the other. He took the tray from her hand and put it back on the shelf, and then he put his hands on her shoulders, facing her, looking into her big and now startled eyes.

"Jane," he said, "are you happy?"

She hadn't resisted his touch. Her eyes were wide open, her lips slightly parted, but they were quivering. She answered almost in a whisper,

"Yes—of course—why?"

His own voice was steady.

"*Were* you happy, before we met in the post office, this afternoon?"

She stared at him. She caught her breath and then said rapidly,

"No—no. I was utterly miserable!"

"And you're really happy now? Because *I* am. I think you're the loveliest woman in the world. I'm just completely in love with you, Jane. I just want you, want you forever. What do you say to that? Are you going to be shocked?"

She just looked at him, her eyes seeming to grow bigger and bigger and to shine with joy. Then she put her hands on the lapels of his tunic and drew herself to him and raised her face to his and, with their lips nearly touching, she said passionately,

"Oh Edwin—I love you. I want to be with you forever!"

3

SHE'D GOT Jane's letter in the morning, just before dinnertime, but luckily before Tom had come in from his work on the top fields. Jonty had got a lift in a military car taking rations (and mail) to the new searchlight post up on High Batts moor. It had enabled him to reverse his usual round and make the farm his first instead of one of his last daily calls. It was a very hot day. He was feeling his years (he was long past retiring age) and he was glad of the cup of tea and the piece of cake she'd given him, glad of the chance to sit down in the kitchen for a spell while he gave her his unusually grim budget of news. She had taken the letter (and one addressed to Tom from the Ministry of Agriculture & Fisheries) from him quite calmly, putting it down unopened on the sideboard, and going on with her work while he talked. Things were bad, aye, things were very bad. The Germans were advancing everywhere. It looked as though they were going to have as easy a job in Belgium as they'd had in Holland. The Belgian king had given in. This after asking the British and the French to come to his help! The Germans had taken Lille and "Wypers" (he'd fought there himself in the last war). They claimed that they'd taken Ostend. They were already in Boulogne. It looked as though they'd got the British and French almost surrounded against the coast. Almost as though they'd got us beat. Next thing would be they'd try invasion. But they'd find that a different job, like Napoleon and the Spanish Armada had done. He only wished he was twenty years younger himself and he could be having a go at the Huns. The latest village news was that young Jack Harrison, one of poor Kit Harrison's lads, was feared lost (his ship was ten days overdue and the owners had written his mother); that Jonty's wife had been sitting up all night with Mrs Bunny, who'd now had a stroke and wasn't expected to last much longer; and that the Government had taken over the old Wesleyan Chapel and were going to turn it into a hostel for "foreign" evacuees. . .

She was a well-practised listener. She had made such signs and comments as would satisfy Jonty that she was taking an interest in everything he said, but all the time her mind had been on the letter. He had said when he had handed it to her, laughingly,

"From Jane, eh? I ought to know that handwriting!"

She had known that he would have very much liked her to have read it at once, and told him if there'd been anything of interest, anything that could be added to his budget of news to take on to the other farms, to his wife, and to the village. She had noticed how, when at last he'd got up to go, he had glanced towards it and she'd wondered if by any chance he and the village had heard anything, but decided no. He was a gossip-monger, but not malicious, and if he had known anything he wouldn't have been able to resist telling. But she had gone to the door with him and watched him climbing the stile into the pasture, and she had seen that Tom had only just left the top fields before she'd gone back and opened it. She had known that Tom would see Jonty, know he had called, but that they wouldn't meet and that he would not know there had been any other letter except the one for himself.

When he had come in the first thing he had said was,

"Jonty's early today, Ella. What is there?"

Outwardly she was quite calm and her voice steady.

"Only that Government thing for you!"

"Nothing from Jane again?"

"No."

He glanced at his letter on his way to the sink. He was wearing flannel trousers and a cotton shirt open at the neck, and he was grimy from the smoke and charcoal of the whins he had been burning and clearing. The sweat had washed streaks in the grime down his face and neck.

"Only that! I reckon it will be another notice telling us to grow more of something or other. But they won't tell us how we're to get the time to do it! I'm having a job up there in the whins. It takes so long. When you've burnt a whin and got the top stuff off you've got to dig round its roots, some of them are feet deep in the ground. Only it will be worth it. Every square yard of land that'll grow food will be wanted, they say."

He was washing. She was ready to serve out the dinner. She knew what he was going to say next, or very soon, and she was prepared for it. She was not going to speak yet. The letter was too fresh in her mind. She wanted time to think. She couldn't start saying just within a few minutes of having at last made up her mind all that she had to say to him, all that had been bottled up in her for years.

He dried himself, then took his letter and sat down in his chair. He opened it and glanced at it.

"It's a circular about wireworm in new ploughed-up land. I've read all about that in the *Farmer's Weekly*. I wish there'd been some news from Jane. That girl ought to be home. I've said it once and I've said it a hundred times. We should never have let her go. Helping on a farm would be more use than teaching school. She'd be safer here, too."

She placed his dish in front of him. Habit was strong, and waiting until she had sat down too, he closed his eyes and asked a blessing. She said, quickly, as soon as he had said "Amen",

"Jonty says the war news is very bad."

He had started to eat and he did not look at her.

"Aye? What's happened? You can't believe everything he says, remember."

"He says that the Germans have got to the coast of Belgium and that the British and French are almost surrounded. They've taken Ostend."

"It sounds serious, if it's true."

"Well I expect he got it on the wireless."

"If it's true it's another reason why Jane should be home. I still think we ought to make peace with the Germans. I've never thought otherwise. War's no good to anybody. It's against religion. It's against what Christ taught us. If they start invading England and dropping bombs it'll be our own fault. . . Well it's more argument for us going harder at it with the farm, and more for Jane coming back. You'll have to write and tell her straight she's got to come. When I've got this new piece clear there'll be another four acres to add to what we've got. But I'll have to leave it soon to start haymaking. We shan't be able to do without her."

She wanted to be fair to him in her mind. She had to admit to herself that whatever cause she had to hate him he had, according to his own lights, tried to do his best. He was honest. He was kind-hearted and even thoughtful in many ways, and he had never spared himself in the matter of hard work. Nor had he driven her physically. He was still always first up in the morning. He was always offering to do jobs about the house. He'd never see her carrying anything like a bucket of swill for the pigs without trying to take it from her. She knew that he did not want Jane back just for her help. That chiefly and quite sincerely it was her physical and moral safety that worried him. He could not realise that she was grown up. He had set to on the clearing of the hillside adjoining the fields already reclaimed (and now promising to yield an excellent crop of oats) knowing that the Jilsons would be too busy themselves to give him any help. For the past two months he had been working up there digging out the whin roots, levering out huge rocks with a crowbar, then smashing them up with a sledge-hammer, stopping only for the routine jobs of the farm and his meals, coming down at the end of the day only when he was completely exhausted. . . But she had no sympathy for him now, no pity. Her heart had gone cold as her body had been cold for him these many past years. She would keep up the pretence for a little while longer, but only because it suited her purpose to do so, because now she knew she had the strength and the resolution and needed only a further short space in time to consider the practical aspects of her intention. . . She said, deliberately misleading him,

"She can't just give up her job as easily as that, Tom. She gave an undertaking when she went to college that she'd become a teacher. She's getting good pay. She's living in a good home. We don't *know* that the Germans are going to try and invade England and start their bombing. And anyway she's well outside Donbridge. She'll be here for the holidays soon and it's then we'll need help most. I've written and told her how things are and that you would like her to come home, especially if things start looking dangerous. . . I didn't tell you that young Jacky Harrison is feared lost. Jonty says his poor mother has had a letter from the owners. . ."

She said that deliberately. She knew it would hurt him but she had no scruples about doing so to divert his mind (until she was ready) from the subject of Jane. He didn't like to have the war brought home to him in any way that would shake his ideas about it. She had never mistaken his pacifism for physical cowardice. She could have understood and sympathised with him if it had been that, seeing what he had gone through in the last war. The bombing of the trawler which he had seen (three of the crew of twelve who had been killed had been washed up near High Batts and he had been obliged to help the police and coastguards in carrying the bodies up the cliff), the death of Sam Bunny and Kit Harrison had shaken and distressed him, but had made no real difference to his self-righteousness which was one of the things she hated him for.

He said, keeping his eyes on his plate,

"I'm sorry to hear that. I never knew the lad, although I must have seen him about. He'd sail as apprentice with Kit on the *Moor Cliff*, wouldn't he? Did Jonty say what ship he was on?"

"No. I believe they've stopped giving the names of ships even to the relations of those who are on them. I suppose it's in case the information should go to the Germans with their spies."

"Aye, of course. It's a bad business. And coming on top of Kit being lost."

She could not resist adding,

"Her other boy's at sea, too!"

He had gone back after dinner to his work on the hillside. She had told him, without a tremor in her voice, that she would have tea ready at five o'clock. When he came into the kitchen again at exactly five o'clock she was sitting in a chair by the open window darning one of his socks. She was wearing a printed cotton dress and, had he looked at her, he might have thought again that she made "quite a picture" for, in spite of the lines at the corners of her eyes and mouth, the faint streaks of grey in her hair, she was still a very attractive-looking woman. But he did not look at her. He walked straight to the sink and she got up, took a saucepan of hot water from the hearth of the fireside where the kettle was boiling on an oil-stove she used in hot weather, and poured it into a bowl for him. Then she filled the teapot from the kettle and put it on the table which was set ready for him, went back to her chair and resumed her darning. The sweat had been pouring down his cheeks and neck. When he had finished washing there were still smudges of soot under his eyes that increased his haggard expression and it was with a sigh of deep weariness that he sank into his chair. He looked at the plate of ham laid at his place and said,

"What's the matter, Ella? Aren't you having tea?"

"No. I had a cup about four o'clock when I'd finished the washing, and I don't feel like eating anything just yet."

He looked at her sharply and with genuine concern.

"You're not feeling poorly, are you?"

"No. I never feel like eating much in hot weather."

He looked at his plate again.

"It is hot and no mistake. The sun was about as much as I could stand on my back up there. I'll wait till it gets down a bit before I go back. But it's bringing the oats on fine. And that seed hay should be ripe for cutting in another week. By, but I'm thirsty!"

He bowed his head, closed his eyes and said a blessing. Then he poured out half a mug of tea, filled it up with milk and drank it almost in one draught. He fell-to hungrily on the ham and bread and butter. The window where she sat was on his left and he could not see her without turning his face. But she could see him and she was watching him all the time she was darning, quite calmly, for her mind was made up and she knew that nothing he could say or do could alter her decision.

She wasn't even hating him now. She could even feel sorry for him for, apart from looking weary, he *was* unhappy too. He was worried about the war and about Jane being in Donbridge. She guessed that all afternoon while he had been working furiously he'd been thinking about the news that Jonty had brought, and she half-wished that she had refrained from adding that bit about the Harrison boy, for it must have set him thinking about his own brother. She didn't really want to hurt him. She didn't want revenge. He had finished the ham. He had started on a piece of cake and was pouring himself another mug of tea, and he hesitated.

"Are you sure you won't have a cup, Ella?"

"No. Not now."

"All right. I'll finish it. I feel better now. I'll just have this mug and then I'll go and drive the cows in. I've enjoyed that!"

He even turned to smile at her. She looked straight at him and said,

"You'd better not go yet, Tom, I've got something to tell you."

"Aye? What is it, Ella?"

"I told you a lie about not getting a letter from Jane this morning. I did get one. And you've got to know what's in it."

He stared at her, uncomprehending.

"You told me a *lie*?"

"Yes. I got a letter from her. I told you a lie because I wanted time to think and get things worked out in my mind. Jane's married to Edwin Knaggs, Will Knaggs' son, and she's going to have a baby. She's nearly three months gone. Edwin's just gone off to France. He's a pilot officer in the Air Force. Jane wants to come home."

He had swung his chair round and was facing her. His eyes were blazing.

"It's a lie—it's a lie. I won't believe it!"

She didn't flinch.

"It's not a lie. Why should it be? She's grown up. She's not a child."

"Where's the letter. Show it to me!"

"I won't. It's to me, not to you!"

"She's my daughter as well as yours."

"She's neither now, so far as she's concerned."

"You're telling lies. You've admitted telling one. What's the matter with you, have you gone mad, telling me my daughter's going to have a bairn by that chap I nearly took my stick to down on the shore years ago?"

"1 haven't gone mad. I'm telling you the truth. She and Edwin are married."

"How do you know?"

"Jane wrote and told me when it happened—last March."

"And you never said a word to me about it, her own father?"

"No, I didn't. She asked me not to."

"Did she send you the marriage lines to prove it?"

"No. Of course she didn't. Why should she?"

"Why should she—why *should* she? Why should you tell me at dinnertime you'd had no letter from her and then tell me that tale about her not being able to come home because she'd promised to go on teaching because of having been to college? It was you who schemed for her to go to college. It was you who schemed for her to go to Burnharbour School first go off, against all I knew to be right. Now you say she's married, wants to come home and have a bairn. Stop lying. Let's have the truth. I know what that chap is. I know what his father is. Has he got her into trouble and left her and us to face the music? If that's it, then she's not coming here. I'll not have that disgrace. I'll have no scandal in my house."

She said very deliberately,

"It isn't your house. It's mine and it's hers too if she wants to come."

"What do you mean by that?"

"I mean that this farm is mine. Yes—and I mean

something else."

She flung the sock on to the table and she stood up, her eyes flashing.

"I'm finished with you. I'm *finished* with you! I've had enough of you and your ways. You and your Bible reading and your praying and your blessings and looking down at anyone who swears or drinks a glass of beer or who doesn't think exactly about everything as you do. Thinking it's wicked to go to the pictures or listen to the wireless or look at any book except the Bible and Hymns Ancient and Modern. Yes, I *did* scheme to get Jane to Burnharbour School and then to college. And I did it chiefly to get her away from you, so that you wouldn't make of her what you've made of me. Have you forgotten what a fool you made of yourself at the Wesleyan concert when Mrs Jones said she thought that one day Jane might be famous as an actress? It might surprise you to know that she's been trying her best to become an actress ever since she's been in Donbridge, and she might have been one now but for the war."

He pushed his chair back and stood up. He was shaking.

"Shut up—shut up—you wicked woman. How dare you say such wicked things. So that's what you've been at. I might have known it. I always knew there was something bad about you. Working behind my back, cheating me. Encouraging your own daughter to be wicked. And you always so meek and mild. I've done my best for you and her. I know I went down myself. I sank, but I rose up again thanks to Almighty God. I've lived a decent life since then and you know it. I've gone straight. You say it's your farm. So it is. But I made it what it is now. You've never wanted for food and clothing, have you?"

"No I haven't! And I suppose that's all you think a woman wants from a man, food and clothing and a roof over her head and a fire at night to sit by and mend his clothes while he reads the Holy Bible to her. What about love? What do you think I am? Do you think my body's made of stone like yours is? Don't you think I've got feelings like every other woman? Do you think that I've been content and happy having only one baby in my life when I might have had at least another four. Even your Bible has plenty to say about love and about a man lying with his wife and conceiving children."

"Hold your mouth. You're being blasphemous now."

"Then I'll be blasphemous. You're not religious, anyway. You only think you are. It's your sort of religion that drives people into lying and deceiving. You needn't think that I've done without love all these years. I'm not ashamed of it, either. If he'd been willing I'd have run away with him. I'd have left you long ago."

"With—with another man—*you*—"

"Yes *me*—with another man. And it's not my fault it's finished."

"You—you—you can stand there—and say a thing like that. . . Who was it?"

"You'd like to know—wouldn't you? Well you won't and you never will. And no one else will either."

He glared at her, clenching his fists till the knuckles were white.

"You bad woman. You bad woman. If I wasn't a God-fearing man I'd knock you down. . . I'd kill you."

She laughed at him, derisively.

"You tried that once, didn't you! You nearly killed me. But you hadn't quite enough strength, then. But it's queer—I had more respect for you then than I've ever had since. You may have been a drunkard, but you were human. Anyway, I've made up my mind. I'm not going to live with you anymore. Jane wants to come home and have her baby. But I won't have her if you're here. I'm not going to have her upset. I can't make you go. But if you don't I will. I'll go to her. I'll get work where she lives. I'm going to be with her. I'll not sell the farm. You can have it so long as you pay me what's due. But I'm not going to live with you anymore."

They were standing not more than six feet apart. With one stride he could have had her within range of his fist and she could not have escaped. But she did not flinch and he did not move except to take a deep breath through his mouth. And then he said with a strange and sudden quietness,

"All right. You needn't say another word. You're a bad woman and that's all there is to it. I don't know how much of what you've said is true. If you can tell one brazen lie you can tell a hundred. But I'll get to know the truth about Jane. I'll go and see Will Knaggs straight away. I'll find out if she's married or whether that's another of your lies. Don't say another word to me. And don't think I want to go on living with you. I don't want to see you again. All I can say is God forgive you for your badness."

He strode to the door, which was wide open, and he took from behind it his jacket and his old peaked sailor cap. He did not turn to look at her again and she made no sound or sign to stop him as he moved out. He crossed the yard to the cow-house and the stile to the pasture where the cows, knowing it was milking time and anxious to be in their stalls away from the flies and the heat, were crowding to the gate. He moved straight past them as though not seeing them, turning obliquely down the pasture for the coastguard's path.

It was only about half-past four by real time. The sun was still high and hot, the sky an unclouded blue, the bay dead calm. Eastwards the sea was bare of shipping to the horizon. To the north, beyond the heat-shimmering cliffs of Low Batts, was an irregular bank of slowly-rising smoke and the leading escort vessels of a south-bound merchant convoy were abreast of the headland itself. There was a sound of distant aeroplanes on duty with the convoy. From the hillside on his left, and slightly ahead as he strode rapidly north along the path, came the sound of a tractor and mowing machine, and had he looked he could have seen the Jilson brothers cutting their first field of seed hay. But he was using his eyes only for guiding his feet along the twisting undulating path. He was stunned, dazed, moving only mechanically. He felt as though someone had been beating him on the head with a club, blow after blow, that he was only half-conscious, unable to think properly, not knowing what was real and what was imaginary. . . It had happened, of course. He had just finished tea and was thinking about getting the cows in when she told him about Jane. If that hadn't happened he wouldn't be walking now as fast as he could go to Bramblewick to have it out with Will Knaggs. She had started abusing him for being religious, for objecting to drinking and using bad language, and picture-going and the wireless, trying to make out that she'd always been unhappy with him, and she'd told him straight out that she'd been encouraging Jane to become an actress, that Jane nearly had become one, as much as saying that his daughter, instead of living the decent Christian life she'd had at home, had been doing just the opposite. And then she'd told him that she herself had been with another man. And he could see her now, as she'd said that, not looking ashamed of it but actually proud, boasting.

It was a lie of course. If that was the most terrible thing she had said it was also the one thing that was certainly untrue. In all the time they had been together at the farm there had not been a single evening when she had been away from it. There had never been any men visitors to the house. The only men with whom she might have been on friendly terms were the Jilsons, and Joe was engaged. George was not the sort of man to lend himself to a thing like that. Besides, he'd have known if it had been either of them. He had seen both brothers almost every day since he had moved into the farm. They had helped each other. A woman might keep up the deception, but not a man. And Ella was a woman, after all. She had never behaved like this before. Even in the days of his drunkenness she had never raised her voice at him. Perhaps that explained it—just the fact that she was a woman. Perhaps the shock of getting Jane's letter had for the time being unbalanced her mind. She couldn't mean that she wanted to leave him forever. She couldn't mean that she'd been happy and in love with him when he had been a drunken wastrel and that now, when he had proved himself a decent man, she could despise him, hate him. And he had proved himself, in all that he had said and done during their quarrel, a Christian too. She had provoked him almost beyond endurance, but not quite. He had not said that he had forgiven her, but it was in his heart to do so. She was a woman, distraught with anxiety about her daughter, and her conscience too. She had tried to brazen it out. She was to be pitied, not hated. The person or the persons who were really to blame for what had happened were the Knaggs: father and son. Thank God he had kept control of himself; that he had not, as indeed he had been tempted to do, struck her or said anything that could not be withdrawn and mended. When he'd got the truth from Will Knaggs he would go back, and they'd talk the whole thing over quietly and decide what was best to do for Jane's sake.

He did not know that he was ill himself, that he was suffering from acute mental shock; that as one person might involuntarily find escape from intense anguish in tears or hysteria or complete coma he was involuntarily shaping his thoughts so that they were supportable to him and, in some sense, almost agreeable. His pride, his self-esteem had been dealt a mortal blow. To save himself he was creating the illusion that this had not happened. It was of immense help for him to feel that he had done right and that he intended to go on doing right, no matter what Ella had done.

He had walked at a tremendous rate. He was carrying his jacket but even so the sweat was pouring down his face and his exposed chest. His mouth and throat were dry. He had begun to feel intensely thirsty. He was getting near to the wooded gorge of the beck, however. Looking down he saw the gleam of fresh water and temporarily the thought of quenching his thirst took dominance in his mind. It was from this point or near it that long ago he had stood and watched and heard the *Moor Cliff* signalling to the shore. Now, where she had been visible, were the first three merchant vessels of the south-bound convoy following in line behind the escort warship. They were all close in, so close that he could hear the dull throb of their engines across the calm bay, distinguishable from the high-pitched drone of the escorting planes. They were all fine ships, and as he started down the bank towards the beck a fourth one cleared the headland, bigger still and painted white and green with the distinguishing marks of a hospital ship. He knew by the position and rake of her funnels and the shape of her superstructure that she was a converted Cunard liner, and he was almost certain that he knew the name and ownership of at least one of the other vessels, in spite of its camouflage paint. But his observations were almost subconscious and instinctive.

Convoys such as this had been passing up and down the coast regularly throughout the winter and spring. They were the one certain and inescapable daily reminder to him that his country was at war. Occasionally in misty weather they had been attacked by enemy aircraft but never within sight or sound of the farm, and the sinking of the trawler and the grim sequel in which he had been obliged to take part were incidents which he had deliberately forced from his mind. This war was not his war. His only concern with it was the one about which his conscience had been quite clear—farming, growing food. In going back over his quarrel with Ella he had not remembered that before it began she had given him Jonty's war news.

When he got to the beck he found that its water had been fouled by cattle and was undrinkable. The tide was half-way out, however, which meant that he could walk the remaining distance to the village along the shore and the other beck, marked by a projecting nab in the cliff, was not so far away and its water usually was cleaner. His thirst became more than ever the dominant thought in his mind and yet his determination to see Will Knaggs and have it out with him was fixed. He hadn't seen him since the bombing. He might now be out on patrol along the northern beach or cliff, but he would go straight to his house and if he were not there his sister would know where he could be found. The second beck was clean and its water babbling across the shingle looked deliciously cool. He knelt down and lapped it like an animal. He felt the taste of brine on his lips as he went on, for the place where he had drunk had been covered when the tide was up, but it had temporarily slaked his thirst and he felt refreshed and clearer in his mind now as to what he was going to do, what he would say to Will Knaggs when they met. He would keep calm, of course, but he wouldn't mince matters. First of all the truth. If his son had married Jane then they must make the best of it. But if, as seemed more likely, he had just got the girl into trouble then justice must be done. He would see to that. . .

He was drawing near the old coastguard station and the slipway that led up into the dock. There was no one either on the shore or the slipway. The sun was still hot. He was feeling violently thirsty again and tired too. He had been working on the clearing, with breaks only for meals, since eight o'clock, and in the unremitting glare and heat of the sun. He had walked the three-odd miles from High Batts quicker than he had ever done before. He had received a severe mental shock, which by the blind instinct of self-preservation he had sublimated into an unwarranted optimism. Physically he had hardened and grown tough with his farmer's life. Mentally he was almost as ill now as he had been that night long ago when he had staggered up from the landing scaur, kept from collapse only by the thought of the flask of whisky he had hidden under the wash-house floor of his cottage.

He did not know that he was ill. Consciously he was aware only of his intense thirst and that growing physical fatigue, and again it was subconsciously that he was observing the convoy, three more ships of which had now cleared the headland, one of them bearing a strong resemblance in size and rig, in everything save her camouflage paint, to the *Moor Cliff*, the ship now sunk (with Kit and Sam), the ship he might have commanded but for his downfall. And it was with even less conscious interest that he was observing the aeroplane that had suddenly appeared over the top of Low Batts and, following the curving line of the cliff, was approaching the village: flying low, diving, as the German bomber had done with its twin engines at full throttle. It was an Avro Anson, one of the convoy's escorts, and the pilot was making a wide sweep to keep station with the slow-moving ships and another aeroplane flying on their seaward beam. But he may too have had a desire to prove his skill in low flying for he came over the village itself, close over the chimneys of the old coastguard station, and banked and turned seawards immediately above

Tom Bransby's head so that the roar of its engines seemed to shake the very ground. And in that moment of din it was as though he heard a tumult of other sounds, which with their frightful associations he had tried to force from his memory: the hiss and roar of the flames engulfing the bridge of his father's ship, the rending of steel plates and timber as he had deliberately turned his own ship at that red light challenging him in the stormy darkness, the roar of the German bomber's engines, the explosion of its murderous bomb on the defenceless trawler, and the voice of his wife mocking him, telling him she would not live with him again. And something seemed to crack inside him. He had stopped, but only while the plane was immediately overhead. He was within a few yards of the slipway. He almost ran towards it, aware suddenly of only one thing: a fierce overwhelming desire for alcohol.

Two old men (he should have known them) had appeared from the dock at the slipway too, and were gazing at the receding aeroplane. He walked past as though he had not seen them. He reached the dock. A military truck, with several soldiers in battledress unloading rolls of barbed wire from it, stood near the old lifeboat house, watched by a group of children. He turned to his right for the narrow cobbled street that led up past Thompson's (the grocers and post office) towards the old Wesleyan Chapel. The Mariner's Tavern was halfway up it on his left and he could see its sign. Thompson's was closed, but as he reached it a short, tubby, white-headed woman emerged from the telephone kiosk near its private side entrance, looked at him and stopped, blocking his way. It was Polly

Scaife, the postman's wife.

"Well—if it isn't Tom Bransby! It's a long time since I've seen you in Bramblewick. How are you getting on?"

She was as garrulous as ever, too full of information to regard him as anything but a listener.

"Ee—you won't have heard about poor Mrs Bunny! She passed away less than an hour ago. I've just been ringing up t' undertakers at Burnharbour. Both of Willy Hodges' sons have joined up, and Willy's rheumatics are so bad he couldn't promise to do t' job under two days, and that wouldn't be reet in this weather. I was up all neet with her. In spite of her having had a stroke she kept on trying to get up out o' bed. She kept on thinking someone was at t' door with a wire from poor Sam to say he'd got his ticket. Them was her last words. "There's someone knocking at t' door!' I reckon it's a mercy she's gone and that she never knew about poor Sam. Isn't t' war news awful? Jonty thinks t' Garmuns will start invading us this week or next. He'll be sat at home now listening to t' six o'clock news. Ee—there's a lot of lads gone from this spot. And now they're trying to get hold of any chaps they can who've been to sea and no matter how awd they are. Jonty says they're wanting them to gan to France in any craft that can sail to bring our soldiers back. There's two captains from 'Up-Bank' who've gone already, Joe Gibson and Fred Emmerson, and they've both been retired at least ten years. Why Joe must be getting on for seventy by now. And have you heard about poor Mrs Harrison losing her youngest lad? And those soldiers, there, say they're going to put barbed wire along t' cliff edge and they're just waiting for their officers to come."

She had to stop to get her breath. He moved to pass her.

"I'm in a hurry," he muttered.

She seemed to see him for the first time and she said,

"Ee—you're looking upset, Tom. Is owt up? You look poorly."

He did not answer but moved on, leaving her staring at him. The door of the Mariner's was open. He went straight in, turned left to look into the familiar bar-room, saw that it was empty, and banged hard on the door of the tap-room which was standing ajar. The landlord appeared. He was old now, deaf and did not at first recognise his customer, and Tom had to shout hard to make him understand. Whisky? He had no whisky. Nobbut beer, brandy and rum.

"A pint of beer. And a double rum. Quick, too. I'm feeling bad."

He took the drinks, a pewter flagon and a tumbler, one in each hand and moved back into the bar-room, setting them down on the table and then sinking down in the very place from which he had risen unsteadily on that winter's night long ago to go fishing down the landing. But he was not remembering that. He had ceased to think. He put his hand to the flagon, felt the delicious cool of it. He bent his face down and inhaled its strong aroma first through his nostrils then through his mouth. Then not daring to lift it with his hand which was shaking, he put his lips to the flagon, tilted it with both hands and drank. It was empty when the old man came in with the change for the pound note he had given him and he sat back, curling the tip of his tongue round his lips as though to assure himself that not a drop of it had been wasted. He said,

"I'll have another pint!"

The old man was staring at him.

"Why, it's Captain Tom Bransby, isn't it?"

"Aye."

"Thoo 'asn't been in for a long while."

"No."

"Ah thowt not. Did tha say just noo tha was feeling bad?"

"Aye, I want another pint."

"All reet—all reet. Tha seems in a great hurry. Why—I thowt thoo'd gone temperance."

"Never mind what I'd gone. Fetch me that pint."

The landlord picked up the empty flagon.

"All reet. Ah'm not refusing t' serve tha, as I had ti mony a taame yance. Ah'm glad ti see tha, Tom. Ah've not got si mony regulars noo as ah had in them days. There's a lot of 'em like awd Cap'n Christopher'll drink ni mair. And Will Knaggs hasn't been in for months, except ti tak a bottle o' two away wiv him. There's nobbut Jonty you'd call a regular and he only comes in late. You'll knaw that Sam Bunny's gone."

"Aye. Let's have that pint."

As he went, Tom picked up the glass of rum. His hand was steady now. He did not drink it as he had done the beer. He took one good mouthful, then he set the glass down and swallowed slowly. Already he was feeling better. The bar-room was cool as a deep cellar. After the glare of the sunshine the dark smoke-grimed walls and ceiling were like balm to his eyes. The pain of thirst had gone. He was starting to think again, confusedly at first, like someone awakening from a troubled sleep. He was remembering his quarrel with Ella, but at the same time other thoughts flashed through his mind: the new oatfields and the clearing, his walk along the cliff tops, the convoy coming round Low Batts, the hospital ship. He remembered his disappointment at reaching the first beck and finding it dirty, his delight in finding the second one clean; he thought of Jane and Will Knaggs, of the noise that aeroplane had made and how it had suddenly brought back the memory of the sinking of his father's ship, and the collision and the bombing of the trawler. He thought of how the sudden craving for drink had come over him, how he had walked hurriedly up the slipway and through the dock, and how he had met Polly Scaife and he thought of what she had said about Mrs Bunny and the war, and the two retired sea captains answering the call for service.

All these things were flashing through his mind, coming and going, still in confusion as though he were only half awake. But nothing was hurting him as it had done before. The landlord came in and set the flagon down in front of him.

"Is tha feeling better noo, Tom?" he said conversationally.

"Aye. I'm all right."

It must have been clear from the way he'd answered that his unexpected customer did not wish to talk, and with a puzzled glance at him the landlord went back to the tap-room. He at once took a long pull at the flagon, then very deliberately, with a hand that was perfectly steady, he poured what remained of the rum into the beer and sat back, his hands clasped round the cold flagon, his eyes staring into the cool shadows of the opposite side of the room. Then there began to take shape from the confusion of his thoughts a single idea, a plan, a course of action. Swiftly it grew and became clearer. Against it and as swiftly everything else seemed to diminish in importance, his wife and the bitter humiliating things she had said to him, her deceit and her confessed unfaithfulness, her admission about Jane, his very purpose in coming to Bramblewick to see Will Knaggs and have it out with him about Jane and his son. The farm, which by years of labour he had restored from ruin, the land he had reclaimed and sown, his religious habits, his sincere conviction that war was a sin against God and that he as a Christian must play no direct part in it, were things that did not matter now.

He took another pull at the flagon, not greedily, but with the confidence of a man who knows what he is about and that he is master of his own desires. He sat back again, very straight, with his shoulders square, still staring into the shadows, but with his mind completely clear and resolute. He was a sailor, once master of a ship, and still qualified to be master of another. The term of his suspension had been only for two years. Normally that would have debarred him from full command until he had served many years in a subordinate position and wiped out the black mark against his name with an unblemished record. But things were not normal now. He was a competent officer. And even if he had to sail as mate or second mate or bo'sun, or even as an able-bodied seaman, it wouldn't matter so long as he got back to sea and played his part against those devils who'd done for Kit Harrison and his boy, and Sam Bunny, what another generation of Germans had done for his own father and brother, the devils who'd murdered those fishermen who, if Jonty was right, were now driving the British Army into the sea and were planning to invade England itself.

He was not drunk, or even getting drunk. He was not even excited, but cool, capable, resolute, thinking out calmly of what he should do. It was past six o'clock. Normally the Mercantile Marine Office at Burnharbour would be closed, but if Polly Scaife had been right about the sudden call-up of sailors there should be someone there. The offices of several other shipping companies were in Burnharbour too. Failing that there would be the Labour Exchange or the police or the harbour authorities. There'd be someone he could telephone and get information from. He'd offer himself for service straight away. He'd have to go back to Ella and get some gear. But if things were really urgent he needn't even do that. She could look after the farm all right. That's what she'd wanted to do anyway, with himself out of the way, so that Jane could come home and have her baby. But he ought to have things clear about that. Very likely she was married to young Knaggs after all. He'd better go and see Will Knaggs while he was here. But the main thing was getting down to the telephone box. He looked into the flagon. It was now about three-quarters empty. He made the cool decision that he did not want any more and he got up and, as he did so, he heard steps at the door and a familiar voice speaking to the landlord.

"Look sharp. A glass of brandy."

He knew it was the smith. He sat down again, waiting for him to come in. He felt no embarrassment and no enmity. He was glad they were going to meet and have things out about his son and Jane so that he'd be able to tell Ella the truth when he went back. But if he had felt enmity he could not have sustained it. He knew as soon as Will Knaggs walked in that he'd had some grievous shock. He stared at Tom blankly. Then he sat down opposite him and said in an anguished voice,

"Have you heard what's happened?"

He answered quietly, thinking that he understood,

"Aye. My wife had a letter from Jane this morning, but she only told me what was in it about teatime. That's what I came on here for, to see you, and get to know if it was true. I was angry about it, but since then I've made up my mind that it's not my business. I've just decided anyway. I'm going back to sea as quick as I can get a ship. I'd like to know the truth, though. She made out they were married. If they are, well then we've got to make the best of it. They're young but they're old enough to know their own minds. I've been having a drink too, as you may have noticed. It's the first I've had since I signed the pledge. I was feeling very upset. I'm not upset now. You look as though you need a drink yourself. There's some rum and beer in that mug. Take it while you're waiting."

He pushed the flagon over. The landlord had come in, however, and he eyed both men inquisitively as he set the glass of brandy down.

"What thoo having, Tom, same again?"

He said, decisively, in quiet commanding tones,

"No, I'll be off in a minute. But I'd like a flask of rum or brandy to take with me. Have you got one?"

"Aye. We've plenty of either."

"Then I'll have a couple of rum and I'll get them as I go out. Will and me are having a private talk."

"All reet."

The smith had half-emptied his glass. He stared at Tom and said with anguish,

"You don't know about my lad then, that he's gone?"

"Gone? The missus said that Jane had said he'd gone to France. What's up? Has anything else happened? Do you mean he's lost?"

He had asked the question calmly as though with complete personal detachment. The smith said,

"Aye."

He took a piece of paper and a crumpled telegram envelope from his pocket and held the paper out.

"I got this about twenty minutes ago. I was in the smiddy, just clearing up. I've been trying to make up my mind since how to tell my sister Betsy about it. She's fond of that lad. Fond as I am. It says he's missing, believed killed. It's from your own lass. They were wed awhile back, but Edwin didn't write and tell me until he knew he was under orders for France. They neither of them wanted you to know anything about it."

Still perfectly calm Tom took the telegram and read,

Air Ministry has wired Edwin missing believed killed
Jane

He said,

"So they wired to her and not you?"

"Aye. She's his wife and next-of-kin. But he's my son. I knew it would happen. I knew from the first it would happen. If only he'd stayed in Canada. He needn't have been in this do at all."

"It doesn't say he's killed. It says only believed. He

may have been taken prisoner."

"They wouldn't have said believed killed if they hadn't meant it. Some other pilot must have seen his machine hit, coming down in flames."

"You don't know. There were plenty of chaps in the last war were posted missing and thought killed and they turned up safe and sound."

A gleam of hope had dawned in the smith's bloodshot tortured eyes.

"You sound quite calm about it, Tom. You sound calm about everything. What's happened to you? Have you ratted from religion as well as ratting from temperance? Do you still believe in God? Do you believe in praying, that if you're in trouble and you pray there's someone to listen? I've been an atheist all my life. I think I am yet. I want proof before I believe in anything. I can't help it, but I've always wanted *proof*. I don't believe in God because I can't. My brain won't let me. But if I could only believe that lad of mine was safe, I—I could believe anything then. I'm not afraid of death for myself. I'm not afraid of anything that may come after. But that lad of mine. I want him back. I want him safe and sound."

Tom Bransby stood up.

"I hope he's not dead," he said quietly. "Jane's going to have a bairn by him. I'm glad they were married and that's all straight. She'll be coming home. But I'm going back to sea. I *do* believe in God. I've had *my* proof. I was blind once and He opened my eyes. I may have gone wrong in my idea about religion, and especially about other folk's religion. Aye—I've ratted from temperance, but never from God. Maybe it was God who sent me into this pub just now and made me drink so that I could see things in a different way to what I have been doing, especially about this war. I'm off now, so I'll say so long."

He did not look at the smith again. He found the landlord at the tap-room door waiting with the two flasks. He paid for them, put them in his jacket pocket and walked out into the street. He walked erect with his shoulders square, and his whole demeanour calm and self-possessed. He entered the telephone kiosk, and with his hand on the coins in his pocket he picked up the receiver. There was a short wait, then the voice of a female operator. He spoke quite calmly. He wanted the Mercantile Marine Office in Burnharbour. . . Was it a private call? If so there would be some delay as all traffic was subject to military priority.

"I'm a retired ship's officer," he said. "I hear they're calling for volunteers. I reckon that's priority or whatever you like to call it."

"The number's Burnharbour 452. I'll try and connect you."

He was speaking to the Marine Superintendent himself. It was Captain Sowerby who'd once commanded the *Northgate*, his own ship, and the voice at first was diffident.

"Tom Bransby? Aye, we're wanting ship's officers and men. As many as we can get hold of. But you're the Tom Bransby that was in trouble, aren't you? Didn't you lose your ticket?"

"Aye. I got a two-years' suspension from master, but it's getting on for thirty years ago."

"What have you been doing since?"

"Farming. I'm a farmer now, but I've heard you're wanting anyone with sea experience. I'm willing to go straight away. And I don't mind if it's before the mast if it comes to that."

"Have you got all your tickets and discharges?"

"Aye, of course. I've got them at home."

"What's your age?"

"Fifty-seven next birthday."

"What's your health like?"

"I'm fit for anything!"

"Are your eyes all right?"

"Aye. I don't need glasses even for reading."

"Then hang on a minute. Did you say you were ready to get off at once?"

"I'd like a few hours to get home and fix things up and get my gear."

"Then hang on."

He hung on. Glancing through the kiosk window he saw a woman appear from the side entrance of the post office, with a telegram in her hand. She had seen him, and she indicated that the telegram was for him. But the voice came again.

"How soon do you think you could get down to Burnharbour?"

"I've got a three-mile walk home to High Batts. It would take me an hour maybe to fix up things there, so that would make it two hours and I might get a lift down from High Batts on the main road. There'll be no more trains tonight. They've taken off the late train. I could be down before ten o'clock even if I had to walk."

"No need for you to do that. We could send a car for you. Do you know that tug belonging to Burnharbour Harbour Committee, the one they used for towing the mud hopper out, *Fanny Rose*?"

"I ought to. She's almost as old as I am."

"Aye. She's been laid up since the war too, but the Navy's called for any craft that'll float. There's been a gang on her all day, fixing up her engines. She'll be fit for sea before midnight if all goes well. You'll guess what she's wanted for. And I won't pretend it's for a picnic. There won't be any weapons, but the ARP chaps are building sandbags round her bridge. She's got her own engineer. Crew will all be elderly fishermen. It's all that's left. Her skipper went mine-sweeping ages ago, so the berth's going. You're married, aren't you? Any dependents? But you'll be able to tell us that if you come. You'd come under ordinary service compensation, anyway. Are you suited? You'll not get a master's berth in a bigger ship at present, but I can send your name to the Pool. What do you make of it?"

"I'll take it."

"Right. We'll send a car for you to High Batts top at half-past eight."

He stepped out of the box. The woman handed him the telegram. She said,

"It came after closing time, but I saw you from our window go in to telephone, and it sounds urgent."

It was addressed simply Bransby, High Batts. He opened and read,

Edwin missing believed killed. Wire me Greystone House Mountwood Park if all right come to-morrow. Jane.

He said to the woman, who had stood waiting,
"Is it too late to send a wire?"

"It's supposed to be, but we can do it if it's urgent. You

could telephone it of course."

"I'm in a bit of a hurry. I'd be glad if you could do it for me."

He took a pencil and an old envelope from his pocket and wrote on the old envelope,

Jane Knaggs Greystone Mountwood Park Donbridge. Yes come. Love from Mum and Dad.

He gave it to the woman with some money. Then he set off down the street for home.

She was in the kitchen, sitting at the window, darning one of his socks exactly as she had been doing before their quarrel had started. He had noticed as he had walked through the pasture that she had milked the cows, and now that she had got the table laid for supper and that everything was as usual as though they had never quarrelled at all. But he wasn't deceived by this or the quiet way she said,

"Hallo, Tom, you've got back."

He hadn't touched the liquor he had in his pocket. He hadn't felt the need to. The knowledge of the major thing he was going to do had given him the necessary courage to say what he had to say to Ella. He said to her, quite calmly, with neither truculence nor humility,

"Aye, I'm back. And I'm glad I went. I've got something to say to you, Ella. Very important. But first of all there's some very bad news. You'd better read this."

He handed her the telegram. She read it, then stared at him aghast.

"I reckon it was meant for you, but it had just Bransby

on the envelope so I opened it. But I knew before that what had happened. I met Will Knaggs. He told me. Jane had wired to him. She's his wife all right. The news wouldn't have come to her first otherwise. I sent her a wire, telling her to come home, and I signed it from both of us. But *I* shan't be here when she comes."

She continued to stare at him, without speaking, and he went on without any outward sign of emotion.

"You were right about a lot of things you said to me after teatime. I've not been to you as I ought to have been. Maybe after all religion did get me the wrong way. Maybe it went to my head like liquor did once. And that isn't what religion's meant to be. That's what the Pharisees did. I felt pretty bad while I was walking to Bramblewick. There was that big convoy passing. And maybe that was reminding me of something. You'd told me about that lad of Kit Harrison's being lost. Remember that I lost my father and little brother in the last war. Then there was that trawler that was sunk off here. Maybe it was my conscience. I don't know. I was feeling bad, and religion wasn't helping me somehow or other. Then an aeroplane came down low, right over my head like that German bomber had done, and I felt sort of ill, like I used to do after the last war, before I had that collision that lost me my ticket, and I knew that the only thing that would save me from going out of my head was a drink. So I went into the pub and I had one. And then my mind sort of cleared and I saw things as I ought to have seen them a while back. Anyway, I went out and I rang up the shipping office in Burnharbour, and I've got a ship. I've come back to tell you this, and to fix things up with you about the farm. I've had a drink, but I'm not drunk and I'm not quarrelling with you, Ella. I've got to be off before it's dark."

He hadn't expected and he didn't want her to say she was I sorry for anything she had said during their quarrel. He knew that she was deeply upset about the telegram. She said at last,

"I'm very bewildered, Tom. I know you're not drunk or trying to quarrel. I feel dazed. I can hardly think. But I can't say it's not right for you to go. You're a sea captain when all's said and done. I'll not say you're not a good farmer. But you're a sailor first, and the war's looking very bad. It's a terrible shock about Edwin. And I'm thinking about Jane now, what it must mean to her. I'm glad you sent that wire to her. I know she loved him very deeply. *I* didn't doubt about them being married, but it would have made no difference to me if they hadn't been. I'd have still wanted to help her, especially with her expecting a baby. But I don't want you to go to sea because of what I said. If you've changed as you say you have, we might be able to get on all right. But it wouldn't be right to have Jane upset. I'm willing to go to her and leave you the farm. I mean that. Are you sure you're doing right?"

"Aye. My mind's made up, Ella. I don't know how long this job will last. It's not a proper ship. It's only a tug. I may just have to take her somewhere and hand her over to someone else. But if that's it I'll try for another berth. I may be able to get a steamer, I might get a berth as mate, but even if I have to sail before the mast I'm going to be back at sea until this war's over. I don't know how you'll come on about the farm, though. That extra land I've been clearing will have to wait. Harvest won't be for a long time anyway. There'll be the hay. I thought I'd go and see Joe and George about that now. I think they'd be able to mow it, anyway."

She said quickly,

"No, Tom. I'd rather you didn't. They'll have too much to do with their own. I'll manage somehow. Jane will be able to help a bit. She'll be able to do the milking, anyway. It'll help to keep her mind off—off what's happened. Do you think there's a chance—"

"That he's not killed? There is, but not much I reckon. They'd have said just 'missing' if there had been. I'll have to hurry, Ella. They're sending a car for me to High Batts top for half-past eight."

She stood up. She seemed to be as calm as he was.

"You'd better have your supper then, Tom. I'll go and pack your things."

The time came for him to leave. She had packed the few things he had said that he required (they included his master's certificate and discharge book) in a small attaché case, with an old kitbag for his boots and oilskins. He swung the kitbag over his shoulder. He had asked her not to come up the hill with him. She came with him just to the door. There were no tears in her eyes, but her face was pale. They stopped on the threshold and he said,

"Well, I'm off, Ella."

He was facing her.

She caught her breath and said, very quietly,

"Yes, Tom. And I'm proud you're going. You're a sea captain and I always was proud of that. I was always proud when I saw your ship coming across the bay and heard you blowing the horn. I'm proud you're going. I want you to come back safe. I—I didn't mean half the things I said to you this afternoon. I got angry. I tried to hurt you. And I lied too. I lied about that other man. There hasn't been any other man but you."

She was looking him straight in the eyes. He put his arm round her and kissed her.

"God bless you, Ella. Tell Jane I'll be thinking about her and praying she'll hear something different before long."

"Yes, Tom. God bless you and keep you."

He had turned and he had not seen her crying at last, her hands reaching out to him.

4

IT WAS an evening in late June. France had fallen. With grievous loss the British Expeditionary Force had been withdrawn from the mainland of Europe. Inspired and fortified by the words of one great Englishman, Britain waited and prepared for the battle which history was to honour with Britain's name.

The weather had continued good for farming. All the hay but for two loads and the rakings of the last fields was in. Jane had been helping her mother at the stack now being "topped". But she had come in to the house to get supper ready for the War Agricultural Committee tractor-driver and the gang of four land girls who had been loading and leading. There had been nothing to cook, however, and having laid the table, and seen that the kettle was on the boil, she had gone out to sit in front of the house, on the seat her father had fixed there many years ago (it was another relic from a shipwreck he'd found on the beach) and get on with the letter she was writing to Gwen Jones.

She'd tried to start that letter more than a week ago when she'd got one from Gwen herself. But that letter (it had taken many weeks to come from Rhodesia) had been in answer to the one she'd written to Gwen in early spring when she and Edwin had been on holiday in Cornwall, the first real leave he'd had since the three days he'd had for their honeymoon. They'd taken a small furnished cottage near the shores of a cove, miles from the nearest town. The weather had been perfect. They had bathed, and sailed and fished, and gone for rides on ponies lent by the farmer from whom they got their milk and Cornish cream and eggs. They'd lazed in the sun, and at night made a huge fire of driftwood in their cottage. Edwin had started to paint too. He had done some pictures that even satisfied himself, and had sworn that she had inspired them, and for one week they had just been madly happy. She had written pages about it to Gwen, and reading her comments on the letter had brought it back so vividly that she'd scarcely been able to read it for crying, let alone answer it intelligently.

Yet she had realised that next to hard physical work (she was getting plenty of that, and physically she was feeling extraordinarily well) writing to her oldest and dearest friend was the best escape from her thoughts and her grief. Mother was being splendid, but she could never feel with her the same mental companionship she did with Gwen. Besides, mother clearly was finding work her *only* escape. Even at meals she could hardly ever be persuaded to sit down and her conversation was always the farm.

It was getting late and the sun was nearly setting. It was warm, however. A westerly wind had been blowing all day (just right for the hay), but now it had died away, leaving the sea calm as an inland lake. It was nearly low water of a spring tide, and from where she sat she could see nearly the whole length of High Batts scaur, the very place where she had first met Edwin. She could see the place where they had lit their fire, for it was catching the last rays of the sinking sun. She had been tempted one evening to walk down there, but on getting halfway down the path she had been confronted by a sentry, who had explained that the whole beach was now out of bounds except to the military and coastguards. There were trenches and machine-gun emplacements, and coils of barbed wire running everywhere except across the path that he was guarding. He had hinted that even mines were laid in certain places where the Germans might think of landing. She was glad that from where she sat she could not see any of these signs of war. A convoy had sailed north during the afternoon, but now there wasn't even a ship in sight. She started to read what she had already written to her friend, beginning at the beginning.

"I got your letter nearly a week ago, and by this time of course you will have had the cable I sent, telling you the terrible news about Edwin, and now I have to tell you that daddy has gone. He was killed at Dunkirk. I have been trying so hard to be brave about it and remember that there are thousands and thousands of other people who have lost those they love, and they just have to carry on, but I feel that I must tell you, because there is no one else I can tell, who really knows me. I just can't talk to mother either about Edwin or daddy. Especially about daddy because they had an awful row about me and Edwin, and she thinks it was because of that that he went to join in the Dunkirk rescue. I think, in fact I'm certain, she loved him very much in spite of him being so difficult at times. I've tried to tell her that it wasn't that at all that made him go. It was just that his father and all the men of the Bransby family have been sailors for generations, and when the real call came he just couldn't help it. But she won't let me talk about it. She never said a word when the telegram came, saying that he'd been killed. And yet I heard her crying in bed that night. I tried to go to her but the door was locked, and she'd stopped crying and tried to make out I'd imagined it. I feel that if she would let me comfort her then it would be easier for me to talk about Edwin. I am certain she did love him and that she is terribly proud of what has been said about him. One of the old fishermen who went with him on the tug came and saw us the other day. Captain Sowerby who gave daddy the berth on the tug (it was an old tug that used to tow the dredger mud barge out from Burnharbour before the war, although it had been sold to be broken up for scrap) brought him out in his car. He was the only one who escaped when the tug was sunk. He said that daddy was wonderful the whole time. He never once left the bridge from the time they sighted the other ships that were going backwards and forwards between France and England carrying the soldiers. They steamed into the thick of it with shells and bombs bursting all round them, and they made no less than four trips and rescued hundreds of men. A German bomber came down and machine-gunned them once and daddy just calmly went on zig-zagging to dodge the bombs, and one of the crew got a bullet through his head just alongside where daddy was standing but he just went on. A lot of the soldiers they rescued were wounded. The fisherman remembered daddy pulling a bottle of rum from his pocket and telling someone to give a drink to those who were in very bad pain. And they were trying to rescue another ship when the tug was sunk. It was a trawler that had been hit with bombs, and two German planes were flying round it machine-gunning the soldiers who were crowded on its deck. Daddy steered the tug close into it to try and get a rope to it and tow it, and he'd got the rope when a bomb or a shell hit the tug on the bridge where he was standing. The fisherman was blown into the sea and was picked up by a naval launch, but none of the others could have escaped. The tug was blown to bits.

"Dear dear Gwen, I do hope it's not upsetting you reading all this, but when I'm writing to you I do feel I am near you. Since I sent you the cable I had a letter from the Air Ministry saying that there is no hope of Edwin being alive. It enclosed a letter from his squadron-leader. It said that the pilot of another plane actually saw Edwin's plane hit and coming down in flames in the place where a heavy German ground bombardment was going on. He said that Edwin was one of the best and bravest officers in his squadron and that he was recommending him for a decoration. He had done over six flights that day and done some very valuable work. I suppose I ought to feel very thrilled about that. I suppose I am but all I want is to have him, alive and well and this horrible war over.

Oh how I hate it.

"When I read your letter saying how thrilled you and Dai were to hear of our happiness can you imagine how I felt, thinking again of those lovely happy Cornish days? It was never like that again, for we only got week-ends together, and although Muriel was marvellous in letting him come whenever he wanted, there were always other people there. I think what made me happiest of all in Cornwall was the way he suddenly decided he must start painting again. Did I tell you that the first time we met, he told me that he'd met an old sick artist in Florence a long time ago who had criticised his painting, and said that he'd never do anything great until he'd had real unhappiness? I told him that the inspiration of an artist should be love, and not misery, and he reminded me about that when he'd done his first picture. It was of that cove where we bathed, and he'd got me in it, in the nude of course, but just a splash of golden brown colour, and the rocks and the sea and the sky, oh it was just lovely and I've got it now and it's very very precious. We used to talk of what we'd do when the war was over. He wanted to take me to Canada but also he wanted me to go on with my acting, and I said I didn't want to do that any more, that I just wanted to go on being his wife, and helping him to paint beautiful pictures, but I knew even then I wanted us to have a baby. And I'm going to have one. And that's why I should be ashamed of being miserable at all. I didn't tell you in my letter because I wasn't certain then. . ."

It was as far as she had gone. Her eyes were swimming with tears, and she looked up from the letter and felt for her handkerchief. But as she dabbed her eyes she was looking involuntarily down to the shore, to the place where she had first met Edwin, and suddenly she saw a man appearing at the edge of the cliff at the point where the path led down to where she had met the sentry. He was in uniform but he was not a soldier. He was walking quickly. She saw that it was Will Knaggs, and that he was coming direct for the house.

She had never met him. She had written to him, but her letter had not been acknowledged. Jonty had said that he'd started drinking heavily since he had got the news about Edwin, that he'd shut up the smiddy altogether, and had been in trouble for neglecting his duties as a coastguard; that his sister (he'd admitted it himself in the Mariner's) was nagging him all the time he was at home about him being an atheist, and saying that what had happened to him was a judgment. But he was still wearing coastguard uniform.

He was approaching the gate. She stood up. He saw her and stopped. He was panting heavily. The sweat was pouring down his face. His eyes were wild with excitement, but she saw that he was not drunk.

He said, catching at his breath, "You're—you're Jane, aren't you ?"

"Yes."

"My son's wife!"

Her own heart had started to beat wildly.

"Yes—yes—what's the matter?"

He came forward and with both hands leaned heavily on the gate.

"It's news—maybe good news—about Edwin. It's not certain yet. But I believe it's true. I *know* it's true. He's a prisoner of war in Germany, alive and well. I've heard it on the German wireless news tonight, in English. Plain English. It gave his name and rank and his address, Greystone House, Mountwood Park, Donbridge. Isn't that where you lived with him?"

She was feeling faint. She could hardly breathe the word "Yes".

"That's what it said—I took it down in writing. There couldn't be two of that name and address. I've brought the paper with me. As soon as I heard it I went out and rang up the Air Ministry in London. It took me a long time to get through, and then they had to put me through to a special department and the chap I spoke to had to call someone at the BBC. They told me they'd heard it, too. They warned me I mustn't rely on it. I must wait until it came through by the Red Cross. But they confirmed every word I took down. So I came on to tell you. I think it's true. I *know* it's true. I've prayed to God it would happen. I didn't believe in God but now—"

He suddenly put his hands to his face and leaning on the gate began to sob like a child. And she, who had prayed too, suddenly became calm. She put her arms round his shoulders, petted him, told him to come into the house and sit down and have a cup of tea. And as she did so she looked past him and saw the beach still glowing in the sun. And she knew that it was true. That her lover was not dead. That one day there would be no war and that they would be together again.

THE END

About the author

LEO WALMSLEY was born in Shipley, West Yorkshire, in 1892, and was brought up in Robin Hood's Bay on the North Yorkshire coast — the 'Bramblewick' of several of his novels. After serving with distinction in the Royal Flying Corps in the Great War, where he was awarded the Military Cross, he determined to become a writer, beginning with boys' adventure stories.

He lived for a while in London before returning to Robin Hood's Bay in the late 1920s, then settled in Fowey, Cornwall and wrote *Three Fevers* (1932), the first of his 'Bramblewick' novels, followed by *Phantom Lobster, Foreigners, and Sally Lunn.*

In addition to over twenty books, he wrote 200 or so short stories and articles prior to his death in 1966.

Other books available in this series
(see overleaf)

Three Fevers
Angler's Moon
Foreigners
Phantom Lobster
Sound of the Sea

For further information about Leo Walmsley,
or membership of the Walmsley Society,
please visit:

www.walmsleysoc.org

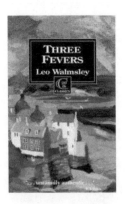

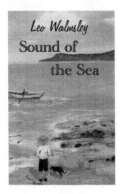

Midden